FIGHT

OR

FLIGHT

A SOUTH SIDE STORY

JOSEPH DURETTE

Editor: Victory Editing
Cover Designer: Streetlight Graphics
josephdurette.com

DEDICATION

Dedicated to the friends of my youth.

*With love to Mom and Dad
and Wendy*

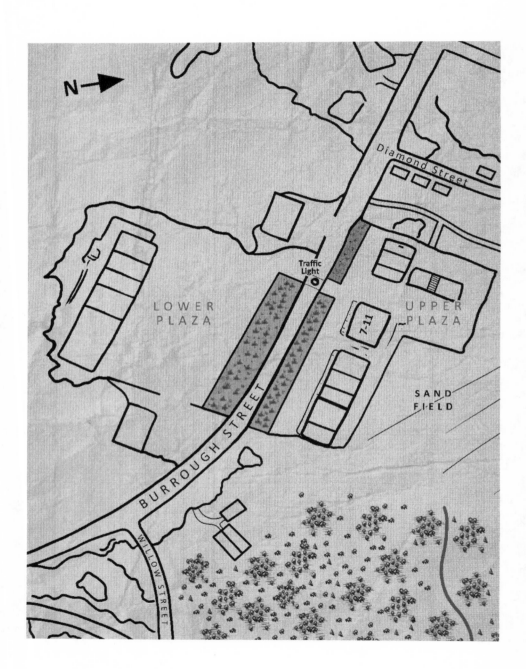

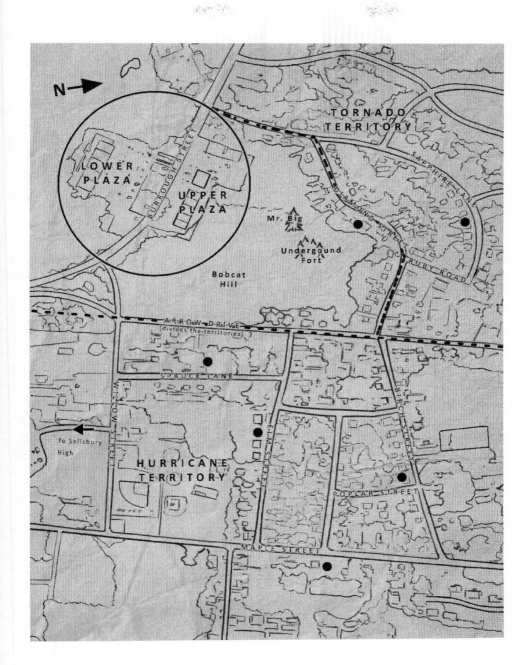

PART I
ESCALATION

PROLOGUE

"**P**OW!" THE RED dart pierced the cherry center of the dartboard, a bull's-eye of bull's-eyes. "See that, Craig? That's Hollister's head."

Craig snuffed out a cigarette on the cement of a basement wall and reached for a can of beer. "You gotta stop talking like that, Curly. We got a truce with them, remember?"

Curly hurled another dart that struck the target an inch to the right of the first one. "I don't care about no truce, and I don't care about no turf. All I care about is Hollister... dead." He lobbed a third red dart, but it bounced off the metal rim of the target before sticking in the worn brown carpet covering the basement floor.

Craig snickered. "Nice shot."

Curly picked up another set of darts from a nearby table and fired them wildly at the target. "Don't worry. Soon it'll be Hollister's head, and I swear I won't miss."

"You're crazy, man. You really are."

CHAPTER 1

T HE WAY THE wind was blowing, the footsteps of the nine
boys could not be heard against the street, nor were their
occasional whisperings any more audible to the neighborhood
residents shut in their homes for the night. The cool autumn air
appeared to swallow the glow of the intermittent streetlights,
with a half-moon barely detectable behind a blanket of stratus
clouds, but the boys seemed at ease with the night rather than
in fear of it. Stealthily they moved along the curbside of the
quiet road, blending with the shrubbery when a car drove by,
then once again slinking down the roadside when the comfort
of darkness returned.

Eight of the boys followed the ninth in front, each clad in a
midnight-blue leather jacket with a white swirl on the back.
Occasionally, one of the boys would move forward to converse
with the leader before dropping back into the pack, but the
leader generally walked alone, ready to utter a command if
needed, his brown eyes keenly searching for the unexpected.
At the moment, he confronted nothing but the cool wind
tousling his wavy brown hair and ballooning the trunk of his

open jacket into the face of a skinny boy strolling directly behind him.

The leader slowed his gait as they approached a row of dark houses. "Which one is it?" he asked.

The skinny boy stepped up beside the leader, his dark hair blowing all about in the wind. "I don't know. The blue one? Mick knows." He turned his head and called out, "Hey, Mick!"

"I'm right behind ya, Crazy Legs. Try not to wake up the neighborhood." Mick brushed a strand of curly blond hair from his face, his steel-blue eyes scanning the dark street. He tapped his leader on the arm before pointing across the street. "It's the white one, Jeff. But we gotta be careful. There's a dog next door."

"Are you sure nobody's home?" Crazy Legs asked.

Mick glared at him. "Actually, there's a hundred people inside. It's a surprise party just for you."

"Relax," Jeff said. "He's just asking."

Mick scoffed. "Well, if he wants something to worry over, he oughta worry about his piece of junk starting when it's time to go."

"It'll start," Crazy Legs insisted.

Mick laughed. "Is that a promise or an uneducated guess?"

"Enough," Jeff said. He turned to face the rest of the group. "Everyone knows what they're doing? Axle? Bumbles?" He glanced at the expressions of the two boys he had just called out, then to the faces of the others gathered before him. Once he was certain of their confidence, he clapped his hands and the gang dispersed, their discipline exemplified by their precise execution of a previously instructed plan. Only Jeff and Mick remained by the hedgerow at the edge of the property, along with Jeff's bodyguard Train, a cheery stack of muscles with sandy-brown hair and a boyish face.

"What are you doing here?" Jeff asked him. "You're supposed to help load the cars."

"Axle wanted to switch," Train said. "He said he didn't feel much like crawling around in the dark tonight. I think this is the best part."

"I don't care what you guys *feel* like doing. I need someone strong to help load the cars."

"Too late now," Mick said, cutting in. "We oughta get started, don't ya think?"

Jeff placed a hand on Train's shoulder. "Did Axle tell you what you're supposed to do?"

Train nodded. "I'm supposed to break down the back door…"

Mick slapped himself on the forehead. "Not break *down*. Break in. You're supposed to find a way in through the back."

"And if there is, you come to the front and let us in," Jeff added. "Are you sure you know what you're doing?"

"Yep! Positive!" Train bolted off toward the backyard of the white house.

Mick shook his head. "Amazing."

Jeff smiled. "At least he won't try anything crazy that might get us caught."

They left the bushes for the front door of the dark house. "Keep talking about getting caught and it's gonna happen," Mick said. "You nervous or something?"

Jeff shrugged. "A little, I guess."

"Better keep it to yourself. If word gets out that the fearless Jeff Hollister is scared of a simple operation like this, you'll have a mutiny on your hands."

"I ain't *scared*. I'm just worried about things going sour. Too many moving parts."

"Like what? The gang? If you're not sure about them, there's still time —"

"I'm not worried about the gang," Jeff answered quickly. He stopped at the base of the front steps. "Why, are you?"

"Me? Hell no. Not in a fight anyway," Mick said, "but I'll

admit all this sneaking around stuff seems a little out of their element."

Jeff climbed the steps and turned about to face his friend. "You'd rather fight than do this?"

"Well, yeah. Wouldn't you?"

"Ha. That's a rush. You sell me on these break-ins and now you're getting cold feet?" Jeff found the screen door open, but the front doorknob was locked. "Besides, nobody's worth the trouble."

Mick shrugged. "The Tornadoes are."

"Craig's gang? I'm not sure they're even together anymore."

"Oh, they're together all right. I'm tellin' you, Jeff, they're up to something. We really humiliated them last time. We'd better squash them before they spell trouble."

Jeff unfolded an ivory-handled hunting knife and bent over to inspect the latch. "We're not gonna start cracking skulls just because we're bored," he said without looking up. "We have a truce, and my word is my word. Now go check out the garage door like you're supposed to."

Mick grunted and descended the steps to the driveway while Jeff pried at the molding with the blade of his knife, simultaneously rattling the knob in an attempt to jimmy it open. The door refused to budge, so he pulled the knife free and stowed it away, knowing he had already spent too much time on the steps. Strangely, the door popped open when he released the knob; he slowly pushed it open with his foot and peered inside to discover Train standing in the foyer.

"The back door was unlocked," he said smugly before turning about and heading back inside.

"Hey, Mick. We're in," Jeff whispered.

He stepped into the dimly lit foyer that opened into a spacious living area with a darker hallway jutting off to the right, while a staircase to the left of the foyer led downstairs into blackness. Mick quietly slipped inside the foyer and eased the door nearly shut, peeking through a sliver of an opening at the empty street outside before latching it closed.

Jeff gathered his friends together and pointed to the great room. "Train, you start here. Mick, head downstairs. I'll be down this hallway," he told them. "No lights. Use your flashlights. Got your gloves on?" Train nodded, and Mick displayed his hands for everyone to see. "Okay, go."

They nodded and split up in different directions as Jeff had instructed. Train scored the first item of value, disconnecting a flat-screen television from the wall and carrying it through a sliding glass door to an elevated back porch. From there, the Hurricanes carried it down the porch steps and across a long, sloping yard to a low post fence at the rear of the property. Another runner carried it across a flat ragweed field to an open lot off a nearby road where three vehicles awaited: a brown van, a blue Camaro, and a white Monte Carlo sedan, all with engines idling. The Hurricanes loaded the television into the back of the van, followed by other valuable merchandise including a desktop computer, a stereo with its speakers, and even a pair of skis.

Soon a frantic report made its way back up the chain to Mick, and he searched desperately throughout the dark rooms of the house until he found his leader rummaging through a dresser in the master bedroom. "Jeff!" he said breathlessly. "We got trouble!"

Jeff stuffed a watch into his pocket. "What's the matter?"

"Bumbles dropped a microwave oven while he was loading the van. I guess it smashed pretty good. Denny said he said he saw a light go on in the house next door."

"How long ago?"

"A few minutes." Mick glanced about. "Still some good stuff here. Your call."

Jeff slid a dresser drawer shut before rushing past Mick out of the bedroom. "We're done. Where's Train?"

Mick followed him down the hallway. "He's on the back porch."

"Good. Let's get out of here." Jeff bolted to the end of the hallway with Mick hot on his heels. They stopped at the glass door and Jeff slid it open, but Mick grabbed his arm and held him still.

"Shhh!" he said. "Hear it? Sirens."

"Cops?" Jeff whispered. "They couldn't respond so fast."

"Maybe someone tipped them off. What do you wanna do?"

Jeff stepped out onto the elevated porch. "Where's Train?"

Mick followed him out and looked around. "Maybe he went back inside."

Jeff stepped up to the railing and peered across the backyard. "I don't see any of them. You don't think — ?"

Suddenly the roar of engines filled the air, followed by the screech of tires on pavement. "They're ditching us!" Mick cried. "Come on!"

Jeff climbed over the railing and jumped from the porch, falling to his hands and knees upon landing. He scrambled to his feet as Mick landed beside him, and together they raced across the dark backyard, hurdling the low post fence in stride. Running through the dusty ragweed field, they saw that only the Monte Carlo remained, rolling slowly toward the road with its headlights off.

"C'mon, we can still make it!" Jeff cried out, dashing ahead of his friend as the sirens grew louder. The coupe reached the road and began to pull away, its tires squealing and spinning dirt into the air. Jeff sprinted through the dust cloud and dove for the car, smacking a clenched fist against the trunk lid before tumbling to the pavement. Red brake lights flashed in his face as the car skidded to a halt on the shoulder of the road.

Crazy Legs jumped out of the car and helped Jeff to his feet. "Are you okay?"

Jeff brushed the gravel from his jeans before shoving his friend back against the car. "Where the hell were you going?"

"Brain said the cops were coming," Crazy Legs explained

quickly. "You said if there was any trouble to just get the stuff outta here, so we did."

Jeff released him. "Use your head. Did you think we were just gonna sit there while the cops came in?"

Mick ran up and hopped into the back seat of the car. "Hey, let's get outta here."

Jeff ducked inside and clambered over the center console to take the front passenger seat as Crazy Legs slid behind the steering wheel and shut the door. Seconds later they were driving away, quickly gaining distance from the scene of the crime.

Jeff glanced about. "Where's all the stuff?"

"In Train's van," Crazy Legs replied. "This car's clean."

Mick kicked aside an empty french fry box. "As clean as it ever is."

"What happened to that microwave?" Jeff asked.

"We picked up the pieces," Crazy Legs said. "Train's gonna ditch it when he gets home."

The car jerked erratically as the engine sputtered and coughed. A bright red light flashed on the instrument panel, and all three boys groaned in dismay.

"I thought you said you filled this thing up!" Jeff yelled.

"I did!" Crazy Legs said. "I swear I did!"

Mick folded his arms and sulked. "He filled it up last month. What more could you ask for?"

"Look! There's plenty of gas!" Crazy Legs pointed to a bright red light on the dash. He shifted into neutral and tried to start the engine again, but the car rolled silently to a stop. "Something's wrong, that's for sure."

"Smells like you fried it," Mick said. "Maybe it's out of oil."

"Great," Jeff muttered. "Way to go."

Crazy Legs turned the key again, to no avail. "Maybe a belt broke or something."

Mick leaned forward. "Maybe someone sabotaged it. Someone like Craig Matthews."

"How could he?" Crazy Legs asked. "How could anyone? I mean, Bumbles and Axle were standing right next to it. If it's sabotage, we've got some pretty dumb friends."

"No comment," Mick muttered.

"Well, we can't fix it now," Jeff said. "Might as well start walking."

Crazy Legs sighed and pulled the key from the ignition switch. "Maybe we can hitch a ride."

They all climbed out of the car and locked it before continuing down the road on foot. Thirty minutes later they had yet to be passed by a single car, and the overcast sky began to spit raindrops on them. Jeff and Mick continued to trudge together along the long, dark road leading back to their neighborhood, but Crazy Legs lagged behind. Finally the skinny boy yelped and sat down on the curb before kicking off his running shoe in disgust.

Mick kept walking, but Jeff turned back. "What's the matter now?"

Crazy Legs banged his shoe with the palm of his hand. "I've had this stupid rock in my shoe for the past half mile, and I'm sick of it!"

"Aw, hurry up, will ya?" Mick moaned. "I wanna get home before the sun comes up."

Crazy Legs slipped the shoe back on and started to tie the laces. "Dammit! My shoelace broke."

Mick grimaced. "C'mon, Jeff. He can catch up."

"Hurry up, Crazy Legs." Jeff jogged up to Mick, and they continued walking. "You'd think with all the running he does, he could stand one little pebble."

Mick nodded. "Maybe we should start calling him Tenderfoot instead." He glanced back to their friend before leaning closer to Jeff. "So what do ya think?" he asked in a hushed tone.

"What do I think about what?"

"You think the Tornadoes sabotaged his car?"

"No, I think maybe a belt broke. Like he said."

"Sure. All of a sudden it just breaks, right?"

"Maybe. Remember how it happened to Train on the way to the beach last year?"

"Kinda coincidental though, don't you think? In the middle of an operation with the cops two blocks away?"

"Man, you're just *dying* to have it out with them again, aren't you?" Jeff shook his head and laughed. "Let's not start busting heads just because Crazy Legs's piece of shit breaks down."

"Why not? If they deserve it—"

"I'm not seeing it. We have a truce. They seem happy with it."

"Really? You think they're happy with two nights a week at the pool hall?"

"Maybe. I'll work it out with Craig if they're not."

"It's more than that, Jeff. Maybe they haven't started in on you, but they sure as hell have been harassing us."

"Harassing? Really? Like, who?"

"Like me."

Jeff laughed. "You cry harassment when your old man tells you to cut the grass."

"Okay then. TJ. And Axle. And who do you think smashed all the garage windows at Denny's house last month?"

"It could've been anyone."

"C'mon, Jeff. You know better."

Jeff shook his head. "You're still jumping to conclusions. When they come out in the open, I'll reconsider. Until then, my word stands. That means *you* don't start trouble."

Mick frowned and looked back for Crazy Legs. "Hey, look. A car's coming."

Jeff turned his head to see. "Still wanna hitch? We might as well."

Mick stopped and gazed into the darkness. "Wait a minute. Is that a — ?"

"Cop! Hide!"

They dove to their right into a dense row of bushes and peered out as the police cruiser stopped beside Crazy Legs. Doors opened, words were exchanged, and doors slammed shut again. The cruiser roared past them a moment later with its colored light flashing but its siren silent as it disappeared over a hill farther down the deserted street.

Mick pulled a thorn from his palm as they emerged from their cover. "You would have to pick a pricker bush to jump into."

Jeff gazed down the empty road and scratched his chin. "They couldn't have arrested him for anything, could they? He didn't even go inside the house."

Mick shrugged. "Maybe they're just giving him a ride home."

Jeff started walking again. "Maybe, but I don't like it. They probably found his car too. Plus he's got his Hurricane jacket on."

"Why should that matter?"

"C'mon, Mick. Ever since that jackass Wellis became the police chief, the cops ain't been nothing but trouble. They know exactly who we are, every single one of us. Hell, they might be knocking on your front door right now."

Mick fell silent for a moment. "You don't think they'd just bring him home?"

"A kid in a Hurricanes jacket?" Jeff laughed. "If you were a cop, would you?"

"So what should we do?"

"Get home. Fast."

Mick glanced nervously to Jeff already quickening his pace, and he responded by breaking into a jog. Soon they were running as fast as their stamina allowed, the urgency of their situation driving them onward.

When they arrived at their neighborhood a short time later, the anticipated police dragnet had yet to materialize, so the Landry residence stood as dark and quiet as the other homes lining both sides of Birch Road. Jeff sighed with relief as they ascended the sloping driveway of Mick's house, noting the smugness on his friend's face as they rounded the corner into the backyard of the property. Only when they stopped outside the back door with the sound of crickets in their ears did Mick deliver the anticipated sarcastic quip.

"Good thing we ran so fast," he said as he slid a key into the doorknob lock. "We almost missed all the action around here."

Jeff cocked an ear toward the door. "Your phone's ringing."

"What—?" Mick threw the door open and dashed across the dim room to snatch the receiver off its hook in the midst of the second ring. "Crazy Legs! Are you some kind of moron? My parents are sleeping!"

Jeff shut the door and stepped to a pool table in the center of the room. "Where is he?"

Mick motioned for silence. "Uh-huh. Yeah, he's right here. Hold on." He covered the speaker of the phone with his palm and held it out to Jeff. "Watch what you say. I think he's being recorded."

Jeff took the phone and held it to his ear. "Crazy Legs, what's up?"

"I'm at the police station," his friend replied.

"Really? How come?"

"They were grilling me about some house being broken into. They asked me all sorts of questions about you."

"Uh-huh. What'd you say?"

"Nothing much. I told them how you and Mick went to the *movies* tonight."

"Cool. So what do you want?"

"I need a ride home."

Jeff bristled. "They brought you there. Have them bring you home."

"The cop who brought me here left on another call," Crazy Legs explained. "They said it might be an hour before they can give me a ride."

"So call your mother."

"I can't call my mother, Jeff! It's after midnight! She'll throw a fit if I call her from the police station. You know how she gets. C'mon, man, I need a ride."

Jeff sighed. "I don't even have my car right now. I let Axle borrow it. He had that *date,* remember?"

Mick rolled his eyes at Jeff's yarn as he bounced a cue ball off the cushioned pool table railing. "Tell him to run home like we did. It's only a mile or two. He's Mr. Marathon."

Jeff frowned and turned away. "Okay, Crazy Legs. If Axle's back with my car, I'll be down there in ten minutes. If I'm not there by one o'clock, start walking. Do *not* call my house, understand? And you better be waiting outside."

"Got it, Jeff. See ya in a few. Thanks."

Jeff hung up the phone and shook his head. "I must be some kind of idiot."

"You're kidding. You're actually going down there to pick him up?"

"No. *We* are."

Mick shook his head. "Not me. Forget it. I'm not gonna go. I won't do it."

Ten minutes later, Jeff slowed his midnight-blue Camaro down Willow Street to a blinking red light hanging over a quiet intersection. Mick glowered in the passenger seat, his arms folded across his chest and his face turned toward glowing plaza lights a quarter mile to their right. "This night keeps getting worse," he muttered. "We just robbed a house, and now we're walking into the lion's den."

Jeff turned the car left onto Burrough Street, a main

thoroughfare in the town of Salisbury. "Relax. We're not even getting out of the car," he said. "You can hide in the trunk if it makes you feel better."

Mick slouched back in his seat and closed his eyes. "Someone's gonna pay for this."

Jeff punched the gas and swerved the car wildly across the center lane. He grinned as Mick opened his eyes and braced his hands against the dashboard. "Don't be napping on me," he said. "This whole housebreaking thing was your idea in the first place."

Mick straightened up in his seat. "Okay, okay. At least we got some money now."

"Well, we better cool it for a while. Fence off the new stuff straight up. I just wanna get rid of it."

"Whatever. You're the boss."

A mile down the road, Jeff turned the car onto a long, winding driveway leading up a gentle incline toward a brick building in the distance. As they crossed the hilltop, the driveway opened to their left into the parking lot of the Salisbury Public Safety Complex. The building stood brightly lit by spotlights in the grass, a smattering of cars parked in the front spaces of the lot and a line of idle police cruisers sitting near the edge of the grass at the far edge of the asphalt. Jeff steered the Camaro to the right and backed the car into a space before killing the headlights.

Mick lowered his window halfway to scan the brick building. "I thought you told him to wait outside."

"I did," Jeff replied. "I have no idea what his problem is. Go in and get him."

"Me? No way. I don't even wanna be here, remember? You go. I'll stay here."

Jeff pulled his keys from the ignition switch and opened his door. "I'll be right out."

"Leave me the keys so I can play the radio," Mick said.

Jeff scowled at him before tossing the keys in his lap. "Keep it down. Don't attract any attention. And no smoking in my car."

"Yeah, whatever."

A fine mist fell upon Jeff's face as he stepped outside the car. He zipped his jacket and strode headlong into a stiff breeze as he located the access sidewalk and followed it to the building's entrance. After passing through double glass doors, he turned left down a long, dim hallway and stopped at the first door on the left, drawing a deep breath to summon his bravado as he pushed the door open to enter the lobby of the Salisbury Police Department.

A young female dispatcher watched him approach from behind a glass barrier. "Can I help you?"

Jeff leaned in toward a speaker embedded in the glass. "I'm looking for Gary Kramer," he said aloofly. "Is he here?"

She pressed a button on her console and adjusted her headset microphone. "Chief? Someone's here for the Kramer kid." She listened to a response and gestured toward a row of chairs lining a wall. "Have a seat please."

Instead, Jeff meandered toward a plaque on the wall, superficially reading its wording as he watched from the corner of his eye a tall man with a thick black mustache enter from a hallway at the rear of the dispatch room. The man polished the lenses of his reading glasses as he stepped up to the speaker behind the glass.

"Well, well," he said. "If it isn't Jeff Hollister, fearless leader of the Hurricanes."

Jeff winced at the sight of the police chief. "I'm looking for Gary Kramer."

"The kid in the snazzy blue jacket just like yours?" The chief slid his glasses in his shirt pocket and leaned over the countertop close to the glass. "He's back in the interrogation room. He's singing like a canary."

Jeff forced a smile. "Funny, I always thought he sounded more like a parakeet. Seriously, where is he?"

The chief's stare did not waver. "I just told you. Interrogation room."

Jeff stretched to peer over the man's shoulder. "Where is that? Across the hall from the torture chamber?"

"Don't get smart, Hollister. I know where you were tonight."

"You were at the movies too? You should've said hi. I would've shared my popcorn."

The chief's eyes narrowed, and he pointed his pen at Jeff's chest. "You weren't at any movie, and you weren't at church bingo either. We know all about your little burglary ring."

Jeff's pulse quickened. He knew his alibi was weak, so he decided to force the chief's hand quickly. "Well, I'm right here." He held his wrists out. "Go ahead and arrest me."

Chief Wellis diverted his eyes. "We're still collecting evidence."

Jeff laughed. "Good idea. You don't have any right now."

"We know more than you think. Your days are numbered, Hollister. I'm gonna lock you up or run you out of town. That's a promise."

Jeff's temper simmered. He started to reply, but a tap on his shoulder cut him off. He whirled about, expecting an officer to grab him, only to see Crazy Legs with a startled look on his face.

"Where were you?" he asked indignantly.

Crazy Legs pulled back. "The bathroom. Why?"

Jeff turned about and stepped up to the counter. He leaned forward until his nose was inches from the chief's face on the other side of the thick glass. "You'll have to try harder than that!" he shouted.

The chief's nostrils flared. "I'll see you soon, Hollister."

The Hurricane leader stormed out of the lobby into the hallway but Crazy Legs ran after him. "Jeff! What's going on?"

Jeff paced with fists clenched. "That bastard said you were in the back, spilling your guts."

"I'd rather die!" Crazy Legs said. "He was bluffing, Jeff. They're grasping at straws."

Jeff's face reddened. "Some stupid transfer cop thinks he's gonna run *me* outta town? I'll show him. I've lived my whole life in this nowhere town."

"Easy, man. They were squeezing me too. They got nothing."

Jeff coughed and pulled at the collar of his T-shirt. His voice cracked as he spoke. "I-I need a drink."

"My father's got some beer at the house—"

Jeff shook his head. "I need water—"

Crazy Legs pointed to the far end of the dark hallway. "Around the corner to the right."

"Mick's in the car. I'll be right out."

Jeff rushed down the hallway in search of cool water to soothe his parched throat. He ducked blindly around the corner and promptly collided with someone walking in the opposite direction. Staggering backward, he reached out to steady the girl he had nearly bowled over. "Sorry," he said. "I didn't see you."

She held a hand to her head. "It's my fault. I wasn't expecting anyone coming this way." She watched him as he continued down the dim hallway. "What are you looking for? Everything's closed up down there."

He cleared his throat. "Water."

She pointed to a water fountain and continued down the other hallway. Jeff stepped to the fountain to gulp down a few mouthfuls of water, wondering why a pretty girl was roaming the dark halls of the Salisbury Public Safety Complex so late at night. Wiping his chin, he hurried back toward the long hallway to catch a glimpse of her before she exited the building. Instead, they collided again just around the corner.

She stumbled back and eyed him suspiciously. "You're dangerous."

He leaned back against the wall. "That's what you get for lurking in the dark."

"I'm not lurking. I'm waiting for someone." She started walking away.

He glanced about the hallway. "Who, the janitor?"

She laughed. "No, I'm waiting for my father."

He grinned. "I'm not going to ask why your father's at the police station at this time of night."

She backed away and smiled playfully at him. "Good, I wasn't going to tell you anyway."

"Well, what can you tell me?" he asked. "How about your name?"

"I don't remember," she said coyly.

He halted, sensing rejection. "Well, if you think of it, let me know."

She stopped and leaned back against the corridor wall. "It's Cindy."

He walked slowly toward her. "Are you from Salisbury? I don't recognize you." He found her deep brown eyes mesmerizing in the dim lighting.

"Well, you should," she said. "I'm in your history class."

He smiled. "Well, that explains it. I'm usually asleep by then."

"We just moved here in the summer," she said. "I still haven't made many friends yet."

Jeff straightened up. "Hey, I got an idea. My friend Train is having a party at his house tomorrow. It's a big white house on Maple Street. Come by and I'll introduce you around."

She smiled. "Your friend's name is Train? Does he like the choo choos?"

Jeff laughed. "No, that's just his nickname. It's a long story."

"I'd love to hear it," she said. She continued down the hallway and stopped at an unmarked door to her right. "Maybe I'll see you tomorrow then."

"My name's Jeff," he blurted out.

"Oh, I know who you are." She opened the door and slipped inside before shutting it behind her.

Jeff walked slowly toward the exit of the building, perplexed by her parting comment but chalking it up to his notoriety at Salisbury High. Outside the building, he jogged through the light mist to the Camaro parked in the shadows, opening the door and hopping into the driver's seat.

Mick eyed him warily. "What are you so happy about?"

Jeff started the engine and switched on the headlights. "I just met the most awesome girl," he replied as he began to drive away.

Crazy Legs leaned forward between the seats. "Girl? What girl? I didn't see any girl."

Jeff smirked. "That's because you're too busy staring at your fancy running shoes all the time. She was right there in the hallway. Her name's Cindy. She's coming to Train's party tomorrow."

Mick snickered. "Jeff, the only girls at the police station this time of night are hookers or drug addicts."

"Or a combination of the two," Crazy Legs chimed in.

Mick laughed. "Didn't your mama ever tell you that?"

Jeff waved them off. "This girl's different. I saw it in her eyes. You guys are idiots."

"You saw it in her eyes?" Mick laughed again. "Was it love?"

Jeff smacked him in the chest. "Shut up."

"Where to now?" Crazy Legs asked.

"Home. I've had it with you guys for one night."

Jeff punched the gas to thrust his friends back in their seats, rankled by the frustrating evening but eager to see what the next day might bring.

CHAPTER 2

TRAIN LAID OUT his cards on the polished dining room table for the boys seated around him to see. "Full house," he announced. "Jacks over threes."

Jeff threw his own paltry cards down in disgust. "Take it, ya big ox."

Train stuck an unlit cigar between his lips and dragged a pile of money his way. "Pleasure doing business with ya."

A doorbell chimed above the rock music playing in the adjacent living room. "Whatever," Jeff said. "Go answer your door. Leave your cash behind."

Train rose and pointed a finger at his fellow poker players. "Touch my money and die," he said with a toothy grin.

The burly boy bounded across the living room through a crowd of dancing partiers before descending a flight of stairs to the front door. He opened the door to reveal two teenaged girls, one with brown shoulder-length hair, the other sporting a short blond crop. The sunshine made him squint as he popped the storm door open and stuck his head outside.

"Hi," he said. "Who are you?"

"I'm Cindy," the brunette replied. "I'm looking for a guy named Jeff."

Train scratched his cheek. "I know a guy named Jeff. I'm not sure he's expecting any strangers though."

She touched his hand upon the door handle. "Oh, I'm not a stranger. He asked me to come by today."

Train froze for a moment from her physical contact. "H-hold on a minute," he finally said before turning upstairs. "Jeff! You got visitors!"

Jeff stepped to the railing a moment later, his poker exasperation melting away at the sight of two pretty girls gazing up at him. "Well, don't just stand there. Let 'em in."

Train held the storm door open. Cindy entered first and held the door open for her friend. "This is Shannon. She's my ride. I hope that's okay."

Train shook Shannon's hand. "I'm Lionel. Pleased to meet ya."

"We call him Train," Jeff added.

Shannon frowned at Train and laughed. "Who named you *that?*"

"I did," Jeff said proudly.

"Lionel the Train." Cindy rolled her eyes as she started up the stairs. "Hope you didn't hurt yourself coming up with that."

Jeff laughed. "It's one of my better ones."

Shannon followed Cindy upstairs and promptly waved to a girl across the living room. "My cousin Linda is here," she gushed. "I'll catch up with you in a little while."

Train watched her mingle through the crowd for a moment before shrugging and following her. Cindy smiled and said, "Looks like Shannon found a new puppy."

Jeff smirked. "Sorry he kept you waiting outside. I didn't tell him you were coming."

"No worries. I wasn't sure of it myself, but here I am!"

A door opened down the hallway to their right, and a muscular boy with rusty-brown hair emerged from a bathroom, zipping his fly with one hand and clenching a plastic cup in the other. "Jeff!" he boomed over the din of the music. He extended an open hand before turning his attention to the girl at his side. "Who's this?"

Jeff clasped his friend's hand. "Cindy, this is Tommy Johnson. We call him TJ."

"Tommy Johnson?" Cindy repeated, extending her hand to him.

His friend spilled a little beer from his cup as he shook her hand. "That's not why they call me TJ," he said with a grin.

Cindy turned to Jeff. "Then why do you call him that?"

TJ slapped himself on the chest. "Because I am The Jock!"

Jeff forced a smile. "He's gonna make the varsity basketball team as a junior."

"Got that right, dude!" TJ grinned, clasping Jeff's hand again and spilling more beer on the carpet.

Cindy turned to Jeff. "Do you play sports too?"

Jeff shrugged. "Nah, sports are for schmucks."

She slapped him on the shoulder. "Hey! I play sports. I'm on the field hockey team."

TJ laughed. "Aren't you afraid of breaking a nail?" He stumbled off toward the kitchen without waiting for an answer.

Cindy stood with her mouth agape as she watched him stagger away. "He's more like the Jerk than the Jock."

Jeff put an arm around her and led her toward the kitchen. "He's cool. That's just the beer talking."

A shorter boy with straight black hair jostled through the crowd, carrying a frothy mug of beer in his hand. "Better hit the keg while the getting's good," he said.

"We're getting there." Jeff grinned and pulled his friend closer. "Cindy, this is my friend Axle Fromm."

Axle sipped the froth from his beer before offering his free hand to her. "It's really Alex, but everyone calls me Axle."

She shook his hand slowly and deliberately. "Ah. Dyslexic, are you?"

Jeff laughed. "No. Axle is my personal mechanic. He takes care of my Camaro."

Axle nodded enthusiastically. "It's a fine car."

Cindy turned to Jeff. "So what about you? What's your nickname?"

"I'm the leader," he said tersely. "I don't need a nickname."

"Jeff's the man with the plan," Axle cut in. "He's the one we count on to keep us on top."

Cindy smiled. "Wow, that's a lot of pressure."

"I can handle it." Jeff looped an arm around his friend's shoulders and turned him aside. "Did you check out Crazy Legs's car yet?"

Axle grimaced. "Sure did. The oil pan plug was missing. The motor's fried."

Jeff's smile vanished, for the sabotage theory rang true. "Where's Mick?"

"He was out back playing Frisbee, but I haven't seen him for a while."

"Well, if you see him, tell him I'm looking for him."

Axle nodded and advanced into the crowd. Cindy pointed to the blue-and-white swirl on the back of his jacket. "His jacket looks like yours. Are you on the same team?"

Jeff took her hand and led her forward. "Yeah. Something like that."

They squeezed through a narrow path of people through the open back door onto a raised deck outside, where an October breeze cooled their flushed faces and spread the sumptuous aroma of food across the porch. To their left a gas grill smoked with roasting burgers and hot dogs while, closer to the porch stairs, a silver keg filled the cups of a small gathering of boys.

"Hungry?" he asked. "My man Denny's on the grill."

"Denny? Like the restaurant?" she asked. "Is that why you call him that?"

"No, not like that at all. That would be totally lame." Jeff stepped up to a folding table beside the grill, close enough for the cook to hear. "His name is Dennis LeRoux. He likes sketching with charcoal and cooking with spices. He refuses to shave off that cheesy mustache, and sometimes he spells his name with one *n* when he's feeling overly chic. So I started calling him Denny. I had to do something. The senior class was ready to vote him Most Likely to Wear a Beret."

Cindy held up a finger. "Or Bake a Soufflé!"

Denny turned to face them with a bead of perspiration glistening on his fuzzy upper lip. "Ha ha. Funny. What do ya need, Jeff?"

"Gimme a cheeseburger. You want something, Cindy?"

"I'll take a hot dog," she said, stepping out from behind him.

Denny looked her up and down. "She's with you?"

Jeff nodded. "This is—"

"Yeah, I know who she is." Denny snatched a hot dog off the grill and slapped it into an untoasted roll before shoving it at to her. "Here."

"Uh, thanks." She took the hot dog from him and shrank by Jeff's side.

Jeff took his cheeseburger from Denny and led Cindy away to a nearby condiment table, frowning in bewilderment at his friend's rude behavior. He squirted a dollop of ketchup onto his burger and handed the bottle to Cindy. "Sorry. I don't know what his problem is."

Cindy lined a thin stream of ketchup down the center of her hot dog. "He's in my English class. I didn't know he felt that way about me."

"Why would he?"

She shrugged. "You'll find out soon enough."

Jeff glared back at Denny. "Oh, I'm gonna find out all right."

"Just let it go." She bit into her hot dog and wandered to the opposite side of the porch.

Jeff grabbed the crown of his hamburger bun from the table and whirled about to follow her. Instead, he crashed into a lanky, freckled boy in a Hurricane jacket staggering toward the keg near the edge of the deck. Jeff reeled back from the impact and regained his balance, only to see his cheeseburger lying on the porch deck.

"You dingus," he said. "Keep away from this guy, Cindy. He's a walking catastrophe."

"Sorry, Jeff. You were standing on the runway." The boy held his plastic cup under the flowing beer spigot while offering his free hand to Cindy. "I'm Johnny Bumbry."

"We call him Bumbles," Jeff added.

She leaned forward and shook his hand the best that she could in his awkward position. "I'm Cindy."

Jeff scooped up his fallen burger from the deck and inspected it with a frown before tossing it over the porch railing. He looked back toward the grill, now surrounded by a group of hungry guests, and instead followed Cindy as she drifted toward the porch railing. She leaned over the railing and slowly chewed on her hot dog with her back toward him.

"What's the matter?" he asked. "Why so sad?"

She shrugged. "I figured you'd know by now."

"Know what? What am I supposed to know?"

Bumbles followed them to the railing with his fresh cup of beer. He wiped his chin after a long swig. "Is this the new girlfriend everyone's talking about?"

Jeff cringed. "Isn't there something you need to go trip over?"

Cindy cut in. "I'll be right back. I need to use the bathroom."

Jeff watched in silence as she entered the house, dumbfounded by the sudden chill in her mood. He turned to the last person to see her smiling. "Hey, Denny! What's your problem?"

Denny handed the tongs to a bystander before sidling up to him. "Do you know who that is?" he whispered.

"Yeah. Her name's Cindy, and she's with me. You got a problem with that?"

"Her name's Cindy all right," Denny said. "Cindy Wellis. You know, as in Police Chief Wellis? As in 'Vote for me and I'll clean up this town.' *That* Chief Wellis."

"That's his daughter?" Bumbles gasped.

Denny patted Jeff on the shoulder. "Sorry, dude, but I figured you oughta know."

Jeff mulled the news for a moment before turning back to the porch railing. "So what?"

"So what? Are you crazy?" Denny stepped closer. "We don't even have all the stuff outta here yet. What if she starts snooping around? What if she snitches that Train's got a keg here? My brother's ass is on the line for that keg."

Jeff slammed his fist on the porch railing. "She ain't gonna snoop, and she ain't gonna snitch. She's with me, and that's that. Got it?"

"Okay, fine." Denny started back toward the grill. "I'm just sayin.' Mick's gonna go ripshit when he finds out."

"Mick ain't running the damn gang." Jeff fended off an eavesdropper with a scowl. "Where the hell is he anyway?"

Bumbles shrugged. "I don't know. I haven't seen him for half an hour."

"Find him. Tell him I wanna see him. Now."

"You got it, Jeff."

Bumbles left the porch for the backyard while Jeff stepped up to the keg and filled two plastic cups with beer. When he turned about, he saw that Cindy had returned to the porch, so he walked over to her as quickly as he could without spilling from the cups.

"Beer?" he asked.

She smiled and took a cup from him. "So did your friends tell you who I am?"

Jeff nodded, sipping slowly from his own cup.

"I'll leave if you want me to," she said. "I don't mean to make you feel uncomfortable."

Jeff set his cup on the porch rail as he mulled his answer. "Last night you told me you knew who I am."

"I sure do. You're that no-good, rotten gang leader, Jeff Hollister. My father calls you Public Enemy Number One." She took another sip of beer and swallowed slowly. "My first day at Salisbury High, someone pointed you out and told me to watch out for you."

"Yeah? So why didn't you?"

"Because I don't like having other people tell me who I should talk to and who I shouldn't. I like to make up my own mind about people."

Jeff took another sip from his cup. "So how do I know you're not spying on me for your father?" he asked.

She looked him straight in the eyes. "Honestly, Jeff, if my father knew I was here with you right now, he'd probably disown me."

He scanned her face for a telltale flinch. "I'm not so sure I should believe you."

She shrugged. "That's your choice. But I was willing to give you a fair chance even after all I'd heard about you. At least you could give me the same chance."

He hesitated until the silence felt awkward. "Fair enough," he finally said. "Tell you what. How about, just for today, I just be Jeff and you just be Cindy? All that other stuff can wait until tomorrow."

"That sounds really good, Jeff." She slipped her arm around his waist, inadvertently knocking his cup off the railing, and together they watched it splash onto the lawn below. "I'm sorry," she said with a laugh. "It's just not your day. Here, take mine."

Jeff gazed down at his beer cup lying on the ground below,

then he spotted a boy with wire-rimmed glasses crossing the backyard toward the house. "Hey, Brain!"

"I know him," Cindy said. "That's Brian Murray. He's in my calculus class."

"Yeah, he's a total egghead. We call him—"

"Brain." Cindy groaned.

Brain peered up from the lawn. "Hey, Jeff. Where ya been?"

"Playing poker. You seen Mick or Crazy Legs?"

"Have I? Oh man!" Brain stepped closer to the porch and lowered his voice. "We were tossing the football around out back, and we started getting pelted by BBs. You know what that means. Mick and Crazy Legs flushed two guys out of the bushes and chased after them. I lost them, so I came back here."

"Any idea who they were?"

"Yeah. Tornadoes."

Jeff frowned. "If you find Mick, tell him to come see me."

"Gotcha," Brain said before running off.

Cindy straightened up. "Who are the Tornadoes?"

"They're the other team." Jeff turned toward the grill and signaled for Denny to join him.

Denny handed the tongs off to a friend and slid up beside his leader. "What's up?"

"We got a Tornado sighting. Tell Bumbles and TJ to be on the lookout."

"You got it." Denny scurried off down the porch stairs.

Cindy stepped up and rested a hand on his shoulder. "Something wrong?"

"No. Everything's fine." Jeff took a plastic cup from a nearby stack and stuck it under the spigot of the keg before pulling the tap down. A part of him wanted to run off and join in the action, but he knew Cindy would probably leave if he did, and normally he wouldn't care. Gang matters took precedence over social activities, even if it meant breaking off a date, because there would always be another girl. Cindy felt different though, different from any girl he had ever dated before. As his cup filled with beer, he admired how the sunlight glistened off her golden-brown hair and how her thin lips curled in a smile with her cavernous brown eyes gazing back with affection...

"You're spilling," she said.

He rushed to shut off the tap as cold beer ran across the back of his hand. "Guess I spaced out for a second."

She winked. "I have that effect on people sometimes."

He sipped an inch from the top of his beer and wiped the foam from his lip. "C'mon, let's go back inside. I'm not hungry anymore."

They walked back into the house and through the kitchen to find Shannon and Train huddled closely and chatting in a corner of the living room. Jeff took Cindy's hand and led her through the crowd, stopping beside his bodyguard and leaning close to his ear. "Something's up," he murmured. "You might wanna head outside."

"Don't leave," Train told Shannon before bounding downstairs and out the front door.

Shannon leaned closer to Cindy and gestured to the crowd dancing in the living room and partying throughout the house. "There must be a hundred people here," she said.

Cindy slipped an arm around Jeff's waist. "It's a great party. Thanks for inviting me."

"Train and I were just dancing," Shannon told her. "He's really a sweet guy."

Jeff laughed. "Train was dancing? Wish I could've seen *that*."

The beat of the music changed, and Shannon gestured to the living room, where the dancers were moving closer to their partners. "It's a slow song. You guys should dance."

Jeff shook his head. "I don't think so—"

"What's the matter?" Shannon asked. "You got webbed feet?"

Cindy placed her cup on a nearby table and took his hand. "C'mon. I love this song."

"All right." He set his cup beside hers and wrapped an arm around her waist, pulling her closer as they drifted into the center of the living room. She slid her hands up his back and clung to his sturdy shoulders, swaying in his grasp as he rocked her from side to side to the beat of the music. He closed his eyes and nestled his face close to hers, letting the sweet perfume in her hair waft into his nostrils. Together they wandered to an open area by the picture window as she pressed her lips close to his ear.

"Not bad for webbed feet," she purred.

"Quack, quack." He closed his eyes and squeezed her closer. When he opened his eyes again, he looked out the picture window to see Crazy Legs running across the front lawn toward Maple Street, chasing a boy in a maroon jacket with a brick in his hand. Jeff swayed to a halt as he recognized the tightly spun black locks and bushy eyebrows of Curly McClure, the Tornado lieutenant, crossing the street for Train's front lawn. Behind him, a passing car cut off Crazy Legs's pursuit, and he shouted to Axle, who sprinted in from the adjacent lawn, but Curly eluded Axle's dive and continued across the front yard toward Train's house. He stopped and glared up at Jeff before cocking the brick behind his head and hurling it toward the picture window.

"Look out!" Jeff shouted. He pulled Cindy to the floor as the brick crashed through the window, showering them with shards of glass as the other dancers ran screaming from the room. His body shielded her from most of the flying glass, but the brick itself landed on her left foot.

"Ow!" she moaned. "My toe—"

Shards of glass trickled from his jacket as he sprang to his feet and rushed to the gaping hole in the picture window. The front lawn was now clear, although he could see some boys running toward the right side of the house. He turned about and asked her, "Are you all right?"

"I-I think so," she said, cautiously picking broken glass from her torso.

"Don't move. Stay here." He looked up at Shannon standing a few feet away with her mouth agape. "Help her."

Shannon rushed forward and crouched beside Cindy while Jeff dashed out of the living room and down the stairs, bowling past curious guests on his way out the front door. He followed the commotion to the side of the house, where a circle of spectators stood around two boys wrestling on the ground. Stepping closer, Jeff saw that the boy in the superior position was Train, pinning a boy in a maroon jacket to the ground with all his weight and strength.

"You're gonna pay, ya bastard!" he yelled, pummeling his adversary with his fists.

Jeff broke through the crowd. "Don't kill him. Not yet."

Train mashed his foe's goateed chin into the dirt. "Easy for you to say! You don't have to pay for that window. I'm gonna get my money's worth right now!"

"Lemme talk to him first. Who is it?"

Crazy Legs stepped forward from the crowd. "It's Justin Jenkins."

"JJ?" Jeff glanced up to his lieutenant standing on the other side of the circle. "Curly threw the brick. Where is he?"

"Ahh, he got away," Mick said in disgust.

Jeff squatted to lift JJ's head by a fistful of hair. "Hey, scumbag. Give Craig a message. The truce is over. We're gonna fight! The Tornadoes will be done by next week."

JJ gnashed his bloody teeth. "You'll be dead before that, Hollister."

Train drove a fist into his ribs. "Shut up! Who said you could talk?"

Jeff rose and patted Train on the shoulder. "He's all yours.

Try not to kill him." The beating resumed as he stormed back toward the house with Mick and Crazy Legs buzzing behind him like horseflies.

"So we're good?" Mick said. "Open season on the Tornadoes?"

"When's the fight?" Crazy Legs asked.

Jeff pondered. "How's Saturday night?"

"Kind of short notice," Crazy Legs said. "Some of the guys might be rusty. You know, signals and whistles, stuff like that."

Jeff stopped. "You guys can handle that, can't ya?"

"Sure. No problem," Mick answered quickly.

"Good. Do it." Jeff rounded the front corner of the house and spotted Cindy and Shannon waiting for him on the steps.

"Whoa. Who's that?" Crazy Legs asked.

Mick caught his leader's scornful look and tugged on the skinny boy's sleeve. "C'mon. We got work to do," he said before they ran off together.

Jeff hurried across the driveway to help Cindy hobble down the front steps as Shannon carried her friend's shoe from behind. "Do you wanna go to the hospital?" he asked.

Cindy shook her head. "I'm okay. I don't think anything's broken. I'm going home to put some ice on it. Looks like the party's over anyway."

Jeff nodded. "I guess a brick through the window will do that." He watched the guests leaving the yard in droves. "Hey, I'm really sorry —"

"It's not your fault," she said. "We were having a good time, up until the end."

"It was a great party," Shannon said. "Lots of people here."

He sighed. "Train's a popular guy."

"Can you tell him goodbye for me?" she asked.

"I will. He's a little busy right now." He turned to Cindy. "Sorry it ended like this."

"I'll be fine," she said. "You've got more important things to worry about."

Jeff shrugged. "Being Public Enemy Number One isn't all it's cracked up to be."

"Yeah, but for a no-good, rotten gang leader, you're not so bad." She leaned over and kissed him on the cheek. "I'll find you at school tomorrow."

Jeff watched silently as she hobbled down the driveway with her friend's help. He felt angry that she had become a victim of his affairs and wondered if she truly would see him again. When they were finally out of view, he turned about and marched back to the mob gathered around the side of the house as he stewed in anger. Train might be getting his money's worth out of JJ, he thought, but Craig and Curly would soon pay dearly as well.

Jeff cracked a door open, and a sliver of light cut into a pitch-black bedroom. "Ma? You awake?"

A sigh of exasperation preceded the reply. "What is it, Jeff?"

"Have you seen my keys?"

"You lost them again? What about your spares?"

"Those were my spares," he said. "I never found the other ones."

"That's too bad."

Jeff paused. "Can I use your car? It's raining, and I'm almost late."

"I need it today. I'm getting my hair done. You'll just have to walk."

He hesitated again. "I need some money."

"I put some in the jar last night. Now let me sleep."

Jeff squeezed the door shut and retreated to the kitchen. He took a cookie jar from atop the refrigerator and removed a twenty-dollar bill inside before placing the jar on its perch again.

Walking to school wasn't so bad, he mused as he stuffed the bill into his pocket, and the Camaro was probably better off staying in the garage in light of the alleged sabotage to Crazy Legs's car. Living close to the high school had certain advantages, like avoiding the indignation of riding the yellow bus, but as he bounded down the half dozen steps to the foyer he could see through the front-door window sheets of rain cascading along Spruce Street outside his house. He took his Hurricanes jacket from a wall hook and donned it, then he slipped a gray backpack over his shoulders before opening the front door. He pulled a navy-blue baseball cap tight upon his head, eyeing the rainwater pooling on the soggy lawn as he stepped out onto the front steps and shut the storm door behind him.

Ten minutes later, he arrived at the schoolyard with backpack, jacket, hat, and hair all soaking wet. He cursed the advantages of walking to school, although he reserved a few mutterings of contempt for his mother as he shivered along the covered front walk of Salisbury High School. Inside, he found his reception equally chilling: the lone figure in an otherwise deserted hallway of Vice Principal Lloyd Stammer, impatiently tapping a shoe on the hard black tile with one hand buried in the pocket of his checkered brown blazer. The vice principal's face grew stern as he took a pink pad of paper from his jacket pocket.

"You're late," he snapped. "You were late all last week too."

Jeff shrugged. "Well, I heard it was fashionable to be late, and you know how I like to keep up with the times."

Stammer's nostrils flared as Jeff walked past. "Well, I wouldn't want you to miss out on the latest fad. Here." He scribbled onto the pad before tearing off the top sheet and holding it out.

"What's this?"

"It's your official invitation to detention hall this afternoon."

Jeff snatched the slip of paper from Stammer's hand. "You know what your problem is? You're too official. You should wear a whistle around your neck or something."

"Come to the office and I'll give you a pass." The vice principal sauntered down the shiny hallway to the office door, where he suddenly stopped and whirled about. "Where's that slip of paper I gave you?"

Jeff glanced back to a crumpled wad of pink paper in the middle of the hallway. "I officially threw it on the floor."

Stammer yanked the office door open and grabbed his sleeve. "Come with me!"

Jeff jerked his arm free. "Let go! Keep your mildew to yourself!"

"Get in here, Hollister, or you're in big trouble." Stammer stormed through the office between the desks of startled secretaries before disappearing into a back room, leaving the door ajar behind him.

Jeff followed reluctantly. Stammer could be more than a thorn in the side if his ego was jolted enough, and the last thing the Hurricanes needed was a nosy vice principal just when activity against the Tornadoes was heating up. He retraced Stammer's steps through the reception area as the secretaries pecked idly at their keyboards with their eyes following him. Once he entered the vice principal's office, he pushed the door shut and turned about to see Stammer reclining in his leather chair, a grin upon his face and a large black oxford shoe propped upon his desktop.

Jeff eyed him suspiciously as he sat on the edge of a chair with his backpack still on. "What's so funny?" he finally asked.

"That was easy," Stammer said. "I thought you'd be harder to corner than this."

"What are you talking about?"

"Let me lay it on the line, Jeff. There are some kids in this school aren't angels, but with a little work we can straighten them out. Then there are those who tend to have influence over these kids. The bad apples, so to speak."

Jeff removed his baseball cap and shook the excess water off it. He took out a comb and began to comb his wet hair back. "I thought you were gonna lay it on the line. I still have no idea what you're talking about."

Stammer dropped his foot off the desk and leveled a finger at him. "I'm talking about you, Hollister. You and your hoodlum friends. You might think you own this town, but I'm not gonna let you take over this school, understand?"

Jeff frowned. "Take over the school?"

Stammer folded his hands across his chest. "Coach Reynolds informed me that he caught Mick Landry and Lionel Armstrong beating on Phil Jennings in the boys' locker room at seven thirty this morning. That was the second such report I received today."

"So? I was eating my corn flakes at the time. What do you want from me?"

Stammer leaned forward and narrowed his eyes. "Here's the deal, Jeff. From this day forward, I'm holding you personally responsible for the actions of your... er... *gang.* Any more incidents on school property involving your cohorts will result in their immediate suspension as well as your own, whether or not you're directly involved."

"You can't threaten me like that," Jeff shot back. "I'll go to the board of ed."

"Feel free. I already have their, er, *unofficial* support..." Stammer's voice trailed off as he pondered his reply. "Let's just say that, with eight months left until graduation, you'll be fighting an uphill battle."

Jeff slipped off his backpack and sank back into his seat. "Something tells me you're not just upset about a locker-room scuffle."

The vice principal leaned back and nodded slowly. "Very perceptive, Jeff. As a matter of fact, I bumped into Chief Wellis yesterday. He told me he suspects your gang was involved in a housebreaking incident Saturday night."

"So I've heard. I was at the movies with Mick."

"Well, he's not convinced. There were several sets of footprints in the adjacent lot, but they were all destroyed by the rain. Still, they think at least five or six people were involved. Naturally, you're the most logical suspect to have committed the crime."

"I'm flattered," Jeff responded.

"Well, you're probably safe unless they nab you with the goods." Stammer leaned over the desk again. "But consider yourself warned, Jeff. The whole town is watching you. Sooner or later you're going to screw up, and then it's bye-bye, Hollister."

Jeff mulled over the vice principal's admonition. He stood up and slung his backpack over his shoulder before opening the door again. "You sound pretty sure about everything. I guess the presumption of innocence ain't so fashionable anymore."

Mr. Stammer glared back at him. "Don't forget what I told you. About the suspension."

Jeff slammed the vice principal's door shut, causing the secretaries to jump in their seats. He stormed out of the main office and slammed that door too, rattling the glass office windows as he entered the hallway. A few hallways farther, he stopped at his locker and dropped his backpack on the floor, his teeth still grinding from the conversation. He yanked open his locker door to toss his wet jacket and hat inside, all the while hoping he could catch Mick before the end of the first period to tell him what had just happened.

He zipped his backpack open and reached inside for a book, spotting the keys to his Camaro lying at the bottom of the bag. With a sigh of disgust, he tossed the backpack into the locker and kicked the door shut, taking just three steps away before the shrill period bell resounded throughout the hallways. Muttering to himself, he stepped back to his locker and rummaged through the backpack again as students spilled from their classrooms into the hallway. As he pulled out another book, he felt an unexpected tap on his shoulder, prompting him to spin around with a clenched fist, ready to crack a knuckle across an unfriendly face.

Cindy shied away. "Don't shoot."

Jeff shut the locker door again. "Sorry. I'm a little strung out today."

"No worries," she said. "I shouldn't have sneaked up on you like that."

He sighed. "Yeah, I almost flattened you. You're the last person I expected to see. If I were you, *I* wouldn't even talk to me after what happened yesterday."

She frowned at him. "Do you talk to yourself a lot?"

"No! I mean — Well, you know what I mean." He finally smiled. "So how's your foot?"

She held it out and flexed the ankle. "It still works. Don't worry about it, I don't blame you for it."

"Well, you gotta admit it wasn't the best ending to a party," he said.

"I didn't like getting my toe squashed," she said. "It was fun being with you though."

"Really? Does that mean you'll go out with me again?"

She squeezed her books and flashed her eyes up at him. "No, dummy. It means I never want to see you again."

He laughed. "Awesome! How's Friday night?"

She thought for a moment. "Sounds good. Where are you going right now?"

He stuck out his tongue in disgust. "Physics. You?"

"Chemistry."

"Wanna walk with me?"

"Only if you'll carry my books," she joked.

He waved her off. "Forget it, I'll go by myself."

She smiled. "I'll still go with you. You'll probably just drool all over them anyway."

They started down the crowded hallway together with their books in hand, her stack noticeably larger than his. Jeff glanced over his shoulder to be sure no one was watching, then he took the thickest book from her stack and added it to his own books. She smiled and nestled closer to him while he shifted the stack to the opposite hand, but as he reached for her waist with his free hand, he lost control of the books and they spilled into the center of the hallway.

"I'm having a bad day," he told her. He knelt down and gathered the books before they were trampled by the student body. As he rose to his feet, he saw Crazy Legs run up beside her.

"Jeff, you gotta come quick," his friend panted. "Mick and Curly are gonna fight in D stairwell."

"So? Mick can handle himself."

Crazy Legs leaned closer and whispered, "They've got knives, Jeff! You know how quick Curly is! There's gonna be trouble."

Jeff rolled his eyes in exasperation before handing all the books to Cindy. "I'll be right back," he promised her.

He ran off before she could object, darting after Crazy Legs through every opening of students swarming the hallways. They squeezed against the corridor wall and jostled classmates from their path until finally Crazy Legs shoved open the door of an outlying stairwell. He rushed halfway down the first flight of stairs, but Jeff entered the stairwell more cautiously, spotting the familiar faces of Hurricanes and Tornadoes, drawn apart like filings on a magnet. In the center stood the lieutenant of each gang, facing off on the midlevel platform of the stairwell with knives in hand. The advantage lay clearly with their adversary as six Tornadoes crammed behind Curly on the landing with only Axle, Denny, and Bumbles backing Mick.

Jeff brushed past Crazy Legs to the last stair above the platform. He grappled the end of the railing and leaned close to his lieutenant's ear. "Mick, what the hell are you doing?"

Mick tightened his grip on the knife without losing sight of

Curly. "Stand back, Jeff. I'm gonna erase this sorry son of a bitch."

"Not here. Wait till Saturday."

Curly slackened his posture and glared impatiently at Jeff. "C'mon, Hollister, kiss your pal goodbye and lemme finish him off. I'll do you next."

"Don't be an idiot. Where's Craig?" Jeff hopped to the platform beside Mick and spotted the Tornado leader lurking over his lieutenant's shoulder. "School's off-limits, Matthews."

"Of course it is," Craig said cheekily, "but your boy started it."

Mick nudged Jeff's ribs. "Stand back and I'll run 'em both through," he murmured.

The Tornadoes' sudden aggression puzzled Jeff. He kept Curly in the corner of his eye as he inched his lips close to his friend's ear. "Put the knife away. Now."

"No way. I'm gonna kill him. Stay back."

Jeff gritted his teeth and pressed his chest against his lieutenant's arm. "I said now!"

Mick shot a glance at Jeff before quickly returning his line of sight back to the knife in Curly's hand. Finally he said, "I will if he will."

Jeff turned to face Curly still four feet away. "How about it, buddy? Wanna put it away?"

"I ain't your buddy, Hollister," Curly said. "You'll be dead real soon."

"We'll see."

Curly stepped forward threateningly. "C'mon, Hollister. Fight me now. You chicken?"

Jeff recoiled, the exchange with Stammer still fresh in his mind. As much as he hated high school, suspension wasn't on his agenda. "You wouldn't get it if I told you."

He nudged an elbow into Mick's ribs as he sensed Curly's hand tightening on the black handle of his switchblade knife.

Mick grunted in reply, ready to lunge at their enemy if his leader suddenly dove out of the way. Standing between two adversaries with both wielding deadly weapons, Jeff still felt in control, confident that his lieutenant would defend him with more speed and precision than any other Hurricane.

Upstairs, the stairwell doors crashed open and Train rushed to the railing, his face red and sweaty. "The SRO is coming! And he's got backup!"

Distracted, Jeff looked up to see Cindy rushing to the upper railing beside his bodyguard. He winced at the thought of embroiling her in another gang confrontation, but she pointed down toward the landing behind him. "Look out!" she screamed.

Jeff spun about, already certain Curly was attacking. A blur of silver shot toward Mick's gut, a blur the Hurricane leader could not deflect, only intercept. Mick staggered back unscathed, but Jeff yanked his hand back with a cry of pain, twisting away with the switchblade knife stuck in the palm of his left hand. Curly scanned the floor in astonishment for his missing weapon, but Craig alertly stepped forward and shoved Jeff backward down the lower staircase. He heard Cindy's frantic scream resounding throughout the stairwell as he turned to break his fall. Instead, his head slammed against the fourth step down, and he rolled into a crumpled heap at the bottom of the lower staircase.

The Hurricanes rushed forward to aid their leader, only to be met squarely by the advancing Tornadoes. Still holding his knife, yet suddenly jostled to the back of the group, Mick rushed to the railing to glimpse his fallen friend before looking up in despair to Train and Cindy. The overhead stairwell doors burst open, and the graying student resource officer barreled into the stairwell, flanked by three other police officers wielding batons and shouting orders to submit. Cindy and Train fell back against the railing as Mick snapped his blade away and retreated to a row of exit doors lining the midlevel platform. He kicked the closest door open to reveal a rainy courtyard outside.

"Hurricanes, break!" he shouted before dashing outside.

Axle and Denny sprinted out into the courtyard after him. Bumbles finally broke free from the clutches of the Tornadoes to slip outside, trailing his friends by a dozen steps as they ran off through the rain. Inside the stairwell, Crazy Legs backed against the wall as the Tornadoes stampeded out into the courtyard. Train and Cindy rushed downstairs behind the policemen as they hit the landing and filed outside in pursuit.

Train grabbed the last officer by the arm before he left the building. "Jeff's hurt. Help him."

The startled officer reached for his club before spotting Jeff's crumpled body at the bottom of the staircase. "Sergeant Hyrst!" he called out. "Victim down!"

The trailing policeman stopped in the courtyard and returned to the stairwell doors. "Where?"

"This way." Crazy Legs slipped past the officer to the bottom of the lower staircase, where Jeff sat propped up against the basement wall. He moaned softly with his legs stretched out and his eyelids fluttering, his hand cradled against his shirt and the switchblade knife lying on the floor beside him. Blood streamed down his face from a welt on his forehead, and he seemed oblivious to those gathering around him.

Train knelt beside him. "Jeff? Are you all right?"

Sergeant Hyrst scratched his fuzzy gray crew cut before turning to Cindy. "That's Jeff Hollister! But you're—"

"Cindy Wellis," she said.

Hyrst folded his arms across his chest. "Why are you running around with this ilk?"

She stood up. "I'm not running around with anyone. Jeff tried to break up a fight and he got hurt. Do your job and take care of him."

"Do my job," the sergeant muttered in disgust. He stared

down at Jeff and stewed for a few seconds before clicking his collar transmitter. "Dispatch, this is Hyrst. I need an ambulance at Salisbury High, Stairwell D, for a 10–53."

"Copy," his radio crackled in reply. "Ambulance to Salisbury High. Stairwell D."

Hyrst eyed Cindy skeptically before pointing his baton at Crazy Legs and Train. "We'll take care of him. We're gonna take care of *all* you delinquents. As soon as we catch your friends, somebody's going down to the station. You just better hope you're not involved."

Crazy Legs shuffled closer to Train as the sergeant knelt down to attend to Jeff. "Fine with me," he whispered, "but I sure hope Mick has his running shoes on."

Proper footwear was the least of Mick's concerns as he led his friends off school grounds through the steady rain. He had stretched the Hurricanes' lead to fifty yards over the Tornadoes and the two policemen on their trail, enough to see Willow Street, the western edge of their home turf, looming ahead. "Keep off the streets," he warned them. "More cops will be on the way."

They crossed Willow Street at its intersection with Spruce Lane and quickly veered into the backyard of the first property on their left. Slipping through a hedgerow into the next yard, Mick stumbled over a protruding root and fell to his knees in the muddy soil. He quickly scrambled to his feet but not before yielding his narrow lead to his friends.

Denny pulled him along by the arm. "Where to?"

"Jeff's garage," Mick panted. "But keep quiet. His mother's probably asleep."

"I saw the Tornadoes splitting up," Axle said. "What do you think they're up to?"

"Who cares? As long as they're behind us," Denny said.

They entered a third yard, slipping beneath an elevated deck of a raised ranch with the Hollister residence set beyond a row of evergreen bushes. Axle glanced over his shoulder. "Where's Bumbles?"

Denny looked about. "He was right behind me. He must've fallen down."

"Or the Tornadoes got him," Axle said.

Mick waved them on. "No time to go back. Cops are coming. Keep moving."

They passed through the evergreen bushes and ran through the Hollisters' backyard to the far end of the house. Denny darted around the corner and stopped at the first basement window, placing his hands flat against the glass and silently sliding it open for his friends. Axle passed through the window first, followed by Denny and lastly Mick, who dropped quietly to the garage floor before sliding the window shut again. They sat on the floor in front of Jeff's idle Camaro, saying nothing and listening intently. Only after several minutes did anyone dare to speak.

"We must've lost them," Denny said. "It makes no sense. Everyone was right behind us, and now they're gone."

"The cops must've gone after Craig," Axle said.

"Good," Denny said. "I hope they bust every one of the Tornadoes after what they did to Jeff. Talk about cheap shots."

Mick rose to his feet. "Curly thinks he can pull a knife on whoever he wants. I'm gonna take care of him personally." He took out a cigarette and stuck it between his lips as he wandered toward the garage door. Fumbling in his pocket for a lighter, he peered out a high window to scan the front lawn. "Holy shit!" he exclaimed as the cigarette tumbled from his mouth. He unlatched the garage door and rolled it open, disregarding his own directive of silence as he ran out into the driveway. "C'mon!"

His friends scrambled to their feet and hurried out of the garage with Axle quickly rolling the door shut on his way out. At the far edge of the front yard beside the border row of hedges, Bumbles stood alone beside the two policemen, one white and the other black, both lying motionless at his feet.

Mick rushed up to his lanky friend. "Bumbles! What'd you do?"

Bumbles threw his hands up in despair. "It wasn't me! It was the Tornadoes!"

Mick knelt down and rolled the trim black patrolman onto his back, revealing the name BOYD on his name tag. He bent an ear to the man's lips. "This guy's out cold."

Denny pointed down at the second officer sporting a bleeding cut along the graying hairline of a fair scalp. "It's the SRO!"

Axle ran up. "Oh shit! What the hell happened?"

"The Tornadoes ambushed them," Bumbles explained quickly. "Curly, JJ, Happy Jack, and Zak. They looked pretty slick doing it too."

"Yeah, real slick. Four on two." Mick bent beside the school resource officer, and pressed a finger against his neck. "They're alive. Let's split before they wake up."

"Look!" Denny cried out. "Their guns are gone! And so are their billy clubs."

"Seriously?" Axle said. "Tornadoes got guns now?"

Mick frowned. "Looks that way. C'mon, let's go."

Bumbles motioned to the unconscious policemen. "We can't just leave these guys like this, can we?"

"They'll live. We better go before more of them show up."

"But why? We didn't do this, the Tornadoes did."

Mick turned to face him. "Did you see where you're standing? You think the cops care about who's a Tornado and who's a Hurricane? All they're gonna know is that two of their men got their asses kicked in Jeff Hollister's front yard. We're gonna catch the heat for this, not Craig."

Bumbles shook his head. "We'll be better off in the long run if we tell the truth."

Mick patted him on the shoulder. "Okay, hero. You stay here and tell the truth. We'll take up a collection for your bail. Me, I'm lying low. I ain't going anywhere that the Tornadoes can take potshots at me. That includes school."

"What about the fight?" Axle asked. "Are we gonna have to cancel it now?"

"Not necessarily." Mick smiled wryly as he led them off through the raindrops. "The Tornadoes just raised the stakes. The question is, do we fold or call their bet?"

CHAPTER 3

RADIANT SUNLIGHT SHONE through the painted front window of Crusty's Pizza Shop and onto Mick's frowning face as he sat in the corner booth of the restaurant. He propped his chin upon his palm and glanced over to Train tapping his stubby fingers on the tabletop as Crazy Legs shoved a ham grinder into his mouth, completely oblivious to their frustration. Finally Mick slapped his palm down on the tabletop hard enough to make the plates and glasses rattle. "Will you hurry up? I'm sick of waiting for you!"

Train nodded. "I've never seen anyone eat so slow in my whole life."

Their skinny friend remained unflappable. "You're the ones who dragged me out of bed to come down here. Now you'll just have to suffer with the consequences."

Mick laughed. "Dragged you out of bed? It was eleven thirty!"

"And what's with the whole grinder?" Train asked. "We said we were going for a snack."

"I need to keep my energy up," Crazy Legs said. "I'm in training, ya know."

"Training. Ha." Mick motioned to a young waitress with short black hair passing by with four lunch plates stacked on her arms. "Hey, how 'bout getting these dirty dishes outta my face?"

"I'm a little busy," she replied.

Crazy Legs wiped his mouth with a napkin. "Anyone talk to Jeff lately?"

Mick exhaled a sigh of agitation. "I brought his backpack by his house yesterday, but he was still in bed. His mother said he had four stitches in the hand and a mild concussion. All things considered, he got lucky, I guess."

"I still can't believe it," Train said, his eyes fixed upon a TV monitor mounted near the ceiling over Mick's seat. "So much for the truce."

"I tried to warn him about the Tornadoes," Mick said. "He's too trusting sometimes. You can't turn your back on Craig or that son of a bitch Curly for one second."

Crazy Legs swallowed a mouthful of food. "You know what I think? I think Jeff should just thank his lucky stars and be done with it. Nothing good is gonna come from tangling with the Tornadoes again. We're seniors now. We oughta be thinking about college, not who's king of the hill."

"College?" Mick pointed a thumb to his burly friend staring up blankly at the television set. "You think this lummox has any shot of getting into college?"

"Watch it," Train grumbled without looking down.

Mick leaned over the table toward Crazy Legs. "You know what *I* think? I think you're an idiot if you believe the Tornadoes are just gonna lie low until next June. I think what happened to Jeff is just the beginning if we don't squash those bugs right now." He shoved his empty soda glass toward the center of the table. "I think I'm going out of my *mind* sitting in this bullshit restaurant!"

Train pointed up to the TV. "Check it out. They're talking about us on the news. Turn up the sound."

Mick stood on his seat and reached up to access the volume button. "How's that?"

The waitress returned to their table and began to stack their dirty dishes. "Please don't stand on the furniture. And watch the language."

Mick sat back down. "Quiet," he told her. "We're trying to watch the news."

"I thought this was a school day," she snapped before storming off.

Crazy Legs gazed up with his grinder an inch from his nose while Mick craned his neck to see the screen overhead. An unseen anchorwoman spoke to a young reporter with wavy blond hair, standing in the lobby of a school with a microphone in his hand. "...the fifty-three-year-old student resource officer is listed in stable condition at Madison General Hospital after sustaining multiple injuries in the altercation. Let's go to Rick Flynn with more on this story from Salisbury High School. Rick?"

"Thanks, Melissa," the reporter began. "I'm here with Sergeant Bob Hyrst of the Salisbury Police Department. He's one of four officers who responded to a call on school grounds early Monday morning. Sergeant Hyrst, can you shed any light on what happened here that morning?"

Mick grunted. "That guy's an asshole."

"Hyrst is the worst," Crazy Legs agreed.

The sergeant stepped closer to the reporter's microphone and spoke in a low, gruff voice. "At precisely 8:47 on Monday morning, we responded to a call concerning a disturbance on the school grounds involving approximately a dozen students. Upon our arrival at the school, several of the students fled the scene of the disturbance, and two officers engaged in pursuit."

Mick sucked in his cheeks and bulged his eyeballs at his

friends. "At precisely 8:47," he mimicked Hyrst, to their amusement.

The reporter Flynn spoke into his microphone. "The same officers who were subsequently ambushed?"

Hyrst shifted nervously in front of the camera. "School Resource Officer Steven Ballard and Officer Wendell Boyd followed a group of suspects into a nearby neighborhood and were ambushed by multiple assailants. A 9mm semiautomatic pistol and a .38-caliber revolver were subsequently taken from the officers after they were subdued. We're asking anyone with information on the whereabouts of these guns to contact the Salisbury Police Department immediately."

The reporter turned the microphone back to himself. "Sergeant Hyrst, there's an unsubstantiated report that one student was stabbed with a knife in the altercation, that the student is the leader of a local gang, and that the two officers were ambushed on that very student's front lawn. Would you care to comment on that account?"

Hyrst nodded slowly. "I can confirm that one student sustained non-life-threatening injuries as a result of the school altercation. He was treated at a local clinic and subsequently released. I'm not at liberty to comment on the student's identity or any affiliation at this time. Our investigation is continuing."

The camera panned away from Sergeant Hyrst to focus solely on the reporter. "Knives and guns and gangs—scary stuff for this quiet bedroom town. Rick Flynn, live from Salisbury. Back to you, Melissa."

Train frowned. "They're continuing their investigation? You guys hear anything since Monday?"

Mick chuckled. "Some investigation. Hyrst came by my house yesterday with a list of questions. I offered my usual spirit of cooperation. That moron couldn't find a bagel in a doughnut shop." He spotted a businessman eavesdropping on their conversation from a nearby booth. "Hey, you got a problem?"

The man quickly looked away, but the waitress returned to their table with a remote control and lowered the TV volume with it. "If you're gonna harass the customers, you're gonna have to leave."

"Ahh, we're done anyway." Mick sucked the final remnants of soda through his straw with a loud slurp. He pulled a twenty-dollar bill from his pocket and handed it to the waitress. "Keep the change," he said with a wink.

"Can I have a refill?" Crazy Legs handed his soda glass to the departing waitress before sinking his teeth into the grinder again.

"A refill? We've been waiting twenty minutes for you to finish!" Mick cried.

Crazy Legs tried to answer, but mayonnaise and lettuce dribbled down his chin. He laughed at his own spectacle while Mick turned away in disgust. Train threw some money onto the table and stood up from the booth. "I'm outta here. I think I'm gonna puke."

"I'm with you," Mick said. "See ya later, slob."

"Hey, wait! Where ya going?" Crazy Legs called out.

Mick donned his jacket and pulled a pack of cigarettes from the pocket. "Outside. You got two minutes to finish or else."

"Or else what?"

"Or else I'm gonna come back and finish it for you," Train said with a grin. "And you've already wasted ten seconds."

Train and Mick marched out of the restaurant and stopped on the sidewalk as the glass door shut behind them. Mick stuck a cigarette in his lips and offered the pack to his friend. "Want one?" he asked.

Train took one. "Thanks. Got a light?"

Mick lit his own cigarette before extending the flame to his friend. "Want me to smoke it for ya too?"

Train puffed the cigarette to life before exhaling a cloud of smoke into Mick's face. "No, thanks, pal."

"You jerk." Mick socked his friend in the chest. "I'll make you eat it."

Train laughed and backed past the windows of a tattoo parlor to the end of the sidewalk, where a short brick wall abutted a gravel embankment rising around the side of the building. He leaned back casually and drew another drag from the cigarette, but his smile faded as he exhaled the smoke again.

Mick frowned quizzically at his friend's sullen expression. "I'm just kidding, ya know."

Train held up a finger for silence, tilting an ear closer to the building. Mick held his breath as he crept forward, straining to hear a conversation around the corner. As he stepped closer, he could hear several voices interrupting and arguing with one another, but Curly's voice boomed above the rest.

"Hey, I took the chance," he said. "I'm keeping them *both*."

"You don't need both," said another voice that sounded like Craig.

"Curly's been playing too much *Grand Theft Auto*," said a third voice. "He's gonna shoot up the world."

Mick and Train craned their necks to the left to hear more, but they both cringed at the sound of the familiar voice calling out from behind. "Hey Mick!" Crazy Legs shouted from the doorway of Crusty's. "Whatcha doing?"

Train whirled about. "Shut up!"

"Too late! Run!" Mick broke into a sprint with a thumb pointed back at the Tornadoes already filing around the corner of the building. He jumped off the sidewalk and darted among the cars in the parking lot, while Crazy Legs and Train whirled about and bolted off together down the sidewalk past Crusty's.

Mick made a beeline for Burrough Street and the Lower Plaza on the other side of the road, where a bustling parking lot presented more cover than the Upper Plaza lot from which he fled. Nearing the busy road, he glanced over his shoulder to see Zak and Curly following him, although the rest of the

Tornadoes pursued Crazy Legs and Train down the sidewalk. Zak's bulky stature minimized his threat in a footrace, but Mick knew Curly was one of the Tornadoes' fastest runners, and the verity that he possessed at least one of the stolen guns made him all the more dangerous. Crafty though he was, he could not outwit a bullet if its mark was true, nor could he hope to maintain his frantic pace long enough to escape Curly's sights.

At the curb of Burrough Street, he glanced back to see Zak predictably lagging behind but Curly gaining ground. Horns blared and tires squealed as he dashed out among the approaching cars, but he arrived unscathed on the other side of the street, leaving Curly waiting for the cars to pass. Mick dashed down a grassy slope to the edge of a wide parking lot that stretched nearly fifty yards to the storefronts of the Lower Plaza chain mall, heading for a pharmacy at the center of the strip where the pedestrian traffic seemed heaviest.

Curly finally crossed Burrough Street, while Mick ducked behind a nearby car and kept his head low, weaving a haphazard course between the other parked cars until he reached the storefront sidewalk of the Lower Plaza stores. He cast open the glass door of the pharmacy and glanced back to locate his pursuer, promptly collided with a woman toting two shopping bags in her hands. They toppled to the ground in a tangle of arms and legs as the contents of her bag scattered onto the sidewalk.

"Sorry," Mick muttered. He helped the woman gather her items until he saw Curly sprinting toward the door, so he scrambled to his feet and ran farther into the store. Seconds later Curly tromped past the woman and her scattered items before bowling past another startled customer and rushing down the center aisle toward the rear of the store.

A pharmacist spotted the approaching ruckus and stepped out from the prescription counter to confront the boys, but Mick ducked his head and barreled into him, leveling the smaller man and stepping over him on the way to the back room. He passed through a brown swinging door and rushed down a hallway to the left, darting around a blind corner only to confront a gray metal fire door that did not readily open. Behind him, the swinging door crashed open to signal Curly's arrival, prompting Mick to drive a hard shoulder into the fire door that finally separated it from its sticky jamb. He stumbled into a dim storeroom and slammed the door shut behind him as Curly rounded the blind corner.

A corridor led to the right, past a row of freestanding metal racks stocked with assorted products and supplies. Mick grabbed the final rack and yanked it over as he turned toward the rear of the storeroom, just as the fire door burst open behind him under Curly's brute force. Aerosol cans and plastic containers tumbled onto the floor as the rack fell against the opposite wall and into Curly's path. He tried to hurdle the toppled rack at its lowest point, but he tripped on the far edge and tumbled to the stockroom floor with a profane shout.

Another metal door equipped with a crash bar stood in Mick's path, with sunlight leaking through the imperfections in its frame. He ran forward and leaped triumphantly into the air, striking the crash bar with his heel and casting the door open to a blinding blast of sunshine and the promise of escape. His jubilation quickly soured as he landed on a short loading platform guarded only by a thin metal chain that readily snapped from the weight of his body. Bracing himself for the fall, he landed on the asphalt three feet below, scraping his palms and tearing the knees of his jeans. He rolled to his feet, dazed from the jarring impact but motivated into action by the sight of Curly standing in the doorway with his stolen pistol in hand.

Back inside the stockroom, the pharmacist pushed the fallen metal rack aside. "Hey!" he shouted. "Get back here!"

Curly sneered back in defiance. He stepped out onto the loading dock and slammed the door shut with his foot, while Mick sprinted for the far corner of the building to the right. As he ran past the rear door of an adjacent liquor store, a German shepherd sprang after him from the shadows of a dumpster, barking furiously with its chain rattling against the pavement. The dog lunged and bit his calf just before the chain snapped taut on its collar, jerking it away. Mick shouted and limped on toward the rear of the adjacent supermarket with his leg throbbing. He looked back to see Curly running beyond the perimeter of the vicious dog's reach and the pistol held freely in his hand.

Tired and aching, Mick staggered past the final establishment in line, the Salisbury branch of the Madison Savings Bank. With fading hope, he ducked around the corner of the building and fell flat against the building. He struggled to control his labored breathing as he inched back toward the corner of the wall, listening intently beyond the barking dog for the sound of panting or footsteps upon the asphalt. When he thought he heard something close enough, he clenched a fist and swung it blindly around the corner, relishing the feeling of solid contact that was swiftly followed by a groan and a thud. He waited a few seconds before peering around the corner to see Curly lying flat on his back with the gun lying harmlessly on the ground a few feet away.

He gasped in surprise and sprang over his enemy to scoop up the gun, marveling at it in his hand for a moment before aiming it down at Curly. Rather than pull the trigger, however, he simply tucked the gun away under his waistline and concealed it beneath his jacket. He brushed the gravel from his knees and spat down at his adversary before turning about and continuing merrily on his way.

Crazy Legs and Train didn't share their lieutenant's glee as they ran full stride across the Upper Plaza parking lot with six angry Tornadoes in swift pursuit. Their course had continued straight where Mick's had turned left, down the sidewalk past a nail salon and a bicycle shop, across a delivery access driveway, and behind a 7-Eleven store set like an island in a sea of asphalt. From there, they ventured to their left across a wide, empty section of the parking lot, their twenty-step lead over the Tornadoes waning as the skinny boy lagged behind.

"Why are you running so slow?" Train called back.

Crazy Legs winced. "I can't breathe. I got a cramp."

"That's what you get for stuffing your face." Train pointed to another row of shops ahead. "Head for the pool hall. Maybe Denny and Axle are up there."

"Good idea."

Train drew a deep breath and quickened his pace, lumbering down the gentle decline of the parking lot toward the rectangular two-story building, the longer leg of a disjointed ell that faced Burrough Street with its shorter leg. The storefront windows shimmered from the late October sun, briefly blinding him as he hopped onto the sidewalk. He turned about and backed up to a glass door with POOL HALL painted in silver lettering, pulling it open to reveal a red-carpeted staircase leading upward.

"Hurry," he urged his friend. "I saw Willie and Phil circling around back."

Crazy Legs hopped onto the sidewalk and glanced at the four remaining Tornadoes still heading their way. "This might be our best chance," he said breathlessly. "Let's take 'em on right here."

"Are you kidding? We'd get creamed." Train pointed his thumb inside. "Go!"

Crazy Legs slipped inside the foyer and started up the carpeted staircase, while Train pulled himself upward along a brass railing behind his friend. As they rounded the midway landing, the glass entrance door rattled open behind them, and the four pursuing Tornadoes filed into the foyer below. Train followed Crazy Legs up the second flight of stairs and stopped at the top to catch his breath, only to spot Happy Jack's spiked blond hair bouncing up the stairs at the front of the Tornadoes.

At the top of the stairs, Crazy Legs held open another glass door with POOL HALL lettered in gold and the image of an eight-ball painted beneath it.

"Hurry," he said before ducking inside.

Train pushed off from the railing and followed him in as the Tornadoes neared the top of the staircase. They halted as a dozen pool players scattered around the pool hall turned to acknowledge their tumultuous arrival, while a bald, wrinkled man looked up from behind a countertop. "Hey! No colors in here!" he grumbled. "You two know better!"

Crazy Legs held up his hands as he backed to the center of the hall. "Sorry, Otto. Just passing through."

The skinny boy turned forward again and promptly collided with a tattooed player in a motorcycle vest who was lining up a shot at a solitary nine-ball. The biker stumbled forward as he shot, glancing the cue ball with his stick and sending it straight into the side pocket. Furious, he threw his stick onto the table and grabbing Crazy Legs's wrist before he could slip away.

"That game was for twenty bucks," the biker fumed. "You owe me twenty bucks!"

Crazy Legs tried to twist his hand free. "I-I haven't got it!"

The biker looped an arm around his neck. "Then I'm gonna take it out of your ass, toothpick!"

"Train! Help!"

Train glanced back to see the four Tornadoes gathering by the front desk. He picked up a cue stick from a vacant table and stepped up behind the biker, cracking the butt end of the stick across the biker's buttocks, while Otto shouted in objection. The man howled and grabbed his stricken butt cheeks, allowing Crazy Legs to break free and retreat toward the rear tables, while Train backed toward him with a wary eye on the other patrons in the room.

Otto cussed and started out from behind the counter, but Craig shoved him back onto his stool as the other three

Tornadoes fanned out across the room. Train tossed the broken stick aside and retreated to the emergency exit at the rear of the room; he drove an elbow into the crash bar and kicked the door open to reveal a metal catwalk outside.

"Hurry!" he shouted. "Willie and Phil are coming!"

Crazy Legs stopped at the last pool table, littered with a dozen balls from an abandoned game. The angry patrons glowered at him from about the room, while the four Tornadoes continued to approach: Tony Spanelli and Happy Jack flanked the walls to either side of the room and Craig strode confidently down the center aisle ahead of JJ. The tattooed biker approached with the butt of the broken cue stick in hand, as his bearded partner circled around their table with his fists clenched by his sides.

Crazy Legs scooped up three balls from the nearby pool table and launched them in rapid succession across the room. Tony cried out as a green ball ricocheted off his elbow, while a blue-and-white-striped ball whizzed past the biker's ear before crashing into the fluorescent lamp over the table behind him. Craig jumped back from the shower of sparks and glass and into the path of a flying yellow ball a split second before it glanced off his collarbone.

"Ow! Kramer, you're gonna die!" he cried out. Tornadoes and patrons alike chimed in with their own shouts and threats.

Crazy Legs grabbed two more balls from the table before retreating to the emergency exit. "These might come in handy," he said, clacking them together.

"Go!" Train grabbed him by his jacket and threw him outside before slamming the door shut behind them.

To their right, the catwalk led to a rusty staircase that Phil was already ascending, while to their left the metal grating stretched to the end of the building at a point that overlooked the alley between the two buildings at the junction of the ell. Crazy Legs peered over the metal railing to see Willie standing below, waiting to pounce if they attempted to jump.

"We're trapped! Now what?"

Train headed left. "This way."

"Hold on." Crazy Legs cocked back a solid black ball and called out, "Eight ball, center pocket." He cast the ball with all his might at Phil running down the catwalk, striking him squarely on the forehead and knocking him flat on his back.

The emergency door burst open again, casting Crazy Legs back against the railing as Craig led the angry mob out onto the catwalk. The grating shook with every step of Train's beefy legs as he bolted for the far end of the fire escape, while Crazy Legs whirled about and sprinted after him with the incensed throng thundering along the grating, hot on his heels. Train turned about at the end of the catwalk and stretched out his arms to his friend sprinting at him full tilt. Crazy Legs leaped forward and, in one fluid motion, Train lifted him over the safety railing to place him deftly upon the metal lid of a dumpster in the alley below. Train grabbed the railing with his sturdy hands and swung his feet over it like a gymnast on a sawhorse, nearly kicking Craig in the jaw with his giant shoe before landing on the dumpster lid with a clang.

Crazy Legs clambered safely to the ground, but Willie quickly jumped him from behind and latched onto his back. Train dropped to the asphalt and peeled Willie away before twirling the diminutive scout about and flinging him into tall stacks of empty beer bottle cases that crashed down upon him. Crazy Legs grabbed Train's sleeve and pointed to the Tornadoes laboring over the catwalk railing with the pool hall patrons muddling among them. "Way to go, Train! We're home free!"

He ran out of view around the dumpster toward the parking lot again, but his departure was marked by a thump and a muffled cry, followed by an orange-striped billiard ball trickling out into the center of the alley. Train darted around the corner to find Zak lying on top of his friend and mashing his face into the grimy asphalt. He tried to knock the rugged

Tornado from his perch as Crazy Legs squirmed to break free, but one by one the other Tornadoes joined into the fray. Soon Train also lay pinned to the ground, twisting and writhing while four Tornadoes held each of his powerful limbs immobile. Craig hovered over them with eyes gleaming, his Tornadoes joined by a half dozen pool players with smirks of satisfaction upon their faces.

JJ squeezed Train by the jaw. "How do ya like me now, Armstrong?" he asked, his left eye still sporting a shiner from his thrashing at the keg party.

Phil stooped beside Crazy Legs with a noticeable welt growing on his forehead. "I'm gonna make you eat this!" he yelled, pressing the orange-striped billiard ball hard against the skinny boy's nose.

Craig squatted between his two captives. "Time to teach you Hurricanes a lesson. We ain't playing games anymore."

Crazy Legs grit his teeth and wriggled beneath his captors' hold. "We ain't afraid of you, Matthews."

"That's your first mistake." The Tornado leader stood upright and kicked him in the thigh before stepping back and lighting a cigarette. He drew a deep drag and exhaled dramatically before snapping his fingers, and the true pain began. Neither strength nor agility spared either boy from the punches and kicks that rained down upon them, and all they could do was shield their faces while Craig stood back, smoking his cigarette and chatting amicably with the pool players.

Finally, beaten nearly senseless by his enemies, Crazy Legs flinched as a gunshot resounded through the alley. Fearing the worst, he rolled over and cast a wary eye toward Train, expecting to see him lying dead on the pavement. Instead, Train rose to his knees as their assailants scattered from the alley like a flock of frightened birds. He leaned back upon his heels and sucked on a bloody lip as he watched a familiar face entering the alley from a gap in the short stockade fence bordering the sidewalk. "Where did you come from?" he asked the Hurricane lieutenant.

Mick grinned with his newfound pistol still pointed toward the sky. "You guys looked like you needed help."

Crazy Legs wiped his bloody nose on the back of his hand. "Where'd you get the gun?"

"Like it? Courtesy of Curly McClure," he said proudly.

"Great idea, shooting it like that. What if Craig had the other one?"

"Then he'd be dead," Mick snapped. "Maybe I should've stood by and let you carry your teeth home in your pocket."

Crazy Legs struggled to his feet and brushed the dirt off his pants. "I'm just saying. You shouldn't have fired it. Now they'll think you'll do it again."

"So what? Maybe I will. We ain't exactly playing kickball with them, freak."

Train glanced about the plaza. "Can we argue later? We should get the hell out of here."

Mick stuffed the pistol under his belt. "I save the kid's ass, and he nags me about it. I can't win." He backed through the fence opening and trotted off across the open parking lot in the direction of Hurricane territory. Train glanced to Crazy Legs, who rolled his eyes in return before they ran off after their friend with the gun.

CHAPTER 4

"Ready?"

"Yeah. Let's go."

Crazy Legs pulled the front door of his house shut, donning his Hurricane jacket as he joined Mick on the steps. Together they hopped to the lawn, skipping the bothersome steps in between, and jogged across the empty driveway to Elm Street. Only when they passed the adjacent Spruce Lane to their left did they slow to a walk, glancing down toward Jeff's house with vague curiosity. Not since Jeff's tragic stairwell plunge had either Hurricane seen his leader, but they knew his absence was soon to end, for it was his phone call that prompted their venture in the first place.

Continuing northward, they soon crossed Arrow Drive, a long, hilly road that separated Hurricane territory from Tornado grounds at points farther east. The land directly across the street from them was considered neutral turf by both gangs, rising from the small golden field before them to a triangular section of woods spanning a square mile that separated both neighborhoods from the Upper Plaza. At the far edge of the golden field, a familiar dirt path divided a pair of forsythia bushes before winding into the outskirts of the woods, where young poplar trees stood only as tall as the two boys. The farther they hiked into the woods, the more the sunlight dimmed, obscured by colorful foliage of taller oak and maple trees overhead.

Deeper into the woods, they came upon a clearing covered with fallen cones and needles deposited by the tallest tree in the woods, a landmark pine dubbed Mr. Big by the gang. Here, their path was intersected by four other pathways around the large, protruding roots of the tree. The main path continued past the giant tree, following a ridge atop the sloping forest bed toward the rear of the Upper Plaza, while a thinner trail jutted off to the right, running downhill across a stormwater gulley before rising on the other bank into thick brush near the edge of Tornado territory. A well-worn path rose behind their left shoulders toward an elevated clearing known as Bobcat Hill, offering a panoramic view overlooking Salisbury High School, parts of Hurricane territory, and the Lower Plaza. Lastly, a rabbit path barely discernible cut back at an acute angle toward Arrow Drive, down the hillside slope toward the deepest end of the rainwater gulley.

The two boys turned sharply onto the rabbit path, holding their arms overhead to avoid contact with the prickly bushes to either side. The path wound down to a long-fallen tree spanning the ravine before widening on the other bank, gradually rising to a flat clearing of soft pine needles set like a blanket before a semicircle of four modest pine trees. Crazy Legs stopped at the brink of the clearing, fumbling inside the pockets of his Hurricane jacket as if in search of something.

Mick wandered into the center of the clearing. "Don't tell me you forgot it."

"No, I got it," the skinny boy said as he pulled out a single key on a string. He sank to his knees and brushed the pine-needle bed aside, uncovering the edge of a plywood board. Tracing the edge with his fingers, he located a brass padlock clasped to a rusty latch and unlocked it with the key before removing it and tossing it aside. He brushed the dirt from a small brass handle beside the latch and flipped a plywood door over, revealing a square hatchway leading into a black hole underground.

"I knew you were good for something." Mick knelt down and peered into the darkness. "Gimme your flashlight."

"I thought you brought one," Crazy Legs said.

Mick shook his head in exasperation. He sat on the edge of the hatchway and dangled his feet into the dark hole, swinging a foot about as if wading in a pool. After a moment he lifted the foot up to reveal the first rung of a rope ladder dangling from the toe of his sneaker. Grabbing the top rung for support, he set his feet upon the lower rungs and then swiftly descended to a plywood floor ten feet down into the darkness. He struck a flame with his cigarette lighter to reveal a small wooden table to his right with an oil lamp set upon it. After removing the glass chimney from the lamp, he set the flame to the wick and a hazy orange glow spread throughout the pit, chasing back the shadows. He adjusted the burner and lit a cigarette off the flame, replacing the glass chimney onto the base of the lamp as Crazy Legs dropped to the floor beside him.

"Get the other one," he said, flipping the lighter to his friend.

Crazy Legs waved his hand in front of his face. "Do you have to smoke in here? It's gonna stink for a week now." He crossed the room and stepped upon a carpeted platform at the opposite end of the room, where another oil lamp stood on a wooden stand set in the corner of the fort. Moments later, a bright flame burned in the second lamp, driving the lingering shadows farther into the corners of the pit while he snapped the lighter shut and tossed it across the room to his friend.

The underground fort was little more than a rectangular hole with a plywood ceiling and thinly paneled walls, dry and secluded housing for an assembly of chairs within. An old brown sofa lined the short wall to the left of the hatchway and a raised platform across the room supported a wooden tripod with a stack of charcoal sketches on white poster boards. Halfway down the long wall, an open sheet metal box was embedded in the plywood wall, with a four-inch-wide aluminum pipe boring up through the dirt for ventilation to the surface. To the right of the makeshift fireplace, a pair of yellow skis leaned against the paneling with their bindings facing out and tips pointing up.

Crazy Legs ran his finger gently along one of the ski's edge. "You didn't get rid of these yet?"

"I had a deal, but it fell through," Mick said, clearly agitated by the question. He drew a long drag from his cigarette and exhaled. "Those are good skis. I ain't gonna sell 'em just for the sake of selling 'em. I'm sure Jeff would agree."

"We'll see." Crazy Legs said. "We'll see what he says about your gun too."

Mick shrugged. "What about it?"

"Ever since you got it, you've been struttin' around like you're Clint Eastwood or something."

"What should I do? Give it back to Curly?"

"Well, you don't gotta carry it everywhere, do ya?"

"It won't do me any good at home," Mick said. "I coulda been shot yesterday just going out for lunch. I ain't taking any more chances."

Crazy Legs sighed. "Great. Now we got two idiots running around with guns."

The fort darkened a shade as a pair of legs dropped through the overhead hatchway. A moment later, TJ climbed down the rope ladder and jumped to the floor, his rusty-brown hair bobbing as he landed. "Hey, guys," he said. "Where's Jeff?"

"I don't know," Crazy Legs said. "He just said to meet him here."

Axle descended the ladder next and dropped to TJ's side. "Hey, what's up with the pool hall? Last night Otto told us that the Hurricanes are *persona non grata* now."

Mick pointed a thumb at Crazy Legs. "Nimrod here decided to run an obstacle course through the place yesterday. I'll talk to the old coot. He'll go belly up without us."

Crazy Legs laughed. "Mick makes it sound like Field Day. He forgot to mention I had half the Tornadoes on my ass."

Denny climbed down to the floor and steadied the rope ladder for Brain to descend. "The Tornadoes? Really? What happened?"

"Well, for one thing, I got this." Mick pulled out the stolen pistol for everyone to see.

"Awesome!" Axle exclaimed. "Can I hold it?"

"How'd you get it?" TJ asked.

Mick held the gun out. "Curly tried to shoot me with it, but I turned the tables on his ass."

Axle spoke like a movie gangster from the corner of his mouth as he took the pistol and lifted it toward Denny. "Okay, Bugsy, your number's up!"

Mick grabbed his wrist and stripped the gun away from him. "It ain't a toy, ya know."

Axle withdrew defensively. "Ow! I was only kidding around."

"Yeah, no shit," Mick said. "That's how friends get shot."

Crazy Legs laughed. "And if there's any shooting to do, Mick's gonna do it."

Denny stroked his thin mustache. "Better keep that under wraps. Especially with Jeff's new girlfriend around."

Mick tucked the gun away again. "You mean that chick he met at the police station?"

Denny shook his head. "No, the chick whose father *runs* the police station. You didn't see them together at the party?"

"I barely saw Jeff at the party." Mick turned to Crazy Legs. "Why didn't you tell me about this?"

Crazy Legs shrugged. "It's none of my business who Jeff goes out with. If he thinks he can handle it, it's fine with me."

Brain gazed up through the hatchway opening. "I think he's here."

The boys fell silent at the sound of scuffling feet on the plywood rooftop. Mick drew another drag on his cigarette and exhaled toward the fireplace in a half-hearted attempt to exhaust the smoke through the vent. Crazy Legs plopped down on the center cushion of the couch while TJ and Axle took seats on either side of him. Denny settled into a wooden chair beside the fireplace as Brain leaned back against the opposite wall, polishing his glasses with the tail of his shirt.

Another pair of legs started down the rope ladder, and although everyone looked up in anticipation of Jeff's arrival, Bumbles dropped to the plywood floor instead, sporting a familiar freckled grin. "Hey, guys. Jeff's right behind me."

Mick pointed to a sneaker fishing for the rope ladder overhead. "Don't stand there like a dork. Help him out."

"I can do it," Jeff said from above. His foot caught the ladder, and he cautiously descended four rungs until his entire torso was inside the fort, his bandaged left hand looped around the top rung of the ladder. He reached back through the hatchway with his right hand to grasp the inner handle of the hatchway door, pulling it shut before continuing down the ladder. When he was low enough, he jumped to the floor, but he landed awkwardly and stumbled back into the outstretched arms of Brain.

"I got ya, Jeff," he said.

"Thanks." The Hurricane leader smiled humbly as he stood upright. He scanned the faces in the fort and asked, "Where's Train?"

"Haven't seen him all day," Crazy Legs said. "I thought he was with you."

Mick checked his cell phone. "I texted him earlier, but he never answered."

"How's your hand, Jeff?" TJ asked.

Jeff held out his bandaged paw for all to see. "It hurts like hell. The doctor said I'm lucky there wasn't any major damage." He nodded toward his lieutenant. "I think Mick oughta be the one who considers himself lucky."

Crazy Legs smiled at Mick. "He's right, ya know."

"I don't know," Mick said coolly. "I can take care of myself in a fight. I took on Curly all by myself yesterday, and I'm still here."

"So I heard," Jeff said. "Lemme see it."

Mick glowered at Crazy Legs before looking back to Jeff. "You gonna give it back?"

"I'll let you know. C'mon, cough it up."

Mick sucked one last drag from his cigarette before flicking the butt into the sheet metal firebox. He ponderously exhaled a cloud of gray smoke into the confines of the room as his steel-blue eyes scanned the faces of his friends seated before him. Finally, he pulled the pistol from beneath his jacket and held it out at arm's length to his leader.

"Wow!" Bumbles said. "Where'd you get that?"

"It fell out of my cereal box this morning," Mick quipped.

Jeff pinched the butt of the gun like he was holding a dirty diaper. "You took this from Curly?"

"Like candy from a baby."

Jeff gripped the handle more firmly and strolled forward to step up onto the raised platform. He held up his bandaged hand for all to see. "If this isn't enough proof how serious the Tornadoes are"—he lowered the hand and raised the pistol in the air with his good hand—"then this gun oughta be. Curly already threatened to shoot Mick with it yesterday."

"Hard to imagine, after all the good times we've had together," Mick joked.

Jeff waited for the smattering of laughter to die down before continuing. "You guys have always had my back and done whatever the gang needed you to do. But we've never faced something like this before. There's another gun out there, and we have no reason to think they won't try to use it. At first I figured it'd be suicide fighting against two guns, but now that we have one, I'm not so sure. Maybe they won't risk using it now that we have one. Or maybe it's crazy just taking that chance."

Denny frowned. "So what's your point?"

"No point," Jeff said. "I just wanna know what you think. Should we fight or what?"

"*Or what?* You mean, like, *back out?*" Mick asked. "We can't back out, Jeff! We gotta see their ugly faces at school every day."

"You won't see much with a bullet in your head," Crazy Legs said. "Although it might be an improvement."

Mick scowled at him. "The Hurricanes don't back down from no one. The Tornadoes think they're tough with guns. Well, we got one now. Let's see how tough they really are."

"Okay," Crazy Legs said. "You stand in front."

"Fine, I will. I ain't afraid of nobody. If we back out now, we ain't nothin' but yellow." Mick jabbed his thumb into his own chest. "And I ain't yellow!"

"Okay, I know where you two stand." Jeff turned to his friends. "How 'bout everyone else?"

Mick pulled out another cigarette and stuck it between his lips. "What is this, a vote?"

Jeff turned indignantly to his lieutenant. "I just wanna know what they think. Is that all right with you?"

The hatchway door opened again before Mick could reply. Jeff squinted in the rush of daylight to see Train descending the rope ladder. His bodyguard pulled the hatch shut behind him before climbing to the floor and turning to face the ensemble.

"Sorry I'm late," he said.

"Where ya been, ya big ox?" Mick asked. "We've been looking for you all day."

"Around," Train said quietly.

"Like where?"

"Just around." Train stepped to the couch and tapped Axle on the shoulder, deliberately avoiding eye contact with everyone else.

Jeff scrutinized his bodyguard for a moment. "Everything all right, buddy?"

Train looked up. "Huh? Yeah, Jeff, I'm fine. Other than the fact that Axle's in my seat." He waited for Axle to move before sitting at the end of the sofa. "So what'd I miss?"

Mick huffed. "We were just having a *vote*. On whether to fight Saturday night." He waved a hand mockingly in the air. "Who wants to fight? Let's see those hands, girls!"

Jeff frowned at him before turning to the gang. "You heard him. Who wants to fight?"

The befuddled Hurricanes glanced about each other's faces, waiting for someone else to speak first. Finally TJ raised his hand. "I'll still fight. I ain't afraid of them."

Denny nodded. "Me neither."

Axle shrugged and raised his hand. "Mick's got a point. We can't back down."

Jeff looked about the room. "Anyone else? Bumbles? Brain?"

Crazy Legs spoke up. "I don't think they wanna fight. And neither do I."

"I expected that from you wimps," Mick said, "but we still got the majority."

"How do you figure? I only count four."

"Well, Train's gonna fight after they trashed his party. Right, Train?"

Train stared down at his feet. "Um, no. I don't think so."

"What?" Mick cried out.

"Sorry, Mick. I just don't think it's a good idea right now."

Mick lit the cigarette and exhaled the smoke slowly before

turning to his leader. "Okay, Jeff. Looks like it's up to you. I can't believe my lying ears, but it's your decision anyway. So what do you say? Fight or flight?"

Jeff shuffled his feet beneath the pressure of Mick's loaded question. Finally he looked up to his friends. "Look, I know you guys are nervous, but the Tornadoes are bold and getting bolder. We gotta squash them now before things really get outta hand. The fight's still on."

Brain folded his arms and leaned back against the wall again. "We're asking for trouble, Jeff. You know it."

"We gotta stand strong. They won't just go away." Jeff held out the gun to Mick, who gladly accepted it and stuffed it under his belt again.

Crazy Legs gasped. "You're giving it back to him?"

Mick smiled. "He just did."

"You should hold it, Jeff," Crazy Legs said. "At least we'd know it's in safe hands."

Jeff shook his head. "I don't want it. And Mick's not gonna use it without my say-so. Right, Mick?"

His lieutenant held up three fingers with his cigarette dangling from his lips. "Scout's honor, Jeff!"

"I mean it." Jeff turned to the rest of the Hurricanes. "Look, I know Craig Matthews. If we show restraint, I think they will too. They might just be over their heads on this. Maybe we can give them a way to save face and keep everyone safe."

Crazy Legs sprang to his feet. "Are you kidding me? Safe? It's just a big game to you guys, isn't it?"

The Hurricanes squirmed in their seats as their scout stormed toward the rope ladder, but Mick stepped forward and grabbed him by the shoulder. "Where do ya think you're going?"

Crazy Legs jerked himself free. "I don't wanna hear this crap. I'm outta here."

"Let him go," Jeff told Mick before narrowing his eyes on his skinny friend. "Just be here Saturday night."

Crazy Legs turned and scurried up the rope ladder, throwing the hatch open and climbing outside without another word. The others watched his departure in silence until the hatchway door slammed shut on them.

Jeff glowered at his friends. "Anyone else wanna leave?"

Mick plopped into the vacant seat on the couch. "Don't worry, he'll be here. He's in this just like the rest of us. What's he gonna do, hide in his basement for the next six months?"

Jeff smirked at the notion. "So I want everyone to be here at sunset on Saturday night. We'll go over the plan then."

"You mean you don't have a plan yet?" Mick asked.

Jeff glanced to a charcoal sketch of the plazas set upon the easel. "I got some ideas. I just haven't decided on them yet."

Mick glanced about his friends with incredulity. "Um, the fight's in two days, Jeff."

"Yeah? So?"

"You're always the man with the plan. What's so different this time?"

"Give him a break," Train said. "Look at his hand."

"Nothing's different," Jeff said. "We meet at sunset, we fight at ten. That's the plan. You need a dress rehearsal or something?"

The Hurricanes snickered, but Mick persisted. "Why can't we go over things tomorrow? We got nothin' going on."

"You don't. I do."

Mick smiled with realization. "Oh, I get it. You got a date with Miss Law and Order?"

Jeff frowned. "Why? You wanna be our chaperone?"

"You're out of your mind. There's a dozen chicks who would go out with you in a heartbeat, and you gotta pick the police chief's daughter."

"I don't like them. I like her."

"But what about the risk? Your timing couldn't be worse, dude."

Train sprang up from the couch. "Don't take this crap, Jeff! It's none of his business who you go out with!" He stormed to the rope ladder and began to pull himself up with his thick biceps.

"Where are ya going now?" Mick asked.

"Crazy Legs had the right idea." Train pushed the hatchway door open and climbed out, letting it fall shut by its own weight.

"Sheesh," Mick said. "What's eating him today?"

"Maybe it's you," Axle said.

Mick laughed. "What can I say? I bring out the best in my friends." He turned back toward the Hurricane leader. "How about you, Jeff? You gonna storm out too?"

Jeff shook his head. "I can do better than that. You guys get lost. Meeting's over."

"But we just got here," Bumbles said.

"Just be here on time Saturday night. Now beat it. I got stuff to do."

The Hurricanes rose grudgingly from their seats and filed toward the rope ladder, grumbling among themselves as they climbed out, but Mick remained behind. "It's good to see you again, Jeff. Thanks for taking the hit for me at school the other day."

Jeff nodded before pointing a thumb to the skis against the wall. "How much did you get for the other stuff?"

"Nine hundred," Mick replied coolly. "Best one yet. We got about seventeen hundred in the account now." He watched the last boy climb out of the hatchway while Jeff flipped through a large pad of Denny's hand-drawn maps set upon the easel. "You want your bankbook back?"

"You can hang on to it for now," Jeff said.

Mick backed to the rope ladder. "Okay then. See ya Saturday."

"See ya." Jeff turned back to the map as Mick scaled the

ladder. The Hurricane lieutenant had just poked his curly blond hair through the open hatchway when Jeff called out to him. "Hey, Mick."

Mick ducked his head back inside. "Yeah?"

"Remember what I said about the gun."

"I already promised ya, Jeff."

"Good. I'm trusting you. One more thing."

"What's that?"

"Get rid of these skis. I don't want 'em in here. We're done with the break-ins."

"You got it." Mick clambered out of the fort and slammed the hatchway door shut with a defiant flick of his wrist. Jeff glanced back with chagrin before turning to the charcoal maps again, to contemplate a plan of attack for the impending fight Saturday night.

Jeff turned his midnight-blue Camaro onto Hillside Drive for a third time, having already driven around the block twice without stopping at his destination, the Wellis residence. Cindy had assured him over the phone that her father would not be there, but as he approached the brown ranch dwelling to his left, he noted an unmarked gray cruiser still parked in the sloping driveway of her house. He tightened his grip on the steering wheel as he imagined Chief Wellis gunning him down like John Dillinger as he fled for his life across the front lawn. If ever there was a time to stand a girl up, this was it, but as he drove by the house, he saw the living room curtains separate to reveal her peeking out at him. He had been spotted; his doom was sealed.

Jeff felt as if he might barf up a butterfly as he parked alongside the police vehicle and climbed out of his car. At the front of the driveway, a steep flight of cement steps led him up to the front door and a lighted doorbell button. He swallowed hard and reached for the button, but before he could depress it, the door popped open to reveal Cindy in a dark green sweater and black jeans. He backed away as she pushed the storm door open.

"What took you so long?" she asked.

He nodded to the cruiser in the driveway. "You said your father wouldn't be here."

"He isn't." She stepped outside and pulled a white windbreaker onto her arms before shutting the front door. "He's at a fundraiser with my mom. They took her car."

Jeff stepped aside as she shut the front door. "Fundraiser? What do you mean?"

She started down the steps. "He's running for county sheriff. That's why we moved here in the first place. You know, gain exposure. Make connections. Shore up his résumé. All that crap."

He followed closely behind. "So you thought that dating a hoodlum might help you get his attention back?"

"What? Jeff, I'm not fourteen anymore."

He smirked. "Sorry. I have a big mouth sometimes."

"Well, shut it and get moving," she told him. "We're gonna miss the movie."

He laughed. "Okay, okay!"

They climbed into the Camaro and he started the engine, glancing into the rearview mirror before backing up the driveway. Once they were on Hillside Drive, he shifted into gear and pulled away, lowering his visor to block the blinding sunset in his eyes.

"So how long do we have tonight?" he asked.

She squinted and pulled her visor down. "Until midnight. But we should try to get back before them."

"Let's shoot for eleven. We don't wanna come down on the wrong side of the law," he quipped.

He spotted a curl of amusement upon her lips as he turned the car onto the main road and punched the gas. She's all right, he thought as they drove away, the girl's all right.

Jeff slipped his arm around Cindy's waist as they stepped up to the sidewalk of the Madison Cineplex 12. "Wow, this place is packed tonight," he said.

Cindy nestled closer to avoid the jostling crowd. "I think we left too late."

They passed through the glass doors to the carpeted lobby of the theater complex. Jeff stepped into line and gazed up at the box office board. "Aw, look. It's sold out."

Cindy studied the board for a moment. "Looks like everything good has already started."

"What do you wanna do?"

"Let's just go."

He returned to the glass doors and pushed one open for her. "Sorry. I guess I blew it."

She stepped outside and reached for his hand. "That's okay. We'll go another time."

They held hands as they crossed the driveway and entered the parking lot, but a cold breeze prompted Jeff to button his jacket as they neared his car. Cindy crossed to the passenger side and stood patiently while he fumbled for his keys. "What time is it?" he asked.

She shivered. "Quarter to eight. Why?"

"Do you wanna go home now?"

"I thought you'd never ask."

He winced. "Ouch."

"Well, what kind of a question is that? Do *you* wanna go home now?"

"Of course not." Jeff glanced back to the theater. "I guess we could go see a bad movie."

She leaned back against the trunk of the car. "I don't wanna see a bad movie."

Jeff sighed and opened his door. "Well, let's go."

A few moments later they sat in his idling Camaro, waiting at a traffic light before leaving the cinema parking lot. He glanced over to her, sitting quietly with her hands folded in her lap. "So where do you wanna go?" he asked her.

"I don't care. Anywhere."

The light turned green, but they continued to idle at it. "You're a big help."

"Well, you asked me out. It's up to you to figure out what to do."

A horn tooted behind them, stirring Jeff into a right-hand turn. He sighed. "I guess you're right."

"What's the matter?"

"I hate first dates. I never know whether to take the girl bowling, try to get her drunk, or run out of gas down some deserted street."

She narrowed her eyes at him. "How about none of the above?"

"The only other option was to drop her off at eight o'clock, then go home and punch myself in the head."

"How about talk to her and get to know her?"

"Is that before or after we run out of gas?"

She smirked. "Before. You run out of gas and you're walking, buster."

"All right, all right," he said. "So what do you wanna talk about?"

She scowled playfully. "Is this your first date, Jeff? I mean your very first?"

He laughed. "Gimme a break!"

"Well, you're not very romantic."

Silence fell over them as he drove away from the Cineplex and concentrated on the surrounding roads bustling with evening traffic. When the silence grew awkward, he glanced over to gauge her boredom, but she seemed content toying with the radio. Nevertheless, he squirmed in his seat at the bright lights of the cinema fading in his rearview mirror.

"We could just cruise around," he finally said. "It's a beautiful night."

She grabbed his arm. "Hey, I know a great spot where we can hang for a while."

"Cool. Can we bowl there?"

"No, but we can run out of gas there." She winked at him. "Only for a little while though."

He glanced at the fuel gauge. "I got half a tank. We shouldn't run out for too long."

She snuggled closer to him. "Follow Dexter Road through the next intersection. Then turn right on Portland Village Road. It's about a half mile past the light."

Jeff followed her instructions through a green light and soon slowed the car for the right-hand turn, switching on his high beams as they accelerated down the dark road devoid of streetlights. The beams sliced through the inky darkness, sporadically confronted by a reflective street sign or a brief wisp of fog.

He gripped the steering wheel tighter. "This is way more romantic. When do the grizzly bears attack?"

She squeezed his arm. "I didn't know bad ol' Jeff Hollister was afraid of the dark."

"I'm not. I just like to see where I'm going."

"Well, slow down. There's a sharp turn ahead."

Jeff tapped the brake pedal and turned the steering wheel to maneuver the imminent turn, a near right angle leading to the left. He shuddered at the sight of a simple steel guardrail preventing them from a steep plunge into a twisting ravine. To his immediate left, a rising rock wall obscured a blind turn to the left that deterred him from edging the Camaro too far from the guardrail. Only after they completed the hairpin turn did he ease back into his seat, loosening his grip on the steering wheel and exhaling with relief as the dark mountainside pass receded in his rearview mirror.

"Wow, that's one hairy corner," he said.

"We call it Life Star Lane." She patted his knee reassuringly. "You wouldn't have been the first to wreck there, that's for sure."

"That woulda sucked," he said. "This car is my dad's legacy."

She took a prolonged moment to behold the Camaro. "It's a beautiful car. What does your father do?"

Jeff stared at the dark road ahead. "Not much. He's dead."

"Oh." Cindy fell silent for a moment. "I'm sorry. I didn't mean to pry."

He forced a smile. "Nothing wrong with asking me about my family."

"You don't mind talking about it?"

He shrugged. "Not much to say. I was only ten when he died. He was walking to his car after work one night, just minding his own business, and some thugs stuck him with a knife for his wallet. Like he didn't even matter."

"That's terrible," she said. "Did the police arrest anyone?"

"Nope." Jeff's gaze fixated on the yellow line in the center of the black road. "I guess it was a bad year for homicides. Or maybe it was just a bad year for cops. Anyway, my mother tried to keep the pressure on them, but after a while it just seemed like no one gave a shit anymore. I think she just ran out of energy."

"I'm sure it's been hard on her," Cindy said.

Jeff nodded. "She picked up a second job bartending in Madison so she could keep the house. She says she's just hanging on until I graduate. I don't know what the big deal is. My brother Billy left for California three days after he graduated, and I ain't seen him since. I just wish she would let the whole thing go. I hardly even see her these days. We're not much of a family anymore."

She laid her hand upon his knee. "I'm sorry. It must be lonely."

Jeff shrugged. "The Hurricanes are my family now. They're always there when I need them. Just forgive me if I'm not fond of cops. I have my reasons."

"Oh." Cindy withdrew her hand to her lap.

He mulled his words for a moment before patting her softly on the knee. "C'mon, let's not dwell on my past. I just wanna have a good time tonight. We can still do that, can't we?"

She flashed her brown eyes up at him. "Sure we can, Jeff."

The road straightened at the bottom of the mountainside, leading them over a small stone bridge spanning a babbling stream. A roadside marker announced Portland Village two miles ahead, but a mile along the way a secondary road came into view beneath a dim streetlight. She pointed to the street marker on the corner. "Quarry Road. Turn here."

He steered onto the dark road. "Are you taking me out to shoot me?"

"We'll see." She leaned forward to see better out the front windshield, studying the passing foliage on the right side of the road. A mile down the road, she pointed to a thick oak tree with a faded brown sign nailed to it. "There it is!"

Jeff braked the car to a hard stop, lurching them firmly against their seat belts. He turned the steering wheel sharply to the right and slowly advanced the car into the mouth of the dirt road, where a wooden sign nailed to a thick tree read WEST SHORE BOAT LAUNCH.

He squinted into the inky darkness. "Really? You wanna go down here?"

"What else can we do?" she asked. "We're miles from the nearest bowling alley!"

Jeff grinned as he continued to drive along the gradual descent of the dirt road with the headlights slicing through the night. He scanned the road for imperfections that might damage his tires, but it was wide and firmly packed as if to accommodate large trucks or heavy machinery. The density of the forest waned farther down the gentle slope, and soon gaps in the foliage revealed shining stars in the clear sky overhead. Finally, they came upon a split in the road with two white signs nailed to a pine tree in the center of the fork. One of the signs read BOAT LAUNCH, directing them to the right, and the other sign read PORTLAND MINING CO., pointing to the left. Jeff braked the car to a halt at the fork and peered down the road to the left, captivated by the glimmer of a tall metal structure running through the woods a quarter mile up the road.

"What is that?" he asked with his eyes fixed upon the shiny object.

"Oh, you don't want to go down there," she said.

He laughed. "Why? Are there ghosts or something?"

"No, Jeff, it's just—"

He turned the steering wheel sharply to the left and hit the gas, driving up the left leg of the forked road until the towering silver fence forced him to stop. "Wow, look at the size of that thing!" he said. He parked the car and opened his door, leaving the engine running and the headlights on as he started out of the car.

She reached over and grabbed his arm. "Jeff, please."

Her reaction startled him. "Relax. I just wanna check it out." He pulled away from her and continued out of the car, gazing up at the fence as he meandered toward it.

Cindy opened her door and stepped out of the car. "Be careful, Jeff. It's electric."

"Electric? Really?" Jeff glanced to the edge of the headlight beams, where warning placards read KEEP OUT and NO TRESPASSING. He stepped up close to the silver metal mesh and cocked an ear toward the fence before reaching out and grabbing the metal mesh with both hands. "Yaaaa!" he screamed with his arms shaking violently.

Cindy rushed forward to help him. "Jeff!"

He laughed and shook the fence with both hands. "Ha! It's not even on."

She backhanded him on the shoulder. "You jerk!"

He slipped an arm around her waist and pulled her toward the fence. "Wanna explore the other side?"

She resisted his tugging. "No, I don't want to."

"C'mon. Where's your sense of adventure?"

Cindy stepped back defiantly. "No!"

He whirled about for an explanation, but she looked away with her arms crossed. Finally he threw his arms up in the air and stormed past her. "Well, forget it then. I don't wanna go either."

She followed him back to the Camaro. "Jeff, don't be mad."

He stopped at his car door and waited for her to reach her side of the car. "I'm not mad, I'm just curious. A fence like that out in the middle of nowhere."

They climbed back into the car. "This isn't the middle of nowhere," she said solemnly. "This is where I grew up."

Jeff shifted into reverse and backed the car to the fork. "I'm sorry. I didn't mean it like that. I'm just saying, there's probably more bears than people out here. I mean, what are we even doing out here?" He shifted into gear again and drove forward down the right leg of the fork, only to hit the brakes a hundred feet ahead for a fallen sapling spanning the road. "Aw, damn. Now what?"

"We could walk," she said. "It's just up ahead."

"Are you sure? It looks spooky dark out there," he quipped.

"Well, take your flashlight." She reached up and pulled an ivory handle from a sheath strapped to his sun visor, but her mouth dropped open as she beheld a four-inch hunting knife in her hand. "Oops, my mistake."

Jeff took the knife from her and returned it to its sheath. "Probably won't need that, unless we find a grizzly bear."

"Or one finds us!" she mused.

He flicked the high beams on and off, but neither setting seemed particularly effective in viewing the road beyond the fallen tree. "Is there any other way down this road?"

She shook her head and popped her door open again. "C'mon." She shut the door and walked down the lighted path to the fallen tree, straddling it before turning back to the Camaro and shielding her eyes from the headlights. "Come on, slowpoke," she called before continuing down the road on the other side of the fallen tree.

Jeff frowned. He shut off the engine and headlights before climbing out of the car and following her down the dirt road now solely lit by bright moonlight. Ahead, the dirt road cleared the last of the trees before dipping gently toward water, where the starlit sky draped Cindy's shoulders like a shawl. At the end of the dirt road, she stepped upon a wooden dock jutting out over the shimmering lake and walked to the edge, where she sat down with her feet dangling over the water. He stepped up behind her and she tugged at his hand until he sat down beside her.

"You asked me why I brought you here," she said. "I brought you here for this—" She pointed an open hand to the panorama of Almond Lake, serene like glass beneath their feet yet refracting the moonlight with minute ripples stretching out across the waters before them. The nighttime horizon sparkled with so many stars Jeff could not discern familiar constellations, while the warm yellow glow of cottage lights glimmered through the maples and pines on the southern shore to their right. He could even smell a whiff of cherrywood wafting along a breeze from a cottage chimney to the right.

"—and for this." She leaned close and kissed him on the cheek, her eyelashes as soft as caterpillar feet upon his skin.

His heartbeat thumped in his ears as he kissed her lips, and he wondered how he could've been angry with such a beautiful girl who chose to share a cherished place with him. "It's a beautiful lake," he said. "I wish it were mine."

She laughed. "You can't own a whole lake!"

"Why can't I?" He pointed to a towering rock formation on the northern shore. "I'd put a diving board on that cliff and make double reverse flips into the water all day long."

She slid an arm behind him and drew closer. "Sounds like an ambulance ride to me."

He continued to marvel at the landscape, noting the lack of lights for a lengthy portion of the northern shore. "Is that all part of the mines?"

She nodded. "The local kids used to like playing in there after hours," she explained. "One day a kid fell and got hurt pretty bad. He almost died. It was scary. His parents sued the owner and won, so the company put up the fence to keep other kids from climbing over."

"No, they'd just electrocute themselves instead."

"It's not that strong, dummy. Just enough to keep someone from climbing over it."

He eyed her with playful suspicion. "How do you know all this?"

"The owner knows my dad. He was putting a lot of pressure on the police to keep the kids out, but Portland doesn't have the people for that. Then the environmentalists started complaining about runoff into the lake, and he just kinda threw his hands up in the air and walked away. I don't think they even opened up this year with all the legal issues they were having."

Jeff pointed to the lights lining the shore to their right. "Is that where you used to live?"

"No, we didn't live on the lake." She pointed toward a dark patch on the distant shoreline. "My grandparents own a cottage over there. We still keep our boat in their boathouse."

"You mean, like, a motorboat? Cool. I've never been on a motorboat before."

"Wow, really? I practically lived on ours last summer. I'd go skiing with my friends almost every day. Shannon taught me how to ski barefoot last summer. That was the best!"

"You must miss living here," he said.

She cast her eyes downward. "Well, yeah. I wanted to finish

my senior year in Portland. I had to leave all my friends behind."

"Look at the bright side," he said. "At least you got to meet me."

She patted his knee. "Remind me to thank my dad for that when we get home!"

He slipped an arm around her waist and pulled her closer. "You gotta realize something, Cindy. People like your father, they don't care about what you or I want. You're just a possession to him, and I'm just a stepping-stone to his next promotion. Might as well accept it."

Cindy sighed. "My father isn't all that bad. He's just got a job to do."

"I'm just saying, maybe he oughta worry less about high school kids and worry more about real crooks."

"Oh right. Like you guys never broke the law."

Jeff shrugged. "I never said we were choirboys. All we're trying to do is break up the monotony in that stupid town. But every time we turn around these days, there's another cop breathing down our necks. Sure, we get rowdy sometimes, but we're just letting off energy."

"Keg parties and rumbles are one thing, Jeff. Burglary is something completely different."

He drew away from her. "The only thing people in Salisbury care about is trimming their lawns, washing their cars, and making sure their kids get to the soccer game on time. So if someone takes away some of their toys and gives them a taste of the real world, maybe that ain't such a bad thing."

"I see. So you're Robin Hood."

"No. Not Robin Hood." Jeff felt rankled. "Go ahead, make fun. I'm not asking for your approval."

She slid beside him and rested her head on his shoulder. "I'm not making fun. I'm worried about you. I can't help it after everything that's happened this week."

"Everything's under control," he said. "I know what I'm doing,"

"And the guns?" she blurted out.

"I don't have any guns. I was with you, remember?"

"But look what the Tornadoes did to you. Where would your friend Mick be if you hadn't gotten in the way? If your enemies are willing to go that far, what else will they do?"

"I'm not afraid of them. If I was afraid of the Tornadoes, the Hurricanes wouldn't even exist."

"How so?"

"The Tornadoes were here first," Jeff said. "Wearing their colors around school and bullying people they didn't like. They were just a bunch of arrogant assholes. So I started the Hurricanes with Mick and Crazy Legs and Train. It took a lot of time and a whole lotta fighting, but we recruited the rest of the gang along the way, and we finally put the Tornadoes back in their place. We beat them at their own game, and now we beat them every time." He held out his bandaged hand. "Looks like it's time for another lesson."

"What do you mean?" She looked into his eyes. "You're going to fight, aren't you? Jeff, it's too dangerous."

"Look what they did to me. Look what they did to you at the party. Somebody has to pay."

"My toenail isn't worth getting shot over. And you should just be thankful you're alive."

He frowned. "So like, just call it off? How's it gonna look if the Hurricanes don't show up for their own fight?"

"Who cares how it looks?" she replied. "Just skip the whole thing."

"Yeah. And then what? What happens at school Monday morning? Should we just hide in our lockers? The Tornadoes ain't gonna just go away."

"There's got to be another way. Maybe my father —"

"Your father?" Jeff sensed the conversation getting away

from him, so he drew a deep breath and exhaled. "Look, it's too late to start second-guessing now. I was hoping we could forget about that stuff tonight and concentrate on other things." He wrapped his arm behind her again. "Like you and me."

She lay back against him. "I'm scared, Jeff. I'm just getting to know you, and now—"

He stroked her hair gently. "Everything's gonna be just fine. We're the Hurricanes. We're quicker than they are, we're stronger than they are, and we're smarter than they are. And you know why I'm the leader?"

"Enlighten me," she said without looking up.

"I think fast, I stay in control, and I find a way to win. I'm probably a little lucky too, but don't tell anyone I said that."

She tapped on his bandage. "Looks like your luck is running a little thin lately."

He beheld the injured hand. "This is just motivation. The Tornadoes are gonna be sorry they messed with the likes of me."

"Your reputation is rivaled only by your ego."

"It's not ego," he retorted. "It's self-confidence."

She slapped his knee. "I'm kidding, Jeff! You don't have to tell me about the notorious Jeff Hollister. My first day at Salisbury High, the girls were lining up to tell me all about you."

"Ha. Notice I'm not with any of them tonight," he said.

"No, you're here with me. Why?"

"I don't know. I don't like being someone's badge of honor. You're different. That stuff doesn't matter to you. I haven't completely figured out why just yet."

Cindy rested her head on his shoulder. "Maybe I think you're just a cute guy and fun to be with."

Jeff laughed. "Fun to be with? I'm a gang leader."

She tangled her fingers in his. "Well, maybe there's more to it than that. And maybe I'll tell you about it when I figure it out myself. For now, let's just enjoy tonight, okay? Tomorrow will be here soon enough."

He kissed her on the top of her head and swayed her body in his arms as the calm lake water lapped against the dock posts. Her motives seemed as murky as the Milky Way overhead, but for the moment he felt content to accept her proposal to enjoy a solitary moment in time, and let the troubles of tomorrow fall where they may.

Jeff turned the Camaro onto Hillside Drive again before nudging Cindy with his elbow. "Wake up," he said. "We're almost there."

She lifted her head off his arm. "I wasn't sleeping."

He slowed the car at her driveway, glancing at the blue digits of the radio clock before pulling in. "Ten minutes ahead of schedule," he said. "Not bad for a delinquent."

She sat up straight and peered at the driveway ahead. "We're in luck. My parents aren't home yet."

He pulled alongside the parked gray cruiser and shut the engine off. "Sooner or later you'll have to tell your father about me."

She pecked him on the cheek. "After the election. He's bouncing off the walls as it is."

He raised an eyebrow. "I hope that wasn't your good-night kiss."

She opened the car door. "Walk me up the steps."

"Okay." Jeff glimpsed to the rearview mirror under the glare of the dome light. He shut off the headlights and stepped out of the Camaro to join her at the front of the car, casting an uneasy eye at the quiet street behind them before following her up the steep cement steps.

She stopped at the front door and slipped her arms around his waist. "Tonight was better than being hit by a brick."

"Good to know. I was worried." He drew her near and closed his eyes, pressing his lips to hers as she eased back against his sturdy forearm, but they kissed for only a moment before he sensed a bright light upon his eyelids. He popped an eye open to see headlights approaching the house, then eased his embrace and backed away until only their fingertips touched. "I'd better go."

"Call me," she said.

He nodded and hurried down the steps as the headlights neared the driveway. Fumbling with his keys, he opened the door and climbed back into the Camaro, starting the engine only to be blocked in as a white sedan turned in the driveway behind him. Cindy dashed down the steps toward the driveway as Jeff lowered his window halfway, glaring in his side-view mirror at a car door opening behind the bright headlights.

"Let me handle this," she told him as she rushed past his window. "Dad! You're home early!"

Jeff watched the reflection of Cindy confronting her father in the driveway. "What's going on, Cindy?" the chief's voice boomed. "Whose car is this?"

"A friend's," she explained. "We went to a movie."

Jeff sat motionless, hoping Cindy would resolve everything but knowing things were turning for the worse. A knuckle rapped against the side-window glass, and he lowered the window to see the police chief in a black jacket and tie, standing outside his car. The chief bent forward to peer inside with nostrils flaring.

"Why are you on my property?" he asked.

Jeff fidgeted with the steering wheel. "Um, we went to—"

"Yeah, I heard. Another movie. Who gave you permission to go out with my daughter?"

Jeff drew a deep breath as he struggled to remain calm. He spotted Cindy's mother in his rearview mirror, cutting across the headlight beams in a long black dress. "Look, no harm no foul, Mr. Wellis. She's home, safe and sound. Do you mind backing up so I can leave? I'm kinda tired."

Chief Wellis placed his hands on the roof of the Camaro and leaned in close to Jeff. "Oh, you're kinda tired, huh? Tell you what. I'll get my men to come by and check you out. Go over your documents, check out your car, the whole nine yards. If everything's in order, maybe you'll be home by daybreak."

Jeff lowered the window down the rest of the way and stuck out face an inch away from the chief's. "Why are you harassing me? I haven't done anything wrong!"

Cindy tugged at her father's sleeve. "Daddy, leave him alone!"

Mrs. Wellis stepped forward, her scarlet shawl flapping in the cool breeze. "Matt, what's going on?"

Chief Wellis pointed at the car. "Jeff Hollister is in our driveway!"

"Daddy, please!" Cindy cried. "Leave him alone!"

Mrs. Wellis pressed her hand against her husband's chest. "Matt, it's late—"

"Call Bob Hyrst," the chief told her. "Tell him to come right away. Tell him to send backup."

"Backup? Really?" Jeff asked. "You've got me pinned in!"

Chief Wellis pointed a finger at Cindy. "She's off-limits to you, Hollister, got it? Off-limits!"

"Dad!" Cindy objected.

"Get upstairs," the chief told her. "I'll deal with you later."

Cindy whirled about and stormed up the front steps with her mother trailing closely behind. Jeff eyed them entering the house before turning back to her father. "Get out of my way, Chief. I'm not gonna say it again."

The chief shook his head. "Sorry, Hollister. We're gonna have to do this the hard way."

Jeff watched Cindy shut the front door. "My thoughts exactly."

He shifted into first gear and drove forward, stopping just inches from the garage door as the chief looked on with curiosity. Cutting the steering wheel sharply to the left, he shifted into reverse and hit the gas, nearly grazing the idle gray cruiser and forcing Chief Wellis to jump for his safety. The chief chased after him as he backed over the edge of the driveway and onto the front lawn, skidding to a halt on the grass. He waved to Cindy peering out the living room window at him, then he cut the steering wheel the other way and hit the gas, slinging a wide arc of soft sod against the front of the house. Jeff straightened the wheel and the car lurched forward, sailing off the curb and bouncing on the pavement of Hillside Drive as the chief ran after him, cursing and shaking a fist in the air.

Racing away from the Wellis residence, Jeff wondered for a moment if his friends were right. Maybe he was crazy for dating the daughter of the police chief. The sentiment didn't last long, however, for the only thought on his mind as he drove back to his own neighborhood was when he would see her again.

CHAPTER
5

JEFF SAT UPRIGHT at his bedroom desk, a soft bandage roll set beside a lamp that shone down upon the sutures of his outstretched left hand. He tugged gently at the threads of the stitches with a pair of tweezers and poked at the tender tissue surrounding the wound before clenching both hands tightly into fists. The injured hand felt weaker than the right hand but not enough to prevent its use, so he opened his fists and placed a new gauze pad over the wounded palm. After winding the bandage around the hand a few times to keep the gauze in place, he hesitated for a moment before reaching into the bottom right-hand drawer of his desk. Rifling through its contents, he triumphantly pulled out a set of makeshift brass knuckles and slid them over the fingers of his left hand before sliding the drawer shut again.

Squeezing the fist again, he felt satisfied at the way the brass knuckles helped to alleviate pain by restricting full motion of the fingers. He proceeded to wrap the entire hand with the bandage roll, padding the injured palm and tucking the brass knuckles inside before tightly encasing the whole contraption into a thick, solid paw using long strips of adhesive tape. Finally, he rose from the desk and moved to the center of the room, shadowboxing for a few moments until he heard an abrupt knock on his bedroom door. Before he could answer the knock, the door swung open to reveal Mick standing in the hallway.

"Feel free to just stroll into my house," Jeff said.

"Your mother let me in." Mick followed Jeff back into the bedroom and pointed to his bandaged paw. "How the hell are you gonna fight like that?"

"Better than you could." Jeff resumed his shadowboxing to a lesser degree.

Mick laughed. "Everyone knows I pack a harder punch than you."

"Yeah? Prove it." Jeff turned an arm to his friend. "Go ahead. Hit me."

Mick grinned. "Either hand?"

Jeff grimaced. "Just do it!"

Mick threw a straight punch with his right hand, landing the middle knuckle squarely into his leader's arm. Jeff winced and grunted from the impact but nevertheless maintained his stance before his lieutenant. He rubbed his arm to soothe the pain and then drew his right arm back while Mick dutifully turned his arm to accept the counterblow. Instead, Jeff pivoted and jabbed the left hand forward, driving his paw with the enclosed brass knuckles into Mick's biceps. He grinned as his lieutenant staggered back onto the bed with a howl of pain.

Mick rubbed his new bruise vigorously. "Jeez, did ya glue a brick to your hand?"

Jeff laughed. "No, I taped my brass knuckles inside."

"You asshole."

"You deserved it." Jeff picked up his Hurricanes jacket from the bedpost. "Ready to roll?"

Mick stood up straight. "Hell yeah! I've been ready all week."

Jeff attempted to slip his bandaged paw through the sleeve of his Hurricane jacket, but it snagged on the cuff. He fumbled with it for a moment before turning to Mick. "Gimme a hand."

Mick helped him stretch the cuff over the bandage. "Don't forget who did this to you. And don't think for a second he won't try something like that again."

"Did you bring the gun?" Jeff asked quietly.

Mick patted a lump on his left hip. "Of course. I don't leave home without it."

"Remember what I told you. I don't want any trouble. One of them tries something crazy, that's when you step in with it. Otherwise, we're in and out in ten minutes."

"No problem, Jeff. I wouldn't use it on just anybody. Maybe Curly. After all, he did try to shoot me with it."

"No! That's what I'm talking about. You use it for defense only. I'm trusting you, Mick."

Mick rolled his eyes. "Okay, I promise. In and out in ten minutes. Just like you said."

"Let's go." Jeff shut off the light and headed up the short flight of stairs for the front door with Mick following closely behind him. As the upper level of the house came into his view, he spotted his mother dressed in the black pants and white shirt of her bartending uniform, snuffing a cigarette in an ashtray on the kitchen counter.

"Jeff?" she called as he opened the door. "Where are you going?"

He sighed. "Out. It's Saturday night, ya know."

"We haven't talked in three days," she said. "How's your hand?"

Jeff stopped in the doorway as Mick ducked past him for the front steps. "It's fine, Ma. I gotta go."

She stepped to the railing and glared down at him, her black hair pulled back tight, her mascara thinly veiling the dark circles around her eyes. "Don't stay out too late."

"I'll be home before you," he grumbled before stepping outside and shutting the door.

Mick awaited him at the bottom of the front steps with a cigarette in hand. "You should be nicer to your mother."

"I *am* nice to her. She picked a hell of a time for an update." Jeff leaped from the steps to land by his lieutenant's side. "Like you're the darling son."

Mick laughed. "I *am*. My old man's just too drunk to know the difference."

Jeff glanced up to a gibbous moon before a row of advancing clouds. He drew a deep breath from a warm autumn breeze and hopped off the cement steps to the lawn. The two boys sauntered to the end of the driveway and headed left up Spruce Lane toward a streetlight at the intersection of Elm Street. As they approached its sphere of light, they spotted three figures in blue jackets entering it from the right.

"There's a storm coming!" Jeff called out to them.

"A Hurricane!" the largest one shouted back, thrusting a fist into the air.

Jeff stepped under the streetlight and exchanged fist bumps with each of his three Hurricane followers: Train, Bumbles, and Crazy Legs.

Mick repeated the ritual with Train and Bumbles, but stopped with a smirk on his face when he got to Crazy Legs. "Glad to see no one got cold feet."

Crazy Legs shot back a scornful look, but Train blurted out, "Why don't you get off his case, Mick? He's here. That's all that matters."

Mick flicked his cigarette into a nearby storm drain. "What's your problem? Underwear too tight?"

"I ain't in the mood for any damn bickering tonight," Train said.

Jeff leaned closer to Mick. "Chill out, buddy."

"Right," Mick said. "Don't wanna get too worked up before a fight."

They walked in silence along Elm Street to the intersection of Arrow Drive, crossing the street for the short golden field and the woods beyond. "Keep your eyes open," Jeff said. "They might try to ambush us."

"On our own turf?" Crazy Legs asked. "They're bold, but not that bold."

"Don't sass your leader," Mick said. "You'll make Train mad."

Train grinned and flicked his middle finger against Mick's earlobe. The lieutenant yelped in pain and whirled about to retaliate, but Train swelled his chest and flexed his muscles in a playful yet daunting manner that even Mick respected. "Gonna kick some Tornado ass tonight!" the burly boy shouted.

The Hurricanes whooped with excitement as they dashed across the golden field and disappeared from view down the rabbit path. Jeff quickened his pace after them, pleased to see their anxiety subsiding and their fervor rising. What meager moonlight escaped the clouding sky was virtually lost among the treetops, yet the boys soon arrived at the landmark semicircle of pine trees with nary a stubbed toe. He finally caught up with them at the entrance of the underground fort, where Bumbles shined a penlight down to help Crazy Legs open the hatchway lock. The Hurricane scout pulled the hatch open to reveal the muffled beat of rock music and the orange glow of the burning oil lamps inside.

Mick peered over his shoulder. "Someone's already here?"

"Move back." Jeff brushed Crazy Legs aside with his paw before scaling down the rope ladder. He dropped to the floor and turned to see the rest of the gang sitting around the folding table playing cards.

TJ tossed his cards onto the table. "Hey, Jeff."

Jeff glanced about the faces of the four boys already nestled in the fort. "How'd you guys get in here?"

Axle glanced up sheepishly. "We used the tunnel."

"Well, you better cover it up when we get back." Jeff pointed to the music player set inside the recessed firebox. "Turn that thing off and get rid of this table. We're not staying long."

The four boys sprang into action to follow their leader's orders. Mick dropped into the fort, his blue eyes gleaming in the flickering lamplight. "We ready to go?"

"Not yet. Get everyone in here for a minute." Jeff stepped to the raised platform while his lieutenant instructed the Hurricanes outside to descend into the fort. As the trio filed down the rope ladder, Jeff turned to the flip chart with a sketch of the Upper and Lower Plazas perched upon it. The Hurricane leader's face grew taut as he scanned the room, searching for any hint of uncertainty or apprehension among his friends as they all assembled before him.

"You guys ready to rock?" their leader asked.

Train hopped off the rope ladder, landing on the wooden floor with a resounding thud. "Let's kick some ass!" he bellowed, and the Hurricanes cheered in agreement.

Brain removed his glasses and polished a lens with his shirt. "We're leaving already? It's not even nine yet."

"I wanna be there first. We're gonna be waiting for them." Jeff paused for the chatter to die down. "Okay, listen up. I know some of you are anxious about tonight, but if we keep our wits about us, we'll be fine. I know Craig Matthews. He likes a good fight, but he's not out to kill anybody."

"You mean he likes a good *beating*," TJ said.

Nervous laughter rippled through the fort, but Jeff remained stoic and pointed to the map. "Here's the plan. They like to surprise us with their entry point, but we're gonna cut 'em off quick before they can gain a foothold. Train, you're with me on the south end of the tattoo parlor. We're covering the tree line and looking out for any activity coming up from the south end of Burrough Street. Mick, you're with Bumbles at the 7-Eleven facing west. You're gonna watch the Lower Plaza and any vehicles entering the parking lot."

"Great," Mick muttered. "I get stuck babysitting."

Jeff stared him down before continuing. "Crazy Legs and Brain are the lookouts on the roof of the pool hall. TJ, Axle, and Denny are in the sandpits by the fence watching the back of Gaucho's and Tornado territory. I don't think they'll be that predictable, but they've been pretty brazen lately, so who knows? First Tornado sighting sounds the alert. No phones. They might give us away. Everyone knows the whistle?"

"They're all set," Crazy Legs said.

Jeff nodded. "The target is Curly. We take him out first, and then we mop up the rest of them." He stepped away from the easel to address his friends directly. "If things get out of control, I yell 'break' and we meet back here. Any questions?"

"Remember what they did to our leader," Mick told the gang. "It's payback time!"

The Hurricanes roared in approval. Jeff stepped into the center of the fort and held out his bandaged hand with the palm facing down. Mick placed his palm on top of Jeff's, and each Hurricane added a hand on top of the pile, creating an eerie, spiderlike shadow against the plywood ceiling of the fort. Their leader spoke in a low and determined tone. "Through thick and thin…our blood and skin—"

"—is one!" the Hurricanes chanted as they tore their hands from the pile.

He thrust his paw into the air. "Let's rock!"

The Hurricanes cheered as he stepped past them and scaled the rope ladder with his heartbeat pounding in his ears. A gust of wind struck him in the face as he reached level ground, momentarily throwing him off balance, but he leaned forward to steady himself while his friends gathered behind him one by one. With the lamps dark and the hatchway shut, the nine boys strode along the dark path headlong into wind toward the glow of the distant plaza lights. The surrounding branches and leaves seemed to quiver upon their approach, for these were the Hurricanes, unrelenting and undefeated, and no one would deprive them of a victory tonight.

Leaning back against the white brick wall outside the tattoo parlor, Train flicked the butt of his cigarette with two fingers, watching the glowing red ember bounce to a rest on the crushed gray gravel three feet away. He exhaled a breath of smoke into the night and cracked all the knuckles in both hands before turning to his right. "So when do we go?"

Jeff stood at the front corner of the wall, peering down the sidewalk past Crusty's Pizza Parlor toward the 7-Eleven convenience store in the distance. "We're waiting for a signal," he said without looking back, "unless you see them coming up the tree line behind us."

"You think they're gonna show?"

"We wouldn't be here otherwise."

"Oh." Train took a fresh pack of cigarettes from his jacket pocket and opened it. "So what if we get jumped right now?"

Jeff finally looked back at his bodyguard. "The only way that's gonna happen is if they sneak up along the tree line behind us, and you're supposed to watch out for that instead of talking to me. Now keep quiet, will ya?"

Train glanced to his left, where woods conjoined with a sandy field behind the rear parking lot. Nothing moved except leaves in the breeze, sometimes swirling in miniature cyclones until the life ran out of them. He fidgeted with his cigarette and turned to his leader. "Jeff?" he asked after a moment.

Jeff didn't turn. "What?"

"You ever think about getting back to good?"

"Huh? What are you talking about?"

"Back to good. You know, the way things used to be. The good ol' days."

Jeff stared blankly across the parking lot toward Burrough Street. "I don't remember too many good ol' days."

"Sure you do, Jeff. Remember last year how we'd pick up Mick and Crazy Legs, and we'd all go cruisin' to the park in my van? Or we'd head down to the beach in your Camaro and chuck the football around and scope out the girls?"

Jeff smiled faintly. "You're right. Those were good times."

"I miss those days." Train shifted his footing on the sparse gravel and leaned against the wall. "Seems like all we talk about nowadays is stealing and fighting."

Jeff shrugged. "Times change, I guess."

Train drew another drag and exhaled. "Did Mick bring that gun?"

"Yeah. I wanted him to."

"I wish I had it."

Jeff frowned in thought for a moment before looking back to his friend again. "This ain't the O.K. Corral, Train. He's just bringing it to balance things out."

"Just the same, I wish there weren't no guns here tonight."

"Yeah, me too." Jeff craned his neck to see around the corner again.

Train slid closer to him. "Can I ask a favor from ya?"

Jeff sighed. "Of course."

"Well, I know how you're pretty much on top of things in a fight. I mean, I never see you get beat up or anything. So I was wondering, if I keep an eye out for you tonight, can you sorta try to keep one out for me too?"

Jeff frowned. "You nervous or something?"

"A little, I guess." Train looked down. "Everyone's afraid of something, right?"

Jeff looked his friend in the eye. "Look, nothing's gonna happen. We'll be done and chugging beers at TJ's house in an hour." He scanned his friend's face for some sign of consent, but he wasn't even sure if he believed his own words. Finally he patted Train on the shoulder. "I'll keep an eye out for ya. And we're pulling out at the first sign of trouble. I promise." He returned to his post and peered around the corner, down the sidewalk past Crusty's to the distant convenience store. "Mick's gone! C'mon!"

Jeff hurdled over the short retaining wall and sprinted down the sidewalk with Train hot on his heels. They jumped off the sidewalk at the far end and bounded across the delivery driveway to the cement sidewalk of the 7-Eleven store, slowing to a stop in front of the glass entrance doors. "Where'd he go?" Train asked.

Jeff looked about in search of his friend. "I don't know. Listen for a whistle."

Train pointed inside the store. "He's talking to that girl. Hey, isn't that your new girlfriend?"

Jeff spat on the sidewalk. "It sure is. What's she doing here?"

"Let's find out."

"No. You stay out here and find Bumbles. I don't see him around either."

Jeff threw open the glass door and stormed inside. Cindy and Mick both looked over when he entered, but Cindy turned away while Mick sauntered closer.

"Hey, Jeff," he said. "What's going on?"

"Nothing yet. What's up?"

Mick pointed a thumb over his shoulder. "The stupid cashier said that if I kept hanging around, he'd call the cops on me, so I came in to buy some smokes. Then your girlfriend came in and I—"

Jeff held up his hand to stop Mick's babbling. He stepped over to the snack rack, where Cindy was diligently inspecting a bag of potato chips. "Hey."

"Oh hey, Jeff," she said. "Care for some chips? I'll get pretzels, if you prefer."

"What are you doing here?"

"Shopping," she said. "Is that okay with you?"

"There's a store right down the street from your house."

"I got my mom's car, and I felt like taking a ride." She stared at him for a moment before dropping her gaze in disappointment. "I tried calling you today, but I kept getting your voice mail."

"I've been really busy. How did you even know I was here?"

"Train told Shannon. Shannon texted me. Here I am!" she said. Jeff cast a wary eye back to Train standing outside the glass doors as she continued. "I just wanted to say I was sorry about last night. My father shouldn't have treated you that way."

"You don't need to apologize for him. I don't hold it against you."

"You're not mad at me?"

"Of course not."

She flashed her eyes up at him. "Can I come watch you tonight?"

Jeff glanced uneasily at Mick eavesdropping by the door. "It ain't a baseball game, Cindy. Things could get dangerous. You should go home."

"How are you gonna fight with your hand wrapped up like that? Look at you…"

"Go home. Please."

Cindy sighed and smiled. "Okay. Be careful." She walked to the exit, where Mick opened the door and gestured her outside in an overtly regal manner. Jeff socked him in the stomach as he followed her out of the store, watching from the corner of his eye as his lieutenant slip into the shadows of the parking lot. He stepped from the sidewalk and joined Cindy at the side of her mother's white sedan.

"I'll call you later," he said.

She nodded with worried eyes and kissed him on the cheek before climbing into the car and starting the engine. He waved goodbye to her, watching as she backed the car into the center of the parking lot and pulled forward to the Burrough Street traffic light. Suddenly Mick dashed up to him from the side of the store. "Jeff, we gotta go! Why didn't you tell me Bumbles was gone? The fight's already started! They're in the back alley!"

Jeff cast an anxious glance at the white sedan still idling at the red light before darting off after his lieutenant. Around the corner, Train waited as if they were about to pass him a baton. "Hurry!" the burly boy cried.

Jeff grabbed him by the wrist. "Wait! We can't all rush in together. Train, you circle the bar and come in behind the pool hall. Mick, hang here and keep watch by the fence. I'll head around front and come in from the left. We still target Curly first. Sixty seconds on my mark. Got it?" His friends nodded quickly. "Okay, go!"

Train dashed off toward along the front sidewalk toward the backside of Gaucho's Cantina, while Mick slunk along the dark windows of the corner doughnut shop to the short wooden fence at the front entrance of the alleyway. Jeff ran around the front leg of the ell, past the dark storefronts of a florist and hair salon that both faced Burrough Street. At the far end of the sidewalk, he turned before a faded stockade fence and crept down a dark, littered path along the side of the building. He inched forward until the tips of his sneakers met the shadow line of the alleyway, cast by the lemon light of a rooftop spotlight perched high over the alley blacktop where the two gangs battled.

Two boys tumbled to the pavement directly in front of him, locked like rams and swinging fists that were generally restrained by the other. The boy in the Hurricane jacket broke free and stood upright, his nose running with blood as he looked straight into the darkness where his leader hid. Jeff shrank into the shadows, still waiting for Train's arrival, while Crazy Legs drew back in confusion from what he had seen before his Tornado adversary pulled him back into the fray again.

Jeff glanced across the scuffle to see Train running up so fast that he accidentally stepped into the glow of the alley spotlight; the Hurricane bodyguard quickly sprang back to the cover of darkness, but the Tornadoes were already shouting proclamations of his arrival. Left with no alternative, Jeff whistled and jumped into the alley with fist and paw cocked before him as Train slid beside him and Mick stepped into the gap in the short fence between the two buildings.

Craig flung Denny aside and pointed across the alleyway. "It's Hollister! Get him!"

All of the Tornadoes were already engaged in the clash, so no one could immediately respond to his order. The Tornado leader started toward Jeff, but Mick rushed through the fence opening and tackled him as if blindsiding a quarterback. Craig crumpled to the ground and Mick sprang excitedly to his feet, while Train advanced into the center of the alley, ready to pummel any Tornado crossing his path. Jeff followed him into the throng of combatants battling all around them, wary of threats from all directions.

Their first opposition was Zak, who sidestepped Train to catch his caboose, pulling Jeff by the shoulders backward to the ground. Train spun about to aid his leader, but Happy Jack and Phil jumped him from either side to force him down as well, pounding his body with punches while he struggled to lift his face from the asphalt. Jeff's position was no better, sitting on the pavement with Zak's hairy forearm squeezing his throat. He turned his chin toward his captor's elbow, allowing his windpipe room to breathe, then he yanked a handful of Zak's hair with his good hand and slugged his enemy's face with the weight of the enclosed brass knuckles in his bandaged paw. Zak groaned and loosened his grip, allowing Jeff to peel the thick arm from his neck with a merciless twist of the wrist. He shoved the Tornado bodyguard back to the pavement before rolling to his knees in search of his next adversary.

Craig spotted Jeff and rose to his feet, but Mick flattened him again with a right cross to his head. The Hurricane lieutenant glanced from side to side as he backed up to his leader. "Where's Curly? I don't see him!"

Jeff scanned the shadowy edges of the alley. "Find him!"

Mick dashed off into the dark alley behind Gaucho's as Jeff turned back to fight. He spotted Train on his knees with his face still pressed to the asphalt, rocking his torso as Phil and Happy Jack struggled to restrain his arms. With a ferocious roar, the bodyguard spread his broad shoulders apart and ripped his left hand free, elbowing Phil in the groin and then double-fisting Happy Jack under the chin to lay him out flat upon his back. Jeff leaped over the stricken Tornado and landed in the center of the alley with his weaponized paw leading the way, protecting Train as he rose to his feet. Red and blue jackets swirled about them like fireworks, yet friends and foes were hard to discern in the midst of their violent dance.

With his peripheral vision, Jeff spotted a dark object swinging toward him; he ducked away, but the object still glanced off his head and knocked him to his knees. Stunned, he looked up to see JJ with a sinister grin upon his goateed face and a stolen billy club in his hand. The Tornado drew his arm back to deliver another blow, but Train sprang forward to grab his wrist in midswing, and together they toppled to the ground. Jeff wobbled to his feet and staggered to the shadows of the nearby dumpster, shaking his head to clear his cloudy vision.

As his wits returned, he looked back to see Train lying on his back, fending off JJ's furious billy club assault with his hands and feet. Jeff slid up behind JJ and, with careful aim, delivered a left jab to the back of his adversary's head that knocked him to the ground with all the grace of a bowling pin. Train pried the billy club from his adversary's hand as he lay moaning with his face on the grimy asphalt, while Jeff turned his attention back to the center of the alley to find another Hurricane in need.

Crazy Legs shoved Willie to the ground and backed up to his leader. "Who's got Curly?"

"Mick's looking for him," Jeff replied.

"You mean we're sitting ducks?"

Jeff shuddered from the bluntness of his friend's assessment. He surveyed the battle arena, where Phil lay groaning with his head against the southern fence and Bumbles sat propped up against the short building, nursing an ankle injury. Zak traded fists with TJ and Denny, while Axle squeezed Willie in a headlock and Train pinned JJ to the asphalt with the billy club jacked beneath his chin. The Tornadoes seemed to be losing the fight, but they weren't ready to surrender just yet. Craig, Tony, and Happy Jack remained free to fight Crazy Legs, Brain, and himself, a match he felt confident the Hurricanes would win. Still, he saw no sign of anyone possessing the second gun, and he saw little gain in finishing the fight just to prove a point.

"We're done," he told Crazy Legs. "Spread the word."

Crazy Legs turned about to carry out the order, but a beer bottle crashed over his head and he slumped to the ground; Happy Jack pounced upon him while Brain piled on to defend his friend. Jeff lunged forward to help, only to feel a bicycle chain slapping against his chest. Alertly, he raised his good hand to his neck before the greasy chain wrapped around his throat, but Tony pulled it tight against his hand and dragged him down to the pavement with it. Craig dove in and sat upon his chest, grappling for his throat with sweaty hands as Tony pulled the bicycle chain free to lash his legs with it.

Craig pinned Jeff's head to the asphalt. "Give up, Hollister, or I'll — Ack!"

The Tornado leader gasped as the bicycle chain pulled taut around his throat and yanked him off Jeff. Train stepped over Tony lying subdued on the asphalt before reaching down to grasp Jeff's hand.

"I really saved your neck that time," his bodyguard grinned as he pulled Jeff to his feet.

Jeff sighed with relief. "I owe ya one. C'mon, let's get out of here."

Brain shoved Happy Jack aside and pointed urgently toward the short fence at the front of the alley. "Jeff, look out!"

Jeff whirled about, already fearing the worst. He spotted Curly standing on the sidewalk behind the fence with a crooked grin on his face and a finger already squeezing the trigger on his stolen revolver. A gunshot thundered throughout the alley, and blood spattered upon Jeff's face just as Train knocked him off his feet with a diving tackle. A shrill scream rang out amid the shouts of the scattering boys while Jeff fell beneath the weight of his burly friend, landing with his arms pinned to his side by his friend's grasp. His head snapped back to strike the pavement, and he blacked out.

When Jeff came to, the first sensation he felt was an incredible pressure upon his chest that pinned his back to the ground and restricted his lungs from expanding. Slowly his ears attuned to the sounds about him—the distant shouts of frightened boys running away, the faint wail of a siren drawing closer—and he opened his eyes to see the lemon spotlight blaring down at him. Lifting his head off the pavement, he discovered the weight on his chest was actually Train's thick torso lying upon him.

"I'm okay, buddy," he said as he struggled to free his right hand from beneath his friend's body. "You can get off me now."

Train said nothing and moved nowhere.

"C'mon, man. Get up. I can't breathe." He grabbed Train's shoulder and, with all his might, flopped his friend onto his side to reveal a tattered T-shirt soaked in blood. With a gasp he scrambled to his knees to press his fingers against Train's neck, feeling for a pulse but unsure if he found one. He leaned his ear close to his friend's lips, desperately listening for sounds of breathing but hearing none. Straddling Train's torso, he began chest compressions the best he could with his bandaged hand, but every time he pressed down on his friend's sternum, the gunshot wound on the left rib cage gurgled with blood, while Train's pupils stared listlessly into the yellow light.

The siren grew louder in Jeff's ears with every passing

second. Tired and bloodied, he ceased revival efforts when a hand tugged at his shoulder from behind. "C'mon," Mick panted. "We gotta get out of here."

Jeff pulled away. "No. I'm not leaving him here like this."

Mick pulled at his hair in frustration. "He's dead! Can't you see? We gotta go! The cops are coming! Don't you hear the damn sirens? We'll all go to jail!"

Jeff cradled Train's limp hand in his own. "I don't care. I can't just leave him here…"

Mick straightened up and smeared a tear across his face with the palm of his hand. "He's gone, man. Don't ruin things for yourself too." He turned about and bolted from the alley.

Jeff watched Mick disappear into the darkness, knowing his lieutenant was right. Train was gone. The siren grew clearer as a flash of blue light approached from Burrough Street yet he remained steadfast, solemn in his word to stay by his fallen friend. The blue lights cut through the parking lot toward the far end of the nightclub, and he knew in a moment his life would be transformed forever.

He felt a gentler hand upon his shoulder, accompanied by a familiar female voice. "Come, Jeff. Let's go."

He looked up to see Cindy standing over him, her windbreaker flapping in the breeze and her face streaked with tears. "Why are you here?" he asked. "I told you to go home."

She sank to her knees beside him. Bright headlights and blue flashers lit up the fence as a police cruiser turned in to the alley. She pulled on his shoulder in desperation. "Please, Jeff! I don't wanna lose you like this."

His troubled mind could not sort through all the implications of being caught with the police chief's daughter beside his dead friend's body, but his gut told him to listen to her. He stood and glared down at his fallen friend as the cruiser accelerated down the delivery driveway behind Gaucho's. Finally he pointed to the hole in the stockade fence leading into Tornado territory. "That way," he said.

Cindy grabbed his sleeve and pulled him toward the escape while he lifted his collar to shield his face from the approaching headlights. The cruiser screeched to a halt as its lights came to bear upon the body lying in the center of the alleyway. The passenger door popped open and a stocky young officer hopped out, pointing his gun from behind the cover of his door. "Freeze!" he ordered, but Jeff ducked through the hole in the fence behind Cindy. The officer turned and shouted to his partner behind the wheel. "Man down! Call for backup! I'm going after them!"

Jeff pointed to a dim trail winding away from the other side of the fence. "Go!"

Cindy released his sleeve to claw her way through two overgrown berry bushes pinching the narrow path on either side. Jeff clung to the tail of her jacket, following her down a small hill to a dry ravine, where a wooden plank spanned the gulley and connected the worn path to an empty lot on Diamond Street. The sparsely lit road wound up a hill to their right, into the heart of Tornado territory.

Jeff crossed the plank after Cindy and stooped down to pick up the board. "Keep running," he said.

"What are you doing?" she asked.

"Buying time." He tossed the crude bridge into the ravine and ran after her. "You're pretty quick. We can lose this guy if we play it smart."

She nodded as they headed toward the backyard of the first house and the comfort of the shadows. They could hear the berry branches rustling behind them as the pursuing officer advanced down the path, audibly relaying his position to his partner with his collar radio. Cindy turned back to see if the officer had cleared the ravine, but Jeff pulled her along by her wrist.

"Careful," he said. "We're done if he IDs either one of us."

The next yard offered little cover aside from a few small maple trees, so Jeff hustled through it to hurdle a short post fence at the far end of the property. He slowed up and shot a glance back to locate Cindy, only to find she had already cleared the fence and was now sprinting past him. Looking back over the lawn they had just crossed, he did not readily see the stocky officer, although he was certain the man had not given up. Cindy was now a full ten yards in front, running toward the same post fence at the opposite end of the yard when a blue light flashed off the siding of a house across the street.

"Cindy, duck!" he whispered, running after her.

She cleared the fence and dropped to the ground while he dove over the rail and rolled to her side. They lay flat on their stomachs as a cruiser passed silently down the street with its blue lights flashing upon its roof. When the car was far enough down the street, Cindy readied to dash forward again, but Jeff grabbed her arm and held her back. He pressed a finger to his lips, pointing to the silhouettes of three boys walking toward the back deck of the next house, coming from the direction of the Upper Plaza. They laughed among themselves as they started up the unlit back porch stairs, and Jeff recognized their voices as those of his enemies.

"I think you got him," Happy Jack said.

"I got one of them," Curly said. "I couldn't tell which one."

JJ started up the stairs. "Whoever it was, he went down and he stayed down."

They all laughed again while Jeff gritted his teeth, fighting the urge to rush up behind them and drag them all backward down the porch stairs. He squeezed Cindy's hand tightly as they watched the jovial Tornadoes filing into the house and flicking on the lights inside. Then they heard a loud thud and a discernable grunt behind them, as the pursuing officer knocked a fence rail from its post on his way to the ground.

"The cop!" Cindy gasped.

"C'mon," Jeff said. "This way."

He darted to the left alongside the house, glancing back

when he reached the street curb to be sure she was still behind him. They crossed the street for the backyards of Ruby Road, the road that intersected Diamond Street at the top of the steep slope. A four-foot-high chain-link fence lined the perimeter of the second property; inside the yard, the terrain rose sharply to a tall row of boxwood shrubs at the top of the hill.

He scaled the fence and reached back for her hand. "This way! Hurry!"

She glanced back at the policeman crossing the street in pursuit before climbing over the fence, but Jeff was already running up the hill by the time she landed. He reached the shrubs and turned back for her hand again as she labored up the hill, waiting long enough to grasp her hand and pull her to the top.

"What are you going to do?" she asked breathlessly.

He led her up to the edge of the bushes. "I'm gonna take this guy out."

"Don't hurt him," she pleaded.

"Trust me," he said.

They looked back over the lower lawn to see the officer toiling up the hill. "You!" the panting officer called from the base of the slope. "Stop!"

Jeff ducked between the center bushes before pulling Cindy after him. On the other side, a stone patio surrounded an in-ground swimming pool, partially drained and covered with a vinyl tarp. He pointed at the bushes to her right before crouching behind the low branches of the bush to his left; she nodded and followed his lead. Together they waited in silence as they struggled to control their breathing.

The stocky officer lumbered up the hilltop, his deep breaths and his jingling handcuffs betraying his every step. The bushes rustled as he burst onto the patio with his gun in hand, gasping in surprise at the half-empty pool looming before him. Before he could completely stop, Jeff sprang forward and barreled into his back, sending him over the edge of the pool and onto the vinyl tarp with a curse and a muffled splash.

"C'mon!" Jeff called out, darting past Cindy for the dark backyard, as the officer floundered against the collapsing tarp and the cold water leaking onto it.

Running with renewed vigor, Cindy caught up with Jeff as he jogged toward Ruby Road. "You did it!" she exclaimed, grabbing him by the waist. "We're home free!"

"Not yet," he replied, knowing danger still lurked everywhere. They continued upon the gradual rise toward Arrow Drive, where Hurricane territory began on the other side of the road.

Mick stumbled recklessly down the dark forest path, having already tripped twice and fallen hard upon protruding rocks and roots, but any pain he felt was secondary to his urgent need for refuge. He left the common path before it reached the giant pine, Mr. Big, frantically tearing through stalks of overgrown brush until he emerged scratched and bleeding at the semicircle of pines surrounding the location of the underground fort.

The hatchway door was shut, but he could hear the voices of the Hurricanes inside as he reached for its handle. He opened the door and the voices hushed, while the orange glow from within the fort lit up his face.

"It's Mick," TJ said.

Mick climbed down the rope ladder and dropped to the floor. The Hurricanes milled about and fidgeted upon the couch, many of them sported bruises and cuts, but all of them suffering from a greater emotional angst.

"Where's Jeff?" Bumbles asked. "Is he okay?"

Mick lit a cigarette and drew a long drag from it, exhaling slowly as he walked across the fort. He stepped up onto the platform and turned about to face his anxious friends. "Jeff's okay," he finally said. "I think he got busted."

"The cops got him?" Crazy Legs gasped.

Mick shook his head. "I didn't stick around to find out."

Brain scratched his chin. "Why didn't you —"

"Why didn't *you?*" Mick stared down their solemn faces. "Why'd you all run off like that?"

"We heard a gunshot," Axle replied. "Jeff said if things got out of control —"

"So he didn't follow you back?" Crazy Legs asked.

Mick stared at the floor for a moment, his cigarette loose between his fingers. "He wanted to stay with Train."

Crazy Legs frowned. "So where's Train? Did he get busted too?"

Mick lifted his head and narrowed his eyes at the Hurricanes. "Train's dead."

"What?"

"He's dead!" Mick threw his cigarette into the firebox in disgust. "Do I gotta spell it out for ya?"

Bumbles buried his face in his hands, and Axle wiped his eyes. TJ shook his head and muttered, "Oh my God."

Crazy Legs clenched his teeth and stepped closer to Mick. "Are you happy now? Did you get what you wanted?"

"Don't blame me! I didn't fucking shoot him!" Mick whirled about and stopped at the sketches upon the easel. He slammed a fist into the easel, knocking it to the floor and scattering the poster boards across the floor. "Son of a bitch!"

Denny shook his head. "These fights ain't no big deal. Nobody's supposed to die."

"The Tornadoes aren't acting like they used to," Brain said.

Mick fumed. "Well, ain't that the most brilliant thing you've ever said. Do me a favor and keep your stupid revelations to yourself."

"Don't get hostile with us!" Crazy Legs shouted back. "And don't pretend like you didn't know this could happen. You got us into this!"

"Shut up, Kramer!" Mick roared. "You better watch who you're talking to!"

TJ stepped forward. "Hey, cool it! We're all in this together."

"I'm telling it like it is," Crazy Legs said. "Mick has to own up to it."

Mick clenched his fists and stormed off the platform, but Crazy Legs stood tall in the face of his raging friend. The scout took a hard punch in the gut from his leader and doubled over in pain before falling onto the couch. He gasped and held his stomach as he glared up at the Hurricane lieutenant. "You're a real tough guy, Mick," he said.

Mick leaned forward. "Stand up and I'll do it again."

TJ wrapped his arms about Mick's chest. "Stop it!" he shouted as the other Hurricanes rushed to protect Crazy Legs.

"Let me go!" Mick wriggled free and backed to the rope ladder. He climbed halfway up and stopped with one arm looped around the top rung as he turned a fist back to the gang. "Train's my friend too. Anyone says different and they'll get a taste of the same."

He climbed out into the night and flung the hatchway door shut on the bewildered faces inside the fort, eclipsing the orange glow at the same time. Outside, the breeze felt colder and the woods seemed darker now that the moon had finally lost its scuffle with the clouds. With a shiver, he buttoned his jacket and headed for the forest path leading back to Hurricane territory, far away from the sirens of emergency vehicles still descending upon the plaza. His part in the fracas was likely done for the evening unless — he patted the pistol tucked beneath his jacket with a curl upon his lips — an opportune rendezvous with an unsuspecting Tornado presented itself along the way home.

Jeff burst through the front door of his house and switched on the overhead foyer light. "Hurry," he said. "Shut the door behind you."

Cindy followed him inside and pressed the door shut, while he scrambled upstairs and vanished down a dark hallway to his right. More lights flicked on in various rooms down the hallway as she slowly climbed the staircase in the unfamiliar house. Jeff hurried back down the hallway, past the staircase and across the living room to switch on a corner lamp. Already his torso was stripped of his Hurricane jacket and bloody shirt, with neither article in sight. He grabbed a remote control from the coffee table and clicked on the television set before peering out the picture window up and down the street as far as he could see.

His face was flushed with anxiety as he rushed into the kitchen to grab a pair of scissors from the cutlery block. Cindy fidgeted with indecisiveness as he hurried past her down the hallway and through the first doorway on the right. "Come here," he called to her. "I need you."

She found him in the bathroom, hacking the scissors at his bandaged white paw now stained with blood. "Jeff? Are you okay?"

"Help me get this off. Hurry."

"It's okay. We're safe now."

"We're not safe! You don't know who's out there. The cops, the Tornadoes—"

Cindy took his hand and patiently peeled at the tape with her fingernails. "Let the police handle the Tornadoes."

"Cops can't stop someone from shooting me." He handed her the scissors. "Here, use these."

She started to snip at the bandage. "Don't be so paranoid. The Tornadoes are the ones who should be scared, not you."

"Who do you think the target was tonight? I'm the one he wants dead, not Train."

She freed an end of the tape and began to pull at it. "Who? Who wants you dead, Jeff?"

He took the tape from her and continued to unravel the

bandage as he thought about the ramifications of his answer. "I can't tell you right now. If anyone thinks I used you to tip off the cops, we're both in deep shit."

"Jeff, I'm not going to say anything that you don't want me to."

He threw the ball of tape at the wastebasket and then slid the brass knuckles from his left hand. "I can't believe this is happening. Why did Train have to get in the way?"

"It's not your fault."

"It's *all* my fault, Cindy! How could I be so stupid?" He cast the brass knuckles across the room in a fury, and the crude weapon dented two of the walls before rattling to a rest inside the bathtub. Just then, a flash of blue light cut through the window blinds, originating from the driveway below.

"The cops!" Cindy gasped.

"What took 'em so long?" Jeff listened intently as car doors slammed shut and heavy footsteps clomped up the steps. He stepped to the bathroom window and waited for a rap on the door before sliding it open. "Who's out there?"

"Police," replied a voice from below.

"Hold on a minute." Jeff shut the window.

"I'll handle them," Cindy said. "Follow my lead."

Before he could object, she left the bathroom and walked downstairs to the front door, so he stayed back and hurriedly washed his hands and face in the sink. At the foyer, Cindy switched on the front porch light before opening the door to a flashlight shining in her face. She recognized the two Salisbury lawmen standing on the front steps, a uniformed officer with a trim red beard and DRYDEN on his name tag, and Dan Shelnick, a middle-aged detective with graying sideburns, dressed in a brown sport jacket and a matching fedora hat. She stepped closer to the screen door, and their jaws dropped open as they recognized her.

"Cindy!" the detective exclaimed. "What are you doing here?"

"Oh hi, Dan. I'm just hanging with my boyfriend. I was getting ready to leave, actually."

"Jeff Hollister is your boyfriend?" Officer Dryden asked incredulously.

"Well, kinda. We met down at the pizza shop, and one thing led to another, if you know what I mean." She winked at him.

The two men shifted in discomfort, and Detective Shelnick removed his fedora. "Does your father know you're here?" he asked.

"He thinks I went to the mall tonight," she said. "You're not gonna tell him, are you?"

Their gazes turned up over her shoulder to Jeff descending the stairs, shirtless and barefoot with his hair slicked back as if he had just taken a shower. He stepped beside Cindy and pushed the front door completely open. "Hey, guys," he said through the screen door. "What's up?"

"Whatcha been up to tonight, Hollister?" Dryden asked.

Jeff snuggled up behind Cindy and wrapped an arm around her. "Did you tell them?"

She reached back and stroked the hair on his chest. "Maybe you should, honey."

Jeff started to reply, but the detective cleared his throat. "We just needed to verify your whereabouts. Sorry for the disturbance, Hollister. Have a nice evening."

Jeff acted perplexed. "What's this all about?"

Shelnick shook his head. "Can't say. Good night." He placed his hat back on his head and started down the steps.

Dryden followed him. "That's it?" he whispered. "You're just gonna believe them?"

Shelnick shrugged. "Ken, if you want to tell Matt his daughter is lying to us, go right ahead."

"Dan, wait!" Cindy called out. They stopped and turned around. "Can you give me a ride to my car? It's down at the plaza."

Dryden shot an uneasy glance at the detective, but Shelnick nodded his approval to her before continuing toward the cruiser.

Jeff turned her about and looked into her eyes. "I can take you."

"Don't worry. They'll do it." She brushed his hair back from his eyes. "Just take it easy, okay?"

He forced a smile. "I'll try. Can I call you tomorrow?"

"You better," she replied.

She kissed him, and for one brief moment he forgot about the dreadful event that had just unfolded. That sentiment ended abruptly once she stepped outside and followed the two lawmen into the cruiser, leaving him alone in the quiet house. He watched through the screen as the cruiser backed out of the driveway and drove away. Then he shut the front door and walked about the house, switching off all the lights until the television provided the only source of illumination.

Finally, he slumped into a rocking recliner with the TV remote in his hand, numbly clicking through the channels for an hour before switching the television off. He sat in the glow of a streetlamp shining through the picture window, slowly rocking himself back and forth with a lump in his throat and tears in his eyes, silently watching the quiet street outside until eventually he drifted off to sleep.

PART II
ALIENATION

M ICK CROUCHED LOW in the E basement stairwell of Salisbury High, peering through the crack of a door held ajar by the toe of his sneaker, his eyes fixed upon another door halfway down the shiny black-tiled corridor stretching before him. The door opened, and a lone student emerged amid the buzz of an electric saw, shutting the door behind him before walking down the hall. Mick checked the time on his phone and smiled as Craig passed through a men's room door at the far end of the hallway, right on schedule for his ten o'clock smoke break. The Hurricane lieutenant slipped out of the stairwell and down the corridor behind his adversary, glancing through the window of the wood shop door at the students working industriously on their projects. He continued on to the far end of the hallway, stopping at a door stenciled MEN before slamming it open against its rubber backstop.

Craig whirled about with his cigarette cupped in his hand and a puff of gray smoke rising conspicuously over his head. He raised an eyebrow as he recognized Mick and flicked the butt into a nearby urinal. "What's up," he muttered as he stepped toward the door.

Mick blocked his exit with a straight arm against the wall. "Long time, no see!"

Craig backed up a step. "Hey, Mick. No hassle, okay? School's off-limits, remember?"

Mick nodded slowly. "Oh yeah. I remember. It's all part of the *truce,* right? We wouldn't wanna break the *truce.*"

Craig shrugged as he slipped toward the bathroom door.

"Hey, Craig—"

Craig tilted his head toward Mick, but Mick tilted it back with a right cross flush to his jaw, leveling the Tornado leader to the grimy bathroom floor. He rolled onto his back to see Mick hovering over him with wild blue eyes and a crazed grin. "—consider that a formal invitation. Wednesday night, behind the stores. We fight."

Craig slid back against a nearby wall and dabbed a finger on his bloody lip. "Now you're doing Hollister's dirty work?"

"I'm covering for him," Mick said. "And I couldn't care less about all that diplomatic crap. Know what I mean?"

"Hey, then why don't you just shoot me right here?"

"Great idea." Mick drew the pistol from beneath his jacket and shoved it under Craig's chin. "Say please."

Craig squirmed back against the wall. "I can't believe you brought that to school."

Mick drew the gun away. "Wednesday night. Bring your friends. Especially Curly."

"I don't even know where he is."

Mick tucked the gun away and stepped toward the door. "Liar. Tell him I'll be waiting for him. In fact, he's the guest of honor."

Craig sat up against the wall and straightened his collar. "Hey, Mick."

"What."

"We're all gonna miss you on Thursday."

Mick laughed and yanked the restroom door open, letting it slam against the wall again as he stepped out in the corridor, leaving Craig to nurse his bloody lip on the bathroom floor.

Clad only in white underwear and a powder-blue dress shirt, Jeff stood before a closet door mirror as he fastened the buttons from his neck to his waist. He brushed back the damp strands of hair before his eyes and inspected a fresh cut he had inflicted on his chin with his shaver, wiping the blood on a towel before tossing it beside a crisp pair of navy-blue slacks laid out at the foot of the bed. He hadn't worn the slacks all year, but after stepping through each leg and hooking the clasp around his waist, he found that they still fit comfortably, so he took a pair of blue socks from the dresser drawer and returned to the bed to put them on.

The bed squeaked as he sat upon it, its mattress sagging slightly in the middle beneath his weight, while Jeff stared at the floor for a long moment before loosening the roll of dress socks. *Socks are so hard to put on,* he thought, especially with an evening's destination so dreaded. He placed the first sock over his toes but gave up and fell backward, sprawling across the bed with his head close to the wall beneath the window curtains. Shades of blue surrounded him, from the sky-blue walls to the Persian-blue carpet to the sapphire curtains ready to engulf him in blueness with the pull of a string. His suit was blue, the house was blue, even his damn car was blue. Blue had always been his favorite color, but now he wondered if he truly cared for the hue at all.

The doorbell rang. Cursing and loathing blue socks, he sat up and pulled the first sock over his heel before walking to the bedroom door. He climbed the stairs to the front door and cracked it open, returning downstairs without even looking to see who was outside. Crazy Legs entered the foyer, dressed in a light gray jacket with slacks to match, a crisp white shirt, and a steel-gray tie snug against his neck.

"Hey, Jeff," he said before shutting the door and following Jeff downstairs into his room. "How's things?"

"Awful." Jeff glanced back. "Nice suit. You look sharp."

"Thanks. Almost ready to go? Mick's on his way."

"Do I look ready?" Jeff sat back on his bed and held up the second sock. "We're waiting for Cindy. She's coming from field hockey practice."

"Oh."

Jeff pulled on the second sock, eyeing his friend fidgeting in the mirror. "Hope that's all right with you."

Crazy Legs turned about. "Fine with me, Jeff. Not sure if the rest of the gang feels the same way, her being the chief's daughter and all."

Jeff stood up and stepped to the mirror, where he dragged a comb through his damp hair. "Ask me if I care."

Crazy Legs wandered to the bed and bounced to a seat on the mattress. "You really like her, huh?"

Jeff pondered the question as he slid the comb into his back pocket. "Yeah. She's all right." He smiled faintly. "Not exactly the best time for a new girlfriend, know what I mean?"

"We're in it pretty thick, huh?" Crazy Legs sat up straight with a stern look on his face. "Look, I gotta talk to you about something before Mick gets here," he blurted out.

"Like what?"

"I'm thinking about taking a break from the Hurricanes."

Jeff reached into the closet again and took out his navy-blue tie, calmly running it through his fingers before laying it flat on the dresser. "How come?"

"I just don't like where we're heading. Do you?"

"Of course not. But running away ain't gonna help."

"I'm not running. I'm just..." Crazy Legs searched for words. "I'm scared, Jeff."

"So what? We gotta stick together now more than ever."

"Why? To get even? I feel like we're getting sucked down a drain."

Jeff frowned. "So, like, forget about Train? Let the Tornadoes win?"

Crazy Legs shook his head. "Talk to Craig. It's not too late—"

"It's way too late! You don't know how it feels to have a friend die in your arms."

"Not yet."

Footsteps clomped outside the bedroom door, and both boys looked up as Mick entered the room. He wore a black pin-striped suit and a white tie against a blood-red shirt, his black shoes so polished they glimmered from the overhead light. With every hair in place, each crease in his pants razor-sharp, and a cigarette wedged between his lips, he resembled a picturesque gangster, lacking only a derby for his head and a machine gun for his hands.

"You guys ready or what?" he asked.

"Don't you ever knock?" Jeff replied.

"Sometimes," Mick said. "And sometimes people don't answer, so I just let myself in."

"I didn't hear any knock," Crazy Legs said.

"That's what I said. That's why—Oh, forget it."

Jeff reached underneath his bed and pulled out a pair of dust-laden dark blue loafers. "Whaddya think about these beauties?"

Crazy Legs chuckled. "I think you oughta put them away before anyone else sees them."

Jeff dusted off the shoes with the damp towel before tossing them onto the floor. He had just finished wriggling his feet into them when the doorbell chimed upstairs. "See, Mick? The doorbell works."

"Now why didn't I think of that?" Mick mused.

"I'll get it." Crazy Legs darted out of the room.

Jeff scooped up the tie off the dresser and threw it to Mick. "Tie this for me."

"You're kidding, right?" Mick looped the tie around his neck and began to wrap it into a knot. "You never answered my texts yesterday. Did your mother tell you I called here twice?"

Jeff nodded. "She did. I just didn't feel like calling you back." Mick drew back as if insulted, so he patted his friend on the shoulder. "I was avoiding everyone. I was in a black mood."

"Some of the gang went to the park and chucked the Frisbee around. It seemed to help them a bit."

"Yeah? Did it help you?"

Mick shook his head. "Only thing that helped me was stuffing my gun in Craig's face at school yesterday morning."

Jeff pulled a navy-blue jacket from the closet and laid it upon the bed. He stepped back to the mirror and flipped up the collar on his shirt. "Now why would you do something like that?" he asked.

Mick slipped the necktie over his head and tossed it to Jeff. "I challenged the Tornadoes to another fight tomorrow night."

Jeff's eyes bulged with disbelief. "You *what?*"

"The opportunity presented itself, so I took the initiative."

Jeff fumed. "Last thing we need right now is another fight."

Mick shrugged. "What's the big deal? I thought I was doing you a favor."

"Some favor. My ass is already in a sling."

"We're all in the same boat, Jeff. I was thinking about Train."

"Your timing sucks. They'll probably still be packing the dirt on his coffin."

"Good! All the more reason. Let's crush the Tornadoes while we're still hot about it. If we wait, the guys are gonna start gettin' scared."

Jeff looped the tie over his head and began to adjust it around his collar. "They're already scared."

"Not yet they aren't. Denny and TJ are all for it."

"Well, thanks for telling me before Wednesday."

Mick threw his hands up in the air. "What's that supposed to mean?"

"Don't forget who runs things around here." Jeff paused at the sound of footsteps descending the stairs again. "We'll talk later. Not a word of this in front of Cindy."

Crazy Legs stepped into the room. "Hey, what's all the commotion?"

Mick shot a glance to Jeff. "Nothing. We were just talking about your tie."

"What's wrong with it?" Crazy Legs pulled the tie from beneath his jacket and held it to his sleeve. "My mom picked it out."

Cindy slipped into the room behind him, and Jeff's jaw dropped at the sight of her beauty. Her shoulder-length brown hair, normally combed straight down, was piled atop her head except for a few strands that danced upon the fair skin at the nape of her neck. A black lace shawl covered the thin shoulder straps of a sleek black dress that hugged her slender hips and hung slightly below her knees. Mick looked away after gazing a moment too long, but her eyes quickly focused on Jeff.

She twirled about with her arms extended. "What do you think?"

He greeted her with a kiss. "You look amazing. How about me?"

"Charming," she said, "but your shirt is buttoned wrong."

Mick and Crazy Legs snickered as Jeff turned back to the mirror. After a quick inspection, he fixed the buttons before facing them again. "How's that?"

Mick pointed down. "Great. Now zip up your fly and you'll be all set."

Jeff glanced down and quickly corrected his mindless error. "Better?"

"Much," Cindy said. "Are we leaving soon?"

"Maybe I should run home and get another tie," Crazy Legs said.

Mick pulled him toward the door. "C'mon, moron. You wanna break your mother's heart?"

Jeff watched his friends leave before turning to Cindy. "You really do look fantastic. I wasn't just saying that to make you feel good."

"Of course not," she said. "You wouldn't do something like that."

He pulled the jacket from the bed. "That's not what I meant. Why do I always say dumb things around you?"

"I don't know." She stepped closer and took the jacket from him. "Maybe you like me."

Her deep brown eyes felt like an old familiar tree to lean upon. He drew her close and held her with gentle strength in his arms, but his words hung heavy in the air as he tried to explain how she made him feel. "I'm glad you're here. I haven't had to do this since my father died."

She helped him feed his bandaged left hand through his jacket sleeve, although he was able to don the right sleeve on his own. She adjusted his jacket to fit his shoulders before straightening his tie. "I'll be right beside you. Who else is gonna keep you dressed properly?"

He started to reply, but she held a finger to his lips. She took his hand and silently led him out of the bedroom and upstairs to the foyer. They stepped outside to find Mick and Crazy Legs leaning against the Camaro in the driveway with their shoulders hunched and their hands buried in their pockets, awaiting a ride to a destination as undesirable as it was unavoidable.

Jeff squinted into the setting sun as he slowed the Camaro to a crawl, following the line of traffic past a white lawn sign that read PINEWOOD FUNERAL HOME. "What a zoo," he muttered, eyeing with disdain the stream of cars entering the parking lot.

Crazy Legs leaned forward. "Wow. Look at all the people!"

Mick slid forward to peer out of Cindy's window. "I'll bet half the senior class is here."

Cindy stared in fascination at the bustling funeral parlor. "At least."

Everyone lurched forward when Jeff stomped on the brakes, his face aglow from the red taillights of the car stopped ahead of them. The traffic inched forward again, following the direction of an attendant in a fluorescent-orange vest, waving a flashlight toward the parking lot. Jeff ground his teeth as he eased the Camaro forward, scowling at the attendant before turning wide into the lot and nearly grazing his safety vest as they rolled past him.

Cindy gasped. "You almost hit him!"

"Sorry," Jeff mumbled.

Mick tapped her on the shoulder. "Was that a cop? Are cops gonna be here tonight?"

She looked back at him quizzically. "Why are you asking me? I'm not a cop."

"Close enough," he replied.

"Relax, Mick," Crazy Legs said. "It was just an attendant."

The line of cars moved more swiftly within the parking lot, guided by another attendant waving them toward an open space in the back row. Jeff gunned the engine in frustration before punching the brakes; the front tires of the Camaro slid over the edge of the pavement and onto the adjacent sod. He switched off the motor and opened his door.

"Is he done driving?" Mick asked. "Can I open my eyes now?"

"Shut up," Jeff snapped, squinting at the setting sun as he stepped out of the car.

Cindy climbed out and leaned over the roof of the car. "What's wrong?"

He glowered back at her. "Nothing. I'm fine."

She met him at the rear of the car while his friends clambered out from the back seat. "These things are never easy," she said softly. "Try to take it in stride and sort it out later."

"It's not just the wake. It's... everything." Jeff turned to Mick and Crazy Legs standing beside the car, listening inconspicuously. "Go on inside. We'll be there in a few minutes."

"Sure, Jeff," Crazy Legs said, and Mick waved a hand as they departed.

Cindy watched them walk away. "They look sharp tonight."

He nodded. "Kinda weird seeing them dressed up like that."

She stepped close to him. "So what's wrong? Besides the obvious."

Jeff fell back against the Camaro. "You think half these people actually gave a shit about Train when he was alive? Maybe they were in his gym class or had their locker next to his or whatever. So why the hell are they here?"

She took his hands in hers. "I don't know. Maybe they just want to show they care. Maybe they wanted to be his friend."

He shook his head. "This ain't about being friends. It's the social event of the week. They should've stayed home and sent flowers. I wouldn't want them at my wake."

"It's not your wake," she said. "Don't talk like that."

He slouched against the car. "Well, maybe it oughta be."

"So what do you wanna do?" she asked. "Trade places?"

"The thought occurred to me."

"Well, it's a pretty dumb thought. You don't deserve this any more than he did."

"I could've avoided this whole mess if I'd called off the fight from the beginning."

"That's pretty perceptive, but a little late."

Jeff turned away. "Don't get cute. I ain't in the mood for it tonight."

"I'm sorry. That didn't come out right." She stroked his back.

"I just meant that it's easier to say what you should've done after you know the consequences. You know, hindsight?"

Her touch eased the tension in his shoulders a bit. "Tell me about it. I'd give anything to redo Saturday night." He took her by the hand. "C'mon. Let's get this over with."

They strode across the parking lot to a covered walkway that led them toward the main entrance of the funeral parlor. To the right of the sidewalk, a small group of teenagers stood on the crisp green lawn, smoking and laughing quietly among themselves, but Jeff silenced them with a scowl as he reached for the golden handle of the dual glass entrance doors. The door slid open before he touched it to reveal a bald man dressed in a pin-striped gray suit and thin leather gloves.

"Good evening, sir," the man said.

Jeff grunted in salutation as he led Cindy past the doorman. They walked down a corridor of plush red carpet lit by the soft yellow glow of half-moon torchères positioned near the ceiling. The sweet smell of fresh-cut flowers grew stronger in the air as they walked past the elegant portraits lining the walls, while a wistful piano nocturne cast a melancholy mood into the corridor through hidden speakers. He recognized various classmates as they approached the corner ahead, some of them downcast and bleary-eyed and others casting disparaging glances in his direction as they passed.

Around the corner, a narrow staircase led some guests down toward a basement lounge, while other mourners chatted softly among themselves beneath the arched entrance of the viewing room. Jeff eyed them skeptically as he stepped through the archway with Cindy still clinging to his good right hand. Once inside, he turned to survey the room in search of friendly faces with whom Train fought and died, a camaraderie that felt trivialized by such an expansive crowd. He nervously recited the Hurricanes' unifying pledge under his breath. "Through thick and thin—"

Cindy squeezed his sweaty hand. "Did you say something?"

Jeff shook his head. He stepped to the rear of the viewing line that began at the archway and extended to the right, down the perimeter wall to an open casket surrounded by flowers, photographs, and spectators at the far end of the long room. Guests filled nearly every chair of a thirty-row ensemble in the center of the viewing room, and more people lingered about its edges, some speaking in hushed tones and casting surreptitious looks his way. As the line advanced, he spotted Train's parents on the far side of their eldest son's casket, greeting mourners at the end of the viewing line. Train's little brother, Randy, shuffled and fidgeted in his suit at the tail of the receiving line, just thirteen years old and lost in a sea of despair.

A lump swelled in Jeff's throat as he watched Mick and Crazy Legs turn away from the casket with bowed heads and sorry eyes. They plodded through the receiving line, shaking hands and conversed briefly with the Armstrong family. Mick patted Randy on the shoulder but Crazy Legs wandered past them, his puffy red eyes glancing back to the casket one last time. He looked up to Jeff and Cindy and cut across the room in their direction, no longer able to restrain the tears from running down his cheeks. When he reached them, he buried his brow on his leader's shoulder, and his voice cracked as he spoke. "Those bastards…"

Jeff patted his friend on the back of his head as Mick crossed the room along the same path. "How'd you guys get through the line so fast?" he asked his lieutenant.

"We cut in on some sophomores. They know I woulda pounded them later if they said anything." Mick leaned closer and whispered, "You should go up front. Someone will let you in. You're Jeff Hollister."

Jeff sensed Cindy's discomfort from the corner of his eye. "We're cool. The line's moving pretty good."

"Suit yourself. We'll be downstairs," Mick said before leading Crazy Legs out of the viewing room.

Cindy pointed ahead to a blond girl moving toward the casket. "Shannon's here. I should go see her."

Jeff sensed a dozen eyes turn his way as he stepped out of line to glimpse her friend. "No," he said. "Don't leave me."

She nodded and squeezed his hand again as they edged forward. The line moved along steadily, and soon the last two mourners ahead of them turned away from the casket for the Armstrong family receiving line. Jeff felt numb as he stepped forward, his eyes diverting to a collage on the right, strewn with mementos and pictures in honor of his friend's short life. One particular photograph caught his eye, a picture of himself with his arm around Train, flanked by Mick and Crazy Legs, standing beside the freshly painted midnight-blue Camaro. He recalled that warm summer morning from two years earlier, when Axle had captured the picture shortly before they all piled inside the refurbished car for its inaugural road trip to the beach. Train was right: those were good times, and now they were gone.

"Come, Jeff. It's our turn," Cindy tugged at his sleeve. "Kneel down."

He had no trouble complying with her direction, for his legs already felt wobbly. He dropped to the kneeler and stared down at the face of his friend lying silently upon a lacy white pillow with his hands clasped at his waist. Dressed in a fine suit and tie, Train had never appeared as prim as he did now, but Jeff secretly knew he would've balked about being laid to rest in anything but faded jeans and a muscle tee. He longed to chase everyone away, stick a cigarette in his friend's lips, and bury him on the edge of the student parking lot where he would surely rest in peace. He leaned forward and tried to muster some kind of prayer, but all he could think of was the memory of his bodyguard dying in his arms in a filthy alley under the cold pale glare of a lemon spotlight.

A child's cry pierced the hush of the room. Jeff cast a scornful look in the direction of the commotion, only to espy two classmates snickering over a joke. He looked away to glimpse a teenage girl in line, chomping on gum and tapping a finger on her phone.

"I can't concentrate," he said. "It's like a fast-food joint in here."

Cindy sighed. "Let's come back when it's quieter."

"Good idea." Jeff stood and patted Train's lifeless arm. "I'll be back, buddy."

He stepped away from the casket, following Cindy to the receiving line where Train's parents awaited them. The lump in his throat returned, for the Armstrongs had been a second family to him after his own father's death eight years earlier. Mrs. Armstrong greeted him with her arms and her eyeliner running slightly onto her cheeks. "Thank you for coming, Jeff. It's good to see you again."

He hugged her tightly. "I'm still in shock."

"Is this your girlfriend, Jeff?" Mrs. Armstrong asked with a furtive smile.

Jeff's face brightened. "This is Cindy. She's Train's friend too."

Cindy shook her hand gently. "Please accept my condolences."

Mrs. Armstrong thanked her and turned back to Jeff. "Who could have done this to our son?"

"I-I'm not sure." He felt shame in lying to them, but a crowded funeral parlor was no place for full disclosure. "Nothing from the police yet?"

Mr. Armstrong leaned toward them and pounded a thick fist into his meaty palm. "The damn cops in this town. If that Wellis guy wasn't so busy politicking all the time, maybe he'd actually get something done!"

Jeff cringed and glanced back to Cindy, but she simply nodded in accord before advancing down the line. Her poise and grace impressed him, and he felt proud to have her by his side on such a difficult evening. "I'm gonna find out what happened," he told the Armstrongs. "I promise you, Lionel didn't die in vain."

Mr. Armstrong shook his hand and quietly thanked him before turning to the next guests in line. Jeff stopped before Randy and patted him comfortingly on the shoulder, recalling how Train would often chase his younger brother away when he tried to follow them on Hurricane activities. That boyish enthusiasm was lost beneath his sullen eyes and crestfallen posture.

"I know you know who did this," he said.

"We'll take care of it," Jeff said quietly.

"I wanna be a Hurricane."

Jeff subtly shook his head. "You're too young."

"I'm fourteen next week. Please?"

"I said no. We'll take care of it. I promise."

Randy sulked while Jeff wedged a finger under his collar, trying to loosen the tie that felt like a noose around his throat. He shook the boy's hand and finally stepped free of the receiving line, desperately scanning the crowded room for Cindy. He spotted her standing near the archway beside Shannon, conversing softly with a thin, graying man in a black suit. As Jeff stepped closer, she reached for him with a welcoming look in her eyes.

"There's someone I want you to meet," she said.

Jeff felt his stomach churn as he eyed the stranger dressed in clergy attire with a silver crucifix pin upon his lapel, listening to Shannon speak. "We just met last week," she told the man. "He was going to take me out next week. Hard to believe he's gone, just like that."

Cindy brushed the man's elbow to gain his attention. "Jeff, this is Marty Jameson. He's the reverend at our church. He's conducting the service tomorrow morning."

The reverend turned about and extended a hand, his graying

hair belying his youthful features. "Jeff Hollister. I've heard so much about you. My deepest regrets for the loss of your friend."

Jeff shook his hand coolly. "Thanks for coming."

"I'm not always usually able to attend the viewing," the reverend said, "but I felt a special connection tonight."

Jeff frowned quizzically as he withdrew his hand, but Cindy leaned in. "Marty's a friend of the family. He officiated my parents' wedding."

"Twenty years ago next May, if I'm not mistaken." The reverend winked at her. "I baptized Cindy too."

Cindy cracked a nervous smile as Jeff patted the reverend condescendingly on the shoulder. "Wow. That's fantastic. Listen, I'd love to hear more about Lollipop Land, your holiness, but my world's kinda falling apart right now. So if you'll excuse me—"

Jeff started away, but the reverend furrowed his brow and recited from memory. "The foolish man built his house in the sand," he said. "The rain came down, the streams rose, and the winds blew and beat against that house, and it fell with a great crash."

Jeff stopped and turned about. "Spare me the sermon, Rev. I had a lifetime's worth when my daddy died."

Shannon stood with her mouth agape, but the reverend's stoic face displayed no offense from the remark. Jeff turned about and strode indignantly through the archway, out of the viewing room. but Cindy hurried after him. She grabbed his arm at the top of the lounge staircase.

"That was rude!" she scolded him. "Marty Jameson is a good man! He deserves more respect than that!"

Jeff jerked his arm away. "Is that what this is all about? Save the gang leader's soul?" He sauntered down a few steps before looking back. "Maybe some things just aren't worth saving."

He continued down the carpeted steps while she rushed to the top of the staircase. "Don't you believe that, Jeff Hollister!" she cried before storming away toward the viewing room again.

Jeff waved her off as he plodded downstairs, clinging to a polished wooden railing leading him into the basement lounge. The staircase led him below the ceiling, where a spacious, low-lit room opened to his right. Mick stood beside a dormant fireplace, sucking on a cigarette like a drowning man, while Crazy Legs sat upon a padded chair beside him, waving the smoke away from his face. The other Hurricanes sat upon plush sofas and chairs scattered about the lounge, chatting quietly among the other mourners about the cozy room.

TJ pointed a thumb toward the staircase. "Jeff's here."

Denny waved. "Hey, Jeff. Where's your girlfriend?"

Jeff stepped down onto the carpeted floor and flopped onto the nearest sofa beside Axle. "Ahh, she's upstairs somewhere. I couldn't stand it up there anymore."

Axle nodded. "I can't believe all the idiots here tonight."

Jeff glanced around at the ensemble. "So what's the hot topic down here?"

Denny shrugged. "Just talking about old times."

They all sat in silence for a moment until finally Mick grinned. "Remember how we used to camp out in Crazy Legs's backyard?"

"And go pool-hopping at two in the morning?" Brain added.

Jeff smiled. "Down at the McNaultys' pool."

"Aw, they had the best pool in the world!" Crazy Legs laughed.

Mick flicked his cigarette into the fireplace and patted Crazy Legs on the shoulder. "Remember that time when Old Man McNaulty woke up? And Train ripped your shorts off while you were climbing out of the pool?"

Denny laughed. "Ha! You never ran so fast in your life!" The laughter rippled through the room, and Jeff felt his anxiety ease a little.

TJ grinned. "What about that tree fort the Tornadoes had?"

Brain held up an index finger. "The Impregnable Tree Fortress!"

"What happened to it?" Bumbles asked.

Crazy Legs laughed. "You should've seen this thing. It had camouflage branches and a ladder that rolled up into the fort and gun slots in the walls to shoot at you if you got too close."

Jeff nodded slowly. "It wasn't a *bad* fort. It showed some promise, for the Tornadoes."

Mick shook his head with humorous remorse. "Until they shot Train with that BB rifle."

Bumbles regarded the chuckling Hurricanes with curiosity. "What do you mean?"

"We caught Tattoo Phil and Riga-Tony red-handed, egging the snots out of the Kramer house," Mick said. "We chased them through the woods all the way to the edge of Happy Jack's yard. Until we got to… What'd you call it?"

"The Impregnable Tree Fortress," Brain repeated.

Crazy Legs still sounded remotely irritated. "Four dozen eggs on the front of our house. My father had me scrubbing the siding for a week."

Mick continued. "They beat us to the fort and rolled up their ladder and locked themselves inside. Next thing we know, we're getting plugged by BBs. You know how much those things hurt. We hit that fort with a hundred rocks, but it never budged, so we started to back off."

"That's when Train got it in the ass," TJ cut in. "They must've pumped that rifle up about forty times. I couldn't believe the squeal that came outta his mouth when he got shot. I thought he stepped on a field mouse."

Jeff laughed for the first time in three days. "I never thought Train could hit soprano."

Mick grinned. "Yeah, then he got really pissed. He charged the fort in spite of the BBs, and he didn't stop until he was at the base of the tree."

"The fort had one major flaw," Denny told Bumbles. "The whole thing was supported by a two-by-four nailed to the tree trunk. It was really just a glorified duck blind."

"Not very impregnable at all," Brain added.

Mick nodded. "Train found this big rock and started beating on that two-by-four with it. The Tornadoes kept mocking him and shooting at him whenever they could get a clean shot. Every once in a while they'd get a piece of him and he'd holler about it, but he kept beating at that board until he knocked the nails outta that tree. The whole contraption crashed to the ground with Tony and Phil inside. Twenty feet, splat!"

The boys laughed heartily, joined by a handful of others eavesdropping on the tale. One by one, however, the Hurricanes seemed to remember the gravity of their situation, and they all turned to their leader brooding on the sofa.

"Fucking BBs," Jeff muttered.

He rose from the sofa and leaned back against the polished balusters of the staircase, peeling the strangulating necktie from his throat as the Hurricanes hung their heads in silence. Sitting idly, he watched as people ascended and descended the staircase behind him until he spotted the hem of a black dress swirling about in a whirlwind of commotion at the top of the stairs. A pair of high heels rattled a few steps down the staircase, and Cindy craned her neck beneath the ceiling to peer into the room below. "Jeff! Come quickly!" she called out.

The tone of her voice startled him, and he darted halfway up the staircase to meet her in the middle. "What's the matter?"

"He's here," she whispered urgently.

"Who?"

"Craig Matthews. He came right up to me and asked me where you were."

"Craig Matthews is here?" Mick boomed as he strode toward the staircase.

Jeff held up a palm. "Easy, Mick."

TJ and Denny rushed up behind Mick as he grasped the railing knob, ready to propel himself upward. Brain and Axle filed in behind them, while Crazy Legs and Bumbles grappled the balusters, trying to see upstairs.

"Everyone calm down," Jeff told them. "We don't want trouble here."

Just then the Tornado leader stepped through the doorway at the top of the stairs, dressed in black coat and maroon slacks. He descended the three open steps behind Cindy before spotting the Hurricanes gathering below. His usual flippancy had vanished, and his voice quivered as he spoke. "Hey, Jeff."

Mick pointed a finger at him. "You got a lot of nerve showing up here!"

Jeff braced his right hand against the staircase wall, gripping the railing as tightly as he could with his bandaged left hand. "What do you want, Matthews?"

"I need to see you—" Craig answered hurriedly.

TJ gnashed his teeth. "Yeah? Did you see Train on your way down here?"

Craig kept his focus on Jeff. "We gotta talk—"

"Don't listen to him!" Mick shouted. "He's trying to humiliate us!"

"Shut up, Mick!" Craig snapped. "I ain't talkin' to you!"

Mick rushed upstairs to press his chest against Jeff's arm. "Don't tell me what to do!"

Craig held up his hands defensively. "I didn't come here for a fight, Jeff—"

"Well, you're gonna get one!" Mick bellowed. He thrust a shoulder against Jeff's bracing arm, forcing his palm to slip from the wall and pinning him against the railing as the angry Hurricanes rushed past him. Cindy shrank behind Jeff for safety as Craig turned and bolted upstairs.

Jeff waited against the railing until the last Hurricane had passed before starting after them, but Cindy stepped in his path and pressed her hand against his chest. "Don't go," she pleaded.

"I'll be right back." He eased her aside and rushed up the staircase after his friends.

On the main floor he discovered the swath of destruction the Hurricanes had leveled upon the funeral parlor. Along the hallway to the left, a girl sat propped against the wall, nursing a twisted ankle inflicted by an apparent trampling; around the corner, her companion lay flat on his back with his hands covering his face. A spilled plant littered the carpet with dark potting soil, and multiple pictures hung crooked on the wall. Several guests shouted at Jeff as he weaved a crooked course toward the entranceway, where a gathering crowd stretched their necks and gushed with conversation about why a reckless throng of boys had just sprinted out the front doors of the parlor.

Jeff brushed past a pair of irritated ushers and jogged down the front walk into a light rain that had begun to fall. He found Denny and Brain on the lawn near the end of the sidewalk, but the rest of the gang was nowhere to be seen. "Where is everyone?" he asked.

Brain pointed down the main road. "That way, I guess. This is crazy."

Jeff nodded. "Look, if anyone comes back, tell them to stay out here. We've caused enough trouble for one night." He trotted across the parking lot to the street and found Mick slouching beneath a streetlamp with both hands buried in his pants pockets.

Mick looked up at him before casting his head down again. "I can't believe Craig had the balls to show up here. He's gonna pay, mark my words."

Jeff peered down the road through the rain and darkness. "Where is he now?"

"He had a car waiting down the street. I couldn't keep up with these damn shoes on, but Crazy Legs went after him."

Mick kicked a rock out into the street. "Nothing seems to go our way anymore."

"Here comes Crazy Legs. We're leaving now."

"Fine by me."

Jeff gasped. "Crazy Legs, what happened?"

Crazy Legs stepped beneath the streetlight and extended his arms to display the scope of the disaster. His crisp gray jacket was now smeared in mud, his pants dripping with water and clinging to his legs. "I fell in a puddle!"

Mick laughed, but Jeff saw little humor in the spectacle. "Head to the car. We're outta here," he said. "I gotta find Cindy."

He returned to the parlor walkway and could see through the doors that the crowd had dispersed, but a lone figure in a black dress watched through the glass. He brushed past Brain again and started up the walkway, while Cindy pushed open the glass door and strode down the sidewalk to meet him.

"We're leaving," he announced.

She folded her arms across her chest. "I'm gonna catch a ride home with Shannon."

He staggered back. "What? How come?"

She dropped her hands to her hips. "I'm just real embarrassed right now, Jeff. I'll call you tomorrow." She turned and stormed back toward the parlor entrance.

"Cindy, wait!" He started up the sidewalk as she slipped inside, but the two ushers blocked the front doors with squared shoulders and steely expressions.

The bald usher addressed him coolly. "Good evening, sir."

Jeff waved them off in disgust and turned back toward his friends meandering across the parking lot. A cold gust of wind cut through his jacket as he pulled his keys from his pocket and trudged after them, feeling cheated by no one in particular of an honest farewell for a loyal friend.

CHAPTER 7

THE SUN HAD just dipped below the treetops when Jeff turned his Camaro onto Spruce Lane and pulled the car into his driveway halfway down the street. Nearly an entire day had passed since he had seen any of the Hurricanes, but as he braked to a stop and shut off the engine, he spotted a lone figure lurking in the long shadows of the house, revealed by the red glow of a cigarette tip. Mick emerged from the dim lawn and tossed the butt onto the driveway, crushing it out with the toe of his sneaker as Jeff climbed out of the car.

"Hey, Jeff," he said.

Jeff shut the car door. "Hey. Been here long?"

"Ten minutes. Where ya been? I've been trying to reach you all day."

"I didn't go to school today."

"I meant the funeral. Everyone was there but you."

Jeff shrugged. "I had my fill at the wake last night."

Mick buried his hands in his pockets. "Train's mom was asking about you. I didn't know what to tell her."

Jeff started up the front steps. "You didn't have to tell her anything. I don't expect you to make excuses for me."

Mick followed closely behind. "Right. 'Sorry Jeff couldn't come to your son's funeral, Mrs. Armstrong. He's home playing video games.'"

"I wasn't playing video games," Jeff snapped. "I drove down to the beach."

"The beach? What for?"

Jeff stopped at the front door and sorted through his keys. "You writing a book or something?"

"Well, the guys are worried about you. Hell, *I'm* worried about you, Jeff. You're acting… I don't know… moody."

Jeff unlocked the door and pushed it open. "So how the hell am I supposed to act?"

Mick followed him inside and shut the door. "I've known Train probably as long as you have. I still feel like throwing up ten times a day. But right now we just gotta suck it up and focus. We gotta fight tonight, remember?"

Jeff winced and started to reply, but his cell phone ringer cut him off. He held it to his ear as he climbed the stairs. "Hello?"

"Jeff? It's Cindy."

His phone had displayed her name, but her voice still caught him off guard. "Hi."

"I didn't see you at school today —"

"I wasn't there," he said. "Actually, I'm quitting."

"You're dropping out? But you only have like six months to go."

Jeff knew Mick was hanging on his every word, so he drifted into the dim kitchen and lowered his voice. "I can't talk about it right now. I need to see you."

"Not now. We have an away game tonight."

"Blow it off."

"I can't. My team needs me."

"Then I'll come over to your house later."

"Jeff, no. If my father finds out—"

"Then when?" he said quietly. "I have to see you."

The phone was quiet for a long moment. Finally she said, "I have an idea. One of my teammates was going to give me a ride home after the game, but I'll tell her I got one now. Pick me up outside the gym when the bus gets back."

"What time?"

"I don't know. Probably around seven."

"Okay, seven." Jeff turned away from Mick waving in objection. "See you then."

"Bye." She hung up her phone on him.

Mick stepped into the kitchen. "You're meeting her at seven? What about the fight?"

"You set the fight for seven?"

"No, but we gotta hook up before that. What's the plan?"

Jeff tossed his phone on the counter in exasperation. "You called the fight. What's your plan? Line everyone up and bull rush Curly after he runs out of bullets?"

"Here's my plan." Mick pulled his jacket back to reveal the pistol tucked under his waistband. "I'm gonna find Curly, and I'm gonna shoot him. Pretty simple plan, huh?"

"Awesome. What do you need us for?"

"You know he can't resist a fight. We just gotta draw him out."

"So we're decoys."

"Not decoys, Jeff. This fight's gonna be different. All bets are off now. No more of that gentlemen's honor crap you and Craig got going on. I'm just gonna take Curly out, one way or another. After that, the fight's over."

"And we go to jail."

"The cops don't know who has their guns. After tonight they'll never see this one again."

"They ain't gonna tolerate us anymore, Mick. If they see our colors, they'll arrest us on the spot."

"That's the beauty of it, Jeff. It's Halloween! They'll have their hands full with the amateurs and delinquents all night."

Jeff mulled the idea as he filled a glass of water at the sink. "I gotta think about things. Meet me at the fort by eight."

Mick winced. "How you gonna pull that off if you're meeting her at seven?"

Jeff grimaced. "She's just gonna dump me. I'm too much trouble for her now. The wake was the last straw."

Mick crossed the kitchen to the back door. "Well, don't be late. We're counting on you. Curly's getting bolder by the minute." He exited through the door and shut it behind him.

Jeff drank water slowly from his glass as he watched his friend descend the porch steps, pondering the notion that he had just been given an order from his own lieutenant.

Slouched behind the steering wheel of his Camaro, Jeff peered through the windshield across the student parking lot through the windshield, tapping his thumb impatiently on the stick shift as the stereo clock flashed to 7:10. The radio played quietly as he sat with engine off, idly wondering if Cindy had already come and gone. A fleeting notion panged his heart that perhaps she never intended to meet him in the first place, but before he could build the case in his head, he spotted her approaching his car from the right. He started the engine and switched the headlights on as she crossed the lot toward his car. The dome light flashed on as she popped open the door, and she stuffed a gym bag into the back seat before sliding into the front seat and shutting it again.

She surprised him with a kiss on his cheek. "Sorry I'm late. The game went into overtime. We won!"

"Awesome." He started the engine and proceeded to drive away. She continued to relate the details of the game to him, while he quietly maneuvered the car out of the parking lot and down an adjacent street. Soon his silence grew awkward and he felt like he had to say something regardless of how dumb it sounded. "Thanks for letting me take you home tonight."

"I'm glad you could, Jeff. We need to talk."

"Oh," he said sullenly. "Sounds like goodbye."

"Um, that depends."

"On what?"

"On you," she said. "And on me."

His heart beat faster, and he kept his eyes glued to the road ahead. "Let me guess. You're giving me an ultimatum."

"No, you don't understand. It's not like that." She paused, resting her hand upon his knee as she searched for words. "I like you, Jeff. I like you a lot. But something's gotta give. We're heading nowhere fast."

"You mean I'm heading nowhere fast," he said.

"I didn't say that," she replied coolly.

Jeff noticed a familiar driveway leading to a secluded baseball field. "Look, do you mind if I turn in here for a few minutes? I can't have this talk while I'm driving."

She nodded, so he turned the car onto the gravel driveway, following it through a cluster of trees and finally parking by a short chain-link fence not visible from the road.

He shut the engine off. "Is this okay?"

"It's fine." She clasped his fingers in hers and looked into his eyes. "Remember that day at Train's party? How you were just going to be Jeff, and I was just going to be Cindy, and we weren't going to worry about anything else?"

He smiled wistfully. "I don't think we can do that anymore. You're the police chief's daughter, and I'm the leader of the Hurricanes."

"I can't change who I am," she said. "I'll always be his daughter."

"I can't change either," he said. "The things I've done, the person I've become—I can't just flip the coin like that."

Her brown eyes glistened as she looked away. "Well then. There it is."

The finality of the moment felt palpable to him. He sensed that if he released her hand, he might never hold it again, and that seemed terribly wrong to him. "Well, what if I could change?" he blurted out. "What if I quit the gang and became an A student and turned into the swell guy your father wants for you? Would you still want me around? Could you even stand the sight of me? Maybe you like the way I get under his skin. I've seen it before."

A tear rolled down her cheek as she stared into her lap. "I would like you either way. But I can't battle my father forever. It's tearing our family apart."

"Hey, don't cry." He let her hand go and wiped her tear with his finger. "It's all right. You'll be better off without me."

"Don't say that—"

"I wish it wasn't true. But things are getting out of control now. You saw what happened at the wake last night. That was just the start."

"What do you mean?" Her eyes searched his face as if she were probing his mind. "Another fight? Tell me you aren't planning another fight."

He stared at her blankly. "I wish I could just sit here with you all night, but I can't."

"It's tonight? Oh no. Jeff, don't go—"

"I have to. It's bigger than me now."

"I thought you were the leader. I thought you were in charge."

"I can't stop it. How do I tell my friends to suck up what they're feeling right now? They're gonna fight whether I'm there or not."

"Exactly. So it doesn't matter if you go or not."

"It does matter." Jeff drew a deep breath and exhaled. "Train was a great friend. He was my bodyguard. I owe it to him."

Cindy took his hand again and looked at him in earnest. "Last night I heard you tell Train's parents that their son didn't die in vain. Did you really mean that? Because if someone else dies tonight—if all that comes of this is more vengeance and bloodshed—then his death means nothing."

Jeff gripped the steering wheel tightly and opened his mouth to respond, but no rebuttal came out, for her words rang true.

Cindy slid closer to him. "Do you still wonder why Train took that bullet for you? Maybe he was showing you how much he valued your friendship. What does it say if you throw that away?"

Jeff shook his head in remorse. "We never should have gone to that fight. I'll regret it for the rest of my life."

"Then don't go to this one," she said. She took his hand again. "Your whole life is sitting right before you, Jeff. You know where the Hurricanes are going to take you—the only place they *can* take you. But it doesn't have to be that way. You're smart. You're passionate. You're confident. People follow you because they believe in you."

He laughed. "That's a joke. I'm no leader. I'm a fraud."

"No, you're not. You just need to channel your energy in another direction. Change is hard, but the ones who believe in you will follow you in time." She squeezed his hand. "It has to start somewhere. Let it start with you."

He frowned. "It's no simple thing, what you're asking me to do—"

"But it's worth it, Jeff. There's a whole world waiting for you out there. A world filled with opportunity and fortune..." Her chest pressed softly against his arm as she leaned forward to kiss his mouth. "...and love."

He closed his eyes, recalling the last time she had kissed him that way, on the boating dock at Almond Lake when everything seemed much simpler. The notion that her affection had not died helped to ease his anguished heart, for she was like a beacon in the fog that his life had become. He pulled her closer, his fingers sliding along her back where her soft pink sweater had pulled away from the waistline of her jeans. Her warm back arched from the cool touch of his hand as it ran along her smooth skin to settle beneath her bra strap.

"Stay with me," he whispered. "I need you so much."

"Oh, Jeff, what do you want to do?" she asked breathlessly. "Do you wanna go with your friends and make war, or do you want to stay with me and make love?"

Jeff knew his answer, but it was not the one she wanted to hear. This would not be their first night together, not while the Hurricanes prepared for battle. If he failed to show for a fight on account of a girl, he would be despicable in their eyes, and rightly so. He glanced over her shoulder at the dark face of the stereo clock as he kissed her lips, ruing his decision to shut the engine off and keenly aware of a fine line he toed between loyalty and desire.

Mick paced the plywood stage of the underground fort amid the orange glow of the flickering oil lamps, his reddened face a reflection of the six anxious Hurricanes gathered before him. He searched his pockets in vain for his cigarettes and then checked his phone one last time before turning to address his friends.

"We can't wait any longer," he said. "We have to leave."

"How can we leave without Jeff?" Bumbles asked.

"The hell with Jeff if he can't even show up for a fight," Denny said.

TJ nodded. "We'll get by. We don't have much choice if he's gonna choose some chick over the gang."

Bumbles shook his head. "He's only ten minutes late. He'll be here."

Mick hopped off the platform and strode up to the lanky boy. "Let me explain something to you. Sometimes when a boy meets a girl, the boy disappears from the face of the earth because the girl has things that the other boys don't have." He patted Bumbles condescendingly on the shoulder. "Didn't your daddy ever tell you about that?"

TJ and Denny snickered at Bumbles's expense, but Crazy Legs leaned back against the opposite wall of the fort with his arms crossed. "Funny, Mick. Seeing as how you've written Jeff off, I guess it's your moment to shine."

"You think I'm happy?" Mick asked. "I'd gladly trade you and the virgin here for Jeff right now. I'll even throw in a few of my favorite baseball cards for good measure."

Bumbles hung his head amid the laughter, but Crazy Legs maintained his stare. "Go ahead. Make jokes. I hope you all understand it's not gonna be fun and games tonight. No one in either neighborhood has seen or heard from Curly since Saturday night. We have no idea where he is or what he's gonna do."

Mick stepped into the center of the fort. "Lemme put it this way. The Hurricanes are fighting tonight. Sit here and wait for Jeff if you want, but the Hurricanes leave now."

He turned for the rope ladder, but Crazy Legs stepped up after him. "Don't forget who our leader is."

Mick stopped and turned back to face him. "You know, I remember Jeff standing right here in this very spot, telling us that strong men made the gang stronger and weak men made it weaker. I don't see him here right now. I'm here for Train tonight, and I know for a fact that if it was one of you in his place, he'd be the first in line to avenge you."

TJ hopped to his feet. "And I'd be right beside him!"

Denny stood up beside him. "Hell yeah! We fight now!"

Axle joined them in line. "Tornadoes gotta pay for Train!"

Mick clasped hands with his three supporters and turned to the three dissenters standing across the room. "You guys coming or what?"

Bumbles shot an uneasy glance to Crazy Legs. "Can't just sit here and let these guys get creamed," he said, joining the trio by the ladder.

Brain sighed. "Yeah, I'm with ya. United we stand and all that crap, right?"

Mick clasped their hands in approval before stepping so close to Crazy Legs that their noses almost touched. "What about you? Are you a Hurricane tonight or what?"

Crazy Legs thrust his chest against his aggressor. "Yeah, I'm a Hurricane tonight. I'm always a damn Hurricane, Mick. But I'm Jeff's friend too. You might fool them, but you don't fool me."

Mick snarled darkly at him, but he brightened his expression as he turned about to face the rest of the gang. "Okay, let's go!" he boomed, pointing to the hatchway and striding confidently toward the rope ladder.

"Wait! What about the pledge?" Bumbles held his hand out before the Hurricanes. "Through thick and thin—"

"Aw, stuff it, Bumbles," Mick said before starting up the rope ladder. TJ laughed and Denny playfully shoved Bumbles aside as they headed to the ladder, while their lieutenant flipped the hatchway door open to let it slam gracelessly onto the rooftop. He climbed out into the night, patting the gun tucked beneath his jacket for reassurance as the Hurricanes filed out of the fort behind him. Crazy Legs passed through the hatchway last, crouching to shut the door and fasten the lock.

Mick turned to Brain. "I thought you said the moon would be out tonight."

Brain gazed up through the trees and shrugged. "Looks like some clouds are moving in."

"Yeah, no shit." The Hurricane lieutenant started along the forest path with the gang trailing dutifully behind. They traversed down the gentle hill to the fallen log spanning the dried gulley, crossing it in single file to the northern bank and then uphill again to the main forest path running beneath the massive limbs of Mr. Big. Mick dallied beneath the giant tree, waiting for his followers to catch up before continuing north along the main trail that wound along the ridge of a hillside blanketed with pine needles. Behind him, Crazy Legs jostled swiftly past his friends until he strode alongside their surrogate leader, perhaps more in defiance than in camaraderie. The two boys sauntered side by side to the mouth of the forest path, where they stopped at the edge of the fluorescent glow emanating from the Upper Plaza lights.

TJ stopped up close behind them, cracking his knuckles. "Ready to rock!"

Denny slid up beside him. "Let's do it!"

"Keep the chatter down," Mick said. "No talking unless it's absolutely necessary."

He cast a spiteful eye at the spotty gray clouds obscuring his moonlight as he stood before the open terrain like a warlord surveying his realm. The last few steps of the forest path descended into a field of sand that stretched fifty yards straight ahead toward the parking area of Gaucho's Cantina. The field also stretched a hundred yards to the left, where a stockade fence ran behind the line of the shops facing Burrough Street.

Mick studied the shadows. He finally turned to heed an urgent tugging at his sleeve and a finger pointing down the tree line along the left edge of the sand field. "Spy," Denny whispered.

The lieutenant cocked his head slightly, carefully scanning the tree line with his peripheral vision to avoid alerting the spy that he had been detected. "Flush him out," he told Denny. "Take Bumbles with you."

The two boys nodded and split away from the gang, strolling casually side by side along the tree line toward the southern edge of the Upper Plaza shops. Halfway along the sand field, they darted to their left into the woods, the sound of rustling leaves and snapping twigs followed by a startled cry. A moment later, a dark figure sprinted out from the trees in the direction of the stores, and Denny burst from the tree line in swift pursuit with Bumbles following right behind him.

Axle pointed to the dark figure out front. "Looks like Willie."

"He'll tire out," TJ said. "He's so predictable."

Brain frowned. "That was too easy. What if it's a trap?"

Mick twitched at the comment. "Go after them," he told Crazy Legs. "Hold their man until we get there."

The skinny boy recoiled. "Me? Why me?"

"You're the fastest. Nobody else is gonna catch him."

"But he's at least fifty yards away—"

Mick pushed him forward. "Go, dammit! Do what I tell you!"

Crazy Legs dashed off like a spooked cat down the tree line, but Willie had already traversed the entire length of the sand field and was now nearing the backside of the store chain behind the pizzeria and the tattoo parlor. When he reached the stockade fence, he veered abruptly to the right, running alongside the line of wooden spires eight feet high that separated the sand field from the rear delivery driveway of the stores. Denny pursued him doggedly, so fixated on catching Willie that he failed to notice Bumbles lagging behind.

Mick glanced at the Hurricanes around him, now only three in number. "Follow me," he said before breaking into a slow jog across the sand field.

Far ahead of him, Crazy Legs angled across the field to intercept Willie, soon overtaking Bumbles lumbering through the sand. In contrast, Denny ran so fast his heels kicked up the dry sand as he reached ahead for the collar of Willie's jacket. He finally grasped the collar as they passed a gap of broken slats in the stockade fence, dragging the spy down and landing a few glancing head shots as they writhed in the sand. As he held Willie down, he looked up to see Zak and Phil emerge from the cover of the last fence post at the edge of the parking lot. He sprang up and retreated along the fence line, but as he passed by the gap in the fence, a fist shot through the opening, catching him flush on the jaw and pasting him flat on his back. Craig stepped through the hole in the fence, shaking the sting from his hand as he placed a foot on the side of Denny's head to press his face down into the sand.

"It's Craig!" Mick shouted. "Let's go!"

Mired in the sand halfway across the field, the Hurricanes tried to quicken their pace, but the shifting footing slowed their progress so much they could only watch in futility as Zak and Phil advanced toward their friends. Crazy Legs slid to a halt before the fence and glanced about for help, while Bumbles plodded past him to aid Denny. The Hurricane scout glanced back down the fence line to see Happy Jack and Tony jogging along the fence line behind him, threatening to trap them against the fence before the other Hurricanes could come to their aid.

"Look out, Bumbles!" he called ahead. "More Tornadoes!"

Bumbles stopped and looked back in desperation as Zak and Phil closed in on him. "What do we do?"

"This way!" Crazy Legs lunged upward to grapple the pointed spires of the stockade fence, propelling his body higher with a foot upon its midrail. He swung the other foot up and wedged it between two spires, balancing precariously atop the fence as he waited for his friend to follow suit. Bumbles tried to imitate the maneuver, but he lost precious seconds when his sneaker slipped off the midrail, and his subsequent attempt was thwarted when Phil grabbed his shoulders to pull him down into the clutches of the converging Tornadoes.

Craig pulled Willie to his feet and pointed to the top of the fence. "Get Kramer!"

Crazy Legs sprang from his perch, landing in a crouch behind the 7-Eleven store as Willie slipped through the hole in the fence to intercept him. Happy Jack and Tony spun about to retreat toward the southern tree line, while Craig followed

Willie through the hole in the fence, leaving Phil and Zak to pummel Bumbles against the fence with Denny lying crumpled in the sand.

Thirty yards from the fence, Mick slowed the gang up and pointed toward Happy Jack and Tony rounding the last fence post to the left. "That way," he said. "Come on."

"What about Bumbles?" Brain asked. "He's getting his ass kicked!"

"We're here for Curly," Mick replied. TJ and Axle exchanged uneasy glances, but the Hurricane lieutenant clapped his hands to spur them on. "C'mon, go!"

On the other side of the fence, Crazy Legs launched from his crouch like a sprinter from a starting gun, running straight down the delivery access driveway between the 7-Eleven store and the bicycle shop. He saw that he had a strong lead over Willie, so he eased his pace at the front of the delivery driveway to survey the front parking lot. The hour had passed nine o'clock so most of the stores had closed, but a scattering of vehicles remained parked outside Crusty's, where dinner was still being served. The skinny boy ran straight across the parking lot to the curb of Burrough Street before turning back, only to see that he had completely outrun the protection of the Hurricanes. He trotted southward on the roadside along the grassy median with the wind of the passing traffic tousling his hair wildly about. Looking over his shoulder, he saw Willie angling toward him between the parked vehicles, while Craig stepped from the access driveway onto the sidewalk before the dark bicycle shop.

Any Hurricane that Crazy Legs thought might help him was already preoccupied with the Tornadoes at every turn. TJ and Axle ran around the southern end post to chase Tony back down the other side of the fence, but Mick halted as he emerged from the sand field behind the tattoo parlor. He grabbed Brain's arm and signaled for silence while pointing to a rusty dumpster at the corner of the building. Brain crept around the left side of the dumpster as he circled it from the right, but before he reached the other side he heard shouts of alarm and scuffling feet. He ran clear of the dumpster, but Brain was already chasing Happy Jack up the gravel embankment leading around the corner of the building.

Mick slipped upon the jagged gray rocks as he started up the embankment after them, so by the time he reached the side wall of the tattoo parlor neither boy was anywhere to be seen. He slunk forward along the white brick wall to view the front parking lot, wondering how they might have run so far so quickly. Instead, he spotted Crazy Legs jogging along Burrough Street at the far edge of the front lot. The Hurricane lieutenant cupped his hands to his mouth and blew a short, warbled whistle, then he fell back for cover against the wall, while his scout dutifully turned toward him like a retriever called home to its master.

Brain emerged from the sparse woods of the adjacent property, his face beaming with excitement. "Mick, come here! You won't believe what I saw!"

Mick bristled. "Unless it's Curly hanging from a tree, I don't care."

The sudden roar of an engine diverted their attention, and they turned to see Crazy Legs suddenly illuminated by the headlights of a large green pickup truck parked in the nearest row of parking spaces outside Crusty's. The skinny boy squinted in the bright light, barely able to discern the driver's scowling brow or the bony finger of his goateed passenger pointing through the windshield at him. Quickening his pace, he scanned the shadows beyond the lighted sidewalk of the plaza, desperately searching for friends as the pickup truck lurched forward.

"Mick!" he cried out. "I found Curly!"

Mick rushed past the front edge of the building and waved his arms from atop the embankment to reveal his position to his scout. Brain started after his leader, but Happy Jack sprinted from the sparse woods and shoved him to the ground on his way down to the parking lot. The sight of the Tornado jostling up behind Mick spooked Crazy Legs, and he suddenly turned for the safety of the covered sidewalk as the green pickup truck rolled forward from its parking space in pursuit.

Curly gunned the engine and cut the steering wheel left to slide into the fire lane, while the truck's rear wheels hopped the curb, spraying Mick and Happy Jack with decorative white stones lining the edge of the parking lot. Happy Jack shied away from the projectiles, but Mick seized upon the fleeting opportunity, leaping from the embankment into the bed of the truck as its change in direction rendered it stationary before him. The thud of his body landing upon the metal bed was masked by the loud bang of the truck's bumper striking the short brick wall at the end of the sidewalk. Lying on his belly, Mick gripped the grooves of the steel bed while Curly accelerated along the fire lane, too focused on his fleeing prey to notice his unwelcomed passenger.

Crazy Legs fled down the sidewalk past the storefront windows when the glass entrance door of Crusty's flew open in his path and a tall man in an overcoat emerged with a large pizza box in his hands. "Outta my way!" the skinny boy cried, veering off the sidewalk to avert a collision as the man staggered back, juggling his pizza to keep from dropping it. The Hurricane darted down the fire lane directly in the path of the green truck, while Craig advanced along the sidewalk toward him and Willie fell back through the parking lot to converge upon him. The closed shops to the right offered him no refuge, and the 7-Eleven was too far away to outrun the truck, so he chose his only feasible option: he dodged Craig's outstretched hand and swerved away from Willie before turning down the access driveway, where more Tornadoes surely awaited him.

Curly drove the pickup truck straight between Craig and Willie, skidding to a halt at the mouth of the driveway; he cranked the steering wheel hard to the right and accelerated toward the Hurricane runner. Inside the truck bed, Mick remained flat on his belly, bracing his sneakers against the tailgate as the truck fishtailed wildly to the left—Craig spotted him and shouted futilely to Curly as the truck sped away down the access driveway.

As the truck bed stabilized again, Mick crawled to the rear window of the cab, steadying himself with one hand on the front lip of the bed and pulling out the pistol with the other. Peering through the rear slider window, he could see Crazy Legs through the front windshield of the cab, running for the stockade fence with the truck's headlights shining ever brighter upon the white swirl of his Hurricane jacket.

Once Crazy Legs cleared the rear of the 7-Eleven building, he glanced at his left in hope of making a run for Gaucho's, only to see Zak and Phil emerging from the hole in the stockade fence. To his right, TJ and Axle battled with Tony alongside the fence, while in the distance Happy Jack sprinted back around the dumpster, eager to rejoin the fray with Brain lagging behind him. Caught in a moment of indecision with enemies closing in on three sides, he ran straight for the stockade fence and leaped up to grab its spires again, but this time his sneakers scraped futilely against its painted wooden facing without the benefit of a midrail. Using only the strength in his wiry arms, he pulled his body up high enough to swing a leg and wedge a foot between the saw-toothed spires. He drew the second leg up and assumed a wobbly squat atop the fence before casting a quick look back at the headlights of the truck bearing down upon him, confident he had escaped its threat.

Inside the metal bed of the truck, Mick braced a shoulder against the rear of the cab, expecting the driver to brake hard or swerve to avoid the fence. He flicked off the safety and raised his pistol toward the back of Curly's head, but he was instantly thrown backward as the truck bounced over the rear curb of the driveway amid an enthusiastic whoop from its occupants. He crashed against the metal tailgate and frantically craned his neck just in time to see Crazy Legs staring back with wide eyes at the pickup truck careening toward the fence.

The scout leaped as far as he could into the soft sand on the other side of the fence, falling to his knees before scrambling to his feet and staggering farther into the barren field. A thunderous crash filled the air as the truck sailed through the stockade fence, smashing its right headlamp and sending a shower of wood fragments in its wake as its chassis rocked hard upon its struts. Still clenching the gun, Mick tumbled onto his back again before scrambling to his knees to see Crazy Legs through the windshield, tiring in the shifting sand with the truck bearing down on him. The skinny boy stumbled forward and dropped flat in the sand, clasping his hands behind his head seconds before the pickup truck raced over his body. The base of the drivetrain housing passed so closely overhead that it nicked the knuckle of his middle finger; nevertheless, he gasped with relief when he looked up to see the truck's red taillights continuing past him through the sand field.

Curly checked his mirror for the anticipated remains of the Hurricane scout, only to see the Hurricane lieutenant lurking inside his truck bed with gun in hand. With a cuss, he slammed on the brakes and cut the steering wheel hard to the right, sending Mick hurtling over the left side of the bed into the soft sand, then he hit the gas to spin the truck about nearly a full circle to his right, so that the lone headlight shone down upon his enemy. While Hurricanes and Tornadoes alike lumbered across the sand field toward the truck, Curly popped his door open and clambered to the ground amid a blowing dust cloud, stepping beside the hood with his revolver in hand. He leveled his sights upon Mick, covered with sand and searching for his pistol in the shadows.

"Hey Mick!" the Tornado lieutenant called out. "Trick or treat!"

Mick turned his sullen eyes to see the dim outline of the gun pointed his way while JJ snickered inside the cab. Twenty yards back, Crazy Legs lifted his head from the sand to spot a dark figure in a blue jacket dashing from the murky tree line not far away, running on a beeline toward the Tornado lieutenant.

"Jeff!" he blurted out.

Curly cocked an ear at the sound of Jeff's name, but Jeff tackled him before he could fully react; a single gunshot split the night air, yet Mick dove to the dirt unscathed. The revolver flipped out of Curly's hand from the force of Jeff's blow, landing at the fringe of the headlight beam while they scuffled in the sand, tangled in each other's limbs. Curly broke free and lunged for the gun, but Jeff tripped him by the ankle, causing his outstretched fingers to knock the weapon beneath the truck's front bumper.

Curly rose before the front grill of the truck and spun about with the ivory handle of a switchblade knife already clenched in his hand. "Glad you could make it, Hollister," he said. "I was thinking maybe you weren't so tough after all."

Jeff rose to his feet and slowly backed away as Curly popped the knife open and pressed the switchblade tip closer. The Tornado lieutenant charged forward and swung the knife, but Jeff dove aside to escape the wild slash. He rolled over in the sand and hopped up again, pulling his hunting knife from the sheath on his belt as he turned to confront his adversary. He shook his head in disbelief at his predicament. "Curly, this is crazy." he said.

Curly grinned wildly. "Yeah it is. Let's go insane!"

The onrushing gangs separated from each other as they ran toward the truck with a few of the Hurricanes pausing to help Crazy Legs off the ground. Together they followed the Tornadoes toward the truck, where everyone stopped at the fringe of the headlight beam. Crazy Legs stepped forward with the sand on his jacket glistening in the light. "Jeff, what are you doing?"

Jeff held up his bandaged hand to his friend as his good

hand fidgeted with the white handle of the hunting knife. He inched toward the light of the headlamp, knowing the darkness would benefit his foe. "I really don't wanna do this," he said.

Curly laughed. "Of course not. That's why you're gonna die."

"Kill him, Jeff!" Mick shouted, his eyes still fixed upon the shadows in search of his pistol.

Jeff tightened his grip on his knife, pivoting about as Curly slowly circled him. Behind him, the Tornadoes and Hurricanes egged them on with cheers, seemingly content to let the two fighters settle their differences without interference. He spotted the Tornado leader out of the corner of his eye and called him out without looking directly at him. "This ain't gonna solve anything, Craig. You remember why you came to Train's wake last night?"

Craig folded his arms across his chest. "I remember running for my life!" he scoffed.

Curly frowned at Craig as if the exchange was news to him, but he quickly turned back to the Hurricane leader to viciously swipe the switchblade at Jeff's rib cage. Jeff twisted away, but the Tornado lieutenant followed with an errant backhand slash that left him off balance with his arm overextended. Jeff stuck out a foot and smacked his foe hard between the shoulder blades with the bandaged hand, sending the Tornado lieutenant crashing facedown into the sand, lit by the lone headlight with arms and legs sprawled out. He rolled over and scowled at Jeff, the sand in his bushy eyebrows lending him the appearance of a raccoon caught in a spotlight. The Hurricanes howled in delight at the spectacle, while Jeff failed to suppress a mocking grin despite the gravity of his situation.

Curly gnashed his teeth and squeezed his switchblade handle tighter. He nodded to someone in the crowd, and Jeff's smile quickly vanished as he recalled the stairwell attack at school. He stepped back and cast a suspicious eye at Craig, but he could not account for all the Tornadoes in the shadows. His left eye caught a peripheral blur of motion, and he whirled about to see Happy Jack darting toward him with a knife in his hand, while Curly also sprang forward, timing his attack to coincide with his friend's arrival. Jeff fell back toward the open door of the truck with his hunting knife held defensively by his stomach before they all collided and tumbled to the ground in a heap. Jeff felt his knife being ripped from his hand as they landed, but he felt nothing pierce his body.

Hurricanes and Tornadoes alike stepped closer to get a better view of the threesome entangled in the sand, dimly lit by the dome light inside the cab. Curly sprang up first, clenching his hair with both hands as he backed into the light, his eyes darting with uncertainty between Craig and the two boys still lying on the ground. Finally, Jeff pushed his attacker free from his legs, squinting in the shadows for his hunting knife, while Happy Jack flopped onto his back to reveal an ivory knife handle protruding from his bloody gut.

Curly rushed forward and knelt beside his stricken friend. "You killed him, Hollister!" he shouted. "Hollister killed Jack!"

Jeff hopped up and backed away toward the tree line. "No! I didn't—He—It was an accident!"

The Tornadoes rushed forward and huddled around their stricken friend while the Hurricanes shied away from the truck. Curly screamed in anguish and dove beneath the front of his truck to retrieve the revolver from the sand. "Hollister!" he cried.

"Run, Jeff!" Crazy Legs shouted. "He's got a gun!"

Jeff was already sprinting for the forest path even before Curly had retrieved the weapon, while the Hurricanes dispersed in all directions. Curly started after Jeff, but Craig dashed forward and grabbed him by the wrist. "We gotta get Jack to the hospital! You gotta drive him there!"

Curly tried to pull away. "I want Hollister!"

Craig pushed him back against the truck. "Forget about him! We gotta go!"

Phil and Zak lifted Happy Jack by his limbs with the knife still stuck in his abdomen. They placed him into the bed of the pickup truck and clambered in beside him as Craig slid into the cab alongside JJ. Curly lingered a moment longer to watch Jeff disappear into the woods before tucking the gun away and climbing behind the steering wheel. Doors slammed, tires spun, and the truck sped away, weaving chaotically toward the edge of the plaza parking lot.

The sand field, moments ago a beehive of activity, had quickly turned serene again under the emerging moonlight. The green pickup truck raced up Burrough Street as the remaining gang members scattered in various directions, leaving one Hurricane behind, searching with steady eyes until finally he pulled a pistol from the sand.

"Found it!" Mick exclaimed, brushing it clean. He turned to behold the empty field and shrugged with casual disinterest at the sudden departure of friend and foe. With a sigh of relief, he tucked the gun beneath his Hurricane jacket and strolled off for the familiar cover of the nearby woods.

CHAPTER 8

STUMBLING OVER THE stones and roots that scarred the forest path, Jeff could hear the beat of footsteps closing in from behind. He slipped to one knee upon the soft pine needles surrounding Mr. Big, but he clawed at the hard-packed ground along the ridge to avoid sliding down toward the dry ravine, all the while eyeing the dark path behind him in fear of who might be following. He passed the rabbit path leading to the underground fort to his left, but he kept to the main path, driving his legs upward against a steep slope rising to the right. A few minutes later he reached a clearing at the top of Bobcat Hill and, gasping for air with his hands on his knees, he stared down the path he had just climbed, knowing he could count on one hand the boys from either gang who could outrun him up a hill.

A moment later Crazy Legs emerged from the woods in plain view of him. "Don't make me keep chasing you, Jeff!" he called out. "I've run far enough tonight."

Jeff backed to a hilltop clearing and rested his hands on hips. "Go away," he said breathlessly. "Stop following me."

The runner slowed to a walk and circled about as he sucked in the cool air. "Where are you going? What are we supposed to do now?"

"Figure it out for yourself. Just leave me alone."

"I thought you said we had to stick together," Crazy Legs said. "What was that, a lie?"

Jeff straightened up, irked by the comment. "You wanna know what to do? Get out. Find a way. Don't wait." He started away but turned a forlorn look back to his friend. "It's too late for me now."

Crazy Legs stood agape, splashed in the moonlight atop the modest hill, while Jeff darted off to the mouth of another dark path at the other side of the clearing. The short path led him downhill to the edge of an embankment ten feet above Arrow Drive, where he waited for a car to pass before sliding down an eroded rut and crossing the street for the next yard. As he climbed the sloping backyard to a wooden fence, he felt relieved to see his house dark atop the gentle slope of the next yard, for if the news of Happy Jack's stabbing had already reached the Salisbury police, their first move surely would have been to seek out the most obvious suspects. As he crossed the fence and jogged toward his house, he vowed that this time they would not find him there.

He hurried up the unlit porch stairs and burst through the unlocked back door, kicking it shut once inside. A flick of a switch lit the pendant lamp over the kitchen table, and stretching his arms out beneath the bright bulb, he discovered the right sleeve of his Hurricane jacket was streaked with blood, as well as his underlying T-shirt. Quickly he stripped to his waist, rolling the soiled clothing into a ball as he left the kitchen and bounded down two flights of stairs. He left the light off as he slid into his bedroom, stuffing the bloody clothing under the bed before grabbing a polo shirt and a dark sweatshirt from his dresser. After donning both articles, he ripped a green down vest from a closet hanger and rushed out of the bedroom barely a minute after he entered it, pulling the vest over his shoulders as he climbed the stairs two at a time on his way back to the kitchen.

He stopped at the kitchen sink and switched on an overhead light to inspect his hands. A few specks of blood spotted the white adhesive tape of the dressed left hand, but the bandage remained intact, and there was no time to change it anyway. There was some dried blood on his right hand, but under a gush of hot water he was able to scrub it off with soap and a sponge. Jeff was not oblivious to the fact that he was washing blood from his hands for the second time in a week, and he wondered if he could scrub his conscience of Happy Jack's stabbing as easily as he had scrubbed the blood from his skin. A flick of a switch killed the sink light, and barely three minutes after entering the house he was at the back door again, ready to turn off the last remaining kitchen light. As he reached for the switch, however, a shimmering object in the dining room caught his eye: a crystal decanter set upon the middle shelf of a corner curio cabinet.

That's it, he thought. *Perfect.*

He entered the dining room and stepped around the cherrywood table to the matching glass cabinet set in the far corner of the room. Amid the trinkets and keepsakes placed upon the mirrored shelves was a silver-framed wedding photo of his mother and father set beside a crystal decanter of Scotch whisky. Jeff wistfully recalled the last time his parents had drank from that bottle, toasting their fifteenth and final wedding anniversary following an elegant candlelit dinner while he and his brother gleefully looked on.

The sentiment vanished. He threw the cabinet door open and callously brushed the picture frame aside, grabbing the crystal decanter by its neck before turning about and charging from the room. With a flick of the light switch, he plunged the house into darkness again and closed the back door. Moments later, he squeezed through a gap in the hedges, heading toward the grounds of Salisbury High with the bottle tucked beneath his vest.

He continued through a half dozen backyards, stirring a dog into barking but otherwise traveling undetected to the curb of Willow Street, where he took cover behind a bush from the headlights of an approaching car. The car passed by and he sprang forward, holding the decanter safely in his good hand as he crossed the street for the dormant high school recreational fields. Following the left foul line of a baseball field, he passed the outfield fence and skirted the edge of a basketball blacktop to the tall meshed fences of three dark tennis courts, their monolithic spotlight poles silent and gray against the clearing sky. At the edge of the farthest tennis court, a dirt road led to a distant cul-de-sac of upscale homes abutting the school property, but the forgotten road soon thinned into a scraggly path not wide enough to keep the pine trees on either side from mingling their branches overhead.

Jeff stopped to survey his surroundings. To his left, fifty yards up a gentle hill, a post-and-rail fence separated the boundary of a private horse pasture from a clay oval running track near the edge of the high school property, while to his right the soft white glow of a distant Burrough Street home flickered through the gaps in the trees. Confident of isolation from all directions, he leaned back against a thick tree and slid down its trunk to the ground, stretching his legs out comfortably and resting the decanter in his lap. He popped the glass stopper free and sniffed the whisky inside before raising the bottle up to the moon peeking at him through the overhead branches.

"Here's to a hell of a future," he said, tipping the bottle to the moon.

The crystal decanter weighed heavy in his hands as he raised it to his lips, and the whisky choked him as it rushed down his throat with all the splendor of a hot coal. Gasping and sputtering, he dropped the bottle to his lap and fought the urge to vomit, but soon the discomfort eased and he felt a warm sensation in his belly, followed by a slight numbing in his head. A fair exchange, he mused, the effect of the whisky versus the pain of drinking it.

He gazed back to the moon, imagining for a moment that he sat on one of the overhead branches, looking down upon the pathetic figure propped against a tree trunk. Two weeks ago, he'd felt larger than life, cruising through his senior year with the Hurricanes a respected underground force at Salisbury High. Now here he was, a drunk in a gutter with a bottle of whisky in his lap, but what surprised him most was a feeling of inevitability that he would someday descend to this very place. He felt that such a notion ought to nag at him, yet lying against the trunk of a tree with his legs stretched out beneath the stars, he felt strangely at ease.

Nestling back against the tree, he tilted his chin toward the sky and raised the bottle to his lips again. The whisky still burned his throat, but not quite so much this time. Staring at the moon, he closed one eye and held up the bottle stopper to the other, marveling for a moment at the lustrous kaleidoscopic view of the refracted moonlight through the intricate cuts in the crystal glass, an altered perspective of a familiar sight. Finally, he stuffed the stopper into his vest pocket with his bandaged hand as the fingers of his good hand traced the pinwheel emblem inscribed in the face of the decanter. There was dust within the inscription, for the decanter had sat idle since his father's death eight years ago — never moved, never touched, never enjoyed. Five years had passed since Billy had left for California, four years since his mother had taken the bartending job, and three years since he'd formed the Hurricanes, if only to break the monotony of a lonesome teenage life. There the bottle sat on the same glass shelf, collecting dust like a sacred artifact while a family disintegrated in its midst.

"So much for skeletons in the cabinet," he murmured, raising the bottle to drink again.

In one sense, the Hurricanes had saved his life, or at least his sanity, after his father's death. Three friendships had helped to ease his grief, friendships not based on sports or games but rather upon mischief and defiance, and as a result the framework of the Hurricanes had been formed, in practice if not in name. They had assumed their roles instinctively—the bodyguard's muscle and devotion, the lieutenant's cunning and bravado, the scout's speed and sleuth—and they looked to him as their leader. When the Tornadoes formed in his sophomore year, their bullying ways helped the Hurricanes to form and attract more recruits. TJ and Denny joined first, followed by Axle and Brain, and finally Bumbles.

Confrontations with the Tornadoes had focused the Hurricanes' attention from mischief to combat, a change that Mick readily embraced. With his help, the gang honed their fighting skills and strengthened their resolve while the values of espionage and agility Crazy Legs promoted gradually lost favor with the gang. Admittedly, Jeff preferred fighting to running, and with a smirk he mused that if Crazy Legs spent half as much time lifting weights or hitting a punching bag as he did running around town in his fancy shorts, then maybe he'd be fit to question his leader's loyalty. Especially when that leader could rub his face in the dirt easier than he could wipe it clean.

Still, maybe there was something to following one's own path, even if it meant incurring the ridicule of others. Jeff eased his furrowed brow. "Fair enough," he muttered before gulping another mouthful of whisky.

No one was more apt to follow his own path than Mick. Jeff wondered, with a grunt, how two friends as different as Crazy Legs and Mick could still wear the same colors. As a leader he had tried to meld the various personalities of his friends into a unified force, and the result was a cohesive and versatile gang that had gained a reputation that it was better left alone.

"If only Craig could figure that out," he said.

The face of his rival burned clear in his mind as he raised the bottle for another swig. Manhandling the Tornadoes had become second nature for the Hurricanes to the extent that some of his friends had lost interest in tangling with them. And with the principal members of both gangs entering their senior year, the two gangs had seemed to reach a point of mutual indifference toward each other. So before the school year started, the two leaders and their lieutenants met amid pizza and sodas at Crusty's on a Saturday afternoon to hammer out a truce that would help them tolerate each other until graduation. Hell, they had even shared a few jokes, Jeff recalled with a snort of incredulity. Three months later, the Tornadoes had regressed beyond pesky sabotage and physical skirmishes to a new low of murder. Their motives were beyond senseless, they were downright vicious, and Craig's role in it seemed fickle at best. It just didn't make sense...

Jeff could taste a revelation coming on, but another gulp of whisky quickly dispelled it. Train lay in his grave with Happy Jack soon to follow, and trying to decipher the Tornadoes' motives meant entering a labyrinth of speculation that would ultimately lead him right back to where he sat now, sitting under a tree with a bottle in his hand. A few short hours ago, Cindy had told him of a world filled with opportunity, fortune, and love somewhere beyond the suffocating borders of Salisbury. Now he could only laugh at the thought of such a future, for a simple fingerprint from his knife or a drop of Jack's blood on his clothing could send him to prison for hard time. After years of flying in the face of the police, the irony of being arrested for murder in a fight he had intended to stop was not lost upon him. Even if he could somehow escape arrest, he knew Curly would continue to hunt him with renewed vengeance. His head swam in the warm rush of whisky, but a sobering decision beckoned him: stay in his hometown and risk death or arrest, or live on the lam with a glimmer of hope to remain free, but in complete exile of his current life.

Jeff drew a deep breath and closed his eyes. He pictured himself driving the Camaro along a flat road with the radio playing with a warm breeze blowing through the open windows, and it felt right to him. In the morning, he would retrieve the car from its hiding spot and drive out of town, across the state and country to California, where Billy would hopefully welcome him with a room and a job in his auto-body shop. Graduating with his class felt like a fading dream, but the thought of a liberating cross-country trip rekindled a spark in his heart, for he had longed for such a journey to reunite with his brother. Still, loose ends abounded: money, clothes, and fond farewells. The Hurricanes had battled and bled with him, and as their leader he owed each of them a handshake, if nothing else. His mother would probably object to his departure, especially if it meant dropping out of school, but hopefully she would take comfort in the idea of a brotherly reunion.

Those farewells would be painful, but there was one he dreaded even more. He tilted back and swallowed another mouthful of whisky, but neither the thrill of the adventure nor the burn of the liquor diminished the bitter task of breaking up with Cindy. The joy he had felt from their reconciliation had since been completely blown away, and now he had to concoct a half-hearted explanation of why he had to leave her. If only she would take a leap of faith and go with him, maybe they could find more happiness together without all the pressures that life in Salisbury levied upon them.

"So ask her!" he blurted out before raising the bottle to his lips again.

The whisky dribbled down his chin as he laughed. Of course, there were a hundred reasons why she wouldn't go, several of which he could list even before he swallowed: school, sports, friends, and family. Not to mention the fact that they hadn't even known each other two weeks ago. He laughed aloud at his own foolish expectations — it would take him *two months* to convince her to go, if she didn't reject him outright.

But why not ask? The worst she could do was say no. No, he thought with a crooked grin. The worst she could do was laugh in his face and tell him to get lost, but he planned to do that anyway. He had to ask her, if only for his own peace of mind, or else spend years languishing over what might have been. She was like a soft light in his tired eyes, cool fingers in his sweaty palm, a fresh breeze on a hot summer night. Such comforts were not so readily dismissed.

Jeff exhaled a long sigh of relief. He finally had a plan, and plans always set him at ease, even the murky ones. Suddenly he felt as if he had lingered too long under the pines, so he struggled to his feet with the help of his friendly tree. Already time ran thin, for tomorrow would be a day of preparation and farewells, and by Friday morning he would be gone. The first farewell beckoned him from a mile away, over hills and through fields, to a place where an old friend lay, the only friend who could help resolve the resonant ache in his heart. He clasped the decanter by its neck and staggered farther down the overgrown path beneath the moonlight with the flush of whisky buzzing in his head.

"I'm comin' to see ya, Train," he slurred. "I'm comin' ta visit ya one las' time!"

The clang of a heavy bell jarred Jeff awake, his body shivering and his head pounding. Without opening his eyes, he massaged his temple with his fingers, wondering why the howling wind was so cold and why a bell was clanging in his bedroom, and then the bell clanged again. The hoot of an owl convinced him that he was not in the comfort of his own bed, and his aching brain vaguely recalled staggering through an open field, drinking sloppily from a bottle and hell-bent on some destination he had clearly failed to reach. The third ring of the bell finally prompted his bleary eyes open, although they could not readily help him to fully discern his location. Then the bell rang a fourth time and he mustered the will to roll onto his knees to behold his surroundings. The gray outline of a distant church steeple stood against a star-splotched sky now devoid of its earlier lunar glow, as its bell eased into silence for another hour.

As he struggled to stand, he stumbled over the glass decanter lying at his feet, but he caught his balance before falling to the ground. He lifted the bottle and held it up in amazement, for barely an inch of whisky remained inside, although he couldn't tell how much he had drunk and how much had spilled. In a fit of anger, he hurled it down the hill, hoping it would smash into pieces, but it landed with a dull thud in the darkness.

He turned and climbed to the top of the slope, where he gazed wearily at the multitude of marble gravestones lining the other side of the hill, stretching from the rear of the church grounds to a property fence not far from the curbside of Burrough Street. He shuddered as he started down the hill, mostly from the chill in the air but partly from the notion of walking through a dark cemetery in the dead of night. When he reached the perimeter of gravestones, he found the newer markers panning to his right, so he followed them along a ridge until he came upon a gray marble stone speckled in white, set before a freshly covered grave. The grave lay atop a long, grassy slope that ran past a broad oak tree to the glowing streetlamps of Burrough Street a hundred yards away.

"Lionel James Armstrong. Beloved son," Jeff read aloud, noting the bookend dates of his friend's brief life. He knelt to the ground and pivoted about to sit with his back against the side of the headstone in view of the quiet, distant road. There he remained for nearly half an hour, lamenting a friendship lost, and resting his troubled mind. Finally he felt able to answer his friend's question on that fateful night: there was no way back to good anymore. They had crossed a line from which neither friend could retreat, and there would be no redemption now.

"Nice view you got here, buddy," he said, but his words stuck in his throat as he glared over his shoulder at the rectangular patch of dirt cut in the grass before the marker. A bouquet of white roses lay at the base of the stone, clinging together against the onslaught of the cold November wind. Maybe more flowers would come and more after that, but eventually a day would arrive when there would be no more flowers. Sod would take root on the grave, and more new tombstones would dot the hillside, the inevitable result of a burgeoning and ever-aging township. Who would visit this grave when Train was nothing more than a skeleton and a memory? Who would remember his heroic act when twenty or thirty years had passed?

"I will. I'm gonna do right by you, Train. I don't know how, but I will." Jeff stood up and rested his palm on the tombstone. "And I won't forget what you did for me. I swear."

A stiff wind cut through his open vest like a ghost through a windsock, sending a shiver up his spine. He felt as if he teetered between two worlds, separated only by a nick of time, a minuscule happenstance of fate that determined who lived and who died. What mortal mind could predict how knives might cut and bullets might fly? Certainly not his own, for he had twice washed blood from his hands despite wishing death upon no one. Deep down, he knew the reverend was right: the man with the plan—the one his friends admired so much—was just a fool in a fog, a battered flag flailing against the relentless force of a majestic storm.

The wind offered cool relief for his bloodshot eyes as he turned to face the gentle slope again. He zippered his vest tight and glanced back at his friend's tombstone one last time before walking down the slope for Burrough Street and the town of Salisbury, where the morning sun would soon rise again upon the land of the living.

⌁

Even in the early dawn hours, a passing car was not an

uncommon sight along the arterial road of Burrough Street, so Jeff followed the road under the cover of trees and bushes away from the roadside. With the center of town nearly two miles behind him, he approached the fork of Arrow Drive, walking as briskly as he could with the hangover he bore. He wanted to follow Burrough Street to the left and retrieve the Camaro from its hiding place near the Upper Plaza, but he realized that, in his rush to leave the house, he had left his car keys and cell phone rolled up inside his Hurricane jacket under his bed.

Following a dry gully along Arrow Drive, he soon reached the curb of Willow Street, quickly crossing it for the backyards of Spruce Lane and Hurricane territory once again. Minutes later, he slipped through the hedges of his own backyard, relieved to find the house dark, although he knew that his mother would surely be home and in bed at such a late hour. Rather than risk a confrontation by entering through the back door, he continued to the far side of the house, where the garage window slid open with its usual ease. He climbed inside and closed the window behind him before following the familiar path through the dark garage to the basement door.

Holding his breath, he eased the door open slowly and tried to minimize its predictable squeak as he squeezed it shut. He slunk to his bedroom and switched on the light, but when he reached under his bed for the stashed garments, he felt nothing but carpet. His throbbing head strained to remember—had he left them in the laundry room instead? As he turned to leave the bedroom, he heard the creak of a step that betrayed someone's presence. Before he could exit the room, his mother stepped into the doorway, dressed in a white terrycloth bathrobe. She glared at him with sullen, sleepless eyes, a cigarette in her left hand and his Hurricane jacket in her right.

"I didn't mean to wake you up," he murmured.

"Oh, I've been awake," she said.

"Have you seen my car keys?"

She sucked a deep breath through the cigarette and exhaled

the smoke deliberately. "The police were here tonight. They said a boy had been stabbed and that they wanted to talk to you about it." She held up his bloody jacket. "After they left, I found this under your bed."

"It was an accident," Jeff explained.

"An accident!" She flung the jacket into his chest. "It's no accident the way you carry on with your hoodlum friends!"

Jeff frowned as he fished through the pockets. "He tried to kill me, Ma."

She scoffed in response. "Mr. Stammer called me at work today. He said you haven't been to school all week."

He found his phone but no keys. "I'm dropping out. I don't need his bullshit anymore."

She stepped closer and sniffed. "You smell like booze. Where's your father's Scotch?"

"I drank it, Ma! I figured he didn't need it anymore!" Jeff massaged his aching temple. "Do you have my keys or not?"

The scowl on her face seemed to add ten years to her age. "I want you out of this house today! Do you hear me?"

Jeff simmered. "Loud and clear, Ma. Just gimme my keys and I'll be gone for good."

She pulled the keys from her nightgown pocket and threw them at him, but he snatched them out of the air, frustrating her even further. "Get out! You're no better than the thugs who killed your father." She turned about and stormed up the staircase.

Her words stung worse than a knife in his palm. He threw the jacket on the floor and stuffed the keys into his vest pocket. "You're gonna regret that someday!" he shouted after her.

He stormed down the hallway and ripped the garage door open, flicking the light before slamming it shut behind him. Forgoing departure through the window, he instead rolled up the garage door and let it crash down with the light still on as he stormed off for the side of the house. He quickly sought the cover of the dark backyard, but he stopped when he reached the short fence at the rear of the property, his attention drawn to the porch light flicking on behind him. Straddling the rail for a moment, he watched his mother standing at the porch door window, staring out into the night after him. She switched the light off a few minutes later, and he crossed into the adjacent property as surely as if he was crossing a threshold into a new and uncertain future, with no way back home.

Despite possessing his keys again, he realized that retrieving his car at this hour would be a mistake, for the cops on the graveyard shift would be buzzing the streets like angry hornets in search of his conspicuous Camaro. A sliver of sunlight had begun to pierce the envelope of night in the eastern sky, and soon the people of Salisbury would embark upon their workday routine. An increase in traffic might make the roads safer for discreet travel, but until then the underground fort offered a soft couch, a warm blanket, and refuge from the imminent light of dawn, all means of comfort for his pounding head. He crossed the desolate Arrow Drive and trod across the short golden field for the rabbit path, feeling a little less despondent for the deeds he had done but a little more wary of hostile forces — both lawful and lawless — that were seeking to confront him.

CHAPTER 9

JEFF HAD NO idea what time it was when he awoke in the pitch blackness of the underground fort sometime later, huddled under a thin blanket upon the old brown sofa. He had used his phone to light his way to the couch inside the fort rather than fumble with the oil lamps, but when he found the phone on the cushion beside him, its battery was completely dead. He couldn't even see his hand in front of his face, but he could hear the scuffling of feet upon the plywood ceiling overhead.

"Look," a voice said. "It's already unlocked."

"Don't tell Mick," said another. "I'll never hear the end of it."

Jeff lifted his head from the makeshift pillow his down vest had become and shielded his eyes as a blast of sunlight lit up the room from the opening hatchway. He tossed the phone aside and stripped a blanket from his body to sit up as the Hurricanes began to file down the rope ladder. Brain dropped to the floor first and immediately began to tinker with the nearby oil lamp; once the lamp began to glow, he turned about and jumped back, startled to see his leader sitting groggily upon the couch.

"Jeff!" he exclaimed. "Where ya been? We thought the cops got you!"

Jeff rubbed his eyes. "What time is it?"

Axle descended the rope ladder next. "It's quarter to twelve. You been down here all night?"

"Not all night." He bent over to pull on his sneakers. "What are you guys doing here?"

"Emergency gang meeting," Brain said. "Mick said we needed to find you."

"Well, you found me. Congratulations."

Axle called up to the next Hurricane in line. "Jeff's here. I guess we can go home now."

Crazy Legs ducked his head inside the fort. "Hey, Jeff."

Jeff stood up and ruffled his hair with his fingers. "Where's Mick?"

The skinny boy started down the ladder. "He's coming."

Brain crossed the fort to light the second lamp. "He texted everybody to cut out of school because you were missing in action."

Crazy Legs dropped to the floor and grimaced. "I told him you'd come around when you were ready, but it's like talking to a wall. He doesn't listen to anyone anymore. You gotta set him straight."

Jeff frowned. "What do you want me to do? Beat him up?"

Crazy Legs shrugged. "I don't know. Do something. You're the leader, not him."

Jeff bit his lip, knowing he might be in a different time zone by this time tomorrow. More voices wafted into the fort from overhead, and from their argumentative tones, he surmised that the rest of the Hurricanes had arrived.

"It was probably just a squirrel," TJ said. "Or a rabbit. You know, a bunny?"

"It wasn't a rabbit," Bumbles replied. "The whole bush shook."

"Quit being so paranoid," Mick said from above. He dangled a sneaker into the hatchway, fishing for the rope ladder and finally catching it. Quickly he climbed down the ladder and dropped to the floor, scoffing at the sight of his disheveled friend. "Well, well. If it isn't our fearless leader," he said. "Thanks for stopping by."

Jeff peered up through the hatchway as the next boy started down the ladder. "What's all the arguing about?"

"Ahh, Bumbles says he thought he saw someone following us in the woods." Mick waved off the lanky boy. "It was probably just a rabbit."

"It wasn't a rabbit," Bumbles insisted as he landed on the floor.

"Maybe it was Bigfoot!" TJ yelled from overhead before starting through the hatchway.

Jeff shrugged. "If he thinks he saw something, we should probably check it out."

"We did," his lieutenant huffed. "We spent ten minutes combing the stupid bushes. He's just being a dumbass like usual."

TJ jumped down without the aid of the ladder. The floor shook, and both oil lamps teetered before Axle and Brain steadied them. "Hey, all."

"Don't do that again," Mick growled.

"Sorry," TJ said.

Denny entered the fort and pulled the hatchway door shut behind him before he continued down the ladder. In contrast to TJ's athletic pounce, he struggled with every rung of the ladder, panting and groaning all the way down until he dropped laboriously to the floor. He turned to face the gang with his left eye sporting a shiner, his lower lip puffy and black. "Hey Jeff," he said. "How ya doin'?"

"I'm okay." Jeff looked him up and down. "You look like you got hit by a bus."

Denny forced a smile. "I'm not sure what hit me, but I'll live."

Jeff stepped up onto the raised platform and beheld his friends gathered about him, noting the bumps and bruises some of them had sustained in the prior evening's harrowing fight. He felt a twinge of shame for missing the start of the fight, and he wondered if events might've transpired differently had they not been disadvantaged from the beginning. "You guys rocked it last night. I'm proud of you."

A few of them shuffled their feet and looked away in response. Finally Brain said, "You did too, Jeff. Curly would've been toast if it wasn't for their dirty trick."

"Happy Jack got what he deserved," TJ added.

Brain nodded. "I knew you'd come through, Jeff. I saw your car and—"

Mick silenced him with a cold glare. He pulled out a cigarette and tapped it against the lamp stand before sticking it between his lips, then he cupped the sleeve of his jacket in his palm to remove the hot glass chimney of the lamp. Slowly and deliberately, he bent over the open flame to light the cigarette, its tip glowing bright red as he inhaled. He stood upright and exhaled a cloud of smoke into the fort before placing the chimney back onto the lamp.

"Of course, things might've gone better if you had reported here when you were supposed to," he said.

Jeff winced. "Reported? Who do I report to? You?"

Mick glared back. "Somebody has to do their job around here."

"Well, the whole thing was your idea in the first place."

Mick stepped up onto the platform before him. "Really, Jeff? I set that fight up for Train. Remember him? Or maybe you'd rather forget. Maybe you're okay with some scumbag killing our friend, but I'm not. This is war, whether you like it or not. Train laid down his life for the cause, and I'm willing to do the same."

Jeff gritted his teeth. "The last thing Train wanted was to die in some filthy alley. This ain't war. This is nuts. So spare me the avenging crusader crap, Mick. It doesn't work on me."

"No, the only thing that works on you is some chick. What's her name?"

"Leave her outta this," Jeff said. "She has nothing to do with this."

Mick leaned forward. "No? Where were you last night?"

"Saving your ass. You were the twitch of a finger away from a toe tag, remember?"

Mick nodded slowly. "Yeah, I remember. Lucky for me you're not a total schlep. But why weren't you here before the fight?"

Jeff glanced about at the rest of the gang. Some of his friends seemed shocked by the heated exchange between two old friends, but others looked on in earnest, as if Mick's line of questioning was fair. "I lost track of time," he said.

"Lost track of time?" Mick repeated. He hopped onto the platform and stood nose to nose with his leader, flicking his cigarette aside without breaking eye contact. "Maybe you're too busy following her scent. Maybe you oughta step aside for a while."

Jeff laughed. "Step aside? Mick, I'm stepping out. You wanna shoot it out with Curly? Have at it." He turned to face the gang and pointed a thumb back at Mick. "If you guys wanna end up like Train, just keep listening to *him*. I'm done."

Several mouths dropped open in astonishment, but Crazy Legs rushed forward. "Guys, wait—"

Mick brushed the skinny boy aside and grabbed Jeff's sleeve. "When did you become such a... pussy?"

Jeff whirled about in a rage to land a fist flush against Mick's cheek. His startled lieutenant recoiled from the blow before gnashing his teeth and planting a left hook upon his leader's jaw. The impact knocked Jeff off the platform and he crashed into the sidewall, toppling into the stolen skis. TJ rushed forward to help him as Mick cocked his fists and pressed forward. Denny lunged forward to restrain him while Jeff jerked himself free of TJ's grasp, wiping his bloody lip with the back of his hand and rebuking Mick's sneer with a fuming glare.

Crazy Legs wedged himself between his friends and pushed back at them. "Stop it!"

Without uttering another word, Jeff turned about and jostled past the Hurricanes standing in his way. He scampered up the rope ladder and threw the hatchway door open, allowing it to bang loudly against the plywood rooftop. Once outside, he grabbed the handle on the hatchway door and slammed it shut again, leaving the Hurricanes to stew under the command of their new leader.

So that was that.

Jeff sucked on a fresh fat lip courtesy of his best friend as he stood outside the underground fort, amid the muffled arguments of the boys inside. He turned about and stormed up the path toward the plazas, crossing the log over the dry ravine and climbing the pine-needle slope to Mr. Big.

"So much for fond farewells," he said. He patted his pockets and turned back in a panic. "My keys—" In his impetuous departure, he had left the keys along with his phone and his vest inside the fort.

A humbling return for his personal belongings was unthinkable—even a Tornado pummeling seemed preferable to more Hurricane humiliation. He smirked at the comparison, but already he was envisioning new options available to him without the burden of gang leadership. Peace with the

Tornadoes seemed more remote than ever with Mick in charge now, although he regretted resigning his friends to the same jeopardy that had ultimately cut Train's life short. Their plight was far too perilous to simply abandon them to the whims of a reckless, brazen leader, whether they realized it or not.

A thin path snaked down the pine-needle slope to the left, back across the ravine and up toward Tornado territory, and there was time to kill before he could return to the fort to retrieve his belongings without further confrontation. "It has to start somewhere," he told himself. He swallowed hard and started down the winding path.

Twenty minutes later, he crept through a yard on Sapphire Lane, nearing the rear of a house with his heartbeat in his throat. A California beachfront still beckoned him from the back of his mind, but the Pacific coast felt worlds away from his present location, crouching behind a raspberry bush on the edge of the Matthews property. Unlike his lieutenant, Craig was not completely devoid of reason, and Jeff knew a slim chance for peace still existed if they could simply talk long enough to convince him that Happy Jack's stabbing was accidental.

Jeff drew a deep breath as he rose from the cover of the bush. He followed a barren garden bed down the side of the yellow house to the front gutter, where he peered around the corner before running past a shaded basement window and behind a decorative bush to the front steps. The house appeared unoccupied but he was skeptical, for both gangs often used the illusion of vacancy to protect their strongholds during times of conflict. He yanked open the storm door and rapped on the wooden front door, already wary of his visibility on the cement steps.

Loud footsteps clopped through the house and the basement curtains fluttered, while Jeff leaned toward the window, trying to identify the eyeball staring up at him. The front door opened an inch, and Willie stuck his nose through the crack like a rat sniffing a hunk of cheese. "Whaddya want, Hollister?"

"I gotta talk to Craig," Jeff told him.

"He doesn't wanna talk to you."

"I ain't leaving until he does."

"You by yourself?"

"Yes. I swear."

"Hold on."

The door shut completely for a moment. A moment later it reopened halfway to reveal Craig standing beside Willie. "Talk fast, Hollister," the leader warned.

Jeff drew a deep breath. "I'm sorry about Happy Jack—"

"Not sorry enough." Craig pushed the front door open all the way, revealing Zak standing to his right, cracking his knuckles.

"I quit the Hurricanes," Jeff said quickly. "I'm not their leader anymore."

"Bad idea," Craig said. "Now you don't have any friends."

Zak pushed the storm door open and stepped outside. Without saying a word, he shoved an open palm into Jeff's chest, launching him from the top step. Jeff landed flat on his back upon the front lawn as the three Tornadoes mocked him with laughter. Painfully he lifted his head to see Phil enter the front yard to his left as a garage door rolled open to his right, revealing Tony with a large crescent wrench in his hand.

Jeff rolled to his knees and eyed the Tornado leader in the doorway. "Who's next, Craig?" he asked. "You? Me? One of them?"

Craig stepped outside and stood beside his bodyguard. "Um, you, I think." Willie snickered again, but the Tornado leader was no longer laughing, his reply spoken more as a matter of fact than of mockery.

"You gotta admit, he's got balls coming here like this," Zak said.

Willie grinned. "But not much brains."

Jeff ignored them. "You came to the wake for a reason,

Craig. I know you hear what I'm saying. I'm not in control anymore, but you can still make it happen."

Craig rubbed his chin in thought. "Bring me Mick's gun, and we'll talk."

Jeff stood up and brushed himself off. "Mick's not the killer. Curly's gotta go down. You know it."

The Tornadoes exchanged glances, but their leader leaned back and folded his arms across his chest. "I got an idea. How 'bout we give Curly what he wants and be done with it?"

Craig snapped his fingers, and the Tornadoes rushed forward. Jeff turned and sprinted away from them, running past Phil's lunging grasp into the backyard, down Ruby Road and across Diamond Street, sprinting for the safety of the woods until he reached the mouth of the path into neutral territory. Only then did he stop to catch his breath and look back to see that no one was actually chasing him anymore.

Leaving the dangers of Tornado territory behind him, Jeff descended the wooded hill and crossed the dry ravine before climbing the opposite bank laden with pine cones and needles to the trunk of Mr. Big again. Panting heavily, he sat upon one of its thick, protruding roots to catch his breath, relishing a clearer head from the physical exertion. He shuddered from a breeze cutting through the trees, and he yearned for a sunny day in a faraway place, for life already felt cold enough in Salisbury. His mother's heartless diatribe, his lieutenant's contemptuous disrespect, his friends' cool indifference, his enemies' boorish derision—all would lose their sting as the miles amassed behind him. The immediate plan was simple enough: recover his vest and keys from the fort, return home for clothes and money, and retrieve the Camaro that was hopefully still parked in seclusion near the Upper Plaza. From there, one final obligation stood in the way of the open road calling him.

"If I didn't tell her, I could leave today," he said.

That wouldn't be right, he thought. The Hurricanes might've turned their backs on him, but Cindy hadn't, and he still hoped against hope that he could somehow persuade her to come with him. He had to ask her, for he would regret it forever if he didn't, and he already had enough regrets. Waiting until midnight or early morning to leave town might be a mistake, but it felt like a risk worth taking, and it seemed better than spending a lifetime wondering what might have been.

As the breath returned to his lungs, he gazed up at the towering pine rising over him. The tree was like an old friend to him, a reassuring landmark that home was not far away and safe haven was near at hand. He remembered climbing its limbs with his friends in younger days, and daydreaming with his brother while lying upon its soft needle bed beneath its long branches. The tree appeared the same as it had on the first day he had seen it, although his own life had transformed dramatically during the span of eighteen years, a mere fraction of the massive tree's existence. He suspected he was far less significant to the tree than the tree was to him, yet he still felt a connection to it, and he wondered if he might ever pass its way again.

He rose to his feet and started down the familiar rabbit path without looking back, jogging along the winding trail and across the ravine bridge again. He climbed the gentle slope to the semicircle of pines with every intention of entering the fort through the escape tunnel, but as he approached the clearing, he sensed that someone was still inside the fort, for the hatchway door was not camouflaged in its customary fashion and the lock was missing.

Jeff shrugged. All he wanted was his keys, and if anyone wanted to give him a hard time about it, they could have a taste of his knuckles just like Mick had. He knelt down and pulled up on the handle, noting the hazy glow of the oil lamps inside as the hatchway door cracked open. The door felt heavier than usual and, curiously, a rope had been tied to its inner handle leading down into the murkiness of the fort. He raised the hatchway door higher to get a better view inside, only to hear the sound of a heavy object sliding across wood, followed by the shatter of glass on the floor. The orange glow within the fort suddenly brightened and flickered, accompanied by a startled cry from within.

"Help!" the voice said. "I can't move!"

Jeff threw the hatchway door completely open, horrified by the thought of what had just occurred. He stuck his head through the hatchway to see flames spreading across the carpet, fueled by the oil of the shattered lamp on the floor. Sitting in the far corner of the fort was a boy in a Hurricanes jacket, his wrists tied before him and his ankles bound to the legs of a folding chair. "Bumbles!" he gasped.

"Jeff! Get me out of here!"

Every rung of the rope ladder had been severed, and its two longest lengths had been lashed together with one end tied to the inner handle of the hatchway door, the other wrapped around a leg of the lamp stand now partially suspended from the floor. Jeff spun about on the seat of his pants and dangled his feet inside the fort with flames licking at the soles of his sneakers, for already the oily fire had begun to climb the short wall to the left, while the right arm of the sofa also ablaze. Grabbing the lip of the hatchway, he swung his body inside over the growing flames, kicking the dangling lamp stand into pieces before dropping to the floor clear of the fire.

He rushed to Bumbles's side and dug his fingernails at the knotted ropes around the boy's ankles. "Who did this to you?"

"Curly and JJ. They jumped me while I was closing up the fort." Bumbles wriggled and squirmed. "I knew someone was spying on us!"

"Hold still," Jeff said. "I'm almost done."

Bumbles gazed over him with widening eyes. "Look!"

Jeff glanced back to see black smoke rolling from the right armrest of the couch as fire consumed its fabric. Both of the plywood walls by the hatchway were now ablaze, as was the leg and tabletop of the wooden stand still suspended by the rope. He focused on his friend's lashings with renewed urgency, finally solving the knot and pulled the rope free from the boy's ankles. His eyes watered from the sweltering flames as he tugged at his friend's hands still bound by ropes.

"Follow me," he said. "Stay low."

Bumbles slid off the chair and crawled along the side of the fort, while Jeff grabbed the left armrest of the couch already angled away from the short front wall before them. He jammed the couch hard into the blazing corner, stifling the flames for the moment and providing a more direct path for the smoke to escape through the hatchway.

"You want me to climb out?" Bumbles asked. "I'll fry!"

Jeff pointed to a dark opening in the short wall behind the couch. "That way."

"The tunnel? Are you serious?"

The burning remnants of the lamp stand broke free from its charred rope, bouncing off the cushion of the relocated sofa before crashing in a heap of fire into the center of the fort. Flames spread across the carpet and along the long wall across from them, nipping at the edge of the raised platform. The hatchway could not ventilate all of the smoke, so the air inside the fort continued to foul.

"Go!" Jeff said. "Keep your head down!"

Bumbles crawled into the mouth of the tunnel. "I can't even see where I'm going!"

Suddenly Jeff remembered why he came back to the fort in the first place. "My vest!" he cried, looking frantically about the fort. "Where's my vest?"

"That green thing? Crazy Legs took it with him."

"Why? Dammit!"

Bumbles drew his legs completely inside the tunnel and writhed his way into the darkness. "Oh no," he finally said.

Jeff stuck his head inside the tunnel and inched his way forward on the heels of his lanky friend. "What's the matter?"

"The tunnel's collapsed! It's solid earth. We gotta go back."

"Relax. Reach over your head."

Bumbles sighed in the darkness. "There's a ladder here."

In spite of their predicament Jeff felt a twinge of pride. The addition of an escape tunnel hadn't been a popular decision when the Hurricanes constructed the fort, but his insistence on an extra week of digging had paid off. "Go ahead, stand up."

As Bumbles stood, Jeff grabbed his friend by the ankles and used the leverage to pull himself closer to the vertical shaft. He found the ladder in the darkness and groped his way up each rung to another hatchway door eight feet above the floor of the tunnel. The hatchway did not budge, however, even with the added persuasion of his shoulder.

"What's the matter?" Bumbles asked.

Jeff strained against the hatch. "It's blocked. I can't move it at all. Gimme a hand."

Bumbles held up his bonded hands in the dim firelight. "How?"

Jeff tried once more to open the hatchway, but the best he could do was to raise it an inch, as if a heavy object had been placed upon it. He climbed back down to the bottom of the shaft where the smell of smoke was stronger than ever. "Keep working that knot," he said.

His friend's voice quivered. "Wh—where are you going?"

"I need a lever."

Jeff dropped to his stomach and wriggled back to the entrance of the tunnel to survey the fort. The easel and poster boards burned like a torch upon the raised platform, and most of the sofa was now afire. Thick smoke hovered beneath the ceiling while flames licked the plywood at the edges of the hatchway entrance. He drew a deep breath of tunnel air before entering the burning fort, his eyes tearing from the heat. Sliding along the long wall past the metal firebox, he tripped over the edge of the raised platform and fell hard upon his knees, but he fought the urge to cry out with so much smoke in the air. Instead, he scrambled forward to grab one of the skis leaning against the long wall, nearly knocking the second lamp from its stand as he turned back toward the tunnel with his lever tucked under his arm. By now the ceiling had begun to burn, and his lungs ached for air as he clawed back through the growing inferno that had once been the pride of the Hurricanes. He reached the tunnel unscathed, however, and slid the ski into the dark hole before diving inside after it.

Farther down the tunnel, he found fresher air and a hand to pull him up. "I got the rope off," Bumbles said.

"Good job." Jeff groped the floor in the darkness. "Where's that ski?"

"I have it. We'd better hurry."

Jeff took the ski from Bumbles and lugged it up the ladder. He drove his shoulder up against the hatchway door, lifting it up enough against the heavy weight set upon it. Sunlight eked into the chamber as he wedged the curved ski tip upside down into the gap, while thick smoke began to pour into the tunnel from the fort.

"Hurry, Jeff!" Bumbles urged.

"Help me out!" he cried as he pulled down on the ski with all his might.

Coughing and choking, Bumbles climbed the bottom rung of the ladder to grab the tail of the ski; he pulled down on it as Jeff continued to drive his shoulder up against the hatch. The ladder creaked beneath their weight and the ski bent acutely from the strain of the forces upon it, but the fresh air pouring into the shaft filled their lungs and fueled their energy. Finally, the obstruction rolled aside with a thud and the hatchway door flew open to blinding sunlight. Jeff clambered out and fell upon the forest bed, while Bumbles dropped the ski and crawled beside him a moment later. They rolled onto their backs with their limbs spread out, gulping the cool air as smoke billowed from the burning pit and the tunnel entrance.

Eventually Bumbles sat up and pointed his thumb at the thick log that had blocked their escape route. "They tried to kill me. What did I do to them?"

Jeff rose and walked to the edge of the burning fort, where the plywood ceiling buckled from the fire inside. "You just got in the way. It's me Curly wants."

Bumbles stepped up and gazed down at the smoke and flames. "He said he wanted to kill two Hurricanes with one stone. He's insane. So are you, for climbing in there after me."

"Hey, I was just looking for some marshmallows." Jeff patted his friend on the shoulder. "You'd do the same for me, I'm sure."

"You know it, Jeff. I owe you big-time."

They stood in silence, watching as the fire devoured the plywood ceiling. Inside the blazing pit, the flames finally reached the second oil lamp, and it burst open, spewing a rush of flames with its oil; the ceiling collapsed into the pit moments later. The depth of the fort prevented the fire from climbing to the branches of the nearby pine trees, but a column of thick gray smoke curled high into the air.

"We better get out of here," Jeff said. "Someone's gonna see the smoke."

Bumbles nodded. "Where are we going?"

"To find Crazy Legs," Jeff said. "I need my keys. I'm running out of time."

Ten minutes later, they stood on the back porch of the Kramer residence with the sound of sirens converging upon the thin plume of smoke rising above the woods behind them. Jeff opened the storm door and rapped his knuckles loudly against the back-door window. "He better be home," he said before knocking on the window again.

Bumbles dusted off his dirty jeans with his open palms. "Mick's parents left on a booze cruise yesterday. I think some of the guys were gonna hang at his house."

Before Jeff could reply, the door opened to reveal Crazy Legs, shirtless and barefoot with a stick of celery in his hand. "Hey guys. What's up?"

"I need my vest," Jeff said. "Bumbles says you have it."

Crazy Legs pushed the door open farther. "Wow, you guys smell awful. You crawl through a sewer or something?"

The two boys stepped inside, leaving the door slightly ajar. "Not exactly," Bumbles said. "Remember the fort?"

Crazy Legs chomped on a mouthful of celery. "Of course I remember the fort. I was just there an hour ago."

"Well, it's gone now," Bumbles said.

The skinny boy gagged on his snack and fell into the nearest kitchen chair. "Whaddya mean, it's gone?"

"It burned down." Bumbles scratched his head. "Well, it was already underground, so I guess it really burned up."

"You're kidding, right?" Crazy Legs saw the gravity in their faces and narrowed his eyes upon Jeff. "We all worked so hard on that fort, Jeff. What did you do?"

Jeff drew back a step. "Seriously?"

"Jeff didn't do anything," Bumbles replied. "Curly and JJ jumped me while I was closing up, and they booby-trapped the place. I'd be pot roast if it wasn't for Jeff."

Jeff leveled an icy stare at the Hurricane scout. "Can I have my vest now?"

Crazy Legs left his celery stick on the table and slipped out of the kitchen. He returned a moment later with the green vest and handed it to Jeff. "Sorry. I didn't mean—"

"Save it." Jeff pulled the vest over his shoulders. He felt his keys in the left pocket but nothing in the right pocket. "Where's my phone?"

Crazy Legs shrugged. "I don't know. I didn't look inside the pockets."

Jeff winced as he remembered tossing the phone on the couch inside the fort earlier that morning. "Shit," he muttered before retreating to the back door and pulling it open.

"Where are you going?" Bumbles asked.

"Away from here," he said. "I shoulda left a long time ago."

Crazy Legs started forward. "Jeff, wait—"

Jeff shut the back door on them, for there was nothing more to say. His severance from the Hurricanes was now complete. No handshakes, no parties, no laughter, or camaraderie. It felt like failure to him, but there was no other way. His head drooped in dejection as he descended the porch stairs to the Kramers' backyard.

An aberrant thought made him smile again. Crazy Legs was right about one thing: he did smell awful. His face felt like soot, and his day-old clothes reeked of smoke and whisky. There would be safe haven at his house for a short time, for despite their early-morning spat, he knew his mother would never miss a precious day of work. And besides, he would be in and out of the house in less than a half an hour. He crossed Spruce Lane two properties down from his own residence and circled behind those houses for the back door of his home, where he found his house key still worked on the lock as anticipated. Whatever intentions she had of evicting him, there was simply no way for her to change the locks in such a short time.

Half an hour later, he emerged from the bathroom showered and shaved, with a damp bath towel fastened around his waist. As he passed by the kitchen, he noticed through the rear window a flash of blue lights racing up Arrow Drive as more sirens wailed in the distance. The thought of the police discovering the remains of the fort troubled him, for ample evidence of the Hurricanes' transgressions would certainly be found among the ashes. Then again, such a discovery might actually divert the attention of the police for a while as he sought to retrieve his Camaro from its hiding place, if indeed it was still there.

He hurried downstairs and stripped the towel from his body, tossing it onto his bed before quickly donning fresh clothes and his favorite blue baseball cap. He reached for the roll of gauze on his desktop but hesitated, poking the flesh around his stitched palm with minimal pain. "Good enough," he muttered as he brushed the gauze aside. After filling a gym bag with more clean clothes and backup sneakers, he grabbed what few valuables he owned and stuffed them into his backpack before zipping it shut. Lastly, he grabbed his sunglasses from the dresser and slipped them atop his head before rushing out of the bedroom and up the stairs with both bags in hand.

Returning to the upstairs bathroom, he slipped into his sneakers and pulled his belt from his dirty pants when the telephone rang. He backed into the hallway, glaring at the kitchen phone as he fed the belt through the loops of his jeans, wondering who might be calling. Maybe it was his mother making sure he wasn't loafing around the house, or maybe it was Mick wanting to grill him about the fort. Or maybe it was another stupid cop trick attempting to locate him. In any event, it was nobody he wanted to talk to, unless…

He rushed into the kitchen and snatched the receiver from the wall after the fifth ring, quickly checking the caller ID before answering it. "Cindy!"

"Jeff!" she asked. "Where have you been? Why aren't you answering your cell phone?"

The sound of her voice helped ease his tension a bit. "I lost it. Where are you?"

"School. What's going on? Everyone's talking about some junior who got stabbed last night."

Jeff tucked the phone under his chin as he fastened the belt into place. "Really? What's his name?"

"I'm not sure. Nelson something, I think."

"Don't know him. Listen, I need to see you tonight. Can I pick you up after school?"

"No, Jeff. My father's totally wigged out. I thought his head was going to explode this morning. My mom's not talking either. Something bad is going on. We can't let them see us together right now. Plus I've got basketball tryouts after school."

"But I have to see you."

The line was silent for a moment. Finally she said, "I think he's got some political thing after work tonight. They probably won't be home until midnight. Where do you want to go?"

"I don't care. Anywhere out of Salisbury. You decide."

She was silent for a moment. "Okay, I got an idea. Come by at six. They should be gone by then."

Six?" Jeff glanced at the kitchen clock and yanked at his hair in frustration. "Okay, see you then."

"Stay out of the driveway," she said. "Just in case."

"I will. I promise. Gotta go, bye."

Jeff hung up and pulled out his wallet. He counted just two fives and three singles inside it, but more money was literally within reach. The five twenty-dollar bills hidden inside the cookie jar wouldn't get him to California, but they would at least get him across the state line. He took the jar from atop the refrigerator and reached inside, astonished to find instead that it was completely empty. His mother's unspoken message was clear: no more help. Jeff raised the jar over his head, ready to smash it on the kitchen floor; instead, he set the cookie jar on the counter and placed his house key inside before shutting the lid. He hoped his message was equally clear: the key was no longer needed, because the house was no longer home.

"Cindy will lend me money," he assured himself as he finished tying his sneakers. He took his green vest from a kitchen chair and pulled it onto his back before donning the backpack over it. With his gym bag slung over his shoulder, he stepped to the back door and opened it, stopping at the storm glass window to check his reflection before slipping his sunglasses on. The glasses and ball cap obscured his features fairly well, he thought, and his backpack and gym bag lent the appearance of any anonymous student walking down to the plazas after school. He stepped out onto the porch and shut the door behind him, scurrying down the stairs and across the backyard, over the rail of the fence and through the abutting yard to the curb of Arrow Drive with the gym bag jostling behind him.

He darted across the street and up the steep embankment on the other side to reenter the woods at the mouth of the hilltop path. Within minutes he had ascended to the panoramic view of Bobcat Hill, but he was more interested in the wooded area blocking his sightline to the near side of the Upper Plaza. The main path wound down the other side of the hill into the woods toward Mr. Big, but Jeff knew of another path crossing an acre of birch and maple saplings leading more directly toward Burrough Street.

Soon the Upper Plaza came into view through the sparse trees, and he could see the aftermath of the previous night's skirmish: the gaping hole in the stockade fence, the scattered wood fragments across the sand, and the deep tire ruts where Curly's truck had been driven through it. He spotted the white brick wall where he and Train had last conversed but he quickly turned away, for there was no time for nostalgia now. In the adjacent property, an abandoned, dilapidated house stood facing Burrough Street, where a doorless double-bay garage set fifty feet ahead housed the Camaro, shielding it from the view of the road.

Jeff sighed with relief, thankful that the car had not been discovered by anyone but a Hurricane. He fumbled for his keys as he jogged toward the car, pulling his hat from his sweaty brow as he arrived at the door. Quickly unlocking the door, he stuffed the bags and the hat into the back seat before sliding behind the steering wheel and cranking the engine to life. The stereo clock read nearly three o'clock as he shut the door and fastened the seat belt, still hours away from his rendezvous with Cindy, but at least he had his car back and could drive away from the beehive of activity that the neighborhoods and plazas had become. He backed out of the garage and shifted into first gear, rolling his shiny blue car in broad daylight down the rocky driveway to the curbside of the busy street.

What he failed to notice, as he turned the car to merge with the southbound traffic, was a green pickup truck with a broken headlight parked outside Crusty's Restaurant, in precisely the same space and manner as it had been parked the night before, its two occupants keenly aware of the conspicuous Camaro pulling away.

CHAPTER 10

J EFF EASED THE Camaro to a halt along Hillside Drive and snuffed the radio volume with the engine quietly idling. The sun glinted in his eyes as he studied the empty driveway of the Wellis residence ahead on the left, eager to pick Cindy up and get rolling but respectful of her instructions to keep back. He donned his sunglasses and pulled his ball cap down to his eyes, slinking low against his door as the driver of a passing vehicle ogled his car, remaining motionless until the man finally drove away. A three-hour wait at various hiding spots around town had taken a toll on his nerves, prompting him to wonder if the time might've been better spent on the open road putting distance between him and the town of Salisbury.

"C'mon, Cindy, hurry up," he said with a nervous tap on the steering wheel.

Finally he spotted her stepping out the front door of the house. He shifted into first gear but kept the clutch engaged, waiting until she neared the top of the rising driveway before driving forward. She stopped at the curb and waved, then she pulled a white windbreaker over a saffron sweater while he pulled the car to a stop a few feet away from her. She ran around front to the passenger side, popping the door open and plopping breathlessly onto the open seat before shutting the door and leaning over to kiss him. "Hi," she said.

"Hi," He replied. He leaned toward her but the bill of his cap struck her in the forehead, so he pulled it from his head and tossed it in the back seat. "Sorry," he said before completing the kiss.

She smiled and settled back in her seat. "That's okay."

He shifted into gear and drove forward. "I hate picking you up like this."

"I know, but I appreciate it." She turned to him with a wide smile and excitedly asked, "So where do you wanna go?"

He eyed her coyly. "I don't know. Got anything in mind?"

Her eyes twinkled mischievously as she pulled a key chain from her pocket. "I sure do!"

"What are those for?" he asked.

"The boathouse. Let's take the boat out!"

Jeff glanced uneasily into his rearview mirror as he accelerated away from her house. "Aw, I don't know, Cindy. It sounds complicated."

"Only if you consider a half-hour ride to fly on a rocket ship across a clear blue lake complicated." She slapped him on the knee. "C'mon, Jeff! You said yourself that you've never been on a motorboat. My father's gonna dry-dock it next weekend, and then it'll be too late."

He frowned. "It'll be dark in an hour."

"Even better! We can watch the sunset." She squeezed his hand. "Unless you're still afraid of the dark…"

Jeff cracked a weak smile. Riding on a boat wasn't part of the plan, but if it got them out of Salisbury and gave him a quiet moment to plead his case to her, then it was as good an idea as any. There was so much to say and so much to ask, but a starlit vista over a secluded lake might provide the perfect milieu for a monumental proposal. "Okay, you win. What's the fastest way from here?"

She settled back smugly into her seat and fastened her seat belt. "Get on the highway and take Exit 9."

He steered the Camaro down the winding course of Hillside Drive until it intersected with Archer Road, a long, rural road that ran from Arrow Drive along the outskirts of town. After turning left, they continued another half mile down its gradual slope until it passed over the crest of a ridge and plummeted toward a traffic light half a mile down the hill. The light changed to green as they approached it, permitting Jeff to freely turn the car left onto Route 53, a thoroughfare out of Salisbury.

He accelerated along the state road toward an entrance ramp to the interstate highway still more than a mile away, straining to think of a topic less weighty than his pending flight from town. "So how did the basketball tryouts go?"

"Awesome!" she said. "I think I made the team! The coach really likes me."

His heart sank a little, for every tie she felt to Salisbury lessened the chance he could convince her to go with him. "TJ has tryouts tomorrow. He'll probably make the varsity team."

"You should try out. You're in good shape," she said. "It'd give you something constructive to do."

He frowned. "You sound like my mother."

She fell silent for a moment. "Have you officially dropped out of school yet?"

"Officially? Like, stand up in the auditorium and publicly denounce Salisbury High?" He smiled at the notion. "No, I'm just not gonna go anymore."

"Oh." She pointed a thumb at the bulging gym bag and backpack in the back seat. "Going on vacation?" she asked with a subtle bite in her voice.

He rued his failure to place the bags in the trunk. "I'm going hiking with Mick this weekend."

"Sounds like fun."

He knew that she sensed his dishonesty, but the time wasn't right for the truth just yet. He turned the Camaro onto the highway entrance ramp and then stomped on the gas pedal, throwing them back in their seats as the engine roared and the car swiftly accelerated. She shifted in her seat, but she seemed to enjoy the powerful car, so he turned up the volume on the radio again, hoping to avoid further conversation about his future, at least until they were settled somewhere quieter.

They neared Exit 9 several miles down the road, marked by a yellow caution sign warning of a tight circular turn ahead. Jeff lifted his foot off the gas as he drove up the spiral ramp, glancing to his right as he neared the top to spot a dark pickup truck entering the exit lane below. He dwelled upon the truck for a moment too long and slammed on the brakes when he realized they were about to roll through the stop sign into the adjacent road.

Cindy lurched forward in her seat from the abrupt halt. Her seat belt snapped taut against her shoulder, and she instinctively braced a hand against the dashboard. "Jeff—"

"Which way?" he asked urgently.

"Left. What's wrong?"

He turned onto the main road. "That pickup truck behind us. What color is it?"

She turned her head to see. "I don't know. Black? Green? It's hard to tell in this light."

"Good enough for me." He hit the gas as she continued to peer out the back window.

"He's at the stop sign. He's turning this way."

A busy intersection lay ahead, and the traffic light was red. He tugged at her sleeve. "Which way now?"

She pointed to the left. "Dexter Road," she said.

He tried to identify the occupants of the approaching truck still three cars behind them, but all he could distinguish was the glimmer of a single headlight in the advancing sunset. A green arrow flashed overhead, however a slow car prevented him from cornering through the intersection at optimum speed. Jeff drove the Camaro close to the sluggish sedan's bumper as the arrow quickly turned to yellow.

"Move it," he growled at the car.

The truck closed in swiftly behind them, but instead of following them onto Dexter Road, it continued straight through the intersection. Cindy watched it drive away before patting him gently on the knee. "A little paranoid, are we?"

Jeff shuddered. "Better paranoid than dead. That looked like Curly's truck."

"He's still running around? Shouldn't he be in jail by now?"

He laughed. "You tell me. Your father's the chief of police."

She shrugged. "Maybe he needs more evidence."

"Maybe he doesn't give a shit," he shot back.

She sighed. "My father's not the monster you think he is, Jeff. Maybe if you told him what you know —"

"I don't talk to cops," he said curtly. She drew back and folded her hands in her lap. Way to butter her up, he thought.

A half mile down the road, she pointed to an intersection on the right, across from a streetlamp powering up in the dusk. "Turn here," she said tersely.

He spotted the turnoff to Portland Village Road and slowed the car for the upcoming turn. To his relief, the slow car in front continued past the intersection, offering a clear road ahead after the turn. Moments later, they were coasting over the top of a small rise and onto a straight stretch of road that split a dusty field of broken cornstalks in half. Jeff pointed to a rugged dirt road that bordered the adjacent woods, noting how it vanished over a hilltop toward the street that the pickup truck had taken. "I bet a truck could cut through there with no problem..."

"Jeff, you're scaring me."

He patted her knee. "Sorry, I'm just being paranoid. How far to the boathouse?"

"Not far. A few more miles."

He pressed the gas pedal closer to the floorboard as the cornfields gave way to woodlands. The road began to wind along the rising terrain as they crossed the Portland town line marker. Not long afterward, Cindy reached over and squeezed his hand again.

"What's wrong?" he asked.

"Life Star Lane. Remember?"

He had forgotten, and he let off the gas in a hurry. The road rose to a crest at the corner of the hairpin turn and dropped out of view behind the steep embankment of Badger Mountain to the left. Tires squealed against the pavement as he struggled to keep the fenders off the guardrail with the low orange sun shining brightly against his sunglasses. He groped for his visor as he blindly steered to the left, but the road suddenly dipped into the shade of the rolling hills to ease the glare upon his eyes.

He shuddered. "Not much of a guardrail."

She nestled closer. "But you gotta love the view..."

Darkness had hidden the landscape from Jeff on their first trip to Almond Lake, but as he drove down the backside of the pass, he saw the valley below in the full splendor of an autumnal sunset. A babbling stream gurgled about mossy rocks as it flowed beneath a wooden bridge a half mile away while, beyond the bridge, the cozy cottages of Portland Village basked in the glow of a low sun amid cirrus clouds stroked with shades of indigo and crimson. Acres of maples and pines rolled toward a distant horizon, sporadically dissected by winding gray country roads that were swiftly swallowed up by a blanket of colored foliage.

Jeff pointed toward the lakeside village. "Is that where you lived?"

"No, our house was near the center of town," she said. "That's where the boat lives."

"I didn't notice any of this the first time we came," he said. "It gets so dark out this way."

"Yeah, but if it's clear, you can see a billion stars." She leaned closer to the windshield and peered upward. "I think we'll see some stars tonight!"

The road curved to the right in a wide arc along the rock wall as it descended into the valley, straightening and leveling as it approached the gentle bump of the wooden bridge. Jeff slowed the car as they crossed the bridge, his eyes shaded from the sun's low angle by a multitude of trees lining the banks of the brook. Soon the road curled to the left, revealing a familiar intersection set among a clearing of trees a quarter mile ahead.

"Didn't we turn—?"

Cindy nodded. "Quarry Road. Keep going straight."

He laughed. "I get it. Take him to the public dock on the first date. Don't let him see where you really live."

She grinned. "If you were a total dork, I might've left you there."

He eyed her with playful distrust as they continued past the Quarry Road intersection. Soon he could see, between the pine trees, sparkles of sunlight glistening off the dark blue waters of Almond Lake. The soft glow of electric lights exposed cottages that had been indiscernible from the hilltop pass two miles back, and every fifty yards or so, a dirt driveway branched from the paved road, winding through the trees toward a waterfront that was still not visible. After a dozen such driveways, he spotted a carved wooden sign that read WELLIS nailed to a thick tree.

"Turn here," she said. "Be careful. The road's pretty narrow."

The car lurched as Jeff turned onto the craggy road; he pulled off his sunglasses and switched on the headlights beneath the cover of the trees. Hearty pines littered the road with large cones and gnarly roots that bounced and rocked the Camaro as he inched it along.

"Let me know if anything falls off my car," he said.

She laughed. "What's the matter? City mouse doesn't like the country?"

He shook his head. "City mouse doesn't like shelling out cheese for auto parts."

She nestled closer again. "Don't worry. Country mouse has plenty of cheese."

Jeff raised an eyebrow at her subtle offer of aid, but moreover he despised the need for it in the first place. He thought it ironic that his mother would pull all support from him while a girl he had only met a few short weeks ago would offer it freely to him.

Soon the dirt road turned to the right and ended in a square gravel driveway blanketed with leaves and pine needles. An A-frame cottage stood dark upon a gentle slope overlooking the driveway, its tall front windows facing a grassy clearing that descended toward the lapping waters of the lake. Jeff braked the car to a rugged halt and shifted into reverse, backing aggressively to the edge of the driveway before cutting the motor off.

"Always be ready for a quick getaway," he said with a wink.

She climbed out of the car. "Follow me."

He stepped out and locked the car shut. "Who lives here?"

"My grandparents. They're snowbirds though. They're off down south at the first sign of frost." She smiled furtively at him. "I know what you're thinking, but I don't have the key."

Jeff pocketed his keys and glanced back to the Camaro. "I wasn't thinking that at all. I'm just worried about the car." He winced, realizing just how dumb his words had sounded the moment they escaped his lips.

She laughed again. "You weren't thinking that at all? What's the matter, you don't like girls?"

He grinned and lunged for her wrist. "Come here."

She screamed and ran teasingly across the driveway to the

grassy clearing with her white jacket flapping in the breeze. He chased after her and caught her halfway down the slope, tackling her by the waist and breaking her fall with his own body. Lying on her back, she squirmed in token resistance as he pinned her hands to the ground over her head, but when he tried to kiss her lips, she burst into laughter again, startling him.

Frustrated, he released her and rolled onto his back in the grass, exhaling a long sigh before propping himself upon his elbows. She crept up to him and kissed his cheek, her lips as soft upon his skin as the warm shades of sunset upon his eyes. Across the lake, falling maple and oak leaves wafted in a light breeze above the shimmering water, while the evening stars shone brightly in the early November sky.

"It's beautiful here," he said. "No wonder you wanted to come."

She sprang to her feet and tugged at his hands. "C'mon, it's better on the boat!"

He barely stood up before she released his hands to run off down the hill toward the water, where the grassy slope led to a set of gray slate steps intersecting a well-worn footpath that traced the perimeter of the lake. The trail circled behind a gray boathouse while the slate steps continued down to a red door on the side of the windowless structure. By the time he caught up with her, she was standing at the door, fumbling to insert a key into a brass doorknob.

"I hate this stupid lock," she said.

Jeff took the key from her hand. "Allow me."

He guided the key along his forefinger into the slot, twisting the key to the left while jiggling the doorknob to the right, and the door promptly popped open. Raising an index finger in the air, he said in his best French accent, "Behold ze cat burglar magnifique!" He pushed the door open and boldly entered the black space with a hand groping into the darkness, only to whack his right knee on the corner of a low, sturdy post two steps inside the boathouse. "Ow!" he groaned.

Cindy slipped inside and pulled down on a dangling string. An overhead fluorescent lamp flicked to life to reveal Jeff cradling his knee in pain. She smirked and raised her own finger into the air. *"Le cambrioleur s'est cogné le genou!"*

Jeff fell back against the object of his discomfort, a workbench running the length of the rear wall. "I have no idea what you just said, but you're asking for a swim."

"Do *you* know how to swim?" She took the keys from him and pointed to a pair of orange life jackets hanging from a pegboard wall behind her. "Last chance to confess if you don't."

"I said I've never been on a motorboat. I didn't say I've never been in the water." He nodded to a dark green canoe hanging on the opposite wall. "That's more my speed, though."

Cindy laughed. "Do you want to exercise or do you wanna have fun?"

She stepped down to a gray horseshoe dock surrounding a white-hulled cuddy cabin moored with its bow facing a large aluminum garage door. At the far end of the dock, she unraveled a pulley chain from a wall bracket and pulled it down to raise the metal door, slowly revealing the waters of the lake. A cool breeze rushed inside the boathouse, tousling her jacket and hair while the motorboat danced upon choppy waves like an excited puppy waiting to be let out. She balanced herself with a hand on the windshield frame before hopping down onto the deck, sliding into the captain's chair with the keys in hand. The inboard motors gurgled to life a moment later, and she moved methodically about the cockpit, unraveling the mooring ropes from the boat's hitches.

"Can I help?" Jeff asked.

She ran her fingers along the dewy vinyl of the chair and pointed to the workbench behind him. "Toss me that towel."

"Aye, aye, Captain." He turned about and pulled a white towel from the cluttered workbench, tipping over an empty beer bottle that rolled swiftly toward the edge. He lunged for it but only managed to tip the bottle with his fingertip, cringing as he expected it to smash on the dock; instead, it rattled to a rest upon the hard wood without breaking. Relieved, he picked up the bottle from the dock and set it beside a gas can at the back of the workbench. "Whew, that was close," he said.

Cindy rolled her eyes. "Geez, you're not even in the boat yet. C'mon, hop in. Help me keep the boat off the dock while I drive out."

He lobbed the towel to her and clambered over the port side of the boat, while she quickly wiped down the vinyl seats before tossing the towel back onto the dock. She slid into the captain's chair and shifted the boat into drive, easing the throttle back and steering the boat out of the boathouse. Once the bow cleared the dock, she turned the steering wheel aport, churning through the water at minimum speed until Jeff moved forward to sit on the edge of the other swivel chair.

"So how fast does this thing go?" he asked.

She grinned and pulled hard on the throttle, thrusting him back into his seat. He groped for a hold to steady himself as the bow of the craft rose high in the air and the boat wash gurgled violently behind them. Soon the hull leveled out, setting the boat on a swift eastward course, bouncing across the still water with the last shards of violet from the late sunset streaking across the sky.

"This is awesome!" he shouted above the roar of the wind.

She flashed a smile at him, the same smile that had captivated him in the dark hallways of the Salisbury Public Safety Complex nearly two weeks ago. Somehow, even burglary seemed strangely innocent back then, a time without friends in coffins or blood on his hands. He felt the persistent knot in his stomach ease a bit, comforted by the thought that not everything had changed. Every time he saw her, he longed to see her smile for the curl of her lips, and gleam in her eye disclosed a certain pureness of her soul. Here he sat, racing along the deep blue waters of Almond Lake with the cool wind rushing through his hair, a fugitive with one foot turned toward the open road, yet all that truly mattered to him was her shining smile and cavernous brown eyes. He gazed out across the still waters of the lake, knowing he must truly be insane.

The last sliver of sunlight vanished behind the treetops as more stars dotted the sky. Cindy pursued the same easterly course they had followed since departing the boathouse, despite the murky masses of evergreen trees looming ahead. Her calm demeanor suggested no concern for the approaching shore, but in Jeff's own inexpert opinion they were swiftly nearing a point of no return.

"We're running out of water," he yelled over the rush of the wind.

"Wanna check out the cliffs?" she hollered back. "They're kinda spooky at night."

"Whatever you want," he said. "Just don't kill me."

She laughed. "Relax. I know this lake like the back of my hand."

She cut the throttle and eased the boat in a wide starboard arc less than a hundred feet from the shore. Suddenly she jerked the wheel hard aport and then quickly steered back to the right even closer to the southern bank. Jeff clung to his seat and glanced over his shoulder to glimpse a large gray rock protruding just a few feet above the surface, barely visible in the low light.

"Back of your hand, huh?" he asked with wide eyes.

She turned back toward the open waters. "Don't worry! You wouldn't have felt a thing!"

With no visible coves or inlets breaking its shorelines, Almond Lake resembled a teardrop or, as its name suggested, an almond. As they chased the final glimmer of sunlight down the centerline of the lake, Jeff spotted the Wellis boathouse amid the glowing porch lights along the southern shore, but he found the dark outline of the northern shore far more alluring.

They sped closer to the public boat launch at the westernmost point of the lake, where the terrain rose steadily off the starboard side toward a dark peak only slightly discernible against the deep violet sky of daylight's final moments. The lake seemed sunken into the ground beneath the high banks of its northwest corner, with a stretch of its northern shore consisting of a towering rock wall. Cindy pulled the throttle back and turned the wheel to let the bow pivot slowly toward the cliff.

Jeff gazed up at the cliff. "Wow, that's cool. Ever jump off it?"

"No way. The water's too shallow there. It's private property, anyway. The mining company owns it." She pointed over the starboard rail. "See that beach at the bottom of the cliff?"

He squinted, but all he could see was the dark mass of the cliff. "No."

She pulled a searchlight from its bracket on the windshield frame and flicked a toggle switch on the dash. A powerful beam of light sliced through the darkness and followed the craggy rock wall at her direction, down to a secluded sandy beach dotted with large flat rocks at the base of the cliff.

"That was our favorite spot," she said. "My friends and I used to anchor right here and swim out to the beach. We'd lie out on the rocks for hours and work on our tans. The sand is nice and firm, and the sun hits it just right in the early afternoon." She turned to him with a forlorn look in her eyes. "Not this year though. I haven't seen any of them since we moved, except for Shannon."

"You don't like Salisbury much," he said.

"Not really," she said. "There's only one good thing that's come from moving there."

"What's that?"

"Meeting you."

At last, they had arrived at the perfect milieu, a place in the world that was dearest to her heart. He stood up and stepped toward her as if he was going to embrace her, but instead he reached for the dashboard and shut off the spotlight, returning them to the comfort of darkness. He kissed her on the forehead and gestured to the padded bench seat astern. "Let's sit back there," he said. "There's something I need to tell you."

She nodded and zipped up her windbreaker. "It's a little breezy. I'm gonna drop the anchor so we don't drift."

He nodded and stepped aft to the bench seat, plopping down on its white cushion as she powered the anchor down by an electric winch. When she finished, she shut the engine off and joined him at the stern, falling onto the seat beside him. "So, what did you want to tell me?" she asked breathlessly.

Jeff swallowed against the lump in his throat and stretched an arm behind her shoulders. "Um, so like, I know we've only been together for a couple of weeks," he began, "and I don't wanna scare you by using the L word..."

"The L word?" She pulled back and narrowed her eyes at him. "Are you saying you have lice?"

He laughed and drew her closer to him. She did that so easily, he thought, take his awkward moment and kill it with her wit and cheer. Cradling her in his arms under the stars with the water lapping gently against the stern of the boat, he felt like Jeff Hollister the gang leader was light-years away, and that he was everything he wanted to be: just a guy holding his girl on a beautiful starlit night. Her methods were mysterious to him, but somehow she found a way to cut through all his pretenses and connect with the truer nature of his heart.

She wrapped her fingers between his. "Your hands are warm," she said at the same time he said, "Your hands are cold," and they laughed at their contrasting remarks. For a moment they seemed to sense themselves for what they were: two captives of their own worlds, each clinging to the other as the repelling forces of their spinning orbs worked to tear them apart.

"This place is fantastic," he said. "I hope you don't get in trouble for taking the boat out."

"It's no big deal," she said, "although my father wouldn't be happy if he knew."

"You mean, if he knew you were *with*."

She shrugged. "You're right. But he'll come around, you'll see. He's just got an impression in his mind about you. When he gets to know you, he'll like you. Trust me."

He laughed in disbelief. "*That's* never gonna happen."

"Why not? You could work out your personal differences with him, couldn't you?" She ran her fingers through his hair. "If it meant being with me?"

His stomach churned too much to sit still. He stood up and buried his hands in the pockets of his vest. "I'm not talking about personal differences, Cindy. I'm talking about things we do that we can't take back. Things that change our lives forever."

She eyed him cautiously. "Why? What did you do?"

"I quit the gang," he replied curtly.

"Really? That's great! I mean..." Her initial glee faded to puzzlement. "But your friends—Mick—I thought you were going hiking..."

He searched for words. "After I left you last night, I went to the fight. I *had* to. And I got... involved."

She turned her eyes down. "What do you mean by 'involved'?"

He felt as if his tongue was glued to the roof of his mouth. "You know that kid who got stabbed?"

"Oh no!" she gasped. "You did that?"

"It was an accident," he explained quickly. He gazed up at the sky as he gathered his thoughts. "Curly was gonna shoot Mick. I thought I was gonna lose another friend. I knocked the gun away and he pulled a knife on me. I had to defend myself, so I pulled mine. Happy Jack jumped in, and we all went down in a pile. It happened so fast." He turned to look straight into her eyes. "I didn't mean to do it, Cindy. I wasn't looking to hurt anyone. You gotta believe me."

She sat silently for a long moment as he squirmed. "I do believe you," she finally said, "but what are you going to do now?"

He turned to face the breeze rolling in from the western shore. "I'm leaving town tomorrow. I'm going to California. I'm not gonna stay here to get thrown in jail or let some Tornado put a bullet in my head."

"No, Jeff. Talk to my father. Tell him what you told me. If you run, you'll just make things worse."

"How can things be worse? I've lost all my friends. I'm kicked out of my house. I can't go back to school. I can't even show my face around town anymore. And there's a lunatic out there who's hell-bent on killing me." He backed up against his swivel chair. "My freedom is all I have left. If I go to your father, I can kiss that goodbye too."

Cindy rose from the bench and leaned back against the starboard rail. "Think about that, Jeff. Think about living under an alias. Think about breaking into a sweat every time you see a police car. Or never being able to come home." She bowed her head and wiped an eye. "Think about us never being together again."

Jeff stepped close to her and gazed up at the brilliant sky. "When I was nine or ten, I used to sit outside and look up at the stars like this. I'd dream about my future and what my life might become. After my father died, I stopped thinking about those things." He kissed her softly on the cheek. "You said it yourself. There's a whole world waiting for me out there. I know it looks like I'm running away, but it feels like I'm running to something better. At least I gotta try."

She looked away. "Then I guess this is goodbye."

He took her hands and pulled them close to his chest, for the moment was upon him. "It doesn't have to be like that, Cindy.

We could do this together." He touched his forehead to hers. "Come with me, please. I need you. I'm crazy about you."

"California? Are you serious?" Her pupils darted from side to side as she considered the proposition. "Where would we stay? How would we get by?"

"My brother owns an auto-body shop. He'll give me a job. I can make good money."

"But what about school? What would I tell my friends? And my parents, they'd be worried sick."

Her objections rolled off her tongue faster than he could digest them. He cast his eyes downward. "Look, it was just a crazy idea. I shouldn't have asked."

She rested her hand upon his shoulder. "Don't say that. I didn't say no. You know I want to be with you. But it's a big decision. You're not giving me much time. Be fair to me."

He backed up a half step. "You're right. I'm not being fair."

"Maybe next summer," she said. "After graduation. It's only six months. We could stay in touch until then. It wouldn't be so bad."

He dropped his head. "Sure. We'll keep in touch. We'll write letters." The evening breeze suddenly felt chillier, and he wished they weren't stuck on a boat in the middle of a lake so he could bring her home and get on with his heartbreak. "You know, it's getting late. Maybe we oughta—"

She cut him off. "Shhh!"

He listened quietly for a moment. "What's the matter?"

She whispered, "Something's in the water."

He looked about. "Probably a fish. I've heard some lakes have them."

"Not a fish," she said. "Paddling. Someone else is out here."

Jeff moved astern and knelt on the padded bench to peer out into the darkness while Cindy slid into the captain's chair and switched on the spotlight again. She pulled it from the bracket and pivoted about to shine the beam over his head and across the water.

"There!" he said, pointing to a shimmering object slowly approaching from the south.

"I see it." Cindy zeroed the beam on the object, revealing the dark hull of a canoe. "Hello!" she called out. They heard nothing from the canoe but the lapping of a paddle cutting through the water. Only after she repeated her salutation did a response come forth.

"Hello!" a deep voice said.

"Who are you?" Jeff called. "What do you want?"

A long moment passed as the canoe drew closer. Finally the voice asked, "Do you have any clippers? My partner caught a fishhook in his ear."

Jeff retreated to the swivel chairs. "I don't like it. Let's get out of here."

Cindy shook her head. "They need our help."

He grabbed her wrist as she started to leave. "We don't even know who they are."

She jerked her hand away. "Don't be so paranoid. Throw them a line when they get close enough. I'll get the toolbox." She released the spotlight handle and ducked inside the cabin as the light beam listed into the sky.

"At least start the engine," Jeff suggested, but to no avail. He knelt on her chair and grabbed the spotlight handle, swiveling its bracket about to aim the beam off the port quarter. The canoe steadily advanced, the rider in front facing away and huddled under a blanket that shielded his features from scrutiny. The paddler was barely more distinguishable with the collar of his jacket flipped up and the visor of a camouflage cap pulled low upon his brow. He steered the canoe directly toward the motorboat, alternating the paddle from left to right with skill.

Jeff eyed them warily. A happenstance encounter at night with strangers on a secluded lake smacked of trouble, but maybe Cindy was right: maybe he *was* being paranoid. After all, they'd only been out on the lake for about an hour, so if anyone had wanted to follow them, finding a canoe quickly enough to rendezvous with the motorboat in the middle of the lake seemed pretty implausible.

Unless, of course, they found one hanging on the wall of an open boathouse.

He released the spotlight and zipped up his vest against the stiffening breeze before stepping astern for a closer view. The canoe was visible in the moonlight now, but its color was not yet discernible. "Stop there," he told its riders. "Show me your faces."

The paddler pulled his oar out of the water, letting the canoe glide silently toward the motorboat. "We just need those clippers and we'll be on our way," he said.

Jeff glanced back to the cabin for Cindy, but she was still below deck. "Don't come any closer," he said, adding, "I have a gun."

The front rider sat upright and nodded to the driver, who resumed paddling in fervent strokes that jostled his hat from his head. The canoe rocked from side to side as the rider stood up to let the blanket slide off his shoulders, exposing wavy locks of black hair that fell upon the collar of his maroon Tornado jacket. He turned about to face Jeff with his thick brows converging on his dark, scowling eyes. He held a clear bottle of amber liquid clenched in his hand, its neck plugged by a saturated strip of white cloth.

"You got a gun, Hollister?" Curly said. "I got a bomb!"

Jeff stumbled back and fell onto the deck between the swivel chairs. "Cindy, get out here! Now!"

The light of a thousand stars was suddenly dwarfed by the flame of Curly's lighter as he lit the wick of the Molotov cocktail. "Easy, JJ," he said. "Don't rock the boat."

JJ ceased his paddling, gliding the canoe off the portside of the motorboat, while Jeff clambered into the captain's chair and frantically groped for the key chain still dangling from the ignition switch. Before he could turn the switch, however, Curly pitched the flaming bottle on a low, swift trajectory; it smashed against the base of the chair behind Jeff's feet. The chair shielded him from the flying glass, but a flood of fire surged across the deck in a brilliant flash of light and heat.

Burning gasoline splashed up the legs of his jeans as he climbed onto the seat of the chair. "Cindy! Help!"

She ran out from the cabin and screamed at the spectacle. "I'll get the fire extinguisher!" she said before running back inside.

"No! Don't!"

The heat on Jeff's legs quickly grew unbearable, and he staggered backward off the chair, over the starboard gunwale and into the lake. The water snuffed out his burning jeans, supplanting the pain on his legs with the paralyzing shock of an unexpected plunge into a cold November lake. Struggling against the weight of his wet clothes, he resurfaced near the bow beside the hull hidden from the canoe, gulping for air against the constricting muscles in his chest.

"Cindy!" he called out. He swam back from the hull for a better line of sight. Flames now engulfed most of the cockpit, blocking her exit from the cabin.

Inside the cabin, Cindy pulled the fire extinguisher from a bracket and turned about to fight the fire, only to see the wall of flames awaiting her at the cabin entrance. She backed into the front compartment of the cuddy cabin and cranked open the skylight cover, but it only opened halfway, offering fresh air but no escape. Grabbing the extinguisher with both hands, she stood on her toes and bashed the skylight cover out of its frame, launching it over the gunwale and into the water. She pushed the extinguisher through the hole and clung to its hose as she wriggled through, but the hose slipped through her fingers and the extinguisher slid down the hull to hang upon the portside rail. She pulled her legs free from the hatchway and slid down the hull after it, planting the heels of her sneakers against the rail as she reached down to retrieve it.

"Faster!" Curly bellowed from the bow of the canoe. JJ paddled recklessly, bouncing the canoe off the hull of the motorboat, while Curly jabbed the blade of a second oar at Cindy's midriff.

"Get away from me!" She held the extinguisher out to defend herself as she spotted Jeff floundering in his wet clothing at the tip of the bow. "Jeff, help!"

Curly pointed at Jeff. "Get Hollister!" He stepped to the very front of the canoe and raised the oar in the air, while JJ continued to scrape the canoe forward along the cuddy's hull.

"Leave him alone!" Cindy cried. She pulled the pin from the handle of the extinguisher and fired a blast of powder into JJ's face; he shrieked and dropped his oar into the water as he instinctively reached up to clear his face. Curly spun about and slashed his oar at her, swatting the back of her hand with the flat side of the blade; she screamed and dropped the extinguisher over the rail and into the lake.

"Get it, Jeff!" she shouted.

Jeff dove beneath the surface and groped in vain for the extinguisher as it vanished into deeper waters, then he rose again with the hull of the canoe directly overhead. Clenching his teeth in anger, he burst through the surface with all his fury, grasping the metal lip of the canoe and thrusting it downward to the utter surprise of its two occupants. Curly's oar flew into the air as he tumbled backward into the lake, but Jeff maintained a stranglehold on the rim, pushing the canoe ever downward. JJ clawed at the hull of the motorboat in a desperate attempt to stabilize the canoe, but his feeble grip was no match for Jeff's powerful grasp, so he slid toward the low side of the canoe as it began to fill with water.

He kicked at Jeff from five feet away. "I'll get you, Hollister."

Jeff grabbed the front seat of the canoe and flipped the boat over with a roar, dumping JJ into the cold water with the capsized canoe on top of him. With their assailants momentarily neutralized, he dove beneath the hull to resurface on the starboard side. The entire cabin of the boat was now engulfed in flames while Cindy stood at the center of the bow, staring dumbfounded at the sight of the burning craft and the plume of smoke rolling skyward.

Jeff treaded water. "Jump, Cindy!"

"What about the boat?" she cried.

"It's too far gone! Hurry!"

Cindy glanced back at the two Tornadoes regrouping beside the capsized canoe before diving headfirst into the lake. Her momentum carried her underwater past Jeff, and when she broke the surface, she continued in powerful strokes that left him far behind. He slogged after her, his wet jeans and sneakers weighing down his tired legs as he swam the hundred yards to the sandy beach beneath the cliff wall. Exhausted, he crawled out of the water and onto the sand before staggering to his feet. She stepped up to him, scowling and shivering as she squeezed the water out of her sweater.

He gazed up at her with his hands on his knees. "I guess I could've used that life jacket after all," he panted.

She slapped his face so hard he fell back onto the sand. "Liar!" she screamed. "You'll never change! Look at my father's boat, Jeff! Look at it! How am I supposed to explain that?"

Jeff ran his tongue across his molars to make sure they were still in place. He brushed sand from his wet clothes as he sat up. "I had nothing to do with it—"

"You have everything to do with it!" she screamed. "It's all one big mess and you're right in the middle of it! And you know what's really sad? Deep down inside, you enjoy it!"

He rose to his feet and reached out for her. "That's not true, Cindy! I—"

She backed away. "No! Don't touch me! Just get out of my life! I never want to see you again!"

"Don't be ridiculous. At least let me take you home."

"I'll stay at Shannon's. You just stay away from me, Jeff Hollister!" She darted off to the right side of the beach where the perimeter path jutted into the deepening foliage. With a rustle of leaves, she was gone.

Jeff ran to the edge of the path. "Cindy, wait!" he called. "It's not safe!"

Cindy paid no heed as she stormed down the perimeter path, muttering and cursing to herself. The sight of the burning motorboat to her right fueled her anger, but as the flames dwindled, so did her rage. Traveling the dark and rugged path in quest of the faraway cottages on the southern shore, she came upon a large oak tree splitting the path in two, with the second trail disappearing over a hill into the woods to her left. Resting by the tree, she held her breath to concentrate on the sound of rustling brush somewhere behind her.

"Jeff?" she said meekly.

The moonlight had given way to advancing clouds, but in the dim light she could see a teenage boy emerging on the path behind her. As the boy approached, she saw that he was not wearing a green vest but rather a maroon jacket. She gasped and retreated to the perimeter path, only to confront a second figure in a Tornado jacket approaching from the opposite direction. Frantic, she turned about and ran past the oak tree for the secondary path.

"Get her," Curly growled as he met JJ at the tree.

Shortly down the inland path, Cindy met the gate of a chain-link fence secured by a rusty padlock. She turned about and cowered against the fence at the sight of JJ and Curly approaching her, the latter brandishing his revolver.

"Don't scream," he warned her. "Where's Hollister?"

"We... we split up," she said. "He left."

Curly pointed the gun at her stomach. "That's bad for you." He stepped closer and shook the fence with his free hand. "Climb over," he told JJ before waving the revolver at Cindy. "She's gonna follow you."

"What about Hollister?" JJ asked.

"I'm tired of chasing him," Curly said. "We're gonna make him come to us."

Jeff trudged in the opposite direction along the well-worn perimeter path, his waterlogged sneakers squishing with every step he took. The chilly breeze gnawed at his skin as the first cottages of the western shore came into view, but a deeper chill ran inside him, a crushing sentiment that all had been lost. The odds of convincing Cindy to come with him had not been strong, but he never anticipated such a final and painful break. Of all the blows he had endured since Train's death, her rejection was the bitterest.

"You want me out of your life? You got it," he said out loud, as if she was standing right in front of him.

A shrill siren pierced the night as a rescue craft sped across the water toward the smoldering boat. Jeff surmised that Cindy had reached safe haven and called the police, and he hoped she wouldn't be so spiteful as to disclose the location of his car. He arrived at the Wellis property twenty minutes later and scaled the sloping cottage yard to the gravel driveway, relieved to discover that the Camaro had not been vandalized and that he had not lost his keys in the lake. Inside the gym bag in the back seat, he found dry underwear and a dark T-shirt along with the backup sneakers he had been mindful enough to bring.

After stripping naked beneath the waning moonlight, he quickly re-dressed and threw all of his wet clothes into the trunk except for his green nylon vest, which was already almost dry. He tossed the vest inside the Camaro, all the while eyeing the edges of the surrounding foliage for Curly's truck. Lastly, he pulled out a gray hooded sweatshirt with SALISBURY HIGH printed on the front, pushing his arms through the sleeves and pulling it over his head before stuffing the gym bag into the back seat again.

Moments later, he followed the swath of the Camaro's high beams as they cut through the inky darkness, down the winding cottage driveway and onto Portland Village Road, back toward Salisbury. Aimlessly traveling the lonely roads of Portland, he mulled over the downward spiral that his life had taken and wondered how much lower it could possibly sink. With little money and even less gas, California seemed as unattainable to him as the moon overhead, and the thought occurred to him that there might be a simpler solution. A thick tree in the property ahead beckoned him along a different path, and with tearful eyes he pressed the gas pedal down and steered the Camaro onto the shoulder, taking dead aim for the tree trunk near the edge of the road.

"No!" he shouted. He jerked the steering wheel back to the left less than ten feet away from the tree, and its hanging willow branches scraped along the hood of the car as it bounced ruggedly off the curb and onto the main road again. He braked the car to a halt, glaring at the tree in his rearview mirror before scowling at the reflection of his own face. "You're Jeff Hollister," he told himself. "You'll find a way."

He drew a deep breath and exhaled slowly before driving with trembling hands down the dark road again. Self-reliance might not save him forever, but if it kept him alive for one more day, then perhaps he might discover a new pathway to follow. Already he had a plan, another source of money that he'd almost forgotten about. The plan required a return to Hurricane territory, and it wouldn't work until morning, so he turned the Camaro onto the vacant country roads between Portland and Salisbury, searching for an isolated spot where he could park his car and spend one more night in town.

PART III
DESOLATION

CHAPTER
11

THE NEXT MORNING, Jeff awoke in the back seat of his Camaro with a crimp in his neck and a cramp in his thigh. Raindrops pattered against the metal rooftop of the car and streaked down the foggy windows as he shivered beneath the makeshift blanket that his down vest had become. He wiped the sleepers from his eyes and sat up to survey his surroundings, groggily recollecting the events that had led him to bunk in his car in the first place. The boat fire, the icy plunge, the knockdown slap — was it all just a bad dream? He rubbed his tender jaw and recalled the most horrific moment of all: a suicidal collision course with a willow tree, spared from a senseless demise by a last-second stay of insanity. A dangerous concoction of pity and regret had nearly cost him his life, but all he felt now was hollowness worse than a whisky hangover, brought on by Cindy's sudden departure from his life.

That was yesterday, however, and the sun had risen again, albeit hidden behind a thick layer of glowering stratus clouds. Today the open road lay ahead with new opportunities and fresh outlooks. The Camaro's sleeping accommodations had been tight, but they were a vast improvement over the previous night's stay on cemetery grounds, and while the rain might impede his travel, it would also lower the visibility of those who might be looking for him. Such consolations fell short compared to the sting of severed friendships and a broken relationship, but those pains would fade as he built a new life, day by day. Yes, it was already a better day, he thought as he pulled the vest over his shoulders, gloomy skies notwithstanding.

He climbed over the center console and slid into the driver's seat to turn the keys already dangling from the ignition switch. The tachometer jumped to idle as the engine roared to life, but the gas gage presented the first obstacle on his journey to new horizons: a gas tank nearly empty. However, the lack of fuel was only an indicator of the real problem: a lack of money. His soggy wallet spread out on the dashboard still contained thirteen dollars, for although his final evening with Cindy had been a complete disaster, at least it had been free. Thirteen dollars wouldn't buy enough gas to get him out of the state, but what little gas remained in the tank would get him back to Salisbury, and from there his options were clear: either his plan would succeed and fuel his cross-country journey, or he would only get as far as thirteen dollars of gas would take him.

He stuffed the wallet into his vest pocket and shifted into gear, switching on the wipers and defroster as he drove the Camaro around the bulb of an undeveloped cul-de-sac. Once the foggy windshield cleared, he turned onto the main road back toward Salisbury, cautiously accelerating along the rain-slicked pavement and shunning the highway for back roads, with a keen eye on his mirrors for any cars following him. Twenty minutes later, he began the long ascent up Archer Road, past Cindy's neighborhood to the right, continuing onward to the intersection with the eastern end of Arrow Drive.

Moments later, he eased the Camaro onto Birch Road,

returning to Hurricane territory without risking detection by traveling along busy Burrough Street. At the crest of a gentle hill, he passed the entrance of a church parking lot to his left, glad to see that no police cars were parked in a common hideout along the driveway. Coasting downhill past a yellow house on his right, he noted the flutter of the curtains in the picture window as he slowed to turn onto adjacent Poplar Street. He quickly turned into the driveway on the side of the house, driving up an incline to a garage door that was already rolling up before him. Bumbles stepped back to give the Camaro room as it pulled into the vacant bay before quickly rolled the door shut again and peering out an inset window to ensure no one had seen them. Jeff shut off the motor and climbed out of the car, hustling on a beeline for the basement entrance of the raised ranch.

Bumbles trotted after him. "Jeff! What's going on?"

"Where's Mick?"

"Upstairs, I think."

Jeff reached for the knob, but the door burst open to reveal the new Hurricane leader, bare-chested with a dry white towel slung around his neck and an unlit cigarette pinched between his fingers. "What do *you* want?" he asked.

"I need to ask you something," Jeff said. "Can I come in?"

Mick pushed the door open and sardonically gestured him inside. "By all means."

Jeff heard a clack of billiard balls emanating from the adjacent room as he entered the basement hallway. He poked his head into the entertainment room, spotting Axle perched on a tall chair beside the pool table while Denny lined up his cue stick for a shot. Behind them, a television glimmered from its mount against a white wall, facing a reclined sofa chair that obscured all but the shoes of its occupant.

"Hey," Jeff said with a half-hearted wave.

Denny glanced at Mick. "Uh, hey Jeff," he said before striking the cue ball and missing his shot.

The reclining chair swiveled about to reveal Crazy Legs, dressed in a gray nylon running suit and matching running shoes. "Jeff! I figured you were long gone by now."

Jeff stepped into the room. "This is my last stop."

Axle leaned over the pool table and pointed a stick at the cue ball. "What for?"

"Good question." Mick followed Jeff into the room. "Pray tell, Jeff. To what do we owe the honor of your visit? Tea won't be ready for at least an hour."

Jeff returned Mick's smirk with a deadpan glare. "Cut the bullshit. I need the bankbook."

"The bankbook?" Mick lit the cigarette and sucked on it until it was glowing red, then he exhaled a deep breath of smoke toward his feet as if lost in thought. "Sorry, Jeff, I can't do that," he finally said. "That's the Hurricanes' money. And seeing as how you're no longer a Hurricane, well, need I state the obvious?"

"We're not talking about your college fund, Mick. There's dirty money in that account, and my hands are just as soiled as yours. I just want my share."

Bumbles stepped into the doorway and scanned the tense faces about the room. "Hey, guys, what's up?"

"Jeff was just asking if he could cash out the gang's savings account," Mick said.

"Actually, it's my account," Jeff said. "I just let the gang use it."

"We have money?" Bumbles asked. "How much are we talking about?"

"About seventeen hundred bucks," Jeff said. "I'm leaving town, and I need some cash."

Crazy Legs studied Jeff with a puzzled expression. Finally he shrugged and said, "What's the big deal? Let him have it. Let him have my share too. I'm sure he's good for it."

"Well, shoot. He can have my share," Bumbles said. "I owe him more than that."

"Thanks," Jeff said. "I promise I'll pay you guys back."

Mick shook his head. "Time out. There's no shares. It's the gang's money. It was obtained by gang activities, it's exclusively for the gang, and it's the leader's prerogative as to how it's used. Jeff knows that better than anyone because he's the one who set the rules. Ain't that right, Jeff?"

"I never put him in charge of it," Jeff told the others. "He only has it because it was easier for him to make the deposits after he fenced the stuff."

"Yeah, well, timing is everything. I'm the leader now, so it's up to me how the money's used." Mick took another drag from his cigarette and exhaled in Jeff's general direction. "Now it's really sweet that Crazy Legs and Bumbles wanna help you out like that. But it doesn't make much sense to lend money to someone who's literally ten minutes away from skipping town. Sorry."

"Aw, Mick. Cut him some slack," Crazy Legs said.

"The answer's no. Case closed, end of discussion," Mick replied.

"Fine," Jeff stormed down the hallway past Bumbles and yanked open the garage door. "Just remember whose name is on that account. You'll never see a dime of that money once I'm gone."

He slammed the door shut behind him and walked to the garage bay door, reaching down and rolling it open overhead. Rain pelted the driveway with large, splashing drops, and he stared despondently at the water rushing down toward the gutter, wondering what to do next. At the very least he needed to leave Salisbury, so he turned back to the Camaro with his keys in hand, only to see Bumbles standing in the doorway of the basement entrance.

"Mick's getting the bankbook," his friend said. "You must've convinced him."

Jeff smiled faintly as he followed Bumbles back into the house again. They returned to the entertainment room, where

Denny and Axle continued to shoot pool and Crazy Legs flicked through stations on the television set. No one seemed surprised at his return.

"Might as well get comfortable," Axle said. "He'll probably be a few minutes. If you've seen his room, you'd know why."

Denny sank a ball into a side pocket and slid behind the cue ball for another shot. "Who the hell still uses a bankbook anyway?"

"My dad opened that account for me when I was ten. I just never closed it out," Jeff said. "It came in handy for the Hurricanes when we needed an account."

"Until now," Axle said.

Denny pocketed another ball without looking up. "Shit, there oughta be a million bucks in there by now."

"No such luck." Jeff glanced about the room. "Where's TJ and Brain?"

"School," Axle said. "TJ's got basketball tryouts today. Brain was rambling something about wanting an education."

"Go figure," Denny said.

Crazy Legs spun about in the recliner and gestured back toward the TV. "Looks like a good day to hang inside. We're gonna get drenched."

Jeff stepped up for a better view. A radar map displayed a mass of dark green shades sweeping toward their location. "Like I need a weatherman to tell me it's raining outside," he said.

Suddenly the TV emitted a loud beep and the screen cut to a blonde anchorwoman sitting behind a news desk with the picture of a familiar teenage girl set beside her head. "An Amber Alert has been issued for a missing Salisbury girl," the anchorwoman began. "Cindy Wellis was last seen by her parents at their home at five p.m. last night. She is the daughter of Salisbury Police Chief Matthew Wellis, a candidate for county sheriff in next week's municipal election."

Crazy Legs frowned. "Jeff?"

"Shut up!" Jeff grabbed the TV remote from his friend's hand and punched the volume up ten notches while the other Hurricanes gathered behind him.

The inset picture flicked from Cindy's photograph to one of Jeff in a jacket and tie, as the anchorwoman continued. "Police are seeking eighteen-year-old Jeffrey Hollister as a person of interest in Miss Wellis's disappearance. Hollister is the reputed gang leader who was injured in a knife attack at Salisbury High School last Monday. Rick Flynn is at the Salisbury Public Safety Complex with more on the story. Rick?"

The image cut to the young reporter standing beside a familiar plainclothes detective on the front sidewalk of the Public Safety Complex. "Thanks, Melissa," he said into a microphone. "I'm here with Detective Dan Shelnick of the Salisbury PD. Detective Shelnick, it's been reported that a motorboat registered to Chief Wellis was found abandoned and burning on Almond Lake in Portland last night. Is there any connection between that incident and his daughter's reported disappearance?"

Detective Shelnick cleared his throat as the camera and microphone turned to him. "Um, I'm not at liberty to comment on that at the moment. I can say that Hollister is also wanted for questioning in a knife assault that seriously injured a rival gang member Wednesday night. He may also possess one or both of the sidearms stolen from Salisbury police officers last week."

"That's not fair!" Bumbles cried. "They know it wasn't you!"

Jeff scratched his chin. "Happy Jack isn't dead?"

Crazy Legs shook his head, but his eyes remained fixed on the screen as it flashed back to the reporter. "All this with the police chief locked in a tight race for county sheriff," the reporter commented. "How's he holding up?"

Detective Shelnick's expression eased. "We're confident that Cindy will be located soon so that the Wellis family can quickly put this ordeal behind them."

The reporter faced the camera again. "Plenty of cause for concern but hoping for the best. Rick Flynn live from Salisbury. Back to you, Melissa."

The shot returned to the anchorwoman behind the news desk, with pictures of Jeff and Cindy juxtaposed beside each other. "Thanks, Rick. Hollister is considered armed and extremely dangerous. Anyone with knowledge of his whereabouts or that of Cindy Wellis is asked to contact the Salisbury Police Department immediately. Stay tuned for more on this developing story. I'm Melissa Weiss, WCRT news. We'll be right back."

The program switched to a commercial, and Jeff muted the volume before dropping the remote into Crazy Legs's lap. Denny turned toward Jeff with a quizzical look. "Where'd they get that mug shot?"

"It's my yearbook picture." Jeff glanced about the room. "I gotta get out of here."

Crazy Legs tossed the remote aside. "Jeff, what the hell is going on?"

"We were on that boat last night. Curly and JJ attacked us with a Molotov cocktail. The boat burned up, but we got away and swam ashore. Cindy was really pissed. She ditched me and took off. I have no idea where she is now."

Axle gasped. "Curly ambushed you? Does Mick know?"

The Hurricane leader strolled back into the room, still shirtless with the bankbook in his hand. "Does Mick know what?"

"Curly attacked Jeff and Cindy last night!" Axle replied.

"Really?" Mick looked Jeff up and down. "He seems okay to me."

"I gotta go," Jeff said. "That story's been all over town by now. Everyone will be looking for me."

Crazy Legs rose from the recliner. "I don't think so. I've been monitoring the news all morning, and that's the first I've seen of it."

Denny laughed. "Monitoring the news? You've been lying around in your fancy sweatpants watching sports all morning!"

Crazy Legs looked down at his matching gray pants and jacket. "It's running gear. I'm in training, ya know."

Jeff turned to Mick and reached for the bankbook. "Thanks, man."

Mick pulled it back. "Whoa! Not so fast. You get two hundred plus the hundred bucks that was already in there. That's your share, if you wanna call it that."

"I said he can have mine," Crazy Legs cut in, and Bumbles nodded in agreement.

Mick glared at them for a long moment before looking back to Jeff again. "Okay, keep two hundred for each of them. If you stiff me, their asses are on the line for it."

Jeff held out his hand again. "I won't."

"What about the rest of it? How do I know you'll come back?"

"I guess you'll just have to take my word for it."

Mick shook his head. "Sorry, Jeff. Your word ain't good enough anymore."

Jeff bristled. "Then send someone with me. I'll take Crazy Legs."

"I'm not sending one of my men out there with you. It's too dangerous."

"Okay. You tell me."

Mick scratched his chin. "Gimme some collateral."

Jeff laughed in disbelief. "Collateral? Like what?"

"Your keys will do just fine."

"My car keys? Are you crazy? You expect me to walk to the stores?"

"Why not? We've done it hundreds of times."

Jeff sputtered in exasperation as Crazy Legs ambled up to

his side. "Mick, every cop in town will be looking for him. Not to mention it's pouring rain outside."

"Yeah, Mick. Don't be such a ballbuster," Axle added.

"The cops are looking for his car," Mick told them. He turned back to Jeff with a cunning grin. "I'm doing him a favor by keeping it safe in my garage. And who cares about the rain?"

"Some favor." Jeff slammed his car keys onto the pool table and snatched the bankbook out of Mick's hand. "Thanks for nothing."

"Take out all the money and bring me back a grand." Mick picked up the keys and jingled them for a second before stuffing them in his pocket. "Don't be gone long."

"Kiss my ass, Mick." Jeff stomped past the pool table to the back door, but he stopped at the window to gaze out into the deluge of rainwater flooding the yard. He pulled his sweatshirt hood over his head before stepping out into the weather and slamming the door shut behind him.

Mick pulled the towel from his neck. "I'm gonna take a shower," he said. "You guys keep your eyes out for cops. And I don't want you hanging down here playing pool all day." He turned and headed for the staircase again while the Hurricanes stepped to the back window to watch Jeff walk across the backyard until the driving rain swallowed him from view.

A thin wooden door rattled shut, stirring Cindy from a fitful sleep. She blinked her eyes open to face the ragged cushion of an old beige couch with a whiff of mildew in her nostrils. Her hair was in her face and she tried to brush it away, but her wrists were bound together by gray duct tape and her ankles constrained in similar fashion. Beyond the mustiness of the couch, she could smell the aroma of hickory smoke wafting from a crackling fireplace centered in the back wall of the rudimentary cabin.

JJ stood at the thin door, flicking a wall switch up and down and watching a bare bulb attached to the ceiling as it blinked on and off. "We have electricity," he announced.

Curly sat at a plain wooden table in the center of the room, cleaning his revolver with a rag amid a handful of bullets scattered on the tabletop. "What do we need electricity for?" he asked without looking up.

"I don't know. Light?" JJ flicked the switch up one last time to leave the bulb lit. "The main breaker was shut off. I think I fixed the fence too."

Finally Curly looked up with interest. "How'd you do that?"

"I jumped the key switch on the control panel. I think it worked because the power light came on. I'm gonna go check it out." JJ grabbed his Tornado jacket from the fireplace hearth and moved toward the knotty front door; Cindy shut her eyes again and feigned sleep as he strode past her. The heavy front door creaked open, momentarily amplifying the din of the rainfall upon the leaves while a cold breeze quickly chilled the room. "It's friggin' pouring out here," he said as he flipped up his jacket collar.

He stepped out onto the covered porch and latched the door shut behind him. Cindy lay still on the couch, listening as his cowboy boots clomped to the end of the wooden porch, then she cracked an eyelid open to study her other captor sitting at the simple table. Meticulously, Curly stared blankly down at the table, meticulously wiping each cylinder of the revolver with a cloth. When he was finished, he laid the gun on the table and pushed his chair back, scraping its wooden feet across the hardwood floor as he stood. She squeezed her eyes shut as he stepped in her direction, while he stopped and hovered over her for a long moment before kicking the leg of the couch.

"Wake up," he said. "Today's your lucky day."

She opened her eyes and drew a startled breath as if he had surprised her, then she swung her feet off the couch and wriggled into a sitting position to finally see the entirety of the austere cabin. The couch, the table, and its four wooden chairs were the only furnishings inside the long room, dimly lit by the ceiling bulb but more by the murky daylight peeking through the front casement windows. Across the room, a half dozen logs of hickory and oak were stacked upon a brown throw rug with the tip of a hatchet buried in the bark of the top log. The fireplace glowed with embers of logs that had burned all night, drying her captors' boots and jackets on the warm gray stones of its hearth. In the center of the far wall, a sliding wooden hatchway implied the cabin's former function as a weighing station for the mining company's trucks, while the wall behind her was windowless and unremarkable but for a solar clock that seemed reasonably correct. In the corner nearest to the clock, a rudimentary wooden ladder was affixed to the adjacent wall, leading up to a loft through an open hole in the ceiling.

Cindy could not keep her teeth from chattering, for her clothes were still damp from her plunge into the lake. "You know, my father's the chief of police—" she began.

"I don't care if he's the Prince of Wales," Curly snapped. "You're not here because of who your father is. You're here because of who your boyfriend is."

She looked away. "Jeff's not my boyfriend anymore. We had a falling out last night."

"Aw, really?" Curly nodded in the direction of the lake. "Well, you better hope he comes for you, or you might have a falling out off that cliff out there."

JJ burst into the cabin again, shaking the water from his hair as he shut the door behind him. "Man, it's crazy raining out!"

Curly returned to the table and reached for the revolver again. "So does it work?"

JJ smiled proudly. "Sure does. I got a nice little zap from it."

Curly peered through the chambers of the cylinder and blew through one of the holes before inserting a bullet into it. He repeated the routine three times before snapping the chamber back into the revolver. "So how's Hollister supposed to find us now?"

JJ sat down at the table before opening a shallow drawer and fishing through its contents, he pulled out a deck of cards and slid the drawer shut again. "He'll find a way. You know him," he said without looking up. "Everyone else can stay out."

Curly glared at him. "Well, whatever you did, you're gonna have to undo it."

"What for?"

"I have to go get the truck."

JJ shuffled the deck and began to deal a game of solitaire. "Can't we take care of Hollister first?"

Curly nodded. "Sure. Gimme your phone and I'll call him right now."

JJ glared up at his lieutenant. "I told you. I lost it in the lake last night. Remember?"

"No shit, dumbass. You just couldn't leave it on shore, could you? I left mine in the truck, remember?"

"Oh." JJ gestured to Cindy. "What about her? Does she have a phone on her?"

She glowered at JJ through long strands of straggly brown hair. "Do I look like I have a phone on me?"

Curly smirked. "Hey, now. Be a good girl and maybe you'll make it through this. Just because your boyfriend is going to die doesn't mean you have to."

"He's not my boyfriend anymore!" she cried. "He's three hundred miles away from here by now! Your sick little plan isn't going to work!"

The smirk on Curly's lips faded into an ugly grimace, and his pupils began to shift rapidly from side to side. "That's not good," he said. He stood up from the table and stepped toward the couch again, aiming the revolver directly at her. "That's not good for you at all!"

Cindy cringed at the sight of his finger twitching on the

trigger of the revolver. He pulled the trigger back, but the hammer simply clicked upon the pin without firing a bullet, while she screamed in terror and recoiled on the couch.

JJ hopped to his feet. "What are you doing? You can't kill her! We need her to get Hollister!"

Curly whirled about wide-eyed and strode toward his partner with the gun aimed at his chest. "Shut up!"

JJ fell backward over his chair and crashed to the floor with his hands stretched out in defense. "Curly, don't…"

Curly's nostrils flared with a long, deep breath, and he exhaled slowly through his mouth until the crazed gleam in his eyes subsided. "I can do whatever I want. Don't forget it."

JJ quickly stood up and righted his chair. "I didn't mean nothin' by it."

Curly straightened up and stepped to the fireplace, slipping the revolver in his waistband before taking his Tornado jacket from the hearth. He pulled the jacket on as he stepped to the couch to look down at Cindy. "Hey, what do ya know? It really is your lucky day!"

She cowered against the couch with her lip trembling. "Go away!"

Curly turned to JJ. "Here's how it's gonna go. You're gonna shut off the fence now and give me fifteen minutes to get over it. Then you're gonna turn it back on so we don't get any surprises. I'll take the canoe across the lake and call Hollister from my truck."

"I scoped out the lake a little while ago," JJ said. "There's some kind of cop boat out there."

"Whatever. Anyone comes near me, I shoot 'em." Curly pointed at the wall clock. "It's quarter to ten now. You need to shut the fence off again one hour from now so I can get back in. Then turn it back on at eleven. If Hollister's not here by noon, we'll wrap things up here and hit the road."

"You got it!" JJ rushed to the cellar door and cast it fully open, allowing it to rattle against the wall as he dashed down the wooden stairs into the basement again.

Curly smirked at his accomplice's newfound obedience. He stepped across the room and opened the front door before turning back to Cindy. "You better hope Hollister's still around," he warned her, "and that he still gives a damn about you." He yanked the front door open and stepped out onto the porch, slamming it shut behind him to leave her sobbing on the musty couch inside the gloomy cabin.

CHAPTER 12

W ITH HIS SWEATSHIRT hood pulled tight against his forehead, Jeff descended a muddy bank toward the curb of Burrough Street, wishing he hadn't forgotten his ball cap in the back seat of his car. The Lower Plaza lay in plain sight before him, but a Salisbury police cruiser led a line of vehicles toward him from a green light at the plaza intersection, so he ducked behind a large white sign posted near the roadside and lingered there until the line of cars passed. Finally he stepped out into open view, cloaked by poor visibility from the rainstorm, and he glanced back at the large sign that had provided him cover. In large red and blue lettering, it read: MATT WELLIS FOR COUNTY SHERIFF.

Slightly amused, he continued along the shoulder of the road to his right, shielding his eyes from the tire wash of the passing cars. Once the traffic cleared in both directions, he darted across the street to the opposite curb, veering onto the grassy slope toward the plaza parking lot before another line of cars approached. Clearly, the rain had failed to discourage the Friday commerce to any significant degree, so driving his conspicuous Camaro to the bank could've been a glaring mistake. Mick was right to have made him walk, but it irked him nonetheless.

He quickly descended the modest slope toward the supermarket into the parking lot with an eye on the satellite branch of the Madison Savings Bank situated at the far end of the strip. An overwhelmed storm drain gurgled in the middle of the lot, feeding into a large and growing puddle, but Jeff kept to the left of it, intercepting a blowing shopping cart and pushing it toward the supermarket entrance like any shopper might. He spotted a young grocery clerk in a yellow raincoat rustling carts in the wind and launched the cart in the worker's general direction as he continued down the parking lot toward the stores. When he reached the covered sidewalk, he stepped up to the liquor store window and checked his reflection in the glass, straightening his hood and brushing the wet strands of hair from his eyes. Deeming himself bank-worthy, he slipped inconspicuously past the tall glass windows of the supermarket on his way to the bank entrance.

As he reached for the handle, however, the door swung abruptly toward him, and a balding man in a dark gray overcoat strode out of the ATM foyer, inadvertently bumping into Jeff as he struggled to open an umbrella. "Watch it," Jeff grumbled without looking up.

The man whirled about. "Jeff Hollister!"

Jeff froze in his tracks. He turned around to see Vice Principal Stammer frowning down upon him. "Hello, Lloyd," he said drearily.

Mr. Stammer checked his watch. "Surprising to see you out and about on such a lovely school day."

"Oh yeah, school. I thought it was Saturday." Jeff scratched his chin. "Shouldn't you be there too?"

Mr. Stammer grunted in disapproval and continued down the sidewalk while Jeff slipped inside the foyer, wishing for once he could've kept his big mouth shut. He glanced back at the vice-principal, who shot him a contemptuous eye in return before ducking into the supermarket through an automated entrance door. Jeff passed through the foyer and pulled open another glass door to enter the spacious red-carpeted lobby of the bank, where he took a withdrawal slip from a nearby kiosk before heading for the teller counter at the far end of the room.

A young brunette in glasses summoned him forward and pointed to his hood. "Please remove that."

"Sorry." Jeff pulled off the hood again and lowered his head, wary that someone might recognize him.

"Thank you," the teller said. "How can I help you?"

Jeff scribbled a figure and his signature upon the withdrawal slip and passed it over the counter along with the bankbook. "Large bills, please."

She read the slip and checked the bankbook. "I'll need some identification."

Jeff pulled his wallet from his vest pocket and flipped it open on the counter for her to see. He held his breath as she took the wallet and scanned the license closely, exhaling slowly once she handed it back to him. "No fifties. Just hundreds," he told her, slipping it into the back pocket of his jeans.

The teller nodded and pulled a stack of crisp, new one-hundred-dollar bills from her cash drawer, meticulously counted out seventeen of them on her countertop while a printer simultaneously recorded the transaction in the bankbook. Jeff glanced warily at the cameras surrounding him, although no one in the bank seemed alarmed by his presence. She placed the money into an envelope and passed it back across the countertop along with the bankbook. "Have a nice day."

"Thanks." Jeff scooped up the items and turned to leave. On his way out of the lobby, he stopped at a wastebasket beside the kiosk and prepared to toss the bankbook into it, but a memory struck him from many years ago, of the day he and his father had opened the account with his first allowance money.

Only a few dollars remained in the account now, and the bankbook was little more than a memento, but standing over the wastebasket he found himself incapable of letting it go. Instead, he slid it into his vest pocket and continued toward the exit.

As he passed into the ATM foyer again, his sentimental daydream was jolted away by the wail of a siren and a flash of blue light at the farthest visible point of Burrough Street, descending along the hillside ridge toward the plazas. Panic gripped him as a second cruiser followed the first in line, circling the ridge with an additional blur of flashing blue. The first cruiser slowed for the left turn into the Lower Plaza, allowing the second cruiser to close swiftly upon its rear bumper, and then both cruisers sped down the entrance driveway into the parking lot, where they promptly split apart. The lead car headed straight for the bank as the second car followed the edge of the grassy island parallel to Burrough Street, racing in the opposite direction from which it had just come.

With sirens in the air and his heartbeat in his ears, Jeff folded the envelope of money in half and shoved it down into his underwear. He exited the foyer and hastened down the sidewalk, noting Mr. Stammer standing behind a supermarket window with a cell phone to his ear. The vice-principal followed him to the automated exit door and emerged from the supermarket, waving to the approaching cruisers as Jeff frantically scanned the lot for an escape route.

Jeff veered past Stammer's lunging grasp and sprinted down the sidewalk past the liquor store, while the first cruiser fishtailed to a stop outside the glass ATM foyer and accelerated down the fire lane behind him. The second cruiser cut a wide arc past the gurgling storm drain and sped toward the stores with the clear objective of cutting off the sidewalk beyond the pharmacy. The converging vehicles forced Jeff to depart the sidewalk for the open parking lot, into the steady rain.

At the edge of the large puddle, the grocery clerk froze amid the commotion, leaving a chain of twenty grocery carts blocking Jeff's only escape route. Jeff lengthened his strides and sprang high in the air in an attempt to jump over the train of carts, but the toe of his trailing sneaker caught a protruding handle and he tumbled headlong to the asphalt, bracing his fall with his stitched palm. He scrambled to his feet with a wince and pressed forward, while both cruisers swerved to chase after him.

The clerk stood petrified against the carts as the cruisers raced by on either side to close in on Jeff's position. The first car splashed through the puddle and spun to a halt on the high side of the parking lot as the second car brushed past Jeff before skidding to a stop directly in front of him. Sergeant Hyrst leaped from the white cruiser with his pistol drawn, while Officer Boyd popped open the door of his blue patrol car, crouching behind it with his gun leveled at Jeff's chest.

"Don't move!" he barked. "Put your hands up! Do it!"

Jeff slowly complied with the order, scowling at the terrified clerk who had just muddled his escape. He stood motionless except for his darting eyes, wary that he might be shot on the spot if he failed to follow every instruction flawlessly.

Sergeant Hyrst approached him first, his gun aimed with deadly precision. "Hands in the air! Kneel on the ground!"

Jeff complied with the orders, dropping to his knees before lying flat on his stomach with his scraped palms stretched out on the cool, wet pavement. He lifted his head to see a third cruiser rounding the high ridge of Burrough Street toward the plaza intersection as Boyd approached cautiously with his gun still drawn.

"Stay down!" Hyrst holstered his weapon and knelt down to pat Jeff's legs and back pockets, confiscating his soggy wallet and the thirteen dollars enclosed. "Well, whaddya know? It's Jeff Hollister, the catch of the day!" He bent over close to Jeff's ear and whispered, "Chief Wellis wants to talk to you *real bad.*"

Hyrst pinned a knee against Jeff's back and pulled his arms down one at a time to snap a set of handcuffs tightly around his wrists. Boyd bent forward, and together they lifted Jeff by his arms, setting him upon his feet before Hyrst pasted him against the side of the cruiser.

"Take it easy," Jeff groaned. "I'm not resisting."

"Where's Cindy Wellis?" Hyrst asked.

Boyd stepped within an inch of Jeff's face and began to fish his fingers through the pockets of Jeff's jeans. "Where's my *gun?*"

"I don't have any gun, and I don't know where she is," Jeff said. "I wanna see a lawyer."

Hyrst pulled out his club and pointed it at Jeff's chin. "You're gonna wanna see a *doctor* if anything's happened to the chief's daughter!"

Jeff tried to answer, but instead, he doubled over in pain as Hyrst drove the butt of the club into his gut. Boyd stopped searching his pockets to catch him from collapsing to the ground. "Easy, Bob. He's just a kid—"

"He's a no-good, rotten punk," Hyrst snapped. "Read him his rights."

Gasping for breath, Jeff could hardly hear as Officer Boyd recited the Miranda rights from memory. Instead, he focused on the balding vice-principal emerging from a growing crowd of spectators with his black umbrella held over his head. At the same time, the third police cruiser slowed at the intersection, its siren muted as it descended the plaza driveway. Jeff's stomach felt squeamish, not only from the blow of Hyrst's baton but also from the crushing revelation that the gig was up: California was but a dream now.

Boyd snapped his fingers in front of Jeff's face. "Do you understand the rights that I have just read to you?"

"Huh? Yeah, whatever," Jeff replied, his gaze still fixated on the vice principal coming their way.

"Officers!" Mr. Stammer called out as he approached along the edge of the puddle.

Boyd whirled about. "Whoa! Sir, please stay back."

Mr. Stammer halted a few feet away. "I just wanted to thank you for your exemplary effort in removing this, er, *element* from our streets. I intend to write a letter of commendation to both the mayor and the police chief to let them know what a fine job the both of you have done today."

Hyrst puffed out his chest. "Much appreciated, Mr. Stammer."

Jeff rolled his eyes. "Will you hit me again if I puke on you?"

The sergeant yanked open the rear door of his cruiser. "Shut your mouth, Hollister."

Mr. Stammer narrowed his sight upon their captive. "I warned you that this day would come, Jeff. A life of delinquency can only lead to heartbreak and misery. I only hope that you'll learn from this experience and make better choices when given the opportunity in the future."

Jeff longed to kick the vice principal in the knee, but he knew Hyrst would never allow it. Stammer gave each of the officers a congratulatory handshake before starting back toward the supermarket, while the third cruiser sped toward the giant puddle as it pulled around the right side of Boyd's car.

"Uh, Mr. Stammer?" Jeff called out as Hyrst took his arm.

The vice-principal sighed and turned around, clearly annoyed by the beckoning. "Now what, Jeff?"

"Thanks for the advice," Jeff said with a wink and a grin.

The brief delay did the trick. The right front tire of the approaching cruiser caught the edge of the puddle, sending a sheet of rainwater down the slope of the parking lot. The vice-principal cried out as the wave of grimy water struck him and knocked the umbrella from his hand. With his suit completely drenched, Stammer scooped up the umbrella and gestured angrily at the driver of the third cruiser before rushing off in a huff.

Jeff chuckled as he sat down in the back seat of the white cruiser, while Hyrst slammed the rear door shut behind him. He opened the front door and slid behind the steering wheel. "Hope you had a good laugh, Hollister. Probably the last one you'll have for a long time."

Officer Boyd stepped to the open door. "Need me to follow you down, Bob?"

"Nah, I got this." Hyrst shut his door and shifted into drive before pulling the radio microphone from the center console. "Squad Car Two. Suspect in custody. Transporting back to station."

"Roger, Car Two," a female voice crackled in response.

Hyrst waited for the other two cruisers to proceed while Jeff squirmed in his seat, trying to wriggle his wrists in the handcuffs locked painfully tight behind his back. The three cruisers drove up the plaza ramp in succession, turning right onto Burrough Street through the halted flow of traffic, parading their capture before the citizens of Salisbury with full lights and sirens along the main thoroughfare. As they accelerated up the road, Jeff spotted the familiar grill of a blue Camaro parked at the edge of the Upper Plaza lot, facing out toward the street. All three policemen drove their cruisers past the Camaro in oblivion while he held his breath, trying to glimpse the occupants of the car without turning his head too much.

The lead cruiser snuffed its siren and lights before turning left onto Willow Street, but Hyrst continued to follow Boyd's car along Burrough Street toward the Public Safety Complex near the center of town. The sergeant glanced into his rearview mirror at Jeff sitting in the center of the caged back seat. "Nice ride, eh, Hollister?"

Jeff glared at the sergeant's eyes in the mirror. "What?"

Hyrst patted the dashboard. "Brand new Police Explorer Interceptor with a V8 hybrid engine. I had her up to a buck twenty yesterday and she wasn't even breathing hard. Dual airbags, antilock brakes, traction control, GPS. She's even got that new-car smell."

"So what? You want me to buy it or something? You sound like a used-car salesman."

"Did you know you're the first criminal to ride in the back of this fine vehicle?"

"I'm honored," Jeff muttered.

"Don't be bitter, Hollister. You knew this day would come sooner or later. You and your friends used to get away with murder in this town. It's different now that Chief is here. Take this car. We'd never get cars like this. We'd get the used ones from Madison. Now it's a whole new ball game. Matt Wellis is giving us the tools we need to put punks like you behind bars. He's the best thing that ever happened to this town. He's got a plan for law and order in this community, and it's going to take him places."

"Yeah, he's a real visionary," Jeff said.

"He is, Hollister, and he knows what a snake in the grass you are. He knows you've been trying to get at him through his daughter, but he didn't figure you were so evil that you'd murder her when your scheme didn't work."

"I didn't murder anyone. You're out of your mind. Stop talking to me. I just wanna see my lawyer."

"All in good time, Hollister. All in good time."

An ominous feeling gripped Jeff's gut as he realized he was at the mercy of a police force that likely held little concern for his own welfare. Beyond the beating wipers of the rainy windshield, the brake lights on Officer Boyd's cruiser flashed bright red in their faces, its yellow blinker indicating a left turn toward Salisbury High School. Hyrst slowed the squad car and passed Boyd's cruiser on the shoulder of the road before accelerating into the clear lane ahead. Jeff glimpsed back, hoping to see the Camaro outside the rear window, but by now other vehicles had merged into the line of traffic, obstructing it from his view.

As they neared the driveway to the Salisbury Public Safety Complex, Jeff spotted through the front windshield a white van approaching them, its roof equipped with a small satellite dish and its hood stamped in red letters reading WCRT NEWS. He quickly recalled the Amber Alert and slid across the seat to his left, pressing his face close to the side window as the news van whizzed by. Brake lights flashed bright red upon the wet pavement as the van skidded to a halt in the middle of Burrough Street, momentarily cutting off traffic in both directions as it turned about in a wide arc to pursue the police car.

Jeff settled smugly into his seat again, eyeing Hyrst's face in the rearview mirror as the sergeant cursed beneath his breath. The sergeant turned the cruiser onto the winding driveway leading to the brick building on the hilltop, while Jeff slid back to the center of the seat from the force of the turn. The news van followed in swift pursuit, while the rest of the traffic continued straight along Burrough Street past the driveway entrance. As the cruiser raced up the driveway, Jeff spotted the Camaro at the tail end of the traffic line, discreetly following the course of the other cars in line, but his view was quickly cut off as the Interceptor crested the hill.

Over the hilltop, the driveway pitched downward into a rectangular lot smattered with cars, with four idled cruisers parked in the far spaces abutting an open grass lawn. The sergeant kept his cruiser along the curb to the right of the lot, continuing onto the wide asphalt sidewalk leading to the entrance doors of the police station. Twenty feet down the sidewalk, he jammed the shifter into park and popped his door open with the motor still idling and the lights still flashing. He stepped out into the rain, cursing again at the sight of the news van rounding the hilltop.

A moment later Jeff's door flew open. "Get out," Hyrst growled.

Jeff slid over and slowly swung his feet out of the vehicle, cautiously placing them on the wet pavement as he eyed the sky for falling rain. Hyrst grabbed him by his vest and yanked him free of the cruiser with a powerful jerk before shoving him forward into the arms of a boyish policeman approaching along the sidewalk.

"Hey, watch it! Ya big goon!" Jeff shouted. "I got rights, ya know!"

Hyrst whipped out his club and pointed it at Jeff's nose. "You've got as much rights as a bug on my windshield. You'd best start walking with Officer Carmella before I take forcible action against you!"

Jeff grudgingly offered an arm to Officer Carmella, annoyed that such a young and diminutive officer would be the one to finally escort him into custody. Still, with the gargoyle Hyrst lurking behind him, looking for an excuse to bash his skull in, he realized it was better to swallow his pride and comply without further objection. Carmella led him down the same hallway where he had first met Cindy, through the familiar door to the left into the lobby of the police station.

Inside, two more policemen awaited his arrival; they each took him by an arm as the thick metal latch of a heavy wooden door buzzed open. They passed through the doorway into the dispatch room, where Detective Shelnick lingered behind a female dispatcher with a coffee mug in hand. He directed them toward the booking room to their right, but a booming voice from the back of the room halted everyone in their tracks. "Bring him back here," Chief Wellis ordered.

Detective Shelnick shook his head. "No, Matt. No questions until we book him."

Chief Wellis craned his neck to see Sergeant Hyrst pulling the security door shut behind the entourage. "Uh, Bob? Would you bring Mr. Hollister back this way, please?"

"Yes, sir." Hyrst stepped forward and gripped Jeff by the elbow, jerking him away from his subordinates. The sergeant steered him away from Detective Shelnick and toward the entrance of the rear corridor where the police chief stood.

"That's not standard procedure, Matt!" Shelnick yelled. "He hasn't been booked yet!"

Chief Wellis stepped up to the detective. "We're talking about my daughter," he whispered hoarsely.

Shelnick grabbed his arm. "You've worked so hard to get him. Don't blow it now."

As they debated, Sergeant Hyrst escorted his suspect down the corridor, squeezing Jeff's elbow tighter as they walked. They passed two closed doors to the left before slowing for a short corridor to the right that led to three holding cells, each empty with its steel door ajar. Hyrst started Jeff toward the holding cells, but Chief Wellis caught up and tapped him on the shoulder before pointing to a black camera bubble mounted on the ceiling. "Follow me," he murmured as he continued down the corridor.

Jeff glanced back to Detective Shelnick standing at the end of the hallway with his hands on his hips. He tried to call out to the detective, but Hyrst pulled him away from the holding cell corridor and pushed him farther down the hallway. At the end of the long corridor, Chief Wellis unlocked a door on the left with a badge reader, holding it open long enough for Hyrst to shove Jeff inside. The chief shouted an indistinguishable order at Detective Shelnick before retreating into the room and squeezing the door shut with a metallic click.

The hair on Jeff's neck bristled as he scanned his surroundings, for he knew he was in no holding cell or monitored interrogation room. Venetian blinds covered the tall windows before him, fully lowered and tightly drawn shut, allowing only minimal shards of grim daylight through its slits. The soft beige carpet, the pinewood desk, and the collection of diplomas, plaques, and photographs displayed about the walls all led him to the swift and unnerving conclusion that this was the chief's private office, and no one—not even the good detective—would muster the courage to challenge their powerful boss on behalf of a hated juvenile delinquent.

Jeff tried to remain cool despite his heartbeat pounding in his ears. He nodded toward the desk phone and asked, "Is this where I get to call my lawyer?"

The two lawmen exchanged subtle smirks and then Hyrst grabbed Jeff by the collar, hurling the handcuffed boy across the room with all the strength in his beefy arms. Jeff flew over a wooden client chair before crashing on top of the desk, sending the telephone, computer monitor, and numerous picture frames scattering across the floor. He slid across the polished desktop to land prone upon the armrests of a leather swivel chair that promptly toppled over, spilling him onto the floor. Painfully he rolled to his knees, but Chief Wellis was already upon him, lifting him by his vest again and pinning him up against the back wall.

Jeff's face reddened as the man gripped his collar. "You cops are all alike!"

"I'm not a cop now, I'm Cindy's a father!" the chief roared. "Where's my daughter? You son of a bitch!"

Before Jeff could answer he was airborne again, this time careening into the venetian blinds and the hard glass windows they obscured. He backpedaled frantically to maintain his footing before toppling to the floor and landing upon his cuffed hands. Cowering against the wall beneath the windows, he raised his feet in defense of the advancing men, terrified by the chief's rage and the sergeant's sadism, and keenly aware that any rights or standard procedures that might protect him were locked somewhere outside the thick wooden door.

The blue Camaro turned left from Burrough Street onto Sandal Drive, a back road climbing a long, steady ridge rising behind the Public Safety Complex. At the top of the hill, Axle turned the car about across the clear opposite lane and pulled onto the shoulder of a curve overlooking the rear of the police station. He shifted into neutral, letting the engine idle as he turned to his two friends. "So what do we do now?"

Bumbles leaned forward from the back seat. "We gotta say something. We gotta tell the cops."

Crazy Legs maintained an unwavering stare upon the brick building. "That won't do us any good."

"Well, we better do something pretty quick," Bumbles said. "Curly said—"

"Curly said not to tell the cops," Axle snapped. He cast a nervous glance in the rearview mirror. "Look, maybe we should just go back. Mick's gonna throw a fit when he finds out we took the car. If we tell Curly that Jeff's in jail, maybe it'll change things."

Crazy Legs waved him off. "We can't trust Curly for anything. As far as Mick goes, he's satisfied just holing up in his living room. Jeff would be out here looking for opportunities."

"What opportunities? He's busted. It's game over, dude." Axle shifted the car into gear again. "We're gonna get busted too if we sit here much longer. C'mon, let's go."

"No!" Bumbles batted his palm against Axle's headrest. "Let me out!"

"Well, what are you gonna do?"

"I don't know. Something. Anything." Bumbles sighed. "Look, Jeff saved my life. I gotta help him somehow. At least I gotta try."

Crazy Legs scratched his chin. "Whatcha thinking? Fire alarm? Bomb scare?"

Axle shook his head. "They'll never believe it. They'll suspect it was us. And even if we get them out of the building, we'll never get near him."

Bumbles frowned. "Thanks, buzzkill."

"Just keeping it real."

Suddenly Crazy Legs pointed to the building. "Did you guys just see that?"

Bumbles craned his neck forward. "See what?"

"Those window blinds..." The scout's voice trailed off. He studied the building a moment longer before popping his door open. "C'mon, follow me."

Axle killed the motor. "What is it?"

Crazy Legs stepped out of the car and tilted the seat forward for Bumbles to exit. "Maybe an opportunity. Hurry."

The skinny boy barely waited for his friends to join him in front of the car before running down the slick grassy hill toward the windowless rear wall of the brick building. At the far end of the wet lawn two hundred feet long, bright blue lights continued to flash atop Squad Car Two as the two TV reporters huddled beneath an umbrella beside the news van, one holding a microphone and the other a video camera. Crazy Legs reached the cover of the brick wall first, crouching behind the corner to peer down the long side of the building toward the front walk, while the other two Hurricanes slid up beside him a few seconds later.

"Now what?" Axle panted.

"Wait here." Crazy Legs crept forward to the edge of the closest window. As he did, the blinds shook violently as if struck from the other side. He retracted at first, but then he peered through a gap in the newly damaged slats before returning to the cover of the rear wall. "Jeff's in there with Hyrst and Chief Wellis," he whispered. "They're roughing him up pretty good."

Bumbles started forward. "Let's bust him out!"

"Wait!" Crazy Legs grabbed him by the arm before pointing to the four idle cruisers at the edge of the parking lot. "They got guns and they got cars. How far do you think we'll get?"

Axle frowned. "We need a diversion."

Bumbles stepped to the corner of the building. "What's the one thing a politician hates?" His friends shrugged, and he smiled at them with a mischievous twinkle in his eye. "Bad press."

Crazy Legs nodded. "I like it! But what about all those cop cars?"

Axle pulled a Swiss Army knife from his pocket and opened the blade. "I'm on it!"

"Hold on!" Crazy Legs said. "What if we all don't make it back?"

"I left the keys in the ignition." Axle patted Bumbles on the shoulder. "Ready?"

Bumbles drew a deep breath. "Let's go!"

The two boys trotted off through the rain in separate directions, while Crazy Legs crouched low beside the corner of the building, waiting for their opportunity to fully develop.

Inside the corner office, Sergeant Hyrst pressed Jeff up against the blinds with a forearm beneath his chin. "Tough gang leader," he said. "Not so tough now."

Chief Wellis folded his arms across his chest and leaned against his desk. "What part about staying away from my daughter didn't you understand?"

Jeff strained to speak. "I'll tell you what I know. But you gotta do something for me first."

Hyrst grunted. "Mention your lawyer again and I'll pop your head like a zit."

Jeff turned to reveal the handcuffs behind his back. "Take these off."

"Good one, Hollister," Hyrst said. "I don't think so."

"C'mon, they're killing me!" Jeff glanced at the chief. "Where am I gonna go?"

The chief studied Jeff's eyes for a moment. "Take 'em off," he told the sergeant.

Hyrst bristled. "Chief—"

"My daughter's life is on the line. Take them off or give me your keys. That's an order."

Hyrst spun Jeff around to face the blinds, leaning his captive over the wide sill as he fumbled to insert a key into the cuffs. The sergeant bent his wrists sharply for better access to the keyhole, while the chief leaned closer to ascertain the reason for the delay. Wincing, Jeff gazed through the tattered blinds, where he detected a shadow beyond the glass, perhaps even an eyeball peering back at him through a gap in the blinds.

"Jeez, Bob. Why so tight?" the chief asked.

"Public Enemy Number One, remember?" Hyrst snapped the cuffs open and fastened them to his belt. "Let him file a complaint. I'm just doing my job."

Jeff rubbed the welts on his wrists as he turned back around. "What's that, town thug?"

Hyrst grabbed the handle of his baton. "Why, you little —"

"Back off, Sergeant," the chief said. "This is about Cindy. Let's hear it, Jeff."

Jeff swallowed hard. The Hurricanes and Tornadoes had always shared an implicit understanding that ratting to the police was a contemptible act, but the scope of his quandary overrode such juvenile pacts now. "I was with her last night. We were on the boat. We were minding our own business when two guys in a canoe attacked us. They firebombed us. That's how it burned. We jumped overboard and swam ashore."

A glint of hope kindled in the chief's eyes. "She swam ashore with you?"

"Yes. I swear I would never hurt her," Jeff said. "We were on the shore, safe and sound."

Hyrst glared at him skeptically. "So why'd you leave her there?"

"I didn't. She left me. She told me to get out of her life, and then she was gone."

"But if you were just minding your own business, why —"

The chief held up his hand to stifle Hyrst's questioning. He returned to his desk and leaned back against it again, stroking his mustache with his thick fingers. "If what you say is true, where do you think she is now?"

Jeff shrugged. "I don't know. She was pretty upset. She mentioned Shannon."

Hyrst grimaced. "C'mon, Matt. You're not falling for this bull, are you? He's hiding something. It's Jeff Hollister, for Chrissake."

Chief Wellis picked up his telephone from the floor and set it back on the desk. He lifted the receiver and quickly punched in a phone number on the keypad. "I don't know, Bob. Some of it makes sense. The fire marshal thinks an accelerant started the fire, but the gas tank was still intact." He paused a moment before holding the receiver up in the air. "No answer at Shannon's house."

"What about the guys in a canoe?" Hyrst asked. "Can you identify them?"

"I sure can. I can also tell you who shot Lionel Armstrong and who ambushed the two cops in my yard. And you know what? It wasn't me."

Hyrst's face reddened. "Yeah? What about the Nelson kid? Know anything about him? Don't get all righteous on us, Hollister. We've got the goods on you. You're going to prison!" A sharp knock at the door startled him. "We're busy!" he barked.

Chief Wellis stepped to the door and opened it to reveal Officer Carmella standing in the hallway. "What is it, Jason?"

"TV reporters are back, Chief."

"Tell 'em to get lost. I already told them no comment."

"I know, but they're interviewing some kid in a Hurricane jacket on the front sidewalk. He says he saw Sergeant Hyrst roughing up Jeff Hollister in the plaza parking lot and that he's got a video to prove it."

Jeff held his breath. The trailing blue Camaro, the shadow at the window, the commotion on the walk—what was transpiring outside the room?

Chief Wellis glowered at Hyrst. "Four days until the election and you're squeezing a local kid in a public parking lot. What's the matter with you?"

The burly sergeant rushed to the door with eyes bulging and nostrils flaring. He brushed Carmella aside and stormed down the hallway. "Where is he? I'll fix the little twerp!"

"Better hurry, Sarge!" Carmella yelled. "I think they're streaming live!"

Chief Wellis stepped to the doorway to watch Hyrst storm down the hallway. "Call the Portland rescue team," he told Carmella. "Tell them they can stand down for now."

Carmella raised an eyebrow. "Good news about your daughter?"

"Maybe. Keep an eye on Bob. He's pretty wound up."

The chief shut the door and ambled across the room, stooping to retrieve a family photograph from the carpet before setting it on the desktop again. "I know this probably feels like the end of the line, Jeff," he said, picking up his stapler from the floor. "But it doesn't have to be that way."

Jeff slunk toward the windowsill and peered over his shoulder to glimpse the lawn through the tattered blinds. "End of the line, sir?"

The chief continued to pick up the other items scattered across the floor. "If what you say is true—if Cindy is okay—there might be a chance for you to catch a break."

Jeff turned to face the chief again. "How so?"

"Turn witness against the gangs and help us find the missing guns."

Jeff leaned back against the sill. "That's one way to go, I guess."

Just then there was a loud rap against the glass, and he heard his name shouted from outside the window.

"What the hell was that?" The chief rushed to the window before pointing at the wall behind the desk. "Stand over there!"

The chief spread the blinds with his fingers to peer outside while Jeff backed to the desk. He lifted the telephone from the desktop and stepped up behind the chief, promptly swatting him over the back of the head with a clang. The chief groaned and slumped to the floor as Jeff dropped the phone beside him; he reached up and ripped the center blinds down to reveal Crazy Legs outside the window, frantically waving his arms. The skinny boy glanced urgently toward the front walk before facing Jeff again.

"Hurry!" he called.

Jeff spun about and grabbed the wooden chair set at the front of the desk, raising it high over his head before launching it at the center window with all his might. The chair sailed through the pane with a terrific crash, showering both the chief and the lawn with broken glass. The deafening sound and the sight of the chair tumbling across the lawn caught everyone's attention on the distant walkway, and jaws dropped at the sight of Jeff Hollister jumping from the windowsill onto the muddy lawn. The cameraman pivoted toward the commotion, but Sergeant Hyrst shoved the reporter Flynn aside and drew his service gun. He strode aggressively across the walkway in front of his blinking cruiser and stopped at the edge of the lawn with his feet spread apart and his pistol clenched firmly in both hands.

"Freeze, Hollister!" he ordered. "You are in my sights!"

Jeff stopped, for he knew Hyrst had a clean shot. He raised his hands slowly and warily glanced back toward the front entrance, only to see Bumbles brushing past Flynn and sprinting across the walkway. An errant shot rang out as Bumbles tackled Hyrst to the ground; they wrestled upon the wet grass while Carmella rushed in to assist his superior and the cameraman turned his focus upon the fray.

"Run, Jeff!" Bumbles yelled as Hyrst pinned him to the grass.

Crazy Legs ran up and yanked at Jeff's arm. "This way!"

Jeff dashed after his friend across the slippery lawn as Axle ran on a convergent course to his left. They met at the base of the steep embankment and quickly scaled it to the shoulder of the road where the Camaro was parked. Crazy Legs arrived at the car first; he opened the passenger door and pulled the seat forward while Axle rounded the front of the car and climbed into the driver's seat. Jeff lumbered to the top of the hill and dove into the back seat of the car as the engine roared to life.

Crazy Legs clambered into the front passenger seat and slammed the door behind him. "Go!"

Axle cut the steering wheel to the left and punched the gas, spinning the nose of the Camaro completely about on the wet pavement before straightening the wheels and accelerating up Sandal Street. "We're just gonna leave Bumbles behind?"

"We have to!" Crazy Legs said. "He'll be okay."

Jeff looked out the back window before leaning forward between the seats. "What the hell were you guys thinking? You're in deep shit now!"

"We had no choice," Crazy Legs told him. "We gotta get you back to Mick's."

"No way. No time for that." Jeff reached down his pants and pulled out the folded money envelope from his pants. He slid the bills out and peeled off seven of them before tossing the remainder in his friend's lap. "Here's the money. I gotta get outta town fast. Pull over somewhere and I'll drop you off."

Crazy Legs folded the bills in his hand. "You don't understand. It's not about the money."

Axle glanced into the mirror. "Curly called Mick's house ten minutes after you left. He wants to talk to you."

"Yeah, right." Jeff said. "I'd rather sing Jingle Bells on the chief's front steps than talk to that son of a bitch right now."

Crazy Legs looked him straight in his eyes. "He says he has Cindy. He says he's gonna kill her if you don't talk to him by ten o'clock."

The scout's words hung heavy in the air, for the worry that had been nagging Jeff the past hour was now directly in his face. Still, he continued to deny the notion. "He's bluffing. He probably saw the news. He's just messing with my head."

"Are you gonna take that chance?" Crazy Legs asked. "Without even talking to him?"

Jeff shook his head. "We'll never make it. This car sticks out like a sore thumb. The cops will be all over us in two minutes."

Axle pulled out his phone. "I can call in an accident across town. It might tie 'em up."

Jeff frowned. "Too late. What about the cars back there?"

"I cut the valve stems on their tires. It'll give you a head start anyway."

"Good work. Don't know if it's enough."

"It all comes down to one thing," Crazy Legs said. "Whether you give a damn or not."

Jeff sighed with exasperation, for he knew his friend was right. He pointed at the stereo clock on the dashboard. "You'd better step on it, Axle. We only got five minutes to get there."

Axle tossed his phone into the skinny boy's lap. "Call Denny and make sure he's ready for us." He hit the gas and they all slid back in their seats while the Camaro raced even faster up and down the slick hills of Sandal Street, back toward Hurricane territory.

Moments later the Camaro careened onto Poplar Street and splashed through the gutter to race up the Landrys' driveway. The garage door rolled up swiftly before it, and Denny pulled the door down just as quickly after the car slid to a stop inside the bay. The three boys climbed out of the car, and Axle handed Jeff the keys. "Sweet ride," he said. "Glad I got to drive it one more time."

Denny brushed past him for the entry door to the house. "Mick wants your asses upstairs now. He's plenty pissed."

He bounded up the staircase to his right while Axle rolled his eyes and dutifully followed. Crazy Legs squeezed between the front bumper and the garage wall before entering the house after them. Jeff dallied behind, closing the door and climbing a short flight of carpeted stairs to the front landing of the split-level home.

Mick's voice boomed from the upstairs living room. "...so you just steal the keys out of my pocket when I'm in the shower?"

Axle stood erect at the top of the stairs. "I didn't steal anything. They weren't yours in the first place."

"Don't get smart, Alex. I'll lay you out right here!" Mick turned to the skinny boy arriving at the top of the stairs. "So, where's Bumbles?"

Crazy Legs stepped up to Axle's side. "The cops got him."

Jeff climbed the second flight of stairs and stepped to the edge of the living room behind Crazy Legs. He locked eyes with Mick standing bare-chested beside the burgundy picture window curtains with the Hurricane leader's face turning brighter shades of red. "How the hell did *that* happen?" he asked.

"Jeff got busted by the cops," Crazy Legs explained. "We broke him out but Bumbles got caught. He knew what he was doing."

Mick stared Jeff up and down. "So I'm losing my men to spring this deserter out of jail?"

Jeff winced. "I'm not here to make nice, Mick. I'm here about a phone call. Feel free to rant all you want once I'm gone."

Mick leveled a finger at him. "Cut the attitude, Jeff. You come over here uninvited asking for money, you get one of my guys arrested, and now you're on the verge of blowing our cover and dragging the rest of us down with you. The cops have been down this street three times already, and I got your big blue car sitting in my garage. I'm the leader of the Hurricanes now, so you're gonna listen to what I have to say. Got it?"

Jeff folded his arms across his chest. "Fine. So what's up with Curly?"

Mick's agitation mellowed to plain disgust. "He called right after you left. He didn't say what he wanted. He said he'd call one more time and that you'd better be here when he did. You know where the phone is."

Jeff furrowed his brow and backed into the kitchen where a cordless phone hung on the wall. Crazy Legs leaned back against the staircase post in frustration, clearly abashed by the volatile dynamic between his friends. Mick turned to peer through the split in the center of the drawn curtains, snapping his fingers a moment later and motioning his friends forward. Denny sprang from the recliner to join Axle by their leader's side.

"Check it out," Mick said. "Spy."

Axle squinted through the foggy window at the windswept church grounds across the street. "How can you tell?"

Denny pointed and laughed. "Look! His sneakers are sticking out at the bottom of that bush. What a moron!"

The shrill ring of the kitchen phone pierced their conversation. Jeff snatched the receiver off the hook before the second ring. "Yeah?"

Curly's voice screeched in his ear. "Hollister!"

Jeff wandered back to the top of the stairs as the Hurricanes looked on intently. "What do you want?"

"Aw, c'mon, Hollister. You don't sound too happy to hear from me," Curly said. "What about all the good times we've had? Like that tender moment out on the lake last night. Big bad Jeff Hollister and Little Miss Law an' Order cuddled up like two lovebirds on a boat. Now one of the lovebirds is locked up, all alone and scared. She's a very pretty girl, Hollister. Too bad she made the mistake of going out with you."

"She's not going out with me anymore."

"So I heard. It's all the same to me, Jeffy. If you don't care, then don't worry about it. Maybe you'll read about her someday. You know, skeletal remains, dental records. Stuff like that."

Jeff squeezed the phone. "You bastard. I'm gonna—"

"Don't threaten me, Hollister! You are in no position to threaten me! Now, if you do exactly what I tell you, she might live. You won't, but she might."

Jeff drifted into the living room. "Let me talk to her—"

"Yeah, that ain't happening. She's not even with me right now. Hopefully JJ's treating her right, but I can't guarantee anything. Let's just assume she's okay."

"You're bluffing."

"Okay then. See ya."

"Wait!" Jeff blurted out. He closed his eyes and drew a deep breath. "What do you want from me?"

"Real simple. Your life for hers. You got until noon to meet me. The Portland Mining Company. There's a cabin on the hilltop. Don't be late." Curly paused. "And no cops. If I see any cops or any Hurricanes—anyone at all besides you—then I'm not gonna treat her so nice anymore. Got it?"

"Yeah, I got it. Portland Mines. I'll be there."

"I'm looking forward to it, Hollister."

The line clicked dead, and the color drained from Jeff's face as he returned the phone to its hook on the kitchen wall. He walked back to the top of the stairs and stared numbly across the living room at the Hurricanes.

Crazy Legs stepped forward and shook him by the arm. "What did he say?"

He struggled to say the words. "I gotta meet him by noon or he's gonna kill her."

Axle and Denny gasped, but Mick simply turned back toward the picture window. Crazy Legs slipped past Jeff and snatched the kitchen phone from its mount. "That's it. I'm calling the cops," he said.

"No! No cops! He's gonna kill her if he sees a cop." Jeff drew a deep breath. "I have to go by myself. That's what he said."

Axle grimaced. "Right. He's got a hostage, he's got an accomplice, and he's got a gun. Sounds fair to me."

Jeff absorbed Axle's blunt assessment and hung his head in despair while his three friends mulled his predicament, all at a loss for words. Finally he looked up to the solitary figure at the window and walked across the living room to him. "I need a favor from you," he said.

Mick pointed outside. "Spy's gone. Curly calls and he splits. Coincidence?"

Jeff strained to comprehend his point. "I don't know. Listen, I need the gun."

Mick pulled a fresh pack of cigarettes and took one out before stuffing the pack back into his pocket. "Don't get too worked up, Jeff. You can't trust Curly one bit."

"I hear you. I'm asking you for a favor. As a friend."

"He probably saw the news, and now he's just messing with your head."

"I can't take that chance. Can I have the gun?"

Mick lit his cigarette and took a long drag before exhaling slowly, "Sorry, Jeff, I don't think that's in anyone's best interest right now," he said earnestly.

Jeff digested Mick's response for a moment. He straightened up abruptly and bolted for the staircase with his car keys in hand.

Axle followed him. "What do you want us to do, Jeff?"

"Just stay outta my way!" Jeff growled. He bounded both flights of stairs and slammed the inner garage door shut as he exited the house. A moment later everyone could hear the sound of the rolling garage door rumbling through the house, followed by the roar of the Camaro's engine.

Crazy Legs turned to Mick. "What did you say to him? Why'd he run out of here like that?"

Mick shrugged, aloof. "He wanted the gun, I said no. It's my gun. I'll do what I want with it." He snapped his fingers and cussed. "The money! He didn't give me the money! Denny, go stop him! Quick!"

Denny broke for the stairs, but Crazy Legs grabbed him by the arm. The skinny boy pulled the wad of hundred-dollar bills from his sweatpants pocket and threw it across the living room. "There's your stinking money!" he cried.

Mick watched in astonishment as the bills fluttered to the carpet. "Hey!" he objected.

Crazy Legs rushed downstairs to the landing and yanked open the front door, but he stopped to point up through the balusters at his leader. "He's your best friend! And you're just going to sit here while he heads off to die!" He pushed the storm door open and grabbed the knob of the front door. "If that's what being a Hurricane is all about, then I'm ashamed to call myself one!"

The skinny boy stormed outside and slammed the door shut so hard it rattled the glass in the picture window. Mick pulled the curtains back to watch his scout running after the Camaro racing up Birch Street, while Denny and Axle diverted their eyes away and occupied themselves with retrieving the scattered bills from the carpet.

Finally the Hurricane leader turned away from the window to face his two remaining friends. "Who's got a car?"

Axle took the money from Denny and laid the entire pile on the coffee table. "Not sure. Brain said his mother has the flu. Maybe she stayed home from work."

Mick turned to Denny. "Text him. Get him out of class."

Denny shook his head. "Can't. He's in calculus right now. His teacher has a no-phone policy."

"Then go to school and get him. Don't take no for an answer. Text me with an update." Mick turned to Axle. "Where's TJ right now?"

"I don't know. Gym, probably."

"You guys are supposed to know this stuff." Mick took a final drag from the cigarette before snuffing it out in an ashtray. "Find him and meet me at the fort in half an hour."

"What fort?" Axle asked.

Mick clapped his hands at them. "C'mon! Move it!"

Denny and Axle jumped at his prodding and rushed downstairs to the foyer landing, Once beyond their leader's view, they exchanged keen nods and fist bumps before rushing outside into the rain to embark upon their newly assigned duties.

CHAPTER 13

T HE SMART THING to do was to get out of Salisbury while the getting was good. As the Camaro slid to a stop at the intersection of Arrow Drive, Jeff knew his quickest escape route lay to the right, on the back roads of Salisbury toward Route 53 and eventually to Interstate 88. At best he had ten minutes to leave town, for in spite of Axle's handiwork, there were still police cruisers in service, and they would surely be converging on Hurricane territory before long. He also knew that Sergeant Hyrst's manhandling would feel like a Swedish massage compared to what he could expect if the cops had another crack at him. They might even try to kill him.

As he readied to turn the car onto Arrow Drive, however, he spotted through the beating wipers Willie Freeman sprinting across the street fifty yards to his right, straight for Craig's home on Sapphire Lane. Jeff had assumed that the Almond Lake attack was a rogue operation orchestrated by Curly, but a Tornado spy in Hurricane territory suggested that Craig still had his finger in the pie somehow. He gritted his teeth and hit the gas, rocking the Camaro on its suspension as it sailed over the crest of Arrow Drive to land upon Diamond Street in Tornado territory.

Half a minute and two squealing turns later, he skidded to a halt outside the Matthews residence before backing swiftly into the empty driveway. He hopped out with the motor still running and dashed up the slippery cement steps to the front door, where he heard frantic footsteps bounding down the staircase from inside the house. The doorknob turned, but he met stiff resistance from the other side, so he lowered his shoulder and rammed it hard against the door. The jamb splintered and the door burst open, knocking Craig backward onto the staircase rising behind him.

"What do you want?" he cried with his hands held out defensively before him.

Jeff stepped into the foyer, towering over the Tornado leader as he kicked the broken door shut. "You know what I want! Call Curly off!"

"I don't know what you're talking about—"

"You're lying!" Jeff pulled him from the staircase by his collar and slammed his back against the door. "I know you're in on this somehow!"

"I don't know where he is! He's on his own page now!" Craig regained his composure in spite of Jeff's grasp on his collar. "Why do you think we didn't beat you down yesterday? I still want a truce."

Jeff sneered. "I've heard that line before—"

Craig managed a smirk. "So, it was kinda fun duking it out with you guys again. But I didn't want Armstrong to die, and I don't want this. It's all gone too far."

Jeff eased his grip. "Yeah? Then why the spy?"

"We saw the news. We were just looking for information," Craig said. "That's all, Jeff. I swear. Tell me where they are, and I'll do whatever I can to help."

Jeff glared into his old adversary's eyes. He wanted to

believe the Tornado leader, but there had been too many lies in the past to trust him now. Instead, he mashed Craig's face against the door with an open palm. "Just keep your nose out of it. If anything happens to her, I'm coming after you!"

He pushed Craig aside and forced the broken door open, stepping outside just as Willie ran up the cement steps. Without another word, he shoved the spy off the top step into the nearby bush before running across the front lawn and climbing into his car again.

Craig emerged from the house and stood on the front steps, watching the Camaro back out into the street and race away as Willie climbed out of the bush. "Find the others," he told his spy. "Meet me outside the pool hall in twenty minutes. And don't let anyone see you this time!"

As Willie ran off down Sapphire Lane, the Camaro raced back up the hill to Ruby Road. Jeff sped down the short road to Diamond Street, blowing through a stop sign in a sharp left turn on his way out of enemy territory. He braked to stop at the Arrow Street intersection again, this time from the opposite direction, but a long flatbed trailer stacked with lumber reached the intersection before him and slowly accelerated toward Burrough Street. Jeff spotted his baseball cap on the back seat and grabbed it, pulling it on his head and cursing beneath his breath in frustration as the flatbed truck inched forward. When it finally cleared the intersection, he prepared to turn left again, only to spot Crazy Legs splashing through the rain in his gray running suit, his arms flailing as he ran downhill along Birch Street.

"Jeff, wait!" he cried out.

Jeff diverted his eyes and accelerated up Arrow Drive. "Sorry, buddy. I'm on my own now."

As he sped away, he spotted in his rearview mirror the reflection of his friend standing at the intersection with his hands on his hips, the white wisps of his breath swirling in the cold, moist air. The car passed over a crest in the road, and

Crazy Legs vanished from view, but not before Jeff glimpsed him starting to run in the same direction. He regretted leaving his friend behind, but the time had come to stop relying on the Hurricanes, and Crazy Legs was still a Hurricane, after all.

A shudder rattled his spine as he focused on the slick road ahead with peril on his mind. He fastened his seat belt and switched on the radio to calm his nerves, tightening his grip on the steering wheel and pressing the gas pedal closer to the floorboard, while the Camaro rolled along the hills of Arrow Drive as reckless as a roller-coaster, with the wind and weather beating down upon it.

The clock on the cabin wall read ten forty-five, but it offered no second hand for Cindy's benefit as she gnawed at the duct tape binding her wrists. "One minute," she counted quietly before chewing at the tape again.

Footsteps clomped up the wooden cellar stairs, followed by the creak of the flimsy wooden door to the left of the fireplace; JJ returned to the room and shut the cellar door as she rested her hands in her lap with a blank stare at the glowing embers. Seventy seconds had elapsed since he first headed downstairs to disarm the electric fence again.

He tried to follow her listless gaze. "What are you staring at?"

She rolled her eyes toward him. "I was just wondering. Why does Curly hate Jeff so much?"

JJ pulled the hatchet from the bark of the thickest log and sank it into the center of a smaller length of wood. He beat the shorter log against the shale hearth, splitting it in half and tossing one of the halves onto the hot coals. "Everyone hates Jeff. Curly just hates him a little more."

"Do you hate him?"

"He's a Hurricane. Of course I hate him."

"What if he wasn't a Hurricane?" she asked. "What if he was just another guy in school?"

"Jeff Hollister? Just another guy?" He tossed the other half of the log into the fire. "See, you don't really know him yet. You don't know what the Hurricanes have done to us over the years."

"Enough to make you want to kill him?"

JJ shrugged. "It's Curly who wants him dead."

"But just helping him makes you an accomplice to murder. That alone will get you twenty years. Not to mention the kidnapping charge."

"We didn't kidnap you. We're just holding you until Hollister gets here."

"Okay, unlawful restraint. And do you really think Curly will let me go if he kills Jeff?"

JJ set another log on the hearth and drove the blade of the hatchet into the center of its end. He beat it hard against the hearth until it split in half, throwing one of the pieces into the fire and burying the tip of the hatchet into the bark of the other piece. "Don't ask me so many questions," he finally said before stepping to the wooden table.

Cindy fell silent, for she had clearly rattled him. She peered out the casement window to her right and was able to see the very beginning of a dirt road heading down the hilltop toward Quarry Road over a mile away. Soon Curly would return along this path, and his arrival would eliminate any reasonable hope of escape. "Curly's gonna fall sooner or later," she said. "There's still hope for you, but you have to get over your fear of him first."

JJ sat at the table and chuckled. "I ain't afraid of him."

"You looked pretty scared when he pointed that gun at you," she said.

He scratched his goatee as he mulled her remark. "Yeah? What about you?"

She glared at the tape that bound her hands. "I'm scared to death of him. I'd be dead right now if there was a bullet in that chamber."

JJ reached for the deck of cards again. "He knew it was empty. That's why he did it."

"You sure about that?"

He glared at her. "Curly's no monster. He just gets angry easy."

"And then kills people over it?"

JJ looked down to the wooden table and resumed dealing his solitaire game. "You know, it's too bad that big doofus Armstrong had to get in the way. Otherwise, Hollister would be dead already, and I wouldn't have to listen to you right now."

She studied him for a long moment as he began to deal solitaire. "You know, my dad's chief of police—"

"A lot of good that's doing you right now," he said without looking up.

"I'm just saying. I've been around cops all my life. So I learned a little along the way."

"Yeah? So what have you learned so far?"

"Guys like you never fare very well," she said.

He finally looked up. "What do you mean, guys like me?"

"You know. The ones who go along for the ride. The ones who think they can just step aside when the walls come down. My dad says they always look like they got hit by a bus when the judge sends them off to jail. The sad part is they could've changed their fate if they would've just stood up to their bully friends before they got in too deep. But they never do."

JJ laughed. "You think the cops are gonna care who killed Jeff Hollister? They won't even find the body. There's a dozen quarries up the road where the water's five hundred feet deep. A few bricks and a roll of duct tape, and it's sayonara Hollister."

Cindy fell silent again. She studied everything about him as he dealt solitaire on the table: his scraggly goatee, his plaid flannel shirt, his worn-out cowboy boots, even the glowing green hands on his chintzy wristwatch. He acted as if he were an unwitting mule for his lieutenant, but by disclosing their plan to dispose of Jeff's body to her, he revealed his complicity in a plan that Curly intended to kill her as well.

"It's eleven o'clock," she finally said.

JJ kept his eyes cast down. "So?"

"Weren't you supposed to turn the fence back on or something?"

He continued to deal the hand of solitaire as if he had not heard her, but she noticed that the toe of his cowboy boot began to tap subtly on the hardwood floor. Finally he set the cards down and pushed his chair back from the table before standing up and sauntering to the cellar door again. He opened the door and flicked on the cellar light, unaware that her seventy-second count was about to commence for a second time.

As he started down the stairs, she rolled from the couch onto her knees, steadying herself against the armrest with her bound hands until she was able to stand upright. She shuffled quietly across the room to the fireplace mantel and squatted to pull the hatchet from the bark of the thick log. With the count of passing seconds upon her lips, she backed to JJ's chair and sat with the hatchet clenched between her hands. Then she flipped the hatchet over in her lap, cradling it between her knees with the blade facing upward, slicing the tape upon the blade to free her wrists with thirty seconds left in her count. By the time a full minute had elapsed, she had freed her ankles as well.

The sound of boots clomping on the basement steps turned her attention back to the cellar door. Despite her predicament, she did not possess the bloodthirst to wield the hatchet against her captor, so she dropped it on the floor and pushed the table toward the cellar door. The sound of the wooden legs scraping across the hardwood floor sparked a quickening of bootsteps up the stairs, but she jammed the table beneath the latch, pinning JJ on the staircase before he could open the door. Shouting and cursing, he drove his shoulder into the cellar door against the weight of the table, cracking the door from its top hinge.

Cindy ran to the cabin door and threw it open to face the hard rain battering the hilltop outside. She stepped out onto the covered porch and ran past the casement window to her left, stopping at the brink of the rainfall to survey her location for the first time. The cabin hilltop was free of trees and covered halfway with muddy grass that gave way to gray shale that seemed to meld with a grayer sky forty yards away, where the cliff dropped to the lakeshore two hundred feet below. To her right, the dirt access road dipped to the forest tree line eighty yards down the hill, winding into the forest toward the Quarry Road entrance somewhere in the distance. There, she spotted Curly emerging from the tree line, his eyes cast down upon the loose footing of the muddy road. Cold rain pelted her face as she stepped off the porch for the cement pad of a defunct truck scale beneath the windowless wall of the cabin.

Curly looked up from his treacherous footing to see her turn and bolt in the opposite direction. "Hey!" he shouted, breaking into a sprint up the hill.

Cindy ran to the other side of the hilltop, where the access road resumed as a river of rainwater gushing over crevices and stones as it descended into the excavation pits. She hesitated at the top of the slippery chute until a gunshot rang out and a bullet whizzed past her ear. With a scream she dove into the chute, sliding ruggedly down the hill, around a corner, and into a puddle at the bottom. She scrambled to her feet and darted for cover behind a large boulder farther down the road into the mining grounds.

Back inside the cabin, JJ finally burst through the cellar door, barreling past the table and toppling a chair as the playing cards scattered everywhere. He ran out of the cabin and down the porch as Curly reached the top of the hill. "What are you doing?" he asked his cohort.

"What am *I* doing? How did she get away?"

"She tricked me! She locked me in the cellar!"

"You idiot! Hollister's on the way. We need to get her back!"

JJ shielded his eyes from the rain. "Don't shoot her, man! I ain't down with that!"

"You just better hope we find her before Hollister gets here. C'mon!" Curly shoved the pistol in his jacket pocket and started toward the muddy chute with JJ trailing reluctantly behind.

Few cars passed Jeff as he drove along Arrow Drive, for the Friday-morning rush hour had given way to a lull in traffic. The blue light of the stereo clock flashed to eleven o'clock as he turned the Camaro onto Archer Street, its windshield wipers beating out a frantic rhythm against the driving rain. Glowering clouds shrouded his vision as he rounded the highest point of the street and started the long and gradual descent toward a distant intersection. From his vantage point over the valley treetops, he could still discern the red glow of the traffic light at the junction of Route 53, still nearly a half-mile away.

Pangs of doubt roiled his stomach as he sped toward the intersection, for a decision loomed ahead. Accessing the westbound lanes of the interstate highway meant driving straight across Route 53, up a short hill, and beneath an overpass to an entrance ramp on the left. Conversely, the eastbound entrance stood more than a mile to the left down Route 53, toward the Madison city line. Heading west meant the sun-splashed California beaches, a brotherly reunion, and a fresh start just a few thousand miles of asphalt away. In contrast, traveling east meant returning to Almond Lake and the Portland mining site where Curly allegedly awaited, with no guarantee that Cindy was even there. Although his morning had not transpired as envisioned, he still had the money he needed and the open road before him—all that remained to complete his escape was to elude the police long enough to get on the highway and go!

The traffic signal changed to green while he was still thirty yards away, and he punched the gas pedal as if the world might pass him by should he wait through a full red-light cycle. As he neared the intersection, however, an unnerving image flashed in his mind's eye of Cindy, her deep brown eyes staring at him and her lips curled in a warm smile. He couldn't pinpoint the exact origin of the image—maybe it was dancing with him at Train's party or lying together on the boathouse lawn or perhaps simply riding together in his car—but it seemed to encompass the essence of her spirit, halting his breath and jolting his heart just like she had on the night she first met him. Instantly he knew that no decision was required because he had no other choice: he could not leave town with her safety in doubt, even if she despised him, even if it meant sacrificing his freedom or his life to save her. Their split on the lakeshore had pained him immensely, but deep down inside he knew that he was still in love with her. Such a confession surely meant further danger for him, but it also helped to ease the somber ache in his heart.

He gripped the steering wheel and narrowed his eyes on the intersection ahead. "Maybe tomorrow, California," he said under his breath.

Had he continued straight for the westbound entrance, the light at the state road intersection might've stayed green long enough for him to pass beneath it with little notice. As he slowed for the left-hand turn, however, the light flashed to yellow, and it turned red as the Camaro rounded the tight turn onto Route 53, its tires squealing as it slid into the shoulder of the road. Jeff cringed as he steadied the steering wheel and accelerated, eyeing a blue Salisbury police cruiser sitting third in a line of traffic waiting for the light to change green.

Inside the cruiser, Officer Boyd looked up from his mobile terminal to view the blue Camaro whizzing past him. With widening eyes, he switched on his lights and siren, but by the time he maneuvered his cruiser out of traffic the Camaro was already a quarter mile up the road and speeding away. Vehicles in both lanes veered onto the shoulders of the road to clear a path for the cruiser as the officer struggled to turn about and engage in pursuit.

Jeff drove around a slight left curve and moved into the opposite lane to pass a slow orange Beetle, narrowly squeezing back into the right lane ahead of the car as an oncoming commercial van flew by with its horn blaring. His tires gripped better once the road straightened and began to rise, so he gave the engine a little more gas, watching in his rearview mirror as the Beetle pulled aside to give clear passage to Boyd's speeding cruiser. As Jeff neared the eastbound entrance ramp to Interstate 88, he spotted another set of flashing blue lights approaching from behind Boyd's cruiser, rounding the distant curve and closing in fast.

Three slower cars ahead impeded him from gaining speed along the spiraling entrance ramp to the interstate, as the two wailing cruisers narrowed the gap on him from behind. Jeff edged the Camaro onto the shoulder of the ramp, passing the first two cars on the right and nearly striking the third as he swerved across its nose for the open lanes of the highway to his left. Boyd followed him along the right shoulder past the slower cars, while the second cruiser cut sharply over the left shoulder of the entrance ramp; it bounced ruggedly over the inner curb before sliding across three lanes of wet pavement to settle into the passing lane behind the Camaro.

Jeff glimpsed in his rearview mirror at the familiar white Police Interceptor closing in fast, but he also spotted a third flash of blue lights approaching along the passing lane from a point behind the entrance ramp. The Interceptor pulled close to his bumper, blocking his view of the third cruiser as the Camaro inundated its windshield with tire wash, yet Jeff could still discern the distinctive crew cut and the menacing scowl of

Sergeant Hyrst leaning over the steering wheel of his prized new car. Jeff looked forward just in time to veer the Camaro around a slower taxicab, but his sudden move into the center lane forced a heating oil truck to career away in avoidance, consequently hindering the path of Boyd's cruiser as it advanced along the right lane.

The cab driver gestured profanely as the Camaro sped by, while Hyrst blew past him on the left shoulder before steering back into the passing lane. For a brief moment the center lane was clear for Jeff, but even his muscle car could not match the power of Squad Car Two advancing on his left, not without pushing his tires beyond the limit of their grip upon the wet pavement. Hyrst pulled his car even with the Camaro before turning sharply to the right, forcing Jeff to swerve away just inches from the steel front bumper of the oil truck. The truck's horn blared as it lurched even farther to the right, forcing Boyd's cruiser to the fringe of the saturated grass to avoid a collision.

Amid the chaos, Jeff shot a glance at the mirror again. He was finally able to discern the source of the third blue light, a state police cruiser weaving through the braking traffic to close in on Boyd's car. Squad Car Two edged slightly ahead of the Camaro, and Jeff knew if Hyrst could pull the Interceptor completely ahead, he would intentionally spin it out to block the center lane. An overhead highway sign indicated that the Exit 9 ramp was two miles ahead, but Jeff resisted the urge to accelerate toward the ramp, for he could already sense his tires spinning too fast for the slippery conditions. All about him, commuters reacted erratically to the three speeding police cars flanking the highway, slowing and swerving in attempts to give them clear passage.

He saw his open lane rapidly diminishing with the iron bumper of a tractor-trailer looming directly ahead, but a slowing minivan in the left lane prompted Hyrst to duck his cruiser back into the center lane behind him. The minivan blocked his access to the left lane as Boyd's cruiser squeezed him from the right, tailed closely by the state trooper's gray sedan. Hyrst inched his car closer to the bumper of the Camaro, pressuring Jeff to drive ever closer to the chrome rear doors of the truck, while the heavy wash of its mud flaps began to overwhelm the pace of his windshield wipers. The sergeant dropped back a car length and gunned the engine again, prompting Jeff to brace for impact with his elbows locked and his hands gripped tightly upon the steering wheel. The Interceptor slammed hard into the Camaro's rear bumper, sending the car fishtailing side to side as he fought frantically to maintain control.

Hyrst charged the Interceptor forward again, and Jeff cursed as the grill of the cruiser crashed hard enough into his bumper, briefly lifting his rear wheels off the pavement before they settled again. With the chrome doors of the tractor-trailer looming tall before him, he craned forward to glimpse another green highway sign overhead, this one announcing the Exit 9 ramp just a quarter-mile away. Hyrst backed off for another run and Boyd inched his cruiser closer to the Camaro's front tire, while Jeff clenched the steering wheel even tighter, eyeing a sliver of daylight between Boyd's rear bumper and the front grill of the state trooper's car. The Interceptor surged forward yet again, but this time Jeff tapped the brakes and cut the steering wheel sharply to the right, clipping Boyd's rear bumper on his way toward the exit ramp.

Boyd's cruiser slid sideways along the right lane, away from the point of contact, while Hyrst stomped on his brake pedal in a panic, the soft target of the Camaro's trunk swiftly replaced by the cast-iron bumper of the tractor-trailer. The wet pavement prevented a quick stop, however, and the Interceptor slammed hard into the bumper, buckling its hood on the right side and deploying the airbag into the sergeant's face. The Interceptor spun wildly to the left until its tires caught the spongy grass at the edge of the freeway median; it flipped into the air and landed upon its hood, snuffing its flashing rooftop lights with a terrific pop. The car rolled over twice before landing on its wheels in a cloud of steam and smoke in the center of the median.

Jeff had no time to gloat over Hyrst's demise, for Exit 9 was already upon him. He clung to the steering wheel with white knuckles as his tires hopped the curb and sailed over the grassy divider for the rising exit ramp. When the car landed on asphalt again, he cranked the steering wheel hard to follow the turn, but centrifugal force pulled the Camaro's left rear quarter panel hard against the metal guardrail with a sickening crunch. Finally the curve straightened out, allowing him to steer away from the guardrail, but he could feel the ragged fender gnawing at the rear tire as he approached the upcoming intersection. Behind him, the trooper's gray cruiser followed him steadily up the ramp with its siren wailing and lights flashing.

The Camaro blew past the stop sign at the end of the ramp in a wide, squealing left turn onto the main road. A half dozen cars waited at the upcoming intersection for the light to change to green, forcing Jeff to cross over the yellow center line into the clear oncoming lane. Nearing the intersection, he spotted in the rearview mirror the trooper's sedan careening through the exit ramp stop sign in hot pursuit. The green light flashed for the cars at the intersection, but Jeff blasted his horn at them as he turned the Camaro left again in a truncated arc through the intersection onto Dexter Road. The trooper followed in kind, sounding his siren in loud, quick blurts to keep the motorists at bay. He raced past their motionless cars and sped through the intersection to pull up close to Jeff's battered rear bumper.

The siren fell silent in favor of a loudspeaker. "Pull over, Hollister!" he ordered. "There's nowhere to go."

Of course, the trooper was probably right. Somewhere ahead, roadblocks surely awaited with armed policemen hell-bent on stopping him from his desperate flight. Soon his run would likely end and perhaps his life as well, but for now he faced just one state cop and a lagging Salisbury townie with the turnoff to Portland Village Road looming ahead. Whatever limited options remained viable for him, surrender was not one of them, for if Curly was true to his word, then such capitulation might cost Cindy her life.

The trooper pulled even with the Camaro and abruptly turned to the right, ramming into the front quarter panel of Jeff's car with its right fender. Jeff jerked his steering wheel hard against the cruiser to stave it off from running him into the gutter, as the acrid smell of rubbing tires began to fill his car. The cars ground against each other with locked fenders for nearly a hundred feet until Jeff spotted the turn to Portland Village Road; he ripped the steering wheel back to the right, separating their cars as hubcaps flew down the street. The Camaro spun to a halt in the middle of the intersection, directly facing the road to Almond Lake, as the cruiser sailed out of control across Dexter Road; it careened over the shoulder and jumped the opposite curb before crashing headlong into a nearby utility pole. The pole snapped at its base and toppled toward the intersection, severing the overhead power line with a brilliant blue flash and showering sparks upon the road as the nearby streetlamps blinked out.

Jeff stomped on the clutch pedal and shifted into low gear, driving forward as the heavy pole crashed to the pavement behind him. The loosened power lines overhead draped toward his rooftop, but he quickly shifted into second gear, leaving the scene behind as he accelerated up Portland Village Road. He watched in his mirror as the state trooper staggered from his vehicle and pointed down the road after him, while the remaining Salisbury cruiser slowly maneuvered around the pole and the wires to turn onto the road after him.

He shifted into third gear and eased the gas pedal toward the floorboard, grimacing as the steering wheel began to shake in his hands. Passing the cornfield to the right, he glimpsed

Boyd's cruiser swiftly closing in on him, and he knew he could not outrun the patrol car long enough with Quarry Road still several miles away. Nevertheless, he shifted into high gear and drove even faster, concentrating on the road ahead as he gently squeezed the vibrating steering wheel. "C'mon, baby," he begged the car. "Hang on."

The road straightened as it began to climb along the ridge of the steep hill rising to his left while the right shoulder dropped away in favor of a silver guardrail. Ahead, a yellow caution sign reminded him of the imminent mountainside pass, and quickly he recalled Cindy's warnings about Life Star Lane. He let off the gas but was immediately thrust back against his seat as Officer Boyd rammed the Camaro with the grill of his cruiser. Jeff kept a straight course, however, and edged his car closer to the guardrail to keep Boyd from turning him against it. Instead, Boyd slid the cruiser into the vacant oncoming lane and pulled even with the Camaro, turning hard into its mangled front fender to pin it against the metal rail.

Jeff fought for control of his car as it scraped down the guardrail toward the hairpin turn. He glanced over to see Boyd glaring back at him, but the officer's expression quickly changed to sheer horror as he turned to face the road again. The cruiser swerved to the left, allowing Jeff to veer away from the guardrail just as a produce truck rumbled around the corner of the mountain pass. The truck's horn blasted as the driver attempted to straddle the centerline between the two oncoming vehicles but the truck skidded to the right, its front bumper clipping the right front fender of the cruiser. The collision sent the cruiser crashing into the rock wall along the inside of the mountain pass while the truck's bumper crushed its passenger side, pinning it against the wall.

Jeff cringed as he tried to slip his car through the shrinking gap between the guardrail and the thick rear bumper of the truck suddenly pivoting toward him. The bumper grazed the Camaro's left rear fender as it passed, turning the car to the left just as it entered Life Star Lane. Jeff frantically yanked the steering wheel back in response, sending the Camaro at a near right angle toward the heart of the hairpin turn; he cried out in terror as the car ripped through the metal barrier and plunged over the edge of the road for the steep hillside slope. The car pitched left and landed on a clearing along the slope, shearing off a sapling before crashing head-on into a thick oak tree a hundred feet down the hill. His seat belt snapped taut against his chest upon impact and his head smacked the side window as the car rolled left off the tree to stop with its nose pitched downward upon the leafy slope.

Dazed from the impact, he unbuckled his seat belt and slid down painfully against the door. A trickle of blood ran from his temple, but he found his ball cap by his side and pulled it onto his head to cover the wound. He tried to open his door but it would not budge, so he wriggled his feet away from the pedals and climbed from his seat to the steering wheel and then to the center console. Gravity worked against him as he pushed open the passenger door, but he managed to slip his arm outside and pull himself through the opening, wary of a frightening tumble down the hillside should he misstep and fall.

He climbed to the ground and fell back upon the steep slope with the cool raindrops falling upon his face. A full minute passed before he rolled to his knees and staggered to his feet, stumbling forward to behold his father's legacy, pitched forward against the damaged tree with its hood buckled up and its rear wheels still spinning freely in the air. He gazed in astonishment at the tree that had destroyed his car but spared him from a devastating plunge down the steep slope to a gushing stream below. Steam rose from the Camaro's busted radiator, its pristine blue chassis now scarred with dents and scrapes from its battle with the police cruisers along the way.

"Sorry, Dad," he said between halting breaths.

"Hello!" a voice called down from above. Jeff looked up to

see the produce truck driver standing at the edge of the road. The man pulled a cap from his bald head before leaning over the mangled guardrail. "Are you all right?"

Jeff waved a hand over his head, too stunned to shout back.

"I need your help!" the driver cried. "There's a man trapped up here!"

"I can't!" he tried to yell back, but his chest still hurt too much to utter more than a whisper. Instead, he turned and lumbered down the slippery mountainside toward the swollen stream below, leaving the driver to scratch his head in bewilderment at the edge of the roadside.

Mick glared down into the pit of charred plywood and furniture, all that remained of the underground fort. Raindrops pattered upon the colored oak leaves and pine needles over him, but few of them worked their way through the branches to fall upon the Hurricane leader. He stood hunched in silence as if mourning a friend until the rustle of bushes behind him caught his attention. TJ and Axle emerged from the rabbit path and stepped into the clearing, dressed in their Hurricane jackets. They nodded to Mick as they flanked him at the edge of the pit, joining in his melancholy stare into the rubble as the rain fell upon their shoulders.

"Sure was a great fort," Axle said.

TJ kicked a rock into the hole. "Of all their dirty tricks, this was the worst."

"This is just the beginning," Mick said. "I can't tell you what to expect today, but it's probably gonna be dangerous. If you're having second thoughts, speak up now."

"Second thoughts?" Axle said. "What are ya talking about?"

"We're all in, man." TJ glanced about. "Where's Crazy Legs?"

Axle elbowed him gently in the ribs. "Don't ask," he whispered.

Mick's cell phone hummed. He pulled it from his pocket and read it for a moment. "Brain's got a car. They'll be at the 7-Eleven in five minutes. Let's go."

They darted off in single file down the fort path, across the log spanning the ravine now gushing with rainwater. From there, they continued up the slippery pine-needle hill past Mr. Big, over root and rock along the slick forest path until they emerged at the rear of the sand field behind the Upper Plaza. TJ arrived first at the mouth of the path, followed by Axle and lastly Mick, panting from the rapid pace.

"See anything?" he asked with his hands on his hips.

TJ squinted and shook his head. "Not really. It's raining too hard."

"Look at it come down!" Axle exclaimed. "I knew I should've worn my galoshes."

"I'll give you galoshes." Mick stood upright and flicked a finger hard against Axle's earlobe already red from the damp, chilly air. "Quit clowning around."

Axle jerked his head away. "Ow! You asshole!"

Mick grinned and ran out from the cover of the trees, pulling his Hurricanes jacket over his head as he trotted off across the sand field. TJ lowered the bill of his cap and followed, jogging backward and grinning at Axle. "You should've worn a shower cap," he chided his friend. "Then you could've tucked those flappers up inside."

TJ laughed and turned to follow his leader through the deluge of rain, while Axle flipped him a finger before rubbing his painful earlobe between his fingers. He trudged out into the muddy sand field after his friends, but a dozen steps along the way he spotted a shiny metallic object half-buried in the sand. He stopped and scooped up the silvery object and a look of incredulity spread across his face as he realized exactly what he had found. "Hey, TJ!"

TJ turned his head as he continued to splash through the mud puddles. "C'mon, Axle! We ain't got all day!"

"Hurry up, Axle!" Mick bellowed as he neared the stockade fence.

The Hurricane leader jogged past the wood fragments still littering the sand, then through the gaping hole in the fence on his way to the cover of the 7-Eleven store. He leaned back against the red brick wall and peeked around the front corner to see a silver Volvo station wagon idling at the far end of the sidewalk. There were no other cars parked at the storefront, so he stepped out and strolled past the convenience store windows to the passenger side of the Volvo, peering inside the car before opening the door and sliding into the passenger seat.

"Not bad," he said, glancing about the comfortable interior of the car. "Good job."

Brain fidgeted. "I'm dead if my mother finds out I took it. Where's TJ and Axle?"

"They're coming." Mick pulled out a comb and used it to wring the rainwater out of his curly blond hair. "Where's Denny?"

"Inside the store. He told me about Cindy. Unbelievable."

The right rear door flew open, and TJ clambered into the back seat away from the rain. "That Camry by the doughnut shop," he said. "It looks like Zak's brother's car. It might be the Tornadoes."

"You're probably right," Brain said. "I saw Phil and Tony hanging out by the pool hall when I got here, and now they're gone. I also saw two cops drive down Burrough Street, and I've only been here five minutes."

Mick bristled at the mention of cops. He took out a pack of cigarettes and offered it to TJ. "Want one?"

TJ shook his head. "Gotta save my wind for tryouts. You think we'll be back by four?"

Mick shrugged. He stuck a cigarette in his lips and lit it as he eyed the black Toyota across the parking lot. Finally he exhaled the smoke toward the windshield and looked back to

TJ. "As long as the Tornadoes stay clear, you should be back in time. That's all I can tell you."

Brain waved a hand in front of his face. "C'mon, Mick, don't smoke in here! I'll never hear the end of it!"

Mick scowled at him before lowering his window a quarter way down. Axle arrived a moment later, following TJ through the open door into the back seat. He leaned over the seat to display the object he had found. "Check this out," he said. "I think it's Jeff's knife."

"Can't be," Brain said. "I saw it sticking out of Happy Jack's stomach when they threw him in the back of the truck."

TJ took the knife from Axle to inspect it. "Looks clean to me."

Mick mulled his friend's words as he exhaled through the open window. "So what?"

"If Jeff had stabbed Happy Jack with it, there'd be some evidence on it, wouldn't ya think?"

"Who knows? It's pouring rain outside. It probably washed off."

Brain adjusted his glasses and pressed on. "But if it's Jeff's knife, then it clearly exonerates him."

Mick glared at him with petulance. "Exona—*What?* Speak English, bookworm."

Brain sighed. "I *am*—"

Mick held up a hand to silence him and turned to face the boys in the back seat. "Listen to me, all of you. I don't care about your little theories or what you think you saw or any of that crap. You better start focusing now. We got one job to do, and that's to get Curly before he hurts Jeff or his girlfriend. Tell me now if you got a problem with that."

Brain rolled his eyes and TJ handed the knife back to Axle, who tucked it away again. "No problem," they all replied.

"Good," he said. "Now, where the hell is Denny?"

TJ pointed to their fellow Hurricane exiting the 7-Eleven store, carrying a large fountain soda cup in one hand and a bag of potato chips in the other. He scampered to the open rear passenger door of the Volvo in the rain. "Move over," he told Axle.

"I don't want the middle!"

Mick turned and leveled a deadpan stare at Axle, who reluctantly slid over to the center of the seat while Denny climbed in beside him and shut the door. Brain shifted into reverse and backed out of the parking space as Mick craned his neck to look at Denny. "What took you so long? We're already an hour behind."

"I was thirsty." Denny offered him the bag of chips. "Want some?"

Mick grunted and turned forward again while Brain shifted the Volvo into drive before pulling it in a tight circle toward the Upper Plaza entrance. Halfway through the turn, Axle pointed to the black Toyota advancing toward them. "They're following us."

"Step on it," Mick said as the traffic light flashed green. "We gotta lose them."

Brain hit the gas and turned sharply left onto Burrough Street, accelerating quickly until they reached the rear bumper of the next car in line. "I don't even know where I'm going."

"The Portland mines." Denny told him. "I know the way."

"Keep an eye out for cops." Mick told his friends. "And shut your phones off. We don't need anyone pinging us."

The Hurricane leader glanced back to espy the black Camry with its five occupants rolling through the intersection behind them. The Tornadoes quickly pulled up to the rear bumper of the Volvo while Brain squinted through the beating windshield wipers, frustrated by the lethargic traffic constraining them with such an urgent mission ahead of them.

CHAPTER 14

T HE DESCENT FROM the wreckage of the Camaro had been a harrowing and delirious stumble down the steep foothills of Badger Mountain, but as Jeff splashed along the edges of the swollen brook at the bottom of the hill, he felt his wits gradually returning to him. He regretted leaving his bags in the back seat of the Camaro, but more cops were surely on the way, perhaps even with dogs, and he knew his belongings would've only burdened him further. For the moment he heard no sirens or dogs, just the rainfall upon the overhead leaves and the gurgling brook leading toward the cottages of Almond Lake.

He could tell that the cut on his temple was still bleeding, for while blood did not show clearly upon his fingertips when he brushed the wound in the heavy rain, he could occasionally taste it in the corner of his mouth. Ahead, the gushing stream forked in two directions, with its main course continuing south along Portland Village Road and a smaller tributary branching off to the left, flowing beneath the distant wooden bridge. Jeff wallowed along the edge of the powerful stream before wading into the smaller tributary, crossing the shallow leg to a large flat rock that split the waters at the fork. With considerable effort, he climbed atop the sloping rock before collapsing onto his back with the cold rain pelting his face.

Finally he sat up and glanced about his surroundings, reaffirming his solitude before pulling off his hat and stripping down to his bare torso. He tossed his vest and sweatshirt on the wet rock behind him, but he kept his cap in his lap and his T-shirt in his hands, tearing a long strip of cloth from the tail of the shirt and tying it around his head to cover his wound. Satisfied with the fit of the makeshift bandage, he pulled the tattered T-shirt back over his head again and turned for the rest of his clothing, but finding only the vest remaining on the rock. Glancing about in desperation, he spotted his gray Salisbury High hoodie floating away toward the center of the stream, where the rushing current swiftly whisked it from his view.

With a grimace and a curse, he pulled the vest over his shoulders and the ball cap back upon his head, squeezing the cloth bandage tighter against his forehead before stepping from the rock for the far bank of the smaller brook. Following the soggy bank, he passed beneath the wooden bridge, where the tributary snaked through open, grassy banks on the other side, ultimately passing through a wide metal storm pipe leading a robust stream of rainwater beneath Quarry Road toward the lake. He soon emerged from the far end of the storm pipe to behold the glowing amber lights of shoreline cottages, stretching away beneath a dark shroud of stratus clouds. Turning to his left, he embarked on a course parallel to the northern bank, relieved that he would encounter no more public roads on his way to the gate of the mining property.

Now that his car was gone, Jeff figured that the trek to the hilltop cabin would probably take at least another hour, casting Curly's noontime deadline into serious doubt. Wet leaves clung to the legs of his jeans as he trudged through the woods surrounding the northern shore of the lake, while his hands and feet ached from the air temperature that had dropped a full ten degrees since he awoke in the car four hours ago. Still he labored forward, driven equally by the threat of more cops assembling behind him and the relentless timetable of the kidnappers waiting ahead. The more he dwelled upon the passing time, the more his pace increased, from a walk to a trot and finally to a jog amid raindrops that began to feel faintly icy. He pulled the bill of his baseball cap low over his brow and zipped up his vest closer to his neck before dipping a shoulder into the teeth of the wind.

Ten minutes later, he scaled a shallow hill to view the boat launch driveway and the silver gate of the Portland Mining Company stretching beyond the dirt road fork. Rejuvenated by a sense of accomplishment, he ran down the other side of the hill, past the fork and along the muddy road to the chain-link gate of the mining property, where he lunged for its diamond mesh as high as his momentum allowed. He dug his sneaker tips into the holes of the steel mesh while clasping the fence halfway up with his fingers, only to feel the painful shock of electricity coursing across his knuckles. Crying out in pain, he struggled to pull his curled fingers from the mesh as the metal fence recoiled from the force of his lunge. The tips of his sneakers slipped from the fence and gravity broke his painful grip, casting him back onto the muddy access road with an unceremonious splash.

Jeff lay in the middle of the dirt road for a full minute, motionless except for his eyelids blinking in defense of the falling rain. "Ow," he finally said, cradling his throbbing fingers against his belly. He rolled to his knees and rose slowly to his feet, staring dumbfounded at the gate that had just zapped him. A broken chain and padlock lay at his feet amid fresh tire tracks passing through the fence line, yet time had been taken to shut and latch the gate again. These circumstances suggested that Curly might be involved as he so claimed, but Jeff still lacked hard evidence that his enemy's story was true.

Gazing at the treetops overhead, he noticed that most of the limbs had been cleared away five feet to either side of the fence, but one large oak tree farther to the right offered some promise: a high, thick limb that spanned over the fence line. Jeff left the access road and followed the fence about fifty yards to the base of the oak tree, where he promptly jumped up and grabbed hold of its lowest limb. Swiftly he climbed, up the various branches around the tree trunk, until he stood upon the promising bough that stretched eight feet over the top of the ten-foot-tall fence. At first he crawled along the thick branch, but as it thinned farther away from the tree trunk, he flipped over and hung upside down with his hands and ankles wrapped around it like a sloth.

Farther along the diminishing limb, his feet slipped off its wet bark, transferring all his weight to his hands and arms. He dangled for a moment with his back toward the rising hill, clinging to a branch nearly twenty feet off the ground, as he waited for his body to sway to a halt. Once his motion had subsided, he rotated his grip upon the slippery bark to face the hill with the fence four feet away and a foot below his sneakers. Every inch forward made the branch bend a little more, and soon the limb groaned an ominous creak near the tree trunk, prompting him to quicken his pace toward the fence. His soles were directly over the top rail of the fence when the limb partially snapped, but he clung to its failing support long enough to plant the soles of his sneakers upon the top rail of the fence.

A gust of wind smacked his face, knocking the ball cap from his head as he teetered on the top rail. Desperate to cross the fence, he pushed away from the cracked limb and jumped from the top rail into the mining property, eyeing a soft landing in the leaves on the other side. He landed upon his desired spot, but his heels sank into the muddy ground and he staggered backward, rolling onto his buttocks and over his shoulders before finally coming to rest with the nape of his neck squarely against the electrified fence. The angle of the hill prevented a swift break from the fence while electricity danced up his scalp and down his spine.

"Yow!" he cried out as he finally sprang to his feet, hopping mad. He refrained from kicking the fence, if only for fear that it might somehow bite him again, but at least it was behind him now. Peeling the wet leaves from his vest, he glared at his favorite ball cap lying upon the ground on the other side of the fence; frustrated, he pulled the cloth dressing tighter against his forehead before starting up the terrain rising before him.

The colorful maple and oak leaves overhead shielded him from the rainfall as he made his way past craggy gray rocks that protruded from the forest bed with increasing frequency. Soon he reached the bank of a thin rainwater gulley running across his path toward the lake, compelling his weary thighs along a more lateral course that eventually led him back to the muddy access road. Staring up the hill with the cold wind blowing raindrops into his face, he zipped his vest as tight as he could before stepping into a stream of mud oozing down the road.

The access road cut deeper into the rising terrain as he climbed farther up the hill, forming high, eroded banks that channeled the rainwater rapidly down the center of the road. Unable to traverse the muddy road any farther, he crawled up the left bank with the help of an exposed root, and he followed the access road along the ridge of the natural forest bed. He scaled a large mossy rock formation abutting the road and froze in his tracks when he reached its peak, sighting Curly's green pickup truck parked directly below him with a fallen tree blocking its path.

His heart sank. The presence of the truck didn't completely validate Curly's story, but it certainly indicated his role in Cindy's disappearance went beyond a simple crank phone call. Jeff studied the truck for a few minutes until he concluded that it was unoccupied and that Curly wasn't lingering somewhere nearby. After scaling down the rock to the gulley with the help of the fallen tree, he descended the slippery path until he reached the side mirror of the truck with the rainwater gushing past his feet. Sabotage crossed his mind as he inspected the truck, but he quickly abandoned the notion when he spotted keys dangling from the ignition switch, surmising that the truck might serve as a means of escape if needed.

He turned about and climbed over the fallen tree blocking the truck, ruing the loss of his sweatshirt and cap as he continued up the slick access road into the wind and rain. A feeling of dread grew larger in his gut, for any hope he held of avoiding an armed and hostile enemy grew slimmer with every step, as did any optimism that Cindy had somehow eluded the menacing clutches of Curly McClure.

Downcast by his friend's rejection and outfitted in his favorite running gear, Crazy Legs had simply continued to run, if only for the lack of a better idea. He was familiar with the location of the mining property, and the highway was the fastest way to Almond Lake by car, but he also knew the winding route through the back roads of Salisbury to Portland Village Road was nearly two miles shorter on foot. Those divergent courses rejoined again at the Exit 9 overpass and, as he crossed that bridge, he spotted to his right an assembly of police cars, fire trucks, and an ambulance gathered around a wrecked Salisbury police car in the median of the highway. Two emergency medical technicians wheeled a gurney from the battered white cruiser toward the open bay of an ambulance, the driver holding a bandage to his forehead as they lifted him into the bed of the rescue vehicle.

Crazy Legs slowed his gait and craned his neck to squint through the rain, but he could not determine the identity of the officer before the technicians shut the ambulance doors. He checked his pulse and sucked in deep breaths of cool moist air as he passed the junction of the Exit 9 ramp, heartened by the absence of the blue Camaro in the highway wreck. An hour had passed since he'd watched Jeff's car vanish down Arrow Drive, but traversing at a pace of a mile every six minutes, he anticipated his arrival at the mining property to be in another hour or so, if his legs held out.

Traffic gathered at the upcoming signal light, where burning flares blocked drivers from advancing in the left turn lane, however he crossed over the street to the opposite shoulder to run behind the foremost flare. A Madison police officer stood in earnest before a cruiser parked at an angle across the yellow centerline, sternly waving Crazy Legs through the intersection, but when he reached the other side of Dexter Road, he looked back to see the reason for the detour: a toppled utility pole lay across the next intersection, severed by a gray state police car with a buckled hood and a steaming grill. Two more Madison police cars sat in the middle of the intersection, marking the live wires in the road with their flashing blue lights as the officers conversed with the trooper at a safe distance. Still, he saw no sign of Jeff's car.

Rather than risk a confrontation, Crazy Legs slipped into the sparse woods to the right of Dexter Road to keep his pace intact. He soon veered onto the slick asphalt of Portland Village Road past the intersection, with the severed utility pole and its mayhem behind him. The gradual incline of the road nagged at his thighs with ten miles of running already upon them, but he shook his head and wriggled his arms, trying to distract himself from the pain while his running shoes continued to pound the pavement. As he passed the stalks of the harvested cornfield on his right, another flash of blue light caught his eye near the limit of his visibility. He approached the site with trepidation, wary of Jeff's ability to escape a third encounter with the police.

Nearing Life Star Lane, he discovered why the road was so devoid of traffic: a Portland police cruiser blocked both lanes leading into the hairpin turn, while at the far end of the mountain pass an identical cruiser similarly restricted oncoming traffic. At the front of the scene, a Portland officer stood on the left shoulder of the road, conversing with Officer Boyd, who was still trapped inside the Salisbury cruiser crushed by the box truck. A second officer stood at parade rest by the mangled guardrail behind the damaged truck, observing with little expression the growing line of cars on the other side of the pass.

Crazy Legs approached the scene cautiously, wary that one of the officers might confront him, but neither man appeared to notice him as he slowed his gait to a walk. He slid up to the open door of the produce truck, where the driver sat sideways upon his elevated seat with a phone to his ear. The skinny boy rested his hands on his hips to catch his breath as the stocky driver looked down from his seat and fidgeted to end his call.

"Did you see what happened here?" the man asked, patting the top of his bald head with a handkerchief.

"Me?" Crazy Legs panted. "No, I just got here."

"They were coming straight at me," he said. "I had nowhere to go."

"They?" Crazy Legs glanced about. "Is there another car somewhere?"

The driver pointed to the corner of Life Star Lane. "Down there."

Crazy Legs jogged away from the truck to the torn metal guardrail and leaned over to peer down the embankment. There he saw the crumpled remains of the blue Camaro impinging the oak tree, a wisp of gray smoke still rising from its engine. He ran back to the driver of the produce truck. "The guy in that car," he asked breathlessly. "Where is he?"

The driver shook his head. "I don't know. He ran off down the hill. Crazy fool."

The quick blurt of a siren turned the skinny boy's attention back to the road behind him, where a gray sedan slowed to a halt in the middle of the road. Both front doors popped open, with Detective Shelnick emerging from the passenger side and Chief Wellis climbing from behind the wheel. They met at the front of the sedan, the chief with a phone to his ear and the detective wielding a camera connected to a strap slung about his neck.

"Hey you!" the Portland officer shouted at Crazy Legs from the neck of the mountain pass. "This area is restricted. Move along!"

The two Salisbury lawmen looked up to the source of the commotion, but Crazy Legs ducked away before either man could recognize him. He ran behind the produce truck and past the officer on the backside of the hairpin turn, downhill past the growing line of idled traffic on the backside of the pass, just a solitary runner continuing on his way.

TJ glanced out the back window of the Volvo station wagon as it rounded the eastbound entrance ramp to Interstate 88. "They're gaining on us," he said as he watched the Tornadoes' black Camry closing in.

Mick twisted the rearview mirror so he could see the road behind them. "C'mon, Brain. My grandmother drives faster than this."

"Leave it alone! I need it to drive!" Brain turned the mirror back to see out the rear window again, inadvertently allowing the car to drift toward the occupied center lane. A blaring horn caused him to swerve erratically back to the right while the affronted driver gestured profanely at him before speeding away.

Axle braced his hands against the front seats. "Watch the road! You'll get us all killed!"

Denny stuffed a handful of potato chips into his mouth. "Put your seat belt on."

"I can't! It's stuck under the seat!"

TJ lowered his window and poked his head outside for a moment. "They're coming up on the left," he warned.

The boys all turned to see the Toyota inching closer to the rear fender of the Volvo, threatening to pin it behind a slow tractor-trailer, but Brain steered the car onto the shoulder to pass the truck on the right. Zak sped forward in an attempt to block the Hurricanes from reentering the lane ahead of the truck, only to be denied as Brain veered the Volvo back into the travel lane ahead of the truck.

"Don't let them get ahead of us," Mick said. "Go faster."

Brain bristled. "I can't—"

Mick slid over and lifted his leg over the center console to stomp on Brain's foot, mashing the gas pedal to the floorboard. "That's better," he said as they closed in swiftly upon the upcoming traffic.

"Cut it out!" Brain steered frantically around the slower cars on the highway.

Axle grabbed Mick's shoulder. "What are you doing? Let him drive!"

Mick pointed to the Toyota trying to pull even with them again. "Ram 'em," he said. "Spin 'em out."

"Are you crazy?" Brain yelled back. "It'll cause a major pileup!"

Mick grabbed his sleeve. "You wanna lead them to Jeff? Do it."

Brain gripped the emergency brake handle. "No, Mick. Move your foot or I'll stop the car right here."

Mick glanced back to his three friends in the back seat, none of whom offered any objection to Brain's ultimatum. He lifted his foot and settled back into his seat again. "Fine time for you guys to go soft on me," he said.

Brain slowed the car to a safer speed while Axle pointed at the Toyota to their left. "Look! Craig's trying to say something!"

Mick leaned forward to peer out Brain's side window, where he saw Zak driving the Camry with his attention fixed on the traffic ahead. Willie, Tony, and Phil all watched from the back seat as Craig stuck his head out the open front window, shouting at the Volvo through the rushing wind.

TJ lowered his window. "What do you want?"

"Slow down!" Craig hollered as the rain pelted his face. "I gotta talk to Mick!"

Denny shook his head. "Don't trust him. He tried that crap at Train's wake and look where it got us."

Mick folded his arms across his chest. "I got nothing to say to him."

The Camry drifted dangerously close to them. Brain fidgeted to steer alongside the vehicle at such close proximity. "Mick—"

TJ stuck his face outside the window. "Get lost!"

Craig waved him off. "Listen to me, Mick! We need to talk!"

TJ reached across Axle to snatch the giant soda cup from Denny's hand before turning to face Craig again. "I said get lost!" He flung the soda cup out the window and into the Tornado leader's astonished face, showering him with soda and ice before the cup and lid were swept away by the wind.

"Arrgh! Asshole!" Craig yelled as he ducked back inside the retreating Camry.

"My soda!" Denny protested.

TJ powered up his window again. "I did you a favor. You don't need all that sugar."

Brain smiled at TJ in the rearview mirror, but Axle directed his attention forward again as they crested a small hill. "Traffic's slowing down," he said, pointing to the left two lanes where long lines of cars were stacking up.

Traffic swallowed the Tornadoes' car in the center lane, but the right lane continued steadily along, allowing the Hurricanes to progress past the site of the accident. TJ and Brain both lowered their windows to observe the scene beyond the traffic while their friends strained for a glimpse of the wreckage.

"It's a cop car," TJ said. "Looks like a Salisbury cruiser."

Mick tapped Brain on the shoulder and pointed to the breakdown lane. "Keep to the right. Drive on the grass if you have to."

"I don't see the Camaro," Brain said. "Maybe this has nothing to do with Jeff."

Mick pulled out another cigarette and fretfully stuck it between his lips. "Maybe not. But if the cops were on his tail, that's a bad thing."

TJ glanced back. "Tornadoes are coming again."

Brain glanced at his side-view mirror, but Denny pointed frantically to their right. "Don't miss the exit!"

"Hang on!" Brain jerked the steering wheel hard to the right, casting everyone to the left as the Volvo veered toward the Exit 9 ramp. Behind them, the Toyota swerved across the right lane and onto the shoulder to clear the traffic, nearly sideswiping another car before following the Volvo up the winding ramp.

TJ pointed a thumb to a streak of dark blue paint lining the battered silver rail. "Someone did a job on that guardrail."

Brain glanced at the side mirror again to see the Camry's headlights closing in on them. He rolled to a stop at the top of the ramp before pulling out in front of a pair of cars approaching from their right, while the Camry braked to a full stop as Zak waited for the cars to clear the intersection. The traffic signals at the next intersection stood dark, and the left-hand turn onto Dexter Road was now blocked by a pair of police cruisers.

"More cops," Brain groaned. "Now what?"

"Keep going straight," Denny told him. "I know a shortcut."

Mick peered down the barricaded road to the throng of emergency vehicles gathered in the distance. "What's going on down there?"

TJ lowered his window again to see better. "Hard to say. Looks like a car might've hit a pole, but I can't say it's Jeff's."

Brain turned his head for a peek, but an officer firmly gestured for him to proceed forward. They passed straight through the intersection, and he continued to scan the woods to his left as they continued down the ensuing road. "So where's this shortcut?" he finally asked. "I don't remember any other roads off this street for at least another mile."

Denny laughed. "What road? There's a cornfield up ahead. We're going mud-bogging!"

Brain winced. "Oh, man. My mother's gonna kill me."

Mick smirked. "Aww, she's probably sick of carting you around to chess tournaments and spelling bees in this thing." He grabbed the rearview mirror again and pivoted it to see the cars behind them. The first two cars in line turned right at the defunct traffic light, but the Camry skirted around them and sped straight through the intersection in pursuit. "Here they come."

"Mick, leave the mirror alone!" Brain shouted, turning it back toward him.

Denny pointed ahead. "Don't miss the turn! We're screwed if you do!"

The woods to their left suddenly gave way to a clearing of broken stalks and withered shucks, the remnants of the freshly harvested corn crop. Brain coasted the car past the width of the field before turning onto a dirt road running along the edge of its far perimeter. The Volvo heaved and rocked along the muddy road, its tires splashing through large puddles and sliding through the softened ground.

"Hope we don't bust a ball joint," he fretted as they bounced through a dip.

"Don't let up," Mick said. "We gotta lose them before we get there."

The Toyota turned onto the dirt road and swiftly closed in on them, for Zak drove through the cornfield with reckless abandon, but as he pulled closer to the Hurricanes, the Volvo's tire wash inundated the Camry's windshield with mud and debris. Unable to see the dirt road, he drifted into a rut running along the right edge; the jagged terrain battered the tires and made the steering wheel vibrate violently in his hands. In a panic, he swerved the car to the left, across the dirt road into the heart of the cornfield. His windshield readily cleared once they escaped the Volvo's tire wash, but he battled to control the steering wheel as the Camry crashed and bucked through cornstalks and craggy terrain, thrashing the Tornadoes about inside the car.

Fifty yards ahead, Brain braked the Volvo to a halt at the edge of the cornfield. He quickly checked the road in both directions before turning right and accelerating along Portland Village Road. As everyone settled back into their seats, the car cleared a small rise in the road to arrive upon the bevy of emergency vehicles bathing the slick pavement in flashing colors of red, yellow, blue, and white. An ambulance pulled away from the scene and whisked past them toward Madison with its siren wailing, while Brain braked the car hard to slow below the speed limit. Drawing closer to the scene, they saw that another ambulance remained behind, accompanied by two tow trucks, a fire engine, and Chief Wellis's unmarked sedan that was now flanked by a Salisbury cruiser and a pair of Madison K-9 units. A line of burning flares sliced the hairpin turn in half along the yellow centerline, leaving a narrow lane of passage through Life Star Lane, yet no cars presently traversed the pass from other direction.

The foremost Portland officer spotted the oncoming station wagon and moved toward the center of the road to meet them. Brain glanced in his mirror at the Camry passing over the shallow hilltop to close in behind them. "What should I do?"

"Bullshit him," Mick said. He turned to the Hurricanes in the back seat. "Lose the jackets! Fast!"

The three boys hurriedly stripped off their jackets and stuffed them down between their legs, while Mick turned to conceal the white swirl of his own jacket against the passenger door. Raindrops splashed off the wide brim of the officer's hat as he held out an open palm, signaling them to stop. Brain braked to a halt alongside the wrecked produce truck and lowered his window to greet the officer.

The officer bent forward to the open window, revealing his Portland police badge and a name tag reading TINNEY pinned to his jacket. "Where'd you kids come from? This road's supposed to be closed."

The trio in the back seat squirmed, but Brain remained cool. "They just reopened it," he said. "We were stuck back there for twenty minutes."

The officer glanced suspiciously about the interior of the car. "Why aren't you kids in school right now?"

"They let us out early," Brain replied. "On account of the power being out."

A man in an orange poncho approached the car from the right shoulder. "Officer Tinney!"

The lanky officer stood up to look over the roof. "Sir?"

Denny cringed. "It's Chief Wellis!" he whispered.

Mick slid low in his seat and ducked his face away as the chief stepped up to his window, oblivious to the occupants inside the car. "You got a rifle with you?" he asked the officer.

"Yes sir. In my trunk," Tinney replied.

"Grab it and come with me. I've got a chopper five minutes out landing in that cornfield up the road."

Officer Dryden slid up beside his commander. "Sir, Portland Police are reporting they found some clothing floating downstream from here. They think it might be Hollister's."

Chief Wellis turned his eye away from the redheaded patrolman to the woodsy valley beyond the hairpin turn. He turned about abruptly and banged an open palm upon the roof of the Volvo. "C'mon, get these cars out of here!" he shouted before strolling back toward the ensemble of emergency vehicles.

Officer Tinney ducked low to speak with Brain again. "Keep to the right and proceed slowly," he said before gesturing for the black Toyota behind them to follow suit.

"Thank you, Officer," Brain said before raising his window.

TJ patted him on the shoulder as he drove away. "Nice work, Brain. Your mother would be proud of you."

Axle glanced back. "Figures. They're just waving the Tornadoes through."

Denny grimaced. "Dumbass cops."

Mick continued to shield his face with his hand. "Quiet. We're not out of this yet."

The Hurricanes fell silent as Brain drove past the produce truck still pinning the Salisbury cruiser against the rock wall. A paramedic attended to the driver sitting in his cab, while behind them a firefighter stowed a hydraulic extraction tool in a side compartment of the Madison fire engine. The severed roof of the mangled cruiser lay against the rock wall, revealing the empty cabin where Officer Boyd had been trapped.

Across the road, a tow truck backed to the hole in the guardrail to position its winch as close to the edge of the road as possible, as more flares prompted Brain to the left and over the yellow line as he slowly drove through Life Star Lane. The Hurricanes watched Detective Shelnick standing at the edge of the hairpin turn, snapping pictures of the mangled guardrail with his camera, while the two K-9 officers peered over the edge of the pass, each with a uniformed police dog perched dutifully by his side.

"Look!" Denny said. "It's Jeff's car!"

The boys all craned their necks to the right, but only Mick could verify what Denny had proclaimed. A fireman and a policeman inspected the Camaro, now just a crumpled wreck teetering on the hillside in the cold rain. Axle finally leaned over Denny's lap and gasped, eliciting a somber hush throughout the car as they rounded the hairpin turn.

"What is it—?" Brain asked, looking back for a glimpse.

Mick pointed forward. "Watch out—"

Brain looked ahead and quickly jerked the steering wheel to the right, around the Portland officer. He squeezed the Volvo's fenders between the cruiser and the flares before starting down the other side of the mountain, past the long line of cars still waiting to proceed through the neck of the pass.

Axle's voice cracked as he spoke. "Anyone see Jeff?"

Denny cast his eyes down, and TJ turned to look outside his window, but Brain pushed his glasses back and gripped the steering wheel with determination. "Jeff's not done yet," he said. "Why would Chief Wellis call in a helicopter if they already had him?"

Mick pulled his pistol from beneath his waistband and checked the magazine before snapping it back into the gun. "I don't know," he said, "but if something bad's happened to Jeff, we're just gonna have to finish the job ourselves."

Down in the heart of the excavation area, Cindy braced against the storm that continued to thrash her shivering body. The falling temperature rendered her thin white windbreaker all but useless, while the rest of her clothing, still damp from the lake plunge, grew wetter by the minute. Frigid water flowed at her from multiple locations, providing treacherous travel underfoot, but she labored onward under the threat of Curly stalking her with his gun.

Her athleticism had enabled her to maintain a lead just beyond Curly's sightline, but her legs tired against the rising slope of the muddy road before her. Shaking nearly uncontrollably from the cold, she scaled the short hill to reach a fork in the road marked by another boulder, stopping behind the large rock to catch her breath and hide from the wind. Peering back around the boulder, she saw Curly at the base of the slope she had just climbed, clawing his way up the muddy road. He made his way halfway up the slope before losing his footing and sliding back down to the base again, slamming a fist into the mud after washing out at the bottom. Verifying that his gun was still secure, he rolled to his knees and started up the slope again as his accomplice ran up from behind.

"Where is she?" JJ asked.

"This way," he grumbled. He climbed to the top of the slope and stood at the fork as Cindy shrank farther behind the boulder.

JJ crawled up the muddy slope to rise alongside his lieutenant. He looked up each road with his hands on his hips. "Which way did she go?"

Curly pointed toward the sky. "Shut up and listen."

JJ cocked an ear upward. "A helicopter?"

"Must be the cops. Who else would be out in this weather?"

"I thought you told Hollister no cops."

Curly grabbed JJ's arm and pointed back down the muddy access road. "Get back to the cabin. Hollister should be here soon. Hold him there till I get back with the girl."

JJ pulled his arm free. "This is crazy! Forget about her! Let's get the hell outta here!"

Curly scowled at him. "Do it! And don't let that helicopter see you, or we're screwed!"

"All right!" JJ snapped before turning to run back down the access road.

Curly turned back to the fork as Cindy clenched her jaw hard to stop her teeth from chattering. She heard his footsteps splashing through the mud up the lakeward path to her left, so she circled right to the brink of the muddy access road now vacated, pausing for a moment to watch JJ running around a corner toward the hilltop. Once he was out of sight, she emerged onto the access road to trudge along a gentler incline, delving deeper into the open mining grounds against the driving wind and rain.

The heavy rain continued to deluge Jeff as he trudged up the muddy access road—his skin felt taut and clammy beneath his soggy clothes, and his legs ached from the constant rise of the terrain. As he continued to climb, he noticed a thinning of the birch and elm trees around him and, rounding a turn to the right, he discovered that the cover of the forest came to an abrupt end another fifty yards up the hill. Here the slope of the hill rose more sharply, while the woods continued to stretch to his left along the base of the steep rise. The hilltop before him was nearly devoid of all trees, and as he scaled the final eighty yards of the slope, he noted the gray slate rock that seemed blended with the dark storm clouds hovering over the lake. He had finally reached the cliff top that he and Cindy had daydreamed about from the deck of the boat the previous night, but it no longer held any mystical appeal to him.

A dim light glowed from the rectangular windows of a wooden cabin facing the open slope he now climbed, the aroma of burning wood wafting from its chimney down the hillside toward him. He crept forward to the last tree capable of shielding his body from view, an elm tree standing near the top of the access road; from there he studied the cabin for several minutes, but he saw no movement around the cabin and heard nothing but the sound of raindrops upon the leaves of the trees behind him. A gamut of possibilities ran through his mind, some more frightening than others, yet he soon concluded that his only choice was to approach the cabin, regardless of what might await him inside.

"Time to find out," he said.

He stepped from the cover of the elm tree and slinked up the hill with his sight fixed on the covered front porch of the cabin. When the curvature of the hilltop could no longer provide him cover, he sprinted forward and slid up to the windowless sidewall facing the cliff, pressing his back against its halved pine timbers before inching his way back along the cement pad to the edge of the porch. His first step upon the wooden porch emitted a loud creak and he held his breath, ready to dive back around the corner if the front door opened in response. Not until a full minute had passed did he feel confident enough to take another step forward toward the first casement window.

The long porch stretched twenty feet to either side of the cabin door, with a wooden handrail running its full length and open at each end. The cabin itself was of sound construction, but the sagging awning overhead leaked water in several places onto the smooth planks of the porch underneath. Still, the rickety awning offered Jeff the first true shelter from the weather since he escaped from the wrecked Camaro at Life Star Lane. Peering inside the casement window with one eye, he observed the sole room of the main floor, dimly lit by a sputtering fireplace flame and a dingy, bare light bulb hanging from a ceiling fixture. Once he verified the room was clear, he stepped past the window and stopped at the rustic front door, depressing the black gate latch with his thumb and pushing it open with a lingering squeak. He slipped inside and pressed the door shut again before turning to the center of the cabin.

A hatchet lay on the hardwood floor beneath the skewed table amid scattered playing cards and a toppled chair. Jeff crossed the room and picked up the hatchet, examining it briefly, identifying no blood on its blade or anywhere else in the room, although he did note two sliced curls of gray duct tape lying on the floor among the cards. He stared at the glowing embers in the fireplace, wondering where Cindy might be, if not in the cabin. Lost in thought, he sank the tip of the hatchet into the bark of a nearby log and turned back to the disheveled table at the center of the cabin, where a sliver of light caught his eye from behind the crooked cellar door.

The door scraped along the floor as he pulled it open, its top hinge partially separated from the jamb. Standing in the doorway, Jeff flicked the light switch off, listening for some type of protest from the basement. Hearing none, he switched the light back on again and proceeded cautiously down the stairs, noting another bare bulb hanging from a low ceiling, driving the shadows back toward the corners of the cement foundation but not completely away. Much of the basement was occupied by power machinery, construction materials, and workbenches littered with hand tools and hardware, while an open toilet stall set beside a dusty industrial sink contributed to the overall drabness of the cellar.

One item struck him as unusual: a gray metal box bearing a bright green light mounted against the wall in the far-right corner of the room. A closer inspection of the gray box revealed a silver faceplate that read CAPITOL FENCING COMPANY, with an indicator light situated above a silver key switch, glowing green despite the absence of a key in the switch. Jeff tugged at the metal housing of the control panel and found it to be loose, so he removed it to discover a thin white wire with alligator clips on each end attached to the soldered connections of the switch. Recalling his encounter with the fence in painful detail, he pulled the jumper wire free and the green light immediately blinked out. He slid the cover back into place and retreated to the staircase with satisfaction, hopeful that his departure from the mining property would be far easier than his entry had been.

He grabbed the railing and cast one final look around the shadows of the basement before ascending the stairs, still perplexed by the vacant state of the cabin and eager to leave it before someone returned. When he reached the main room again, he noticed the wet footprints he had left on the way in, but as he glanced about for a towel or rag, he spotted the straight wooden ladder stretching through an open hole in the corner of the ceiling. With a wary glance to the front windows, he stepped to the base of the straight ladder to his right and flicked on a light switch mounted upon the wall. A faint glow emerged from the open hatchway overhead, revealing attic rafters that defined the sloping roof of the cabin, and he knew he had to rule out the possibility that Cindy might be up there.

He scaled the ladder quickly and stepped out onto the plywood flooring of the loft with the aroma of cut lumber in his nostrils as another bare ceiling bulb glared in his eyes. Planks of plywood stretched more than halfway down the centerline of the attic, giving way to evenly spaced spines of two-by-six boards with insulation packed in the spaces between them. Near the center of the loft before the fireplace chimney, a knee-high stack of plywood sat before a table saw surrounded by piles of sawdust, while at the far end of the attic the broken slat of a vent allowed a sliver of gloomy daylight inside. A few cardboard boxes and folded chairs lay tucked upon the finished floor near the hatchway, but overall, the attic was free of stored items. His gut told him that no one was hidden here, but he had to check behind the stack of plywood just to be sure.

Stooping slightly beneath the low ceiling, Jeff crept toward the stack when he heard the faint, distinctive chop of a helicopter rotor approaching from somewhere behind the cabin. He held his breath and listened intently as the sound grew louder until finally he determined that it was heading directly overhead. Hurrying down the center of the attic, he met the end of the plywood flooring and gripped the overhead rafters for balance as he hopped along the spines of the floor beams. When he reached the vent at the far end of the attic, he peered through the broken slat to see a dark blue police chopper buzzing past the rooftop of the cabin, flying straight out over the lake before banking sharply to the right and out of view.

The sound of the rotor faded, giving way to heavy panting and splashing footsteps approaching from the left. Hard soles scuffed across the cement, and Jeff glanced down through the angled vent slats to glimpse the heel of a cowboy boot as the runner passed underneath. He spun about and hopped back across the spines of the floor beams, swiftly enough to avoid grasping the overhead rafters. When he reached the plywood flooring again, he dashed down the center of the attic and punched out the bare bulb with his fist, plunging the loft into darkness just before the front door burst open and slammed shut again.

Jeff crouched and held his breath as he listened to the boots clomping across the hardwood floor to a point directly beneath him. The cellar door creaked open, and the footsteps grew fainter as they descended into the basement. He slunk to the edge of the hatchway, pondering an attempt to flee the cabin while the main room was empty, but the footsteps suddenly drummed up the cellar steps with newfound urgency. They ceased momentarily at the top of the staircase before clomping across the hardwood floor to the base of the loft ladder in slow, deliberate steps.

Shrouded in darkness, Jeff peered down from the edge of the hatchway to see a hand flicking the light switch on and off a few times to no effect. A head of wet brown hair came into view, and a tangential view of the young man's goateed chin convinced him that it was JJ, not Curly. He retreated to the table saw and knelt in the sawdust pile, wishing he had taken the hatchet with him as he listened to the boots scraping up the wooden ladder rungs one by one. He quietly backed to the plywood stack and shrank into the shadows behind the table saw, while his adversary climbed through the hatchway with a penlight in his hand. The light beam cut feebly from side to side through the inky darkness as JJ advanced down the center of the loft, but he stopped abruptly when his boot crunched upon a shard of broken glass.

The Tornado swung the penlight to his left to shine upon the plywood stack. "I know you're up here, Hollister," he said. "I know you shut off the fence." He pulled a switchblade from the pocket of his Tornado jacket and proceeded cautiously toward the plywood stack, while Jeff cowered behind the table saw with his hands mired in the sawdust. He hoped his foe would turn back without confrontation, but the penlight pivoted to fall upon him, and JJ stepped forward with the switchblade open. "Gotcha!" he said.

Jeff lunged forward, thrusting two handfuls of sawdust directly at the beam of light. JJ screamed and reached for his stricken eyes, dropping both penlight and switchblade upon the floor. Jeff barreled him over on his way toward the hatchway, but he tripped over his enemy's feet and fell to his hands and knees. A hand grabbed his ankle as he scrambled forward, but he dragged himself to the lip of the hatchway to grapple the top rung of the wooden ladder below.

"Not so fast, Hollister!" JJ growled. He grabbed hold of Jeff's belt and punched him twice in the small of his back.

Jeff groaned from the blows and rolled over to break the grasp on his waistband. He pulled a leg free and kicked his enemy squarely in the jaw, stunning JJ long enough to turn and crawl through the hatchway opening. He pulled his head and shoulders through the hatchway, but as he reached for the next rung, his hips passed over the lip and he tumbled headfirst toward the floor below. His outstretched arms helped divert the impact from his head to his left shoulder, while he flopped painfully onto his back in time to see JJ climbing from the hatchway onto the ladder.

JJ turned about and jumped from the top of the ladder, but Jeff rolled quickly to his right to escape the menacing stomp of his enemy's boot. As he rolled to his feet and tried to run, he lost his balance and crashed hard against the cabin wall, knocking the digital clock from its perch to shatter upon the floor. JJ dashed to the fireplace and pulled the hatchet from the log before rushing back with the weapon in hand.

"Curly's gonna be pissed when he finds out I killed you myself," he said.

Jeff tried to scramble for the front door, but his sneakers slipped on the hardwood floor and he slid to a jarring halt against the short wall beneath the casement window. He rolled onto his back and held his hands out defensively as the angry

Tornado pressed forward with the hatchet in hand. "Wait! Wait!"

JJ stopped a few feet away, his goatee littered with sawdust and his right eyelid clogged from the same. "Crying won't do you no good, Hollister."

Jeff shook his head. "Just tell me where Cindy is and I promise I won't hurt you."

A crazed grin spread across JJ's face as Jeff's words sank in; he rushed forward with a wild shout and the hatchet raised high over his head. Jeff drew a knee to his chest and braced it against JJ's sternum, simultaneously grappling his foe's wrist with both hands before the hatchet could swing down upon him. Using the wrist as a fulcrum, he extended his leg upward, propelling JJ overhead and forward in one fluid motion. JJ screamed a moment before crashing upside down through the casement window and landing outside upon the covered porch in a shower of splinters and glass.

Jeff rolled to his feet and leaped to the windowsill littered with shards of jagged glass. He jumped down onto the porch and stepped over JJ lying among a collage of glass, splinters, and blood. "Can't say I didn't warn ya," he told his unresponsive foe as he retrieved the hatchet from the porch and tucked it inside his belt.

Looking back to the open hilltop, he saw no further sign of the helicopter, only storm clouds hovering over the lake. He ducked to the backside of the cabin, knowing Curly would surely come running if he was within earshot of the horrific crash. Any lingering doubts he had about Cindy's predicament had clearly been obliterated, yet despite rendering one of her abductors incapacitated, he felt no less fearful for her safety now than he had felt when he first left Salisbury.

Mick scanned the sullen faces of the Hurricanes in the back seat of the Volvo station wagon as Brain maneuvered the slick road winding away from the mountain pass. TJ and Denny stared out their respective windows, but sitting in the middle seat, Axle could do little to hide the tears streaming down his cheeks.

"What are you crying for?" Mick asked him.

"Aw, give him a break," TJ said.

Axle wiped his eyes and hardened his expression. "Jeff's dead. I just know it."

Denny fidgeted and patted his friend on the knee. "C'mon, man. Don't say that. He's okay."

Mick nodded. "You can't kill Jeff that easy. Craig pushed him backward down a flight of stairs, and look how he bounced back from that."

Brain eyed the rearview mirror as the black Camry closed in again. "Here they come!"

The Hurricanes turned to see Zak poke the nose of his car into the open lane just behind the Volvo. Brain swerved across the yellow line to cut him off and punched the gas to pull away, but the Camry accelerated in pursuit. Suddenly the Volvo lurched forward and fishtailed wildly while Brain fought to control the steering wheel. He turned the car back into the right lane as Zak fell in line and edged close to its bumper again.

"They hit us!" Brain cried. "I can't believe they hit us!"

"They're trying to spin us out!" TJ said.

"I got this," Mick said. He unbuckled his seat belt and powered down his window before pulling out his pistol and climbing out to sit upon the open sill.

Brain yanked at the cuff of Mick's pants while trying to keep his eyes on the road. "What are you doing? Get in here!"

Brain's plea was drowned out by the wet wind in Mick's face as he curled the fingers of his left hand beneath the rooftop luggage rack, simultaneously raising his right arm high enough in the air for the Tornadoes to see the gun in his hand. Zak veered the Toyota back over the yellow line to hide the car from Mick's sightline, but the blaring horn of an oncoming car forced him back in line. While Mick fussed for a clear shot, the approaching car passed by, and the Toyota swerved across the yellow line into the oncoming lane again.

Brain leaned far to his right and yanked on his leader's cuff. "Mick! Get back in here! Somebody tell him to get back in here!"

Axle braced his hands on the backs of the bucket seats. "They're gonna ram us again!"

Denny pointed forward. "Quarry Road's coming up. Don't miss the turn."

Brain glanced at his rearview mirror. "TJ, climb out and tell him to get in here!"

TJ shook his head. "No way! I ain't getting shot—"

"Brain, don't miss the turn," Denny warned.

"Let Mick do what he wants," Axle said. "He's gonna anyway."

"If he shoots someone, we're all—" Brain lurched forward as the Toyota slammed the Volvo's left rear fender again, harder than the first time. He cut the steering wheel back and forth as he struggled to control the vehicle while his friends in the back seat groped for a steady hold.

Outside, Mick squeezed the luggage rack tighter as the Volvo swerved wildly from side to side. When it finally stabilized on a straight course again, he rested his right wrist upon his forearm to aim the gun away from the wind and rain while Zak weaved and ducked the Toyota behind the Volvo to deny him a clear shot. With his attention keenly focused on the Camry, Mick heard Denny's shout from inside the Volvo as they approached the Quarry Road intersection, "Turn here, Brain!"

Brain stomped on the brake pedal, snapping Denny and TJ hard against their seat belts as Axle tumbled forward onto the front console between the bucket seats. Mick slid forward along the windowsill until his leg pinned against the tapering front corner of the open window, while his hold on the luggage rack slipped along the rail. The Volvo slid to a halt in the middle of the intersection but the Camry flew by in the left lane, its brake lights flashing bright red from Zak's late reaction. Brain jerked the steering wheel hard to the left behind the Tornadoes' car and hit the gas again to turn onto Quarry Road. The force of the turn overpowered Mick's failing grip on the luggage rack and he fell backward, his wedged right knee saving him from falling completely out of the car. The side-view mirror offered shaky support to his elbow as he struggled to maintain a grip on his gun.

"Help!" he cried out.

Axle lunged forward to grab Mick by the ankles just as his elbow slid from the side mirror. Dangling outside with his knees cupped over the sill, he groped for the windowsill with his left hand while still clinging to the pistol with the right. Axle clambered forward and stretched to grapple Mick's left hand as Brain glanced back at the black Toyota careening through the intersection in pursuit. The Camry swiftly closed on the rear bumper of the Volvo before swerving into the oncoming lane again.

"Oh no you don't," Brain muttered. He steered sharply to the left, blocking the Camry's approach, but Zak immediately cut the Toyota back into the right lane and accelerated alongside the Volvo's rear fender to prevent Brain's reentry into the proper lane.

Axle pulled Mick's arm closer to the windowsill and stretched out his right hand. "Reach for me, Mick!"

With his wet fingers squirming in Axle's hand, Mick glared back at the approaching Toyota to see Zak's determined face visible behind the beating windshield wipers. Axle shouted out to his leader again, but Mick pointed the pistol beneath his left armpit and fired two shots in quick succession at the trailing car. The first bullet pierced the Camry's radiator and shattered its flywheel, a shot that would have proved fatal to the engine if not for the second bullet. The second bullet ricocheted off the asphalt and tore through the inner sidewall of the Camry's left front tire with a loud blast. Instantly, Zak's expression changed from steadfast resolve to sheer terror as the car swerved sharply to the left, missing the rear bumper of the Volvo by inches. The Tornadoes cried out in fear as the Camry flew off the left shoulder into a watery drainage ditch, where it bounced and splashed along the trench before rolling off the high channel wall and landing gently on its right side in a stream of rainwater.

"Ha!" TJ said. "Those guys are toast!"

Axle finally pulled his leader back into the car. "Great shot, Mick!"

Mick tucked the pistol away before falling back into his seat. "Nice driving, Brain. Remind me to send a letter of commendation to your mother."

Axle climbed into the back seat again, while Denny pointed at a dirt road to their right marked by the brown-and-white boat launch sign nailed to a tree. "We're here," he said.

"Already?" Brain could still see the overturned Camry in his rearview mirror as the first of the Tornadoes climbed from the wreckage. "So much for toast."

He turned the Volvo onto the dirt road beneath the cover of the woods, squinting through the foggy windshield and the beating wipers as the car bounced along the muddy road to the boat launch fork.

Mick pointed toward the left. "Go that way."

Brain complied and pulled the car to a stop before the gate of the mining property. "It looks like it's locked," he said.

Mick frowned. "What'd you expect, a welcome mat?"

Brain gestured toward the fence in frustration. "So how are we supposed to get in?"

"We climb over it. What's the big deal?"

"What about the car? The Tornadoes are right up the road!"

"I'm sure they couldn't care less about your mom's station wagon, Brain."

Brain shifted into park. "Right. All the more reason for them to trash it."

Mick groaned as he popped his door open. He stepped out into the rain and the three Hurricanes in the back followed him out, donning their jackets as they joined their leader at the front of the car.

"Check this out." Denny lifted the chain with a severed lock from the mud. "Looks like someone beat us here."

"C'mon, let's go." TJ grabbed the fence to push it open before shrieking in pain and pulling away. Cradling his fingers in his gut, he looked up to his friends staring back in bewilderment. "It's an electric fence!"

Axle ran the back of his hand across the metal mesh. "Ow! Hey, he's right!"

TJ shook his head in disbelief. "Did you think I was lying to you?"

Brain opened his door and stepped halfway out of the car with its motor still running. "Now what?"

Denny trotted back to the fork to peer back down the dirt road. "I think the Tornadoes are coming," he called back.

Mick stepped around the front of the car. "Hey, Brain. Help us figure out how to shut this thing off."

Brain stepped forward and adjusted his glasses for a closer look. "There's gotta be some kind of controller around here," he said. "Maybe if we—"

Mick bolted for the open door of the Volvo. "Everyone step back!" he shouted as he slid into the driver's seat and grabbed the steering wheel.

Brain ran after him. "Mick! No!"

Mick shifted into drive and stepped on the gas pedal with the car doors still open. TJ dove to the left and Axle to the right as the Volvo crashed into the gate. The impact ripped the nearest fence post from the ground and buckled the chain-link mesh up onto the hood of the car, opening a gap at the bottom of the fence large enough to crawl beneath.

Mick shut the engine off and hopped out of the car. "Let's go! Everyone inside!"

Brain pointed to the damaged grill of the car. "Look what you did! Why did you do that?"

Mick tossed him the keys. "We're here for Jeff. The car means nothing."

TJ wriggled through the space beneath the fence, but Axle limped over to his leader. "I think I sprained my ankle," he said with a wince.

Denny jogged back from the fork in the road. "The Tornadoes are definitely coming. I couldn't see them, but I could sure hear them. They're plenty pissed."

Mick nodded. "Okay. Get inside."

"Hurry. They're closer than you think." Denny stepped to the battered fence and dropped to his knees to crawl through the gap and join TJ on the other side.

Brain shut the car doors and locked the Volvo with the key fob. "I am so screwed," he said before pocketing the keys and sliding under the fence.

Mick eased Axle to the ground. "You're gonna have to do the best you can," he said. "We don't have the time to mess with Craig."

Axle glanced at the pistol tucked conspicuously beneath his leader's belt. "You're not really gonna shoot anyone, are ya, Mick?"

Mick glanced back to the fork, still absent any Tornadoes, although he too could hear shouts in the distance. "I ain't making no promises," he said before dropping to the ground and following his friends underneath the buckled fence.

On the other side of the cabin hilltop, the dirt access road sliced downward into the mining grounds against a high, sloping wall to the left, cut by heavy machinery or blasted by dynamite in some places. With the hatchet looped through his belt, Jeff descended a footpath along the right side of the road with measured steps, but halfway down, he lost his footing and fell back into the center of the road. He initially fought against the river of muddy rainwater, but finally he lifted his feet out of harm's way and rode down the watery chute on his back, splashing into a shallow brown puddle at the base of the hill. His aching body begged for rest, but the cold water streaming into the back of his pants prompted him to his knees to confront his new surroundings. The land maintained little resemblance to the forest that had once grown upon it, now barren of trees and scarred with gravel mounds and excavation pits covering nearly a hundred acres. The access road continued on a level ridge through the center of the strip mine field while a secondary path jutted off to the right, diverting the rainwater downhill through a row of sparse trees toward the white-capped waters of Almond Lake.

He stood up and glanced about in all directions. "I'm dead if I stay here," he said.

Trudging forward along the muddy access road, he soon encountered a deep pit as wide as a city block. The pit was strewn with rocks and gravel, and puddles collecting rainwater in various locations about its floor. A rusty yellow backhoe loader sat idly at the far end of the pit with its shovel facing him and its bucket resting on the ground near a concave wall, as if awaiting a call to resume work someday. Jeff studied the pit as he trotted past it, but he saw no suitable place for someone to hide or be hidden, so he pressed on.

Beyond the pit, the center access road widened into an array of boulders, gravel mounds, dirt piles, and smaller pits spanning a third of the land along the eastern bank of the lake. Jeff gazed about the convoluted terrain, knowing Cindy was probably nearby but also realizing that finding her would be no easy task. He began a painstaking search but soon despaired over the intricacy of the grounds, knowing that every second ticking away increased his chance of confronting Curly. Finally, he sat upon a rock at the base of a slick rise to collect his thoughts as the cold rain pelted his body. If Cindy had been kidnapped to lure him into a confrontation, he surmised, then killing her meant Curly had abandoned that plan. Jeff didn't doubt his enemy's ability to kill Cindy to get back at him, but if Curly had already done so, then why would he linger at the scene of the crime, and why would he have separated from JJ?

He ascended the troublesome rise to the crest of the muddy plateau and stopped to rest against the same boulder that had hidden Cindy nearly an hour earlier. The long dirt access road that began at the fork by the boat launch finally concluded atop the plateau, strewn with puddles, with auxiliary roads branching out to the left and the right. Ahead, the remnants of the access road withered into another footpath that ended at a steep, muddy slope a few hundred yards past the boulder. Jeff splashed across the plateau and down the path to the base of the muddy embankment, scaling it rapidly at first but tiring halfway up the steep slope. Clawing his way to the top, he grabbed a fistful of exposed roots from the overhanging forest bed to help him climb out of the pit.

He rested for several minutes with his legs dangling off the edge of the natural forest bed, envisioning how the ground might have once sloped to the lakefront before the excavation had mangled the landscape. A few minutes later, he stood up and walked twenty feet through the woods to the perimeter fence slicing through the unblemished forest at the far boundary of the property. He glared at it for a moment before brushing the back of his fingers across its metal mesh, and the bite of electricity confirmed that JJ had indeed reenergized the control panel prior to their brawl in the cabin loft.

He returned to the brink of the pit and sat down on the lip

again while the cold, steady rain fell upon him. From his vantage point, he could see a significant portion of the excavation site, although the cabin hill rose sharply to his right and the cabin itself remained beyond his view. Studying the access road winding down from the hilltop, he longed to pinpoint Curly's location from a safe distance, but the terrain was too fractured and the visibility too low to hold much hope for a faraway glimpse. Gradually he focused on points closer to his own position until finally he looked down upon the slope he had just ascended. His own footprints were easily discernable through the muddy base of the slope, but to his right was another set of footprints, worn away by the heavy rainfall, scaling the same slope at a gentler angle.

Curious, he stood up and followed the edge of the ridge to the right, tracing the fading footprints climbing the lesser incline. The footprints stopped at the top of the ridge before retreating down the slope, apparently thwarted by the overhanging forest bed. He continued along the edge of the pit, shielding his eyes from the rainfall to espy a shadowy crevice tucked between the base of the hill and the converging fence line at the northwest corner of the pit. A white sneaker protruded from the crevice, connected to the leg of a body obscured in the shadows of the overhanging rock.

"Cindy!" he cried out.

He jumped from the ridge into the excavation pit, bounding down the slope in three giant strides before stumbling and falling forward onto the gravelly path at the bottom. Pain shot through his palms as he braced his fall with his hands, but he scrambled to his feet and staggered into the dim crevice where Cindy lay facing away from him, shielded from the rainfall by the overhanging rock.

"Cindy, it's me!" He dropped to his knees and pulled at her shoulder but quickly withdrew his hand at the sight of blood smeared across her white windbreaker. Stunned, he tried to stand but stumbled backward instead to fall ruggedly onto the seat of his pants. He rested his elbows upon his knees and buried his head in his arms. "I'm too late," he moaned.

Cindy rolled over, and her eyelids fluttered open. "Jeff?" she asked weakly.

He lifted his head, revealing a face streaked with rain, mud, and tears. "You're alive!" He lunged forward to gather her in his arms. "I saw the blood and—"

"Blood?" She checked herself and then looked at his hands. "It's not mine. It's yours."

Jeff held up his left hand in the dim light of the shadowy crevice. "I tore my stitches open," he said. He pulled the wet bandage from his forehead and pressed it against his palm. "Are you all right? Did they hurt you?"

"I'm cold," she said. "I'm so cold."

He squeezed her frigid fingers in his good hand. "You're soaking wet. How long have you been out here?"

"I don't know," she said softly. "An hour, I think. Curly shot a bullet at me. I barely got away." She struggled to her knees and tried to help him wrap the wound on his palm, but her fingers trembled uncontrollably. "I knew you'd come back for me."

Jeff took the cotton strip from her hand and finished fastening the cloth around the reopened wound on his palm, pulling the dressing tight before tucking the ends away. He took off his green vest and placed it in her lap. "Take this. It's wet, but it's warm."

She slipped her arms through the holes and pulled it over her back. "What about you?"

He peered out beyond the corner of the crevice. "I'll be all right."

She lay down again and curled into a ball, burying her frigid hands in the vest pockets. "I'm sorry I hit you, Jeff. I was afraid."

He felt a tinge of comfort inside, for all the hardship he had endured on a long and arduous day seemed a little more remote with their reconciliation. He longed to tell her about all that had transpired since they'd split up, but he sensed that she was struggling to maintain coherency under the duress of her deteriorating physical condition. "It was just a crazy night," were the only words he could muster.

She pulled her hand from the vest pocket and held up the stopper from the crystal decanter. "What's this?"

He took the glass object from her hand and raised it to his eye, but it did not hold the same luster that it had on that moonlit night in Salisbury. "It's just a keepsake," he told her. "From a former life."

She closed her eyes. "I don't understand."

He slipped the stopper into the pocket of his jeans and crouched close to her ear. "Cindy, listen to me. I need you to stay here. Don't go anywhere. This is a good hiding place." He pulled the hatchet from his belt and set it on the ground beside her. "Use this if you have to. As soon as I find a way out, I'll come back for you."

"The fence is on," she murmured.

"I know. I'll find a way. I won't let you down. I promise."

He leaned toward the edge of the crevice again and gazed out for any sign of his enemy. As he did, he thought he heard her whisper, "I love you," but when he looked back, she had already turned away from him. She seemed to have drifted off to sleep, so he bent over and kissed her on the back of her head. before turning to the opening of the crevice again. With hope renewed, he gritted his teeth and stepped out in his tattered T-shirt, darting from the hideaway into the weather to face the hardscrabble grounds of the abandoned mining property once again.

CHAPTER 15

T WENTY MILES OF running had taken Crazy Legs from Mick's doorstep to his current location, eastward along the outside perimeter of the electric fence. The solitary journey through the cold rain had helped attune him to his surroundings, so that when he approached the fence he sensed something unusual about it, which he verified by dragging a knuckle painfully across its electrified wire meshing. Since then, he trailed the fence line down the sloping hill toward Almond Lake, where dark storm clouds rolled like smoke over the steel-gray waters and brightly colored trees.

As he approached the lake, he struggled to maintain a course alongside the fence as it rose along the inclining terrain to his left. Soon the fence towered high overhead, while his path of lesser resistance degraded into a chasm of mud and water that ultimately dumped him upon the shore of the lake. With his long physical jaunt finally complete, he rose to his feet and sat on a rock at the edge of the beach, resting his elbows upon his knees and letting the cool rain fall upon his neck, unhindered by the forest trees.

He gazed to his right at the perimeter path that disappeared into the brush, then he rose and trudged to the rock wall on his left. Resting his back against the wall, he could see out upon the lake the silhouette of a rescue boat bobbing in the choppy water, perhaps anchoring a diving team or dragging the lake for a body. He held his breath and cocked an ear to the sky, listening to the faint, rapid beat of an unseen helicopter, but he was unable to pinpoint its location amid the low clouds. Sliding to the far end of the rock wall, he saw that the perimeter fence descended from high, rocky terrain inaccessible from his position on the beach, in a similar fashion to the northern track on the other side of the cliff wall. He placed his hands flat against his hips and leaned back to crack the joints in his stiffening back, scanning the craggy rock wall above as he stretched. From his vantage point, the cliff seemed simple enough to climb, so as soon as he felt rested enough, he began to scale its face.

The base of the wall proved as easy to traverse as a rocky beach point, but as he neared its midpoint, his fingers felt the sting of the stiff wind and stabbing rain. His calves cramped from the strain of keeping his body pinned to the wall, and soon he discovered that some of his anticipated footholds were farther apart than they had seemed from the beach. Leaning forward, he reached for a jagged protrusion of wet shale overhead, but as he grappled it, his trailing foot slipped from a notch in the wall, leaving him dangling by his hands. His rubber soles found little traction against the slick wall, but he managed to pull himself up onto the protrusion perched nearly a hundred feet over the serrated rocks on the beach.

He tried not to look down and instead gazed up in desperation to see a slim ledge ten feet from the top of the wall that seemed capable of supporting his weight. To his left, a thin fissure snaked up to a point just a few feet shy of the ledge, and by shifting sideways, he was able to wedge the toe of his running shoe inside the crack. Meticulously he clawed his way up the crease as the hard rain battered his wet clothing and weary limbs. The fissure tightened as he ascended it, and five feet from the ledge, it narrowed so much he could no longer stick a toe inside it, but a flat rock jutting out from the wall to his right offered him a stepping-stone to the ledge he sought.

The flat rock wobbled as he committed his weight upon it, and it crumbled beneath him as he lunged for the lip of the ledge. Weather and gravity conspired against his wiry fingers as they grasped the slippery rock, but he managed to lift an elbow onto the ledge, with the soles of his running shoes scraping for a foothold against the wall. At last, his toe caught some support against the stone, allowing him to raise a knee onto the shelf, and he stood to rest his back against the cliff wall with an eagle's view of Almond Lake below.

As his beating heart settled, he looked up to see that the remaining wall above him consisted of a sheer ten-foot rise to the apex of the cliff with no apparent footholds to assist him. Reaching overhead, he found that his outstretched fingertips fell a full two feet short of the cliff's edge. The danger of attempting a standing jump two hundred feet off the ground seemed obvious enough, but he also knew there was no safe way back down the cliff with the stepping-stone to the fissure gone. He dried his hands the best he could on his running jacket and rehearsed the body motions needed for a successful jump, knowing there would be no second attempt if he failed. Finally, he coiled low and whispered a quick prayer before springing for the edge of the cliff.

Both hands initially grasped the lip of the slate rock but the right hand slipped off, leaving him hanging in thin air by the left. Again, his rubber soles scraped against the wall for traction, while he mustered all his remaining energy to lift his right elbow back over the edge of the cliff. He spotted a long, scraggly vine protruding through a crack in the flat shale of the hilltop edge and lunged to grab hold of it, but the weight of his body began to pull the roots of the vine from the moist soil inside the crack. Climbing up the vine, yet sliding backward toward the cliff, he glanced across the grassy hilltop to the wooden cabin, if only to glimpse a final, unattainable goal. Instead, the sight of a friend slinking along the cabin wall rekindled his hope.

"Jeff!" he cried out. "Help!"

Jeff nearly jumped from his skin at the sound of an unexpected voice calling his name from the cliff's edge; he whirled about to see his friend sliding away with the vine falling limp in his hands. Crazy Legs gave up on the vine and grabbed for the lip of the ledge, while Jeff dashed across the hilltop and dove toward the edge to save his friend. He gasped with his heart in his throat when he sensed he might have lunged too robustly, but he dragged his toes hard along the slate rock and skidded to a halt at the very brink of the cliff, grabbing the cuff of his friend's running jacket just as the protruding hand slipped free of the rock.

"Gimme your other hand!" he shouted.

Crazy Legs reached up with a groan and stretched far enough to clench Jeff's slippery fingers, even as his other arm began to slide through his jacket sleeve. Jeff stretched farther to grab the waistband of his friend's running suit before leaning back on his heels, using his leverage to pull the skinny boy over the edge and onto the hilltop, where they both collapsed in exhaustion upon the gray rock ledge.

They lay on their backs for a long moment, panting and speechless with the rain falling upon their faces. Finally Crazy Legs sat up and rubbed his shoulder with a wince. "Thanks, Jeff. I was screwed if you didn't come by."

Jeff rolled onto his side. "So what the hell are you doing here?"

"Huh? What do you mean?"

"If I wanted your help, I would've waited for you back home."

Crazy Legs's mouth dropped open. "I just ran twenty miles—"

"So run another twenty back home. Last thing I need is the Hurricanes getting in my way." Jeff rose to his feet and stormed off toward the cabin.

Crazy Legs stood up and trotted after him. "I'm not just a Hurricane, Jeff. I'm your friend too. You can't do this alone."

Jeff spun about to face him. "The hell I can't. I already took out JJ and I found Cindy. You're a complication."

Crazy Legs halted in his tracks. "You found Cindy? Where is she?"

"She's hiding." Jeff glanced toward the mining pit entrance. "We're not safe here. C'mon." He ran across the grassy hilltop to leap onto the cabin porch with Crazy Legs trailing him closely behind, and he stopped abruptly by the front door at the edge of the broken glass from the shattered casement window. A puddle of blood remained on the porch, but he saw no sign of JJ anywhere.

Crazy Legs nearly collided with him. "What happened here?"

"I told you. I took JJ out," Jeff said. "I wonder where he went."

His friend glanced about. "Maybe he's under the porch."

"Well, he better stay there then." Jeff pushed open the creaky front door and peered inside. "I need you to do something for me."

"Anything, Jeff."

"Stand right here and keep guard. If you see anyone— anyone at all—holler your head off."

"You got it."

Jeff threw the front door completely open, unsure if he would find JJ inside but confident that he could subdue his injured foe if he did. He kicked the toppled chair aside on his way to the open cellar door and barreled downstairs two steps at a time. As expected, the power button on the fence control panel glowed green again, beckoning him as he rushed across the cellar floor. He pulled the metal housing free and tossed it to the floor, but instead of disconnecting the jumper wire again, he picked up a small yellow sledgehammer leaning against the cement foundation and proceeded to bash the electrical box into junk with it.

His frenzy was interrupted by a shout from above. "Jeff! Get up here, quick!"

Jeff wiped his sweaty brow and rushed back to the staircase with the sledgehammer still in hand, dashing up the staircase and across the main room again with a shudder of anticipation for what he might find. Outside, he saw Crazy Legs on the left side of the porch, gazing down the grassy hill.

"Look!" his friend said, pointing down the hill.

Jeff gazed down the slope to see a familiar figure climbing the access road through the rain. "Hey, Jeff!" Denny called, waving a hand as Brain emerged from the tree line behind him.

"What the hell are *they* doing here?" Jeff asked.

Crazy Legs stroked his chin. "I guess they decided to come after all."

Jeff smacked him on the shoulder. "You guys are gonna get me killed. C'mon!"

He cast a wary eye back to the mining pit entrance again as they jumped off the porch for the grassy hilltop. Below, the final trio of Hurricanes emerged from the tree line, with Axle limping along between Mick and TJ, his arms looped around their shoulders. When they were midway up the hill, Jeff spotted Willie running out of the woods behind them.

"They brought the Tornadoes too?" he asked Crazy Legs.

The skinny boy shrugged. "I don't know nothin' about that."

Denny pointed a thumb over his shoulder. "We tried to lose 'em, but they wouldn't go away."

"Get up to the cabin and wait there," Jeff said. "Yell if you see Curly or JJ."

Brain came next. "Jeff, you're okay! We saw your car and feared the worst."

"I'm good. Keep following Denny." Jeff watched Craig and the remaining Tornadoes emerging from the mouth of the woods, clad in their colors of maroon and black. He descended the hill to aid his struggling friends with his eyes fixed upon the Tornado leader. "What happened?" he asked the trio.

"Axle broke a wheel," TJ said.

"It's just a sprain," Axle added.

Jeff frowned at Mick. "Why are you here?"

"We came to help," Mick said.

"Looks like you need more help than I do." Jeff tapped TJ on the shoulder. "Get up top with the others."

TJ eased his grip on Axle's shoulder and glanced at Mick. "What about the Tornadoes?"

Mick nodded. "Do what he says."

"C'mon, let's fight 'em right now!" TJ bellowed. "The only reason we're running is because we thought Jeff was in trouble."

"I *am* in trouble," Jeff snapped. "Now move it!"

"Hey, Hollister!" Willie called from below. "How come you ain't dead yet?"

TJ grit his teeth. "You little —" He scooped up a stone from the access road and flung it with all his might at Willie, but it sailed over the scout's head and curved into the throng of Tornadoes farther down the hill. With an anguished cry, Zak covered his face with his hands and sank to his knees. He staggered to his feet with the help of his friends, his face red with blood trickling down the bridge of his nose.

He pointed a bloody finger at TJ. "You're gonna pay for that, chucker!"

Axle shuddered. "Uh-oh. I think you made him mad."

Jeff scowled at TJ and handed him the sledgehammer. "Get your ass up top!"

"All right!" TJ yelled before trotting off uphill.

Jeff took Axle's arm with an eye on the approaching Tornadoes. "C'mon, hop a little faster."

Axle winced. "I'm trying."

"We're gonna have to take them on," Mick said. "They ain't going away."

Jeff glanced at the cabin, still wary about JJ's disappearance. "We gotta get off this hilltop."

"What about what's-her—" Mick caught himself. "Cindy. Did you find her?"

Jeff eyed him skeptically. "She's hiding. She's not well. She needs help."

Mick dropped Axle's arm and backed up the hillside, drawing his gun and waving it in the air to deter the advancing Tornadoes. With all of Axle's weight solely in his arms, Jeff dragged his friend up the remainder of the hill to the windowless wall of the cabin, where the other Hurricanes had assembled. He lowered his friend onto the cement pad and pointed to the mouth of the muddy chute leading into the mine.

"Somebody scout that road," he said. "We gotta locate Curly."

Crazy Legs stepped forward, but Brain hesitated as Mick walked up and cleared his throat. "Hey Jeff," he said. "It's my gang now, remember?"

Jeff threw his hands up in the air. "I thought you said you were here to help."

"Here to help, not here to submit."

"No time to argue, Mick. If you've got a better idea, let's hear it."

Mick eyed the Tornadoes climbing the hilltop and closing ground. "Be careful," he told his scouts. "Watch each other's backs."

The two scouts darted off down the side of the muddy road and quickly vanished around the midway corner to the left. Jeff descended the path to the corner, mindful of the precarious footing as he tried to maintain a sightline with the rest of the Hurricanes above. Peering around the corner, he spotted the scouts on level ground, lingering at the fork in the road.

"Which way?" Brain called to him.

A pang of indecision hit Jeff in the gut. His plan had been simple enough: disable the basement control panel, return to Cindy's hideaway, and lead her over the eastern leg of the de-energized fence. Now there were too many variables, with two dangerous enemies still at large. Leading an entourage to Cindy's hideaway seemed like an obvious mistake, yet her deteriorating condition also demanded quick action. A half an hour ago he had held her shivering body in his arms, but now he feared her rescue was slipping away, and he felt powerless to stop it.

Raucous shouts rained down from above, and Jeff moved away from the edge of the road just in time to avoid Denny and TJ tumbling down the chute, fighting for control of the sledgehammer. They slid around the corner and splashed into the puddle at the bottom of the chute, laughing heartily as they wrestled each other to win control of the tool.

Jeff skated down the remainder of the chute and scowled at them. "Are you guys done?"

TJ grinned sheepishly as he rose with the sledgehammer in hand. "Sorry, Jeff."

Denny stood up, covered in mud. "So where's your girlfriend?"

Jeff shook his head and turned away without answering them. He stepped to the edge of the large excavation pit and peered down the rainy access road, but he dared not advance any farther, knowing Curly would be attracted to the commotion the gangs would undoubtedly create.

"Jeff, what do you want us to do?" Crazy Legs asked.

Mick exited the chute and helped Axle down to level ground before passing the hobbled Hurricane off to Denny. He took a moment to scan the unusual surroundings before stepping up to Jeff. "They're right on our heels," he said. "Get ready to fight."

Jeff pulled him aside. "I can't do this. Cindy needs me."

"We need all the help we can get," Mick replied, "especially with Axle hurt."

Brain pointed back. "They're here!"

Jeff and Mick turned to see Willie washing out into the puddle at the bottom of the hill. The Tornado scout quickly rolled to his feet and sprinted toward Axle as his allies began to spill out from the treacherous chute behind him.

"Look out!" Jeff yelled.

Axle stopped and painfully pivoted a quarter turn, only to be driven from his feet by Willie's charge. The wiry Tornado landed on him and attempted to pin him to the ground, but Denny stepped up and knocked the spy clear with a roundhouse slap to his head. Willie shook off the punch and sprang to his feet, tackling Denny into the mud beside Axle.

As the three boys scrapped on the ground, Mick stepped up and pressed Willie into the mud with a foot between his shoulder blades. He drew his pistol and pointed it down at the Tornado. "You got a death wish or something?"

Willie groaned. "You gonna shoot me in the back?"

"I might!" Mick replied.

Craig led the rest of the Tornadoes from the chute. "Let him go, Mick!"

Mick aimed the gun at him. "Shut up, Craig. Just shut up."

Craig waved him off. "Jeff! We gotta talk."

"I thought I told you to stay away," Jeff said.

"Couldn't do it, Jeff." The Tornado leader stepped around the trio in the mud and pointed a thumb back at Mick. "I ain't gonna just sit back and let some cowboy shoot my friends."

Axle and Denny rose from the ground and backed away from the angry Tornadoes pressing forward, while TJ squeezed the sledgehammer handle tighter as he slid up beside Mick.

"What part of shut up didn't you get?" Mick asked Craig, with the gun still pointed at him. "Go home and you won't get hurt."

"How?" Phil cried. "You killed our car!"

"You rammed us first!" TJ said.

"You shut up!" Zak roared. "I'm gonna pulverize you!"

Jeff glanced about nervously. "Hey, everybody keep it down!"

Tony jumped forward. "What's the matter, Hollister? Don't wanna get shot? Maybe you got it coming to you!"

Denny clenched his fists. "Maybe knocking you out will light up my life!"

He lunged forward and swung a wild punch, but Tony sidestepped the blow and shoved him forward, off the edge of the excavation pit. Denny landed in stride along the steep slope and managed a few long steps in the heavy, wet sand before tripping and tumbling head over heels to the bottom. Tony mocked him with laughter, unaware of another Hurricane sneaking up behind him.

"Bastard!" Axle shouted. He tackled Tony over the edge of the pit to roll arm in arm with him down the hill.

The other Hurricanes stepped forward to protect Mick and Jeff as the Tornadoes recoiled behind Craig like rattlesnakes. Finally Zak stepped up, wiping the cut on his forehead before pointing a bloody finger at TJ again. "It's payback time!"

"See ya." TJ hopped off the edge and ran recklessly down the slope with the sledgehammer still in hand.

"Go get him," Craig ordered.

Willie leaped from the edge in swift pursuit, but Crazy Legs sprang after him, intercepting him halfway down the slope and dragging him down into the gravel. Phil bolted off the edge after them with Brain following closely behind, leaving four boys remaining on the access road.

Craig smirked at the boys tussling in the excavation pit. "What do you say, Hollister? Ready to go at it?"

Mick leveled his gun at Craig's chest. "How about if I just blow you away instead?"

Craig scoffed. "You ain't got the guts." He jumped off the edge for the sloping wall of the pit.

"Wanna bet?" Mick called after him.

Zak stepped to the edge of the pit. "Better hold on to that gun tight, Landry. It's the only thing keeping you alive."

The burly Tornado turned and bounded down the hillside while Mick waved the pistol in the air. "I got one for you too!" he called.

Jeff grabbed him by the sleeve. "You can't fire that gun. You might as well shoot up a flare."

Mick snarled at first, but he quickly softened his expression. "Don't worry, Jeff. I'm saving it for someone special."

Jeff eased his grip on his friend's arm. "Well, Curly's got one too. And we're all in the crossfire."

Mick turned a wistful eye to the two gangs regrouping in the pit. "Things sure have gotten crazy. I miss the days when we'd fight just for the fun of it."

Jeff gazed down into the pit with him. "Those days died with Train."

Mick nodded. "It's not the same anymore. Still, there's something you could do."

"What's that?"

"Fight with the Hurricanes one more time."

Jeff knew this was as close to an olive branch as his friend would ever offer. "Curly's still out there, and Cindy needs our help."

Mick tucked the gun under his belt and offered an open hand. "The sooner we take care of the Tornadoes, the sooner we can help you with your problem."

Jeff narrowed his eyes and shook his friend's hand. "We do things my way, understand?"

Mick smiled wryly. "Of course. I wouldn't have it any other way."

They hopped off the edge of the road and began to descend

the loose soil of the steep slope with the wind and rain at their backs. Down on the watery floor of the pit, Denny and Brain helped Axle to his feet, and together they backed toward the abandoned backhoe that faced the cabin hill rising before them. TJ led them past the backhoe loader to the sheer northern wall of the pit, cut deep and slightly concave by the teeth of the steel bucket now perched idly upon the ground. He turned about to face the Tornadoes gathering at the front end of the backhoe, with the sledgehammer held defensively across his chest.

The floor of the pit declined gently to his right, resulting in a large pool of collected rainwater along its western wall, where Crazy Legs and Willie wrestled at the edge, each trying to push the other into the water. Willie's foot slipped in the mud and Crazy Legs exploited his imbalance, shoving the diminutive Tornado back into the brown puddle with a splash. The skinny boy's grin quickly dissipated when he saw his fellow Hurricanes retreating toward the northern wall with the angry Tornadoes closing in on them. Phil and Tony sauntered forward shoulder to shoulder and Zak lurked behind them with his ire clearly focused upon TJ. Denny stepped alongside TJ and turned about to face Zak's threat, while Brain propped Axle up against the backhoe bucket before sliding up next to his friends.

TJ gripped the yellow sledgehammer like a baseball bat and pointed its head at the approaching Tornadoes. "Stop them," he beseeched his friends.

Brain stepped up first to confront Tony, who caught him off guard with a left hook that cracked the frame of his glasses and dropped him to the ground. Denny rushed forward to help, but Tony grappled him with a bear hug and they fell to the mud together, leaving TJ standing alone before the concave wall with the raging Zak bearing down on him.

Crazy Legs ran up from the right and smacked TJ on the arm. "C'mon!" He stepped up to confront Zak while TJ cocked the sledgehammer back, ready to swing as he entered the scrum. Crazy Legs swung a punch at Zak, but the bodyguard swatted him away, sending him flying into the mud. TJ slid to his left toward the backhoe bucket as Phil closed in from the right.

"Back off!" TJ shouted.

He launched a home run swing with the sledgehammer, but Phil drew his chest back just in time to avoid contact, while the yellow handle slipped free from TJ's hand. The sledgehammer slammed into the boom arm of the backhoe, its steel head snapping free from the handle and sailing over the hood of the backhoe, but the handle rattled off the metal frame of the cab before plopping nearby into the mud.

A roar echoed throughout the pit as Zak pressed forward. "Here it comes, chucker!" he shouted.

TJ flattened Phil with a right cross before pulling Denny off the ground and propping him up in Zak's path. "Keep him away from me!"

Denny struggled to orient himself. "Who?"

TJ retreated to the backhoe bucket and stood Axle upright. "Help me—"

Axle hobbled forward with his fists clenched. "I'm on it!"

Zak stormed toward them with blood still trickling from the knot on his forehead. Denny swung a fist at him, but the Tornado bodyguard blocked his punch and countered with a crushing blow to his jaw that knocked him out cold before his face hit the mud. Axle stepped forward next, but Zak grabbed him and launched him into the metal edge of the bucket, where he collapsed to the ground with a gasp. Zak stepped around the stricken Hurricanes and turned his attention back to TJ, now weaponless and shrinking toward the sheer northern wall.

TJ cowered against the wall, looking for an escape route that was not clearly evident to him. He gulped a breath of air and assumed a boxing stance as his assailant stepped up to him, driving a punch into Zak's muscular abdomen in the futile hope of knocking the wind out of him. He followed with an uppercut that split his foe's lip, but his strikes only seemed to infuriate Zak even more. The Tornado bodyguard threw him back against the wall and drew back a heavy fist, while TJ ducked his face behind his hands and offered his left shoulder as a target. Zak delivered a meaty punch with all his might, striking TJ's arm with an audible crack and pasting him to the ground in one fell swoop.

TJ writhed in pain as he grabbed for his biceps with his other hand. "Ow! My arm!"

Zak turned about to behold with visible satisfaction the subdued Hurricanes scattered about him.. He thumped his chest with a victory cry before turning his attention to the boys still scrapping in the mud by the backhoe.

Mick cried out with alarm as he neared the bottom of the gravelly slope. "We're getting crushed! C'mon!" he shouted to Jeff before sprinting down to the floor of the pit.

He veered behind Craig meandering by the loader and shoved him to the ground as he ran by, while Willie sprang from the edge of the puddle to chase him. Jeff lagged behind, still wary about engaging in a gang fight with Cindy in need and Curly on the loose. As he neared the wide shovel at the front of the vehicle, Craig stuck out a foot, tripping him and jumping on him after he fell to the mud.

"Going somewhere, Hollister?" he asked.

Jeff looped an arm around his adversary's neck. "Tell Zak to shut his trap."

Craig sneered. "I don't take orders from you, and he don't take them from me."

"You're his leader."

"And you were Mick's. For what it's worth."

Jeff pressed Craig's head to the ground. "What's your point?"

Craig grinned in spite of his twisted position. "We're a lot alike, Jeff. We both know there's a limit to our influence."

Jeff squeezed his face harder into the mud. "I'm not like you at all. I kept my word. If you had kept yours, none of this ever would've happened."

Craig laughed. "The truce was doomed to fail, Jeff! I just realized it before you did. Of course, Curly was always ready to put it out of its misery."

Jeff pulled Craig from the ground by his jacket and leaned into his face. "So you released a madman on me! And now Cindy's caught in the middle!"

Craig pushed back at him. "Look, I wanna help you! But you gotta keep Mick's gun outta my face!"

Mick glanced back at the two boys locking horns behind him. "Don't listen to his lies, Jeff!"

The Hurricane leader turned forward again, but too late to avoid Zak's thick forearm from striking him in the chest. The force of the collision knocked him back into the mud, while Zak also fell to the ground with his work boots up in the air. Mick gasped from the blow and rolled to his knees as Willie ran past him to scoop up the yellow sledgehammer handle lying in the mud. He gripped it with both hands and slipped it over Mick's head before pulling the stick back against his chest.

Zak crawled forward to grapple Mick's ankle. "Tony! Get the gun! Get the gun!"

Tony shoved Brain aside and stepped around the other stricken Hurricanes lying in the mud, and he sauntered toward Mick struggling against the yellow sledgehammer handle beneath his chin. Mick leaned back for leverage against Willie, rising to his feet and wriggling his ankle in an attempt to free it from Zak's grip, but Zak only squeezed it tighter. Tony stopped before Mick and looked him squarely in the eye with a greasy smile on his lips as he coolly reached inside the Hurricane leader's jacket for the handle of the gun.

With a frenzied cry, Mick dropped an arm to elbow Willie hard in the diaphragm. The Tornado scout gasped for air and fell back, dropping the sledgehammer handle on the ground behind him. Tony tried to pull the gun from Mick's waistband, but Mick twisted away, and the gun squirted out as they both tumbled to the mud. Mick lurched for the gun but flopped onto his stomach instead, his ankle still hindered by Zak's hold, a condition remedied by a few swift kicks to the head with the other foot. Finally free, Mick scrambled over Tony's back and dove for the gun, but Tony pulled him back with a handful of his curly blond hair.

Jammed against the engine housing of the backhoe loader, Jeff glanced over Craig's shoulder to see the gun lying in the mud thirty feet away. He tried to break away to retrieve it, but his foe scooped up the sledgehammer handle and spun about, striking him across the gut with it. Jeff doubled over from the blow while Craig drove him back against the fender of the backhoe with the stick.

Jeff mashed an open hand into his adversary's face. "Let me go! I gotta —"

Craig pressed the yellow handle harder against Jeff's chest. "You ain't going anywhere."

Pushing back against the handle from an inferior position, Jeff slipped a foot behind Craig's heel and tripped him backward. They tumbled to the ground together with Jeff on top and the sledgehammer handle falling loose in Craig's hands. Jeff grasped the handle with both hands and pushed it down against his rival's throat.

Craig gasped. "I can't breathe!"

Jeff tightened his grip on the handle and pressed down harder. "Call your men off!"

"You first!"

"No." Jeff eased the pressure off his adversary's neck and offered him a hand. "But I won't leave you hanging. I promise."

Suddenly Phil called out from the far end of the pit. "Somebody stop Kramer!"

Jeff looked up to see Crazy Legs darting through the mud,

hopping over Zak and skirting past Tony's outstretched hand to snatch the pistol out of the mud. He turned about and pointed the gun at various Tornadoes as he retreated to the side of the backhoe loader near Axle and Brain.

"Stop the fighting!" he cried out. "Tornadoes, get up against that wall! Now!"

Zak growled as he stood and backed away. "Watch it, Kramer."

"Shut up! Do it!"

The Tornadoes retreated to the concave pit wall while the battered Hurricanes assembled behind Crazy Legs by the steel bucket. Mick stood up and turned to his scout with glowering eyes. "Nice job. Now what?"

Crazy Legs stood firm. "The fighting needs to stop. Now."

"He's right!" a voice called out from behind.

Mick turned to see Jeff forcing Craig to walk with the sledgehammer handle pinned against his chest.

"Listen up! Craig has something to say." Jeff dropped the sledgehammer handle to the ground and shoved the Tornado leader forward. "Say it, Craig."

Craig stumbled forward a step before looking back. "Don't forget your part of the deal."

Jeff nodded. He stepped up to Mick and patted him on the shoulder. "My way, remember?"

Mick eyed him skeptically as Craig addressed the gangs. "Enough blood's been spilled on both sides," the Tornado leader said. "We want—no, we *need*—peace with the Hurricanes." He turned to the Hurricane leader and offered a handshake. "I'm asking for your trust again."

Mick laughed. "Trust? You want my trust? Look what Zak just did to my men!"

Jeff leaned closer. "He's offering you a broken arrow, Mick. We can't fight the Tornadoes and beat Curly too. Not down three men."

"Yeah? Well, we're down three men because of their meddling," Mick said. "He's gonna have to do something pretty fucking heroic if he wants my trust."

Jeff began to reply, but he was cut off by a familiar voice booming down into the pit. "Hey, Hollister! Look what I found!"

All eyes turned up to the brink of the access road to see Curly waving the hatchet high in the air. He stooped forward and lifted Cindy by an arm around her waist, her limp body seemingly unable to stand under its own strength.

Jeff shook a fist at him. "Let her go, Curly!"

"Come and get her!" Curly yanked her like a rag doll out of view toward the hilltop.

Jeff stared at the brim of the pit for a long moment. He lowered his head and turned back to face the gangs, where friends and foes alike stared back in silence. "Look what you did!" he cried. "You ruined everything!"

Mick shrugged. "We were just trying to help, Jeff."

"I never asked for your help! Now I'm a dead man." He stepped behind the backhoe and trudged toward a dirt ramp leading up the far wall of the pit.

Craig joined the Tornadoes gathered at the concave wall, while Brain retrieved the sledgehammer handle from the mud and gave it to Axle for support. TJ bent over Denny and helped his groggy friend from the ground before huddling the Hurricanes together. Crazy Legs ducked beneath the boom arm of the backhoe to emerge at the base of the circular ramp that Jeff had already scaled halfway.

"Jeff, wait!" he called out. "Where ya going?"

Jeff plodded forward. "I'm gonna do what he wants me to do."

Crazy Legs stopped at the base of the ramp. "You can't do that! He'll kill you!"

Jeff turned back to see Mick and Brain walking up the ramp

behind Crazy Legs. "I have to save her from him," he told them. "If that means he wins, so be it."

Crazy Legs threw his arms up in the air. "So you're just gonna surrender? Okay, maybe we screwed up your plan, but come on! You're Jeff Hollister! No one's gonna figure out how to take Curly down if you can't."

Jeff shook his head. "This has to end now. For her sake."

"It's suicide, Jeff. If you go up there unarmed, you're just killing yourself." Crazy Legs held out the gun. "At least defend yourself."

Jeff hesitated. The offer was tempting, but he knew if Curly saw him carrying a gun, it would likely spark him into a higher stage of violence, and he shuddered at the thought of engaging in a shoot-out with Cindy in the line of fire. Instead of taking the gun, he simply turned about and continued climbing toward the access road, leaving Crazy Legs standing in bewilderment on the ramp with the gun still held out before him.

Mick stepped up from behind and snatched the pistol from his hand. "Gimme that."

"Hey!" Crazy Legs objected.

Mick shoved him aside and stuffed the gun back under his belt before starting up the ramp amid moans of displeasure from the Tornadoes approaching the ramp below. Ahead, Jeff peered over the brink of the pit at the top of the ramp, wary that Curly might still be lingering on the access road, but the road was clear.

Brain held a palm up to the sky as he shuffled past Crazy Legs. "Look," he said. "It's starting to snow."

Jeff glanced up. Sure enough, large wet snowflakes had begun to mix with the rain and sleet. The precipitation had finally eased since the morning's torrent, but a raw wind blew in from the lake, cutting through his wet clothing as he climbed onto the access road with his friends trudging after him. He skulked along the road to the base of the chute and gazed up through the icy rain at the treacherous hill rising before him. The thin path on the left edge offered more footing than the stream of rainwater running down the hill, so he lowered his head and stepped to the edge of the path as Craig led the Tornadoes out of the pit.

"Jeff, wait a minute." Mick jogged to the bottom of the rise and looked back. "I need a scout up front!"

Brain held up his broken glasses. "I can't scout much of anything right now."

Tony glanced at Craig and raised his hand. "I'll go." He ran past Jeff to start up the side path.

Mick pointed to Crazy Legs. "Follow him."

Craig laughed as the Hurricane scout darted off. "Don't trust my man, Mick?"

"Should I? That's your lieutenant up there."

Jeff cocked an ear toward Almond Lake. He could still hear the hum of the helicopter rotor over the treetops, but it sounded far away, perhaps across the lake or even farther out over the forest to the west of the Portland Township. "Follow me," he told Mick and Brain.

He started up the path, slipping and stumbling along the perilous footing with the able-bodied Hurricanes and a majority of Tornadoes falling in line behind him. Rounding the midway corner, they encountered the two scouts descending the hill.

"You can get about five feet from the top," Tony said. "Any closer, he'll see you."

"He's up against the side of the cabin," Crazy Legs added. "And JJ's back. He don't look so good."

"What about Cindy?" Jeff asked. "Is she okay?"

Crazy Legs shook his head. "I don't know. She's just lying there."

Jeff grimaced and gestured them backward. "Okay, get in line."

Crazy Legs stepped past him and fell in position behind Mick and Brain. Tony tried to follow in line, but Mick hip-checked him into the center of the road. "Enough baloney, Riga-Tony." He snickered as the Tornado slid down the muddy chute, cursing all the way around the midway corner and out of view.

"Really, Mick?" Craig yelled from below.

"Quit screwing around," Jeff said. He crouched low and inched forward to the brink of the hilltop to see Cindy lying motionless on her right side and facing the hilltop. JJ sat propped against the wall with one hand tucked beneath his bloody flannel shirt and the other lazily clasping the hatchet by his side. Curly paced about with his revolver in hand, barking an order at JJ before rushing near the top of the muddy chute.

"Come on, Hollister!" he shouted out blindly. "I ain't got all day!"

Jeff slid back to his friends as Craig slinked up from behind. "What'd you see?" the Tornado asked. "How does he look?"

Jeff shook his head. "He's wigging out. We don't have much time."

Mick leaned closer. "I can take him out. Just say the word."

Jeff could feel the glare of Craig's eyes upon his back. "No. You might hit her. And if you miss him, there's no telling what he'll do."

Mick frowned and glanced back to Craig. "Looks like we could use some heroics," he said with a wink.

Craig snarled back at him before motioning the other Tornadoes forward. "I'll go talk to him," he said.

"You better not," Jeff said. "He looks pretty unhinged."

"I've been friends with Curly my whole life," Craig said. "If anyone can talk him down, it's me."

Jeff glanced at Mick. "You good with that?"

"Hell yeah," Mick said. "He wants our trust. Here's his chance."

Jeff patted Craig on the back. "All right, go for it. Be careful."

Craig laughed. "I'll be fine."

The Tornado leader continued up the hill with Zak and Phil following him dutifully, while Jeff crept forward to watch with the three able Hurricanes crouching behind him. Craig stopped his men at the edge of the hilltop and whispered instructions to them before leading them out into the open. JJ brightened when he spotted his friends, sitting up as much as his wounded abdomen allowed, but Curly scowled and leveled his revolver at his leader.

"What do you want?" he demanded.

Phil and Zak froze at the tone of his voice, but Craig proceeded with caution. "How about putting that gun down?"

"So you're on Hollister's side now?" Curly asked.

"It ain't about sides," Craig said. "She's innocent. Let her go."

"She ain't so innocent. She's Hollister's girlfriend."

"Look, Curly. The gangs just—"

"Aw, screw the gangs! I saw you getting all chummy with Hollister down there. You're a traitor!"

Craig bristled and glanced back at his friends before edging forward again. "I'm not a traitor, Curly. This has to end."

"It'll end," Curly said. "It'll end with a bullet in Hollister's head!"

Back at the chute, Jeff turned to the Hurricanes huddled behind him. "He's in over his head."

"Someone better get him out of there," Crazy Legs said.

"Phil! Zak!" Jeff called out. "Get him back!"

Zak and Phil heard his shout and exchanged uneasy glances, but Craig signaled them with an open palm to allay their fears. He reached the same hand out to Curly. "C'mon, Curly. Give me the gun."

"Stay back," his lieutenant warned.

"No. Enough's enough. Put it down."

Curly held the gun steady in his hand. "I don't wanna hurt you, Craig."

Craig stopped a half dozen steps away from him. "You're not gonna hurt me. You're gonna give me the gun, and we're all gonna go home."

"Don't come any closer—"

"Give it to me!"

"No!"

Everyone flinched as a gunshot rang out. Craig cried out in anguish and collapsed to the ground with a bloodstain spreading on the left thigh of his jeans. "You shot me!" he wailed. "You son of a bitch!"

"You shoulda listened to me!" Curly shouted back at him.

"He shot him!" Crazy Legs gasped from the edge of the hilltop. "He shot his own friend!"

Zak rushed forward to aid his leader. He pointed a finger at his lieutenant. "You're gonna get it now, Curly!"

Curly turned the revolver to him. "You wanna go next?"

Phil rushed forward with his hands in the air. "Don't shoot, Curly!" he said. He grabbed Craig by the wrists, dragging him back to the mouth of the access road as Zak guarded their retreat. They pulled their agonized leader over the brink of the hilltop and propped him up against the cut rock wall at the top of the chute.

Craig writhed in pain. "He shot me! I can't believe he fucking shot me!"

Tony hustled to the top of the chute and stripped off his Tornado jacket, kneeling down to press it against his leader's bleeding leg. The injury didn't appear life-threatening to Jeff, but he knew his rival would need medical attention before long. He also sensed that they had just witnessed the final act of the Tornadoes' legacy. "It's me he wants dead," he reminded everyone. "No one's gonna stand in his way."

He motioned for the Hurricanes to follow him, but Craig grabbed the cuff of Mick's jeans as he stepped past. "Was that heroic enough for ya?"

"Not bad," Mick said glibly as he yanked his leg free. He followed Crazy Legs to the brink of the hilltop and crouched down with him alongside Jeff. There they watched Curly stomping and fretting about the hilltop, his face beet red with anger and the revolver clenched tightly in his hand. He stopped and glared in their direction, but unable to see them, he stormed back to the cement pad where JJ lay propped up against the cabin wall with Cindy lying motionless before him.

"Hollister!" he shrieked. He drew a foot back and kicked Cindy hard in the midriff with his work boot. She groaned and recoiled into a fetal position, but she did not cry out.

Jeff lunged forward in a fury, but his friends grabbed him and pinned him down. "Let me go!" he cried. "I'm gonna kill him!"

Mick forced him down with a forearm against his jaw. "That's what he wants! He's trying to draw you out!"

"Well, we can't just sit here!" Crazy Legs cried.

A few deep breaths helped calm Jeff's nerves. "Who's left who can walk?"

Mick glanced back down the chute at the injured Hurricanes rounding the midway corner. "Brain's okay. TJ's got a busted arm. Denny and Axle are kinda messed up."

"And the Tornadoes?"

"You're gonna count on them?"

Jeff nodded. "Get 'em up here. I have a plan..."

Curly tapped JJ's boot with the toe of his shoe. "Don't die. I still need you."

JJ rolled his eyes up toward him. "I need a doctor."

"Soon enough. Is she still alive?"

"She's breathing, I think."

"Good. She's our ticket outta here."

"Then don't kick her no more." JJ lifted his finger toward the chute entrance. "Better check that out."

Curly turned to see a line of four Tornadoes shuffling uphill, their squared shoulders obscuring a second row of Hurricanes crouching behind them. He sprang forward and pointed the revolver at the group. "All of you! Get back now!"

The front line muddled to the right, shielding a short run to the nearest corner of the cabin for the back line. "Go!" Jeff yelled before dashing out from the Tornadoes' cover with his head ducked low. Mick darted after him, followed by Crazy Legs and Brain in a sprint, while the Tornadoes retreated toward the chute. Curly turned the corner, ready to fire his gun, only to glimpse the back of the last Hurricane jacket slipping around the far end of the cabin.

Brain fell back against the short cabin wall and wiped his broken glasses with the tail of his shirt. "That was close!"

Crazy Legs poked an eye around the corner. "He's not coming."

"Of course not," Mick said. "He doesn't wanna get shot."

Curly's voice bellowed over the rooftop. "Hollister! She's gonna die!"

Brain perched his glasses back onto his face the best he could. "Now what?"

Jeff crept to the front corner of the cabin. He scanned the long wooden porch before turning to the woods to their right. "Wait for my signal," he said.

He stepped to the cover of a pine tree standing ten feet from the nearby fence. From there, he slid up to a maple tree directly in line with the cabin's front porch, and another maple led him to the brink of the forested slope leading back to Quarry Road. The next tree offering adequate cover brought him in line with the front door, albeit four feet down the hill. At this vantage point, he could see Curly pacing between the cement pad and the front porch as he attempted to guard both sides of the hilltop at the same time. Jeff eyed the elm at the edge of the access road twenty feet away, the same tree that had provided him cover for his initial arrival. He turned back to Mick at the far end of the porch and motioned for him to send the next man.

"You're up," Mick told Brain. The Hurricane leader peered down the front porch, his eyes peeled for any sign of Curly as Brain advanced along the same course that Jeff had taken. Once Brain reached the third tree, Mick turned to Crazy Legs and beckoned him forward with a finger. "Come here."

Crazy Legs cast a final look behind the cabin before slipping down the sidewall beside his leader. "You're next," he said.

Mick shook his head and pointed to the edge of the roof. "Help me up."

"What? That's not part of the plan."

Mick reached for the edge of the awning, unable to grasp its wet shingles firmly enough to climb onto it. "I got my own plan. Gimme a boost."

Crazy Legs folded his arms across his chest. "No way. I'm not gonna do it. I'm doing things Jeff's way."

Mick grabbed Crazy Leg by his collar and jacked him up against the wall with a forearm under his chin. "Now you listen to me, you little twerp. Jeff's doing everything he can to save his girlfriend, and so am I. You're either with us or against us. And if you're against us"—he pulled out his pistol and crammed the barrel against the scout's rib cage—"I'll cap your scrawny ass right here!"

Crazy Legs shrank beneath Mick's pale blue eyes devoid of all compassion. With a quivering lip, he dropped to one knee before his leader and cupped his hands with interlocking fingers, giving Mick a step and a lift to the roof of the cabin. Mick tucked the gun away and reached for the shingles again, while Crazy Legs lifted him high enough to climb atop the flatter roof of the rickety awning.

Jeff finally advanced to the corner elm, where he had a clear view of Mick scaling the cabin rooftop. He turned and waved Brain forward. "What the hell is he doing?"

His friend shielded his eyes from the precipitation to view his leader's escapade. "Trying to be a hero, I guess."

Jeff grabbed his friend's arm and pointed down the front access road. "Go find help. Cops, townies, anyone. Don't let Curly see you leave. He left his keys in his truck. Hurry."

"You got it," Brain said before running off down the hill.

Jeff glanced to the far end of the porch, where Crazy Legs peered around the corner to view the front porch and the hilltop beyond. He caught the scout's eye with a subtle wave and pointed to Mick, but his friend only shook his head and threw his hands up in exasperation.

Up on the awning, Mick backed to the edge of the cabin rooftop rising at a steeper pitch. He dug his palms and heels for traction against the icy shingles, and with the aid of his rubber soles, he methodically climbed his way up to the spine of the roof. He flipped onto his belly to straddle the spine, pulling out the gun again before crawling to the lakeside edge of the cabin. Still unable to see Curly, he rose to his knees and then to his feet, inching to the very brink of the rooftop as the freezing rain pelted his body.

At last he spotted Curly standing near the cement pad directly below him, and he aimed the barrel of his pistol down toward his enemy's head with a single, steady hand. At that very moment a gust of wind, or perhaps the breath of fate, flicked a pellet of ice high upon his right cheek, splashing onto the bottom lid of his dominant eye. He blinked and flinched as he squeezed the trigger, firing a pair of bullets that missed to the right and ricocheted off the edge of the cement pad on a trajectory out over the lake.

Curly dropped low and spun about on his back heel, firing a single shot upward that struck the Hurricane leader in the left clavicle. Mick cried out in pain and instinctively reached for the wound, while the pistol flew from his hand and skittered off the backside of the roof into an overgrown bush behind the cabin, The impact of the bullet knocked him back to the right; he slipped on the icy shingles and fell hard upon his buttocks before somersaulting twice down the front side of the rooftop. He landed flat on his back upon the flimsy awning, promptly crashing through into a heap of splintered wood and broken limbs upon the porch below.

"Mick!" Crazy Legs cried out. He scrambled down the porch over broken glass and slid through splintered wood to gather his friend in his arms. Curly spun to his left and assumed a wide stance at the front end of the porch, aiming the revolver directly at the skinny boy's chest as he cradled Mick's broken body in his lap. Crazy Legs gazed up, wide-eyed and agape at the gun bearing down on him, while Jeff cringed behind the elm tree twenty yards away, waiting for the gunshot that would surely end his friend's life. Instead, Curly lifted the revolver and retreated toward the side of the cabin again, his eyes darting from side to side in search of additional threats.

"Hollister!" he shouted. "Show your face!"

Jeff's mind raced. Curly had yet to display any mercy toward the Hurricanes, so it made no sense that he would start doing so now. Staring at the gun in his enemy's hands, he recalled the news report describing both guns: a 9mm semiautomatic pistol and a .38-caliber revolver. The pistol surely would've been Curly's weapon of choice until Mick took it away from him, and Jeff had seen enough of Mick's gun to know it was no revolver. The revolver held six bullets in its cylinder, which probably would've seemed plenty to kill one enemy, perhaps until now. Jeff realized his theory might be completely faulty, but with Cindy fading on the cement pad and Mick bleeding on the front porch, there was little time to mull alternate lines of reasoning.

So how many shots had Curly already fired? He could feel precious seconds ticking away as he tried to recall. The bullet in Mick's shoulder was the second Curly had shot at him, the first missing its mark in the dimly lit sand field two nights earlier. Cindy had spoken of a shot fired at her during her escape, and Craig lay bleeding at the chute with a bullet in his leg. So that was four.

And Train was five.

Jeff drew a breath and stepped out from the cover of the elm tree with the faint hope that Curly wasn't as crazy as everyone thought he was. A few snowflakes wafted about him as he turned his shoulders toward the cabin. "I'm right here," he called out.

Curly curled his lips into a sinister grin. "It's about time, Hollister. I was beginning to think you were letting everyone else do your dirty work for you."

Jeff edged forward. "You know what I think? I think you only have one bullet left in that gun."

Curly opened the cylinder and snapped it shut again. "Enough to kill you dead."

Jeff smiled faintly at the ease with which his enemy had confirmed his theory. "Maybe. But if you do, count on my friends returning the favor."

Curly looked around and laughed. "I don't see too many of your friends left standing, Jeffy!"

"He's got more friends than you do right now!" Zak bellowed from the edge of the hilltop.

Jeff held his breath with his best poker face on, hoping that Craig's other men would follow suit. Curly turned and wandered toward the chute entrance, where the Tornadoes had gathered in front of their stricken leader with the wounded Hurricanes milling about behind them. He eyed the ragtag group for a long moment before trotting back to the side cabin wall. Kneeling down, he murmured into JJ's ear before handing him the revolver and taking the hatchet in return. Finally he stood up and strode out onto the hilltop, stroking a thumb against the blade of the hatchet. "Problem solved, Jeffy," he said. "Anyone tries anything stupid, the last bullet is hers."

Jeff stepped sideways onto the open hilltop to see the barrel of the revolver pointed at Cindy's torso, but Curly quickly cut off his view, viciously swinging the hatchet at him from side to side with one hand. Jeff twisted away as the tip of the hatchet blade missed his exposed belly by a quarter-inch, but the return stroke nicked his forearm, drawing a thin line of blood and eliciting a cry of alarm from him. Curly pressed forward and slashed at Jeff's chest, but he pivoted away, allowing his adversary to overextend himself before landing a solid rabbit punch to the back of his head. Curly stumbled forward and fell onto his knees, sliding to a halt on the wet grass before flipping onto the seat of his pants with the hatchet still in hand.

"Remember that one?" Jeff said.

Curly gnashed his teeth as he rose to his knees, while Jeff backed toward the center of the hilltop with his fists cocked and blood trickling from his left elbow. He glanced to the mouth of the chute to spot Axle leaning against the yellow sledgehammer handle, desperately wishing he still had the weapon in his own possession. Axle noticed the forlorn expression, and with a wince of pain from his battered rib cage, he pulled a thin white object from the pocket of his Hurricane jacket. He handed the object to TJ, and once TJ realized what it was, he stepped forward and tossed it toward the hilltop with his good right arm.

"Jeff! Catch!" he cried out.

TJ's perfect throw landed the object at Jeff's feet, and with his eyes affixed upon his enemy, he stooped down to blindly grasp it with his fingers. He stood up and gazed down at the familiar white handle of his hunting knife in the palm of his hand.

"My knife!" he gasped. "But how—?" He narrowed his eyes at Curly as the truth dawned upon him. "You stabbed Happy Jack, not me! That was *your* knife in his stomach, not mine!"

Curly glanced at the Tornadoes. "Shut up, Hollister."

Jeff turned toward the rival gang with his palms open, his

knife cradled loosely in his good hand. "He stabs your friend, he shoots your leader, and he's letting your buddy bleed out right in front of you." He shook his head. "Man, with friends like him…"

Curly rose to his feet. "I said shut up."

Jeff clasped the knife handle in his palm again and turned to his enemy with an acerbic eye. "Look at you. Living out of your truck, running from the law. All your friends have deserted you. And I'm still here. Your little scheme hasn't worked."

"Maybe not." Curly tightened his grip on the hatchet. "But I'm not done yet."

The Tornado lieutenant circled him like a scorpion ready to strike, switching the hatchet from hand to hand, while Jeff backed to the center of the hilltop with the wet wind pasting his tattered T-shirt to the small of his back. As he unfolded his knife, Curly lunged forward and swiped the hatchet at him again, forcing him to suck in his gut to avoid the tip of its blade. He countered with an upward slash that slit the sleeve of his enemy's jacket, but Curly whirled about and delivered a backhand swipe as Jeff lunged aside. He spun about to glimpse Curly's exposed torso, but rather than drive his knife into his enemy's belly, he threw a left hook instead, smacking Curly's jaw and cutting his lip.

Curly staggered away and dropped to one knee with the hatchet still in hand, wiping his lip on the back of his hand before nodding in deference to the skill of the punch. Slowly he rose to assume a battle stance again, while Jeff shook the sting from his aching left hand, ruing his impulsive display of mercy and knowing his enemy would never reciprocate such an act.

"You missed your chance, Hollister," Curly said. "Now it's time to die."

With his surly eyes fixed on the tip of Jeff's knife, the Tornado lieutenant faked a move to the right before spinning about and slashing downward from the left. Jeff rolled defensively onto his back and kicked up a foot at the hatchet, striking the underside of Curly's wrist with the toe of his sneaker. Curly grabbed his wrist with a loud yelp, dropping the hatchet to the ground, while Jeff hopped to a squatting position, pointing his knife keenly at his enemy as he lifted the hatchet from the soggy grass.

"You won't be needing this anymore," he said.

He stood up and drew the hatchet back with his injured hand, flinging it as far as he could toward the cliff, but it still landed ten feet from the edge. Cringing, he glanced back at Curly, who stared back at him as wide-eyed as a startled possum. They both broke into a sprint for the hatchet, one longing to retrieve it and the other intent on removing it from the battle arena. Jeff reached the hatchet first and awkwardly swung a foot at it while running full stride, striking his toe against the butt of the handle and punting the hatchet over the edge of the cliff. When he tried to stop upon the slippery rock, however, Curly charged into him and knocked him from his feet. He tumbled hard upon the gray slab of rock four feet from the edge as his knife skittered out of his hand.

Curly jumped on top of him and pinned a knee on his chest, mashing a hand into his face and clawing up his arm for the knife just beyond his fingertips. Jeff cocked his wrist back and flicked the knife away from his enemy's reach, so that when Curly stretched for the knife, he invariably eased the pressure of his knee from Jeff's chest. Jeff slid out from under his weight, and they scowled at each other before simultaneously diving for the knife, succeeding only in knocking it ever closer to the edge of the cliff.

Jeff shoved Curly aside and rose to his knees, reaching for the knife with his enemy doggedly clinging to his ankles. He turned back and pressed his hands against Curly's shoulders as Curly released his ankles and grappled his biceps in return. They pushed hard against each other, each using the other's leverage to rise to his feet while trying to manhandle an advantage upon the other for access to the knife. Finally Jeff's arms buckled, his strength waning from the day's arduous journey, and he slid back along the slippery rock under Curly's power. He bent his knees and tried to slink free of his enemy's hold, but Curly pulled a fist back and drove it hard into his stomach, knocking the wind from his lungs. Gasping for breath, he collapsed into Curly's arms, and his feet slipped over the brink of the cliff as his enemy continued to push him backward. His knees bounced off the slate rock and over the edge as well, while his hands groped at the cuffs of Curly's jeans to save himself from falling.

Curly pulled his legs away from Jeff's flailing fingers, leaving them to grasp the edge of the wet rock with his feet dangled freely in the air. "Bye-bye, Hollister," the Tornado lieutenant sneered. He spat down into Jeff's face and raised a foot into the air, driving the heel of his boot down upon the back of Jeff's right hand.

Jeff cried out in pain as he pulled the hand away, leaving only the fingers of his weaker left hand to keep him from plunging to the rocky beach below. Curly shuffled over and prepared to mash those fingers as well, while Jeff peered down to view his imminent doom. Instead, he spotted the thin rock ledge that had supported Crazy Legs an hour earlier, and he slid his fingers off the lip of the cliff just in time to avoid Curly's second stomp. Dragging his arms along the rock wall, he caught his bloody elbow upon the lip of the ledge, sparing himself from a deadly fall. Wincing in pain and still gasping for breath, he lifted a foot to safety as loosened stones trickled down the face of the cliff.

With the elbow still propped upon the ledge, he struggled to hold his breath as he watched the tips of Curly's work boots protrude over the lip of the cliff. His enemy tipped forward far enough to reveal the top of his bushy black hair, but certainly not far enough to spot his precarious position. A few seconds later, all signs of Curly vanished, and Jeff held still for a long moment before climbing fully onto the ledge, wondering what he had just witnessed. He dragged himself up onto the ledge with his back flush against the rock wall and the toes of his sneakers protruding over the ledge, where he recalled the final words of a close friend.

"Everyone's afraid of something," Train had said. Apparently, Curly was afraid of heights.

The chop of the helicopter rotor resonated more clearly now, emanating from somewhere closer to the south shore of the lake, but he dared not lean forward for a better view. He wiped Curly's bloody saliva from his face to behold it in his palm, and a rage began to grow in his gut. His mashed fingers, his lacerated skin, his bruised and battered body — all these things meant nothing compared to the anguish Curly had inflicted upon Cindy and his friends. This kidnapper — this murderer — who spat in his face and pushed his life to its very edge had failed to accomplish his depraved goal. Spared by the thin ledge from a horrific fall, Jeff knew his only options were clear: conquer his foe or die trying. There was no other way.

The ledge offered only one chance of escape — back up the face of the cliff to the hilltop — but turning around was no easy task on such a narrow precipice. Stepping to his left, he pivoted on the toe of his sneaker, hugging the rock wall to steady himself after his right foot found the ledge again. Fright and rage drove his thumping heart to pump adrenaline throughout his body as he eyed the lip of the cliff, knowing no one could save him if he failed to complete the jump.

Breathing deeply, he crouched as low as he could and then sprang high with outstretched fingers to grasp the edge of the slippery rock. Pain wracked both hands but he held on fast, soberly aware that this would be his only chance to return to the hilltop. Instead, he drove the pain down and fed it into the fury building within him. His adrenaline empowered his arms to pull his torso high enough to swing a foot onto the hilltop, where he rolled to safety on his back. He rose to his knees upon the slate rock to face the cabin, espying Curly standing near the cabin wall, barking orders at the gangs with the hunting knife clenched in his hand. Jeff stood up and darted stealthily across the hilltop, circling behind his enemy's sightline.

"Hollister's dead!" Curly waved the knife at Zak and Tony. "You two, carry the girl down to my truck. The rest of you get back down that hill. Do it now!"

JJ pointed a shaky finger behind him. "Look out!"

Curly whirled about to see his adversary flying at him feet first, just before the soles of Jeff's sneakers struck his chest, knocking him back against the cabin wall with a thud. He staggered forward from the impact and slashed the knife wildly at Jeff scrambling to his feet, but Jeff dodged his strike and pressed forward again, too enraged to succumb to fear of injury. He stunned Curly with a roundhouse left to his jaw and then drove him back with a pair of right jabs that bloodied his nose and loosened a tooth. Curly countered with another wild slash, but Jeff sidestepped the blade and landed a right cross on his enemy's mouth, knocking the loose tooth free and dropping him to one knee.

Curly cursed and charged with the knife clenched before him, but Jeff ducked the crazed lunge and drove a fist so hard against his enemy's ear that he dropped the knife onto the ground. Dazed, Curly swung an aimless fist that Jeff easily deflected before raining a succession of jabs upon his head, his spongy black hair misting rainwater from each blow he took. Teetering with exhaustion, the Tornado lieutenant raised his fists one last time in token resistance until Jeff sent him sprawling onto the wet grass from a solid right hook to his chin. He grabbed his hunting knife from the mud and straddled his enemy, lifting him by his jacket collar and holding the blade to his throat.

"Do it, Jeff!" TJ yelled from the edge of the hilltop.

Curly grinned, his teeth and gums lined with fresh blood. "Yeah, do it, Hollister. Kill me."

Jeff raised the knife over his head as if readying to strike down upon his foe, but he spotted Cindy again, lying still beneath the threat of the revolver in JJ's hand. His rage drained as he recalled matters more pressing than vengeance, and while she did not utter a sound, her words were a clarion call in his head.

"Let it start with me," he said. He pushed Curly to the ground and stood up, straddling his enemy as he folded the knife blade away. "I'm not going to kill you, Curly. You're going to jail." He stuffed the knife into his pocket and stepped away toward the hilltop as his fury continued to subside.

Curly rolled onto his stomach to face JJ. "Shoot him! Shoot her! Do something!"

Jeff froze. He slowly turned about to see Curly's accomplice struggling to his feet with one hand holding the revolver down at Cindy and the other still squeezing his bloody shirt against his torso. JJ stepped over Cindy's legs and shuffled up to Curly before raising the pistol toward the hilltop. Jeff cringed as his foe fumbled with the trigger, but instead the Tornado simply cocked the gun back and hurled it with all his might. Jeff ducked away as the pistol sailed over his shoulder to land near the center of the hilltop.

Curly pounded a fist into the mud. "Why did you do that? You idiot!"

JJ thrust a finger down at him. "I'm not killing anyone for you." He turned about and stumbled toward the onrushing Tornadoes, collapsing into Zak's arms as Curly dropped his head to bury his face in his hands.

Jeff longed to run to Cindy, but he knew he needed to secure the gun first. Jogging to the center of the hilltop, he stopped near the edge of the slate rock and lifted the revolver from the muddy grass as members of both gangs swarmed the cement pad to aid Cindy and keep Curly subdued. He turned toward the porch where Crazy Legs still held Mick in his lap, only to see the skinny boy pointing urgently at the cliff behind him.

"Jeff! Look!"

A blast of wind struck Jeff in the face as he turned to see the police helicopter rising off the cliff's edge, its beating rotors drowning out all other sound, its rotor wash blowing rainwater and mud against the gangs along the cabin wall. The helicopter yawed right to reveal an open side-door panel, where Officer Tinney sat in the rear seat with a scoped rifle in his arms, while Chief Wellis looked on from the copilot seat with a headset over his ears.

"It's Hollister!" he cried. "He's got a gun! Take him out! Take him out!"

Tinney struggled to aim his rifle, for the helicopter rocked against the wind buffeting off the face of the cliff. He fired once, but the bullet whizzed past Jeff's ear before embedding in the cabin wall. Everyone else dove for cover, while Jeff retreated in fright until he realized he still held the gun in his hand. He flung the revolver in the air as a second bullet splintered the corner post of the cabin porch just behind him. The pilot lifted the chopper and rolled left in pursuit, but Chief Wellis pointed frantically at the gathering beside the cabin.

"That's my daughter!" he shouted. "Set it down!"

The pilot nodded and lowered the helicopter's skids over the grassy hilltop as Jeff fled down the front access road in fear of another bullet heading his way. Fifty yards into the woods,, he heard the sounds of distant shouting and barking dogs, but he doubted Brain could've summoned help so quickly. More likely, Chief Wellis had already radioed ahead to cut him off, or the police were simply zeroing in on the shots fired earlier, but in either case he knew he might face additional gunfire. His only refuge lay in the woods to his right, so he left the access road for the eastern line of the mining property, before he could be seen. Soon he scaled the defunct electric fence for the hilly woods of Portland, where he wandered beneath the cover of the treetops amid sparse snowflakes floating down through the branches, the waning sun having never shone its face upon such a cold and miserable day.

CHAPTER 16

T HE FLURRIES CONTINUED to fall as dusk settled upon the
county, and night had taken full hold when Jeff finally
emerged from the cover of the woods, into the wide backyard
of a secluded Portland residence. A few short weeks ago, the
Hurricanes would have relished the chance to burglarize such
a home, but that notion seemed ludicrous to him now. Still, he
could not resist the temptation to take a mechanic's suit and an
unlocked mountain bike from a shed at the rear of the property.
"I'm just borrowing them," he told himself as he donned the
denim suit, noting the property address as he rode the bicycle
down the long driveway and silently into the night. He pedaled
the bicycle along the dark streets on the backside of Badger
Mountain until he stopped on a hillside overlooking the
evening lights of Madison dotting the valley below.

Cycling along the hilly terrain helped to keep his body
warm, and the blue cotton suit broke the wind from his wet
clothes underneath, but as he coasted down the hill, the cold
air bit his cheeks and gnawed at his knuckles that clenched the
bicycle handlebars for control. By the time he reached the

bottom of the hill, his teeth were chattering and his skin felt raw, but as the road leveled on the outskirts of the city, the wind subsided and the flurries ceased. Soon he came upon a motel across the street from a 24-hour truck stop located near an entrance ramp to westbound lanes of Interstate 88. He parked the bike on the sidewalk and entered the motel office, paying a disinterested night clerk for a room with one of the folded hundred-dollar bills still nested inside his front pocket. A few minutes later, he opened the door to his room and flicked on the light, rolling the bicycle inside before locking the door behind him.

He turned up the heater and laid his wet clothes out to dry while he took a long, hot shower to warm his body and soothe his aching muscles. Afterward, he sat on the bed clad only in a bath towel, flicking through channels with the TV remote. He watched the news clip of his harrowing escape from the Salisbury police headquarters on WCRT-News, reveling in the sight of Bumbles tackling Sgt. Hyrst on the lawn, yet he saw nothing about the girl whose disappearance had triggered the Amber Alert earlier in the day. He longed to call his friends for an update, but he feared that they might all be in police custody at the time. The only useful information he obtained came from an admissions nurse at Madison General Hospital, who confirmed that Mick Landry had been admitted to the hospital in serious but stable condition. She would not tell him if Cindy Wellis was also there, despite his persistence.

His hands throbbed with pain as he hung up the phone, and pangs of hunger roiled his stomach, so he slipped into the mechanic's suit again and left the room with the television still on. Across the street, the lights of the truck stop shone brightly in the night, lighting his way down the desolate service road to a complex consisting of a gas station, a large convenience store, and a busy diner that he chose to avoid. Soon he returned to his room with two bags full of food, some clothing, a silver money clip, and first-aid supplies, and for the next hour he dined on corn chips, beef jerky, and soda as he bound his busted fingers together with gauze tape and cleansed his wounds with alcohol. When he was finished, he continued to flick through TV channels for information about Cindy, but eventually he could no longer resist his underlying exhaustion, so he turned down the heater and drifted off to sleep.

Dawn came with a glint of sunshine upon his face eking through a gap in the curtains. He shut off the television and rolled off the bed to place his bare feet on the carpet, with his body feeling the full effect of the previous day's battle. His jeans were mostly dry and his sneakers only slightly damp, so he dressed quickly, throwing his tattered T-shirt into the trash can in favor of a thick flannel shirt and a navy-blue hoodie he had purchased at the truck stop. He left his room key card on the dresser and scribbled the address of the mountain homestead on a notepad, stuffing the note in the pocket of the mechanic's suit before draping the garment over the handlebars of the bicycle. With the sweatshirt hood pulled over his head, he stepped outside and shut the door behind him on his way toward the truck stop, the first steps on a journey toward a new home and a new way of life.

The morning clouds bore brilliant streaks of crimson and indigo, scars of the powerful storm that had since passed, while the puddles he stepped around bore a faint glaze of ice. He walked briskly along the service road to the diner entrance, entering the restaurant discreetly and taking the closest seat at the counter. A waitress brought him a cup of coffee, and he sipped on it with a wary eye on an overhead TV playing the local news, fearful that his story might be next in queue. He struck up a conversation with the truckers around him, and twenty minutes later he was climbing into the cab of a westbound truck, his new money clip fifty dollars lighter but his identity still secure and his Californian quest ready to begin in earnest.

As they drove westbound down the highway, the lonely truck driver showered Jeff with conversation and off-color jokes, clearly excited to have a companion for a change. Jeff obliged him for a short time, but soon his attention wandered from the passing countryside to unresolved matters back home, and an hour later he asked the driver to let him out at an upcoming rest area, just before they reached the state line. The befuddled driver assented and even offered to return the gas money, but Jeff declined and thanked the man as he climbed out of the cab. He shut the door and waited for the truck to pull away before crossing the highway for the eastbound lanes.

The eastward trek proved more problematic than the westward ride had been. He left the interstate for the safety of less conspicuous state roads, and although he was able to hitch a few shorter lifts along the way, he also had to walk for long stretches between rides. The sun fell upon his back as morning turned to afternoon, but the temperature remained close to freezing for much of the day, so the snow coating the ground softened but never completely melted. The aimlessness he had felt in the truck had all but dissipated as he neared the familiar grounds of his hometown. His solitary journey back home left him tired but clear-eyed, and he felt satisfied with his decision to return, not due to any plan but for a deeper purpose he sensed within him. He wasn't sure if it was closure or something else, but he felt angst in his heart that he knew would not be eased by simply accumulating miles upon his sneakers.

As night began to fall again, he passed through a hedgerow at the base of a snowy slope, beneath a clear sky and bright evening stars. On the other side of the bushes, he gazed up at the tombstones dotting the hillside with the white wisps of his breath curling about his face. A cold breeze cascaded down the hill, prompting him to duck his chin beneath the collar of his flannel shirt before starting up the slope toward the cemetery. Halfway up the hill, his foot struck a heavy object, and with a faint smile he lifted up the crystal decanter he had discarded a few nights earlier. He brushed it clear of snow and dumped out the half-inch of remaining whisky before fishing the glass stopper from the pocket of his jeans. With one last look at the full moon through the refractive crystal, he fit the stopper back into the neck of the decanter, reassured by the notion that not everything he touched had been ruined.

He cradled the decanter in his arm and continued up the hill, trusting his cloudy memory on a course past the outermost markers of the cemetery until he finally cast his sober eyes down upon Train's grave. The gray stone glowed amid the undisturbed snow cover, while an inch of snow atop the marker beckoned him to pack a snowball. He placed the decanter on the ground and scooped up a portion of the snow, packing it as tightly as his bandaged hands allowed. An oak tree down the slope taunted him from afar, so he hurled the snowball at it, grimacing as it landed a few feet to the right of the mark. He gathered an equal portion of snow from atop Train's marker and again tried to strike the tree with it, but this time the snowball curled just inches to the left. Determined, he turned back for the final strip of snow atop the tombstone, but his fingertips stung from the cold, so he buried his hands in the pockets of his sweatshirt and sat down with his back against the headstone. The breadth of constellations stretched all about him, and he felt at ease upon the hilltop, lost in his thoughts with his legs splayed out before him.

Ten minutes later, he heard footsteps crunching in the snow behind him. He rolled to his knees and hid behind the marker as he espied the silhouette of a tall man in a dark overcoat approaching him. "Hello?" the man called out. "Jeff?"

Jeff peered out from behind the headstone. "Who's there?"

The stranger did not answer at first. He continued to step deliberately through the crunchy snow until he was close enough to speak in a natural tone. "It's Marty Jameson. I saw you from my office window. I'm the Reverend here."

Jeff held his tongue until he could distinguish the reverend's face in the low light. "From the wake. I remember you."

The reverend stopped behind the headstone. "That's right. Your friend's wake."

Jeff cast his eyes downward. "Yeah, well. Sorry about the way I acted that night. It was a bad time."

The reverend pointed to the ground. "Mind if I sit?" he asked. Before Jeff could reply, he tucked the tail of his overcoat beneath him and sat upon it in the snow. "I looked for you at the funeral but—"

"I didn't go." Jeff snapped. He turned to face the reverend. "Look, if you're here to tell me what a rotten person I am, there's no line and no waiting, so have at it."

"No, that's not what I want." The reverend drew a deep breath. "I've heard many stories about how close Train was with his friends. And from what Cindy's told me, you and he were very good friends. So I was curious as to why you would avoid the funeral altogether."

"I paid him my respects right here on this hilltop." Jeff sighed. "Train was a great friend, but I still don't understand why he took that bullet for me."

The reverend nodded slowly. "There is no greater love than for a man to lay down his life for his friends," he said.

Jeff smirked. The preacher couldn't help from preaching, but his words were of comfort nonetheless. "Too bad you never actually got to meet him when he was alive. He was a pretty likable guy."

"But I did meet him," the reverend said. "He came to my office about a week and a half ago. It was a Thursday. I remember because I was heading to the hospital for sick call. I didn't have a lot of time for him, but he insisted."

Jeff wasn't sure what he found more incredulous, that this man of faith was sitting in the snow beside him or that he had actually conversed with Train in his church office. "What did he want?"

The reverend shrugged. "Just to talk. He seemed apprehensive about something, so I sat with him for a few minutes."

Jeff recalled Train's odd behavior at the gang meeting that same afternoon. "So what did he say?"

"He felt like he had crossed a line," the reverend began. "He said he felt like he wasn't long for this world. He regretted some of the things he had done and wanted to know if—how did he put it?—if he could get back to good again."

A shiver ran up Jeff's spine for the reverend's tale rang true. "What did you tell him?"

"I told him of a way back to good. I told him the light is always on at my front porch." The reverend patted Jeff on the shoulder. "It's on for you as well, if you ever want to stop by."

His words felt like a glowing fireplace in a drafty hall. Ever since that tragic night, Jeff had longed to find some meaning in his friend's death, and at Cindy's behest, he had sought to define it by the transformation of his own life. If Train had truly anticipated his own demise, as the reverend alluded, he still mustered the courage to defend his friends in a dark alley at his own peril. The selflessness of Train's friendship felt too great for Jeff to fully comprehend, but sitting on a snowy, starlit hilltop, his heart basked in the kindred spirit of that camaraderie, and he sensed a greater measure of peace within him.

"Thanks, Rev," he said. "I just might take you up on that sometime."

Before the reverend could reply, more footsteps crunched in the snow behind them. Jeff rose to his knees to peer out over the headstone toward the church. A dark figure waved a hand in the air, and a familiar voice called out, "Hello there!"

"Oh shit," he muttered. "It's Chief Wellis."

The reverend rose to his feet. "I'm sorry, Jeff. I called him before I came out here. Please don't run away."

Jeff stood up beside him and buried his frigid hands in his sweatshirt pockets again. "I'm too tired to run," he said.

The reverend looked up. "Hello, Matt."

"Hello, Marty," Chief Wellis replied. "I appreciate your discretion, as always."

Jeff looked the two men over. "So how do you guys know each other?"

The reverend smiled. "Madison High baseball. State champs two years in a row."

The chief stroked his mustache. "Might've been three if you didn't strike out looking with the bases loaded in the finals."

The reverend laughed. "That pitch was practically in the dirt!" His smile faded when he saw Jeff quietly staring down at the grave. "Well, I'm sure the two of you have a lot to discuss." He brushed the snow from the tail of his overcoat. "If you ever need to talk, Jeff, I'm easy to find."

He patted the chief on the back before ambling off across the snowy grounds toward the church. The chief waited until he was out of earshot before speaking again. "It's amazing how he turned out, with all the trouble we used to get into."

Jeff shook his head. "A cop and a preacher. I can only imagine."

"People change, Jeff. Sooner or later, we all figure out who we really want to be." The chief turned to face him. "So why are you here? Your friends said you were already gone."

"I tried to leave. I really did."

"Well, then why—"

"I couldn't go without knowing she's okay," Jeff blurted out. "Nobody would tell me anything. I couldn't get any information."

"Some of that was by design," the chief said. "We were hoping to draw you out. Most of your gang has been locked up since yesterday. The Tornadoes too. The ones who aren't in the hospital, anyway."

Jeff mulled the reply. "So how is she?"

The chief exhaled a sigh of relief. "She was in an advanced state of hypothermia when she got to the hospital. Another hour out in the cold might've been too much for her. She's got a bruised spleen too. But the doctor said that overall, she's very fortunate. She's being discharged on Monday."

"That's awesome!" Jeff said. "I didn't know what to think."

"She gave us all a scare," the chief said, "but no one's been more scared than the Jenkins kid. He came out of surgery this morning, and he hasn't stopped talking since. Bottom line is Curly McClure's going to jail for a long time. You're small potatoes compared to him."

The thought of JJ ratting out Curly to police detectives pleased Jeff to no small degree. "Glad to hear it," he said.

"Not that you're absolved of all wrongdoing," the chief continued. "We found a burned-out pit just outside your neighborhood containing some remnants of stolen property, and some of your friends confirmed the site was the Hurricanes' hideout. And if you think you can dodge that, I've got other charges on my list for you. Breaking out of custody. Engaging an officer in pursuit." The chief rubbed the knot on his head. "Assaulting a police officer."

"You weren't a cop at the time," Jeff replied. "You said it yourself."

The chief frowned. "You might win that one in court. But I don't think it'll come to that."

"What do you mean?"

"The stories we're getting from both gangs have been pretty consistent. Considering what you were up against, most of your actions seem generally justified to me. The important thing is that we've got Cindy back safely now, thanks to you."

"I was trying to save her. You tried to have me shot."

"You had a gun in your hand. What was I to think?" The chief buried his hands in his overcoat pockets and shuffled his feet in the snow. "Look, Jeff. I know you don't like me very much, but I'm not a man without compassion. Everyone describes your actions as nothing short of heroic. The more I hear about it, the more I appreciate what you did."

"I didn't do it for you. I did it for her."

"I get it. Still, she's alive today because of you. And I think that earns you a break. So I'm ready to offer you a deal."

Jeff bristled. "A deal? What kind of deal?"

The chief looked up again. "The elections are three days away, and I'm in a tight race. Last thing I need right now is a lot of media attention about my sergeant strong-arming some high school kid, even if he is a gang leader. And I've got enough evidence to put Curly McClure away for a long time, without your input."

"Good," Jeff said. "But I'm not a gang leader anymore."

"That's great, Jeff. But I can't just stand back and let you stroll around town either," the chief said. "So here's the deal. I never saw you tonight. We were never here, we never talked. No one else knows we were here either."

Jeff shook his head. "The reverend knows."

Chief Wellis smiled. "Marty Jameson and I have an understanding. He doesn't try to enforce the law, and I don't try to save souls."

Jeff glared back. "So you're just gonna let me go? What's the catch?"

The chief scratched his chin as he chose his words carefully. "I'm not letting you go. I'm giving you a head start. You got forty-eight hours. Go wherever you want to go, and don't come back. I won't come looking for you."

"A head start? But what about—"

"Forget about my daughter. No goodbyes, no texts, no letters, nothing." The chief's face grew stern. "I mean it, Jeff. If I see you near her, I'm hauling you in. And I don't want to see you anywhere near the hospital either. She's endured a traumatic experience, and she needs to heal."

Jeff's eyes widened. "But I'd never hurt a hair on her head! I put my life on the line for her!"

"And I appreciate that, Jeff. I really do. Believe me, I see you in a completely different light now." The chief sighed. "But I still think that, in the long run, you're just the wrong guy for her. I'm saying that as a father."

Jeff glowered at him. "She's not your little girl anymore. She has a mind of her own."

"That's true. Nevertheless, I'm pulling her out of Salisbury High after the election. I'm enrolling her in a private school. She won't like it, but eventually she'll make new friends. I'm guessing whatever there is between the two of you will probably fade by the time she graduates."

Jeff squeezed his fists. "If you cared one bit about the way she felt —"

"That's the deal, Jeff. I think it's mighty generous." The chief pulled his coat open to reveal a set of handcuffs dangling inside. "Or we can go down to the station right now. Either way, you won't be seeing her anytime soon. So what do you say?"

Jeff felt so sick to his stomach that he could not even speak, only nod in acceptance.

Chief Wellis clasped his gloved hands together. "Good. Then I suppose this is goodbye."

He offered a handshake, but Jeff silently turned to face Train's headstone, bracing against the cold breeze until the chief walked off into the night. He pondered the story that the reverend had told him about his friend's last days and, like Train, he also felt as if he was crossing some kind of invisible threshold, but his own passage seemed quite different. Train had sought redemption, a way back from a destructive path that threatened to consume him, and perhaps he had found his way before he died. Jeff sensed his own passing into a murkier world, a world where disputes were no longer settled with fisticuffs, where alliances were not displayed on the back of a jacket but rather held close to the chest, and where powerful men dispensed their will upon the lesser people in their midst with little empathy or concern.

"They find a way to get to ya, Train. They figure out what matters most to you, and they use it against you." He gazed down at the headstone one last time. "But I've got something inside me that's stronger than them. Something they'll never break. And you'll always be a part of that, my friend."

He scooped up the remaining snow atop the headstone and packed it into a snowball, turning his attention to the oak tree still taunting him from the bottom of the hill. He cocked his arm back and hurled the snowball with all his might, watching as it sailed true to its mark, striking the center of the tree midway up its trunk.

"Bull's-eye," he said, marveling at the accuracy of the throw. He picked up the crystal decanter from the snow and strode downhill past the oak tree out of the cemetery, heading home again to return the keepsake bottle to its proper place and hopefully spend the night in the comfort of his own bed.

The silver Volvo station wagon with the cracked front grill backed into a sunlit parking space in an empty lot behind Madison General Hospital. Brain shifted the car into park and shut off the engine. "You sure you have time for this?" he asked his friend in the passenger seat. "Your train leaves in an hour."

"We got time." Jeff pointed to a door set by the nearest corner of a towering cement structure. "Is that the way in? I don't see anyone."

Just then, the door opened and Crazy Legs stuck his head outside. He shielded his eyes from the bright sunlight before spotting the Volvo and waving at it.

"Let's go." Brain popped open his door.

Jeff hopped out and joined his friend at the front of the car. Together they hustled to the door now held ajar by a crumpled paper cup and entered the building. Inside the dim stairwell, they saw that Crazy Legs had already ascended two flights of cement stairs to the second floor.

"How far up?" Jeff asked.

"Ninth floor," Crazy Legs called down. "Watch out for cops. I've seen a few."

"You wanna take the elevator?" Brain asked.

Jeff gazed up the stairwell. "Nah, let's do this."

They charged up the staircase quickly at first, predictably tiring as they reached the higher floors. Panting, Jeff pulled open the stairwell door on the ninth floor to find Crazy Legs standing before a bank of elevators, motioning him to wait. He waved them forward a moment later and said, "All clear."

Jeff followed him along a brightly lit corridor while Brain dallied behind with an eye on the elevators. They walked down a long corridor with windows to their right until Crazy Legs stopped just beyond earshot of a busy nursing station. He pointed his thumb to the left and said, "Room 904."

"You're not coming?" Jeff asked.

Crazy Legs shook his head. "I'll hang back and keep watch."

"Okay. I won't be long."

Jeff turned down the corridor to his left, where nurses and orderlies bustled about their tasks without paying him any heed. He stopped at the second room on the right with Brain still shadowing him and gently rapped his knuckles upon the open door.

Inside the room, Axle pivoted on crutches, his right foot encased in a protective boot. "Hey, look! It's Jeff!"

Jeff stepped inside the room to see TJ, Denny, and Bumbles all sitting beside a hospital bed, where Mick lay in the bed with three bandaged limbs immobilized by a traction device. "Jeff!" he exclaimed. "I figured you were long gone by now."

Jeff stepped into the room and squeezed Mick's blanketed toes in greeting. "You guys look like you've been through a war."

TJ lifted his left arm in a full cast and sling. "Yeah, so much for basketball season."

"Mrrff," Denny replied through clenched teeth.

Bumbles pointed a thumb at him. "His jaw's wired shut."

"Every cloud has a silver lining." TJ grinned until Denny socked him in the stomach.

Axle squeezed his ribs and winced. "Ow! Don't make me laugh!"

Jeff smiled and turned to Bumbles. "I didn't expect to see you here. I figured they'd have you on a bus to the big house by now."

Bumbles laughed. "They charged me with obstructing justice and assaulting a police officer. My dad totally flipped out. He even refused to post my bail at first."

Jeff shook his head. "Sorry about that. I appreciate what you did, though."

"You're kidding, right? I'd do it again a hundred times after what you did for me."

Jeff shuffled his feet and glanced about the serious faces of his friends. "Well, I just came by to say goodbye. I know I said I didn't need the Hurricanes anymore. Truth is, I wouldn't be here right now without you."

"Where's Crazy Legs?" Bumbles asked. "I thought he'd be here."

"He's down the hall," Brain said. "He's keeping watch."

Mick shook his head. "Nah, he's just pissed at me. Funny how sticking a gun in your friend's gut can change his opinion about you."

A few of the Hurricanes laughed nervously, but Jeff sensed the regret in his friend's voice. "Give him time. He'll come around."

"I hope so," Mick said. "I'm gonna need all the friends I can get once I get out of here. I hear the prosecutor wants my ass in a sling over the gun."

"You'll be all right," Jeff told him. "It's not like you actually shot anyone."

"Try as you might," Brain added. Mick snarled at him, while Axle chuckled painfully again.

Jeff laughed but he quickly fell somber. "Anyway, I better go. If the cops find me here, I'm toast."

"Still on the run?" Axle asked.

"Let's just say the chief is gonna look the other way while I slide out of town. On account of my amazing valor in saving his daughter's life." He smiled at his own pomposity and humbly added, "Thanks for flossing his ass for me."

"We just told him how it was," TJ said. "You were awesome. The way you lit Curly up—Man, I was never so proud to be a Hurricane."

"Vree vroo," Denny agreed through his teeth.

Mick nodded. "I wish I had seen it. Seeing Curly sob like a baby would've made all this worthwhile."

Axle frowned. "So what does Chief Wellis get in return?"

Jeff grimaced. "I had to promise him I wouldn't see Cindy again. It's the only reason I'm not in jail. I'm not even supposed to be here right now."

"What a snake," TJ said. "He ain't doing you any favors. He's looking out for himself."

"Does she even know you're leaving?" Axle asked.

"I doubt it," Jeff said. "I don't even know where she is."

"Second floor," Bumbles blurted out. "I saw her friend Shannon on the elevator this morning and—"

Jeff held up his hand. "I'm probably better off not knowing."

"So where are you going?" TJ asked.

"Now *you're* better off not knowing." Jeff smiled. "And if anyone asks, you didn't see me here."

"Well, don't forget about your brothers back home," Mick said. "Let me know if you need some more cash when you get there. You're good for it."

Axle nodded. "And I'll fix your car if you get it towed to my house."

"Thanks. I'll let my mother know. But you got your work cut out for you this time." Jeff scanned the sullen faces of friends contemplating his imminent departure. "Hey, look. I'll always be a Hurricane at heart. And I'll be back again someday. I swear."

An awkward silence swept over the room as the seven boys searched for words to express themselves. Finally, Mick held out his one good arm. "Through thick and thin—"

Jeff stepped forward and clasped the hand firmly. "Our blood and skin—"

"—is one!" the Hurricanes chorused.

Jeff waved goodbye to his friends and left the room. He strode past the nurses' station back to the main corridor while Brain scurried after him. "You really think she's here?" his friend asked. "In this hospital?"

"Makes sense," Jeff said. "It's the closest one."

Brain hustled to keep up. "So what are you gonna do?"

Jeff shrugged. "I gave the man my word, and I gotta catch a train."

As they neared the stairwell door at the end of the hallway, Crazy Legs burst through the doorway with alarm on his face. He rushed to the elevator bank and pressed the call button. "Cop!" he whispered. "I think he saw me!"

Jeff looked about for an alternate escape route but, to his relief, the middle elevator chimed its arrival and its metal doors slid open. Crazy Legs entered the empty car first and frantically pressed the lobby call button as Brain followed him inside, while Jeff entered the car last, instinctively turning to face the front of the car. The doors began to shut, just as Officer Boyd stormed out from the stairwell.

"You! Stop!" he shouted at the trio in the elevator. The doors slid shut in his face, but not before he locked eyes with Jeff standing in the center of the car.

"That was close," Brain said as they descended. "We better go while the getting's good."

Jeff exhaled slowly, unsure if Officer Boyd had identified him. He glanced up to the lighted numbers over the silver doors, watching their descent from the seventh to the sixth to the fifth floor. As they neared the third floor, he reached out a finger to light the number two button on the control panel.

Brain's mouth dropped open. "Jeff, don't! You'll ruin everything for yourself."

"Pull the car around front," Jeff replied. He pulled his hood over his head and turned to Crazy Legs. "Come with me."

"You found her!" Crazy Legs said. "But you can't—"

Brain shook his head. "Jeff—"

The doors slid open on the second floor and Jeff stepped out. "Do it. I'll be out front in ten minutes."

Crazy Legs hurried out as the silver doors shut behind him. "Chief Wellis won't cut you any more slack—"

"I don't care. I have to see her."

He strode halfway down the corridor, but Crazy Legs trotted up and grabbed his arm. "This is a private wing," he explained, motioning to a solitary nurse sitting at a reception desk at the far end of the corridor. "She'll want to know why you're here."

Jeff stopped. "What should I do?"

"Wait here." Crazy Legs motioned to the artwork lining the walls of the corridor. "Look at the pictures or something. I'll see if I can lead her away."

Jeff frowned. "What room is she in? How will I find her?"

His friend shrugged. "I don't know. Follow your heart."

Jeff nodded and ambled up to a seascape hanging on the corridor wall while his friend continued onward to the reception station. He viewed the painting superficially at first, watching from the corner of his eye as Crazy Legs greeted the nurse and began to spin his yarn. After a few moments, however, the blue pastels of ocean and sky lured his thoughts to a shoreline he had yet to see, where vibrant sunsets glistened off deep waves cresting beyond a sandy coast. The painting seemed like a portal he could climb through, offering the promise of a future that demanded the present world be left behind. He felt both anticipation and regret, knowing that one last farewell remained before he could embark on a new reality.

He turned back toward the reception station and saw that Crazy Legs had succeeded in luring the portly redheaded nurse away. Stepping briskly to the console, he spotted them wandering down the corridor to the left, staring down together at the white-tiled floor. The hallway to the right led him toward an older wing of the hospital, where bright sunlight shone through long panes of glass, glistening off the white tiles descending a gentle ramp. At the bottom of the ramp, the tiles gave way to an indigo carpet, marking the transition to the private wing and a half dozen doorways on the left side of the corridor.

He paused briefly outside the first room but felt compelled to move on to the second doorway, quietly inching his way inside the spacious room, its high ceiling reminiscent of the hospital's earlier days. The bed was tucked around the corner of the bathroom, set to face a tall window slightly ajar to help cool the warm room. Peering around the corner into the room, he saw Cindy sitting upright in the bed with her knees bent to support a magazine and a paper bracelet around her wrist. He stared at the soft brown hair tumbling about her fair face as if trying to engrave an image in his mind.

Cindy looked up and gasped. She dropped the magazine on her lap and stretched her arms out toward him. "My hero!"

He stepped up and greeted her with a kiss. "How are you feeling? No tubes or wires, I see."

"I'm okay. I have a big black-and-blue mark on my ribs, but nothing's broken. They said they're going to discharge me this afternoon." She looked down at her lap. "I wasn't sure if you were ever going to come."

Jeff took her hands in his. "It's all I've been thinking about. But I had to work something out first."

"Detective Shelnick told me the whole story last night. Everyone he talked to told him how fantastic you were."

He smiled humbly. "I wasn't feeling fantastic. I just did what I had to do."

"I think I remember some of it," she said. "Maybe I was just dreaming."

Jeff released her hands before drifting away from her bedside to the open window. He gazed out across the groomed front lawn of the hospital, where a few small patches of snow still resisted the bright sunshine. To his left, the silver Volvo circled a horseshoe driveway past the front entrance of the hospital before stopping farther along the curbside, nearer to him. He stared down at the idling car, remembering how little time he had left to be with her.

"I was thinking," she said. "Now that this ordeal is over, maybe we could pick up where we left off. It'd be nice just to be your girlfriend again."

He swallowed the lump in his throat. "That would be nice."

She frowned. "What's the matter? You don't seem very happy."

He returned to the edge of the bed. "I can't see you anymore," he said bluntly.

Her pupils darted about as his words sank in. "Wha — why not?"

He slid beside her and looked into her eyes. "I have to go. This is my last stop. I'm not even supposed to be here right now."

Lines of pain emerged on her face. "Where are you going? When are you coming back?"

"California," he replied. "I don't know when I'm coming back."

She mulled his answer for a moment before wiping tears from her eyes. "So why did you come here? To make me cry? To break my heart?"

"No. Not to break your heart." He drew a deep breath. "I thought it would hurt you more if I never said goodbye."

"Well, say it, then," she sobbed. "Goodbye."

He stepped closer and gently stroked her hair. "Everyone's talking about how I saved your life. Nobody knows about how you saved mine." He kissed her softly on the top of her head and turned to leave. "I'm sorry."

She dried her tears with her hands and furrowed her brow. "Wait a minute," she said. "What did you mean by 'supposed to'?"

He stopped. "Huh?"

"You said you weren't 'supposed to' be here. Why aren't you supposed to be here, Jeff?"

He cast his eyes down and shuffled his feet. "Um, your father said I—"

"My father!" she shrieked. "What does my father have to do with this?"

Jeff cast a nervous glance to the doorway before returning to her side. "He said I can't see you anymore. He said he's gonna pull you out of Salisbury High next week." He squeezed her hands. "He made me agree to a deal."

"What kind of deal?" she asked sternly.

Jeff looked down. "He said he's gonna look the other way while I get out of town. He said he's gonna arrest me if I come anywhere near you."

She threw her blanket off and swung her legs around to sit on the edge of the bed. "Let me tell you something about my father," she said. "My father will twist any arm and step on any toes to get his way. He does it to the crooks, he does it to cops. Sometimes he even does it to his own family. It's how he got to where he is today."

He frowned. "Yeah, I know what you mean."

"Well, I finally met someone who wasn't afraid to take him on," she said. "Someone who could look him in the eye and not back down."

"A lot of good that did me."

She looped an arm around his neck. "He didn't rescue me, Jeff, you did. Don't let him force you to do something you don't want to do. If you just don't want to be with me, I can live with that. But please don't do it because of my father. I love him, but he's controlled my life for too long now."

"He's relentless," he said. "I need something to counter him with."

"You have me." She kissed him on the cheek. "Me and my love."

Once again, her words rang true. Whatever he chose to do, he was stronger with her by his side, and while rejecting the chief's deal seemed wrong, it also felt so right. His anxiety and gloom melted away, replaced by defiance and gallantry, the traits he had always held dearest in his heart. He was, after all, Jeff Hollister.

He stood up with a gleam in his eye. "You wanna take a chance? You wanna come with me?"

She beamed. "To the ends of the earth."

He kissed her lips and tugged at her hands. "Then follow me," he said. "I have a plan…"

The portly nurse led Crazy Legs back toward the central reception station as he continued to scan the floor. "I'm sorry about your necklace," she said. "If you leave me your phone number, I'll have the night nurse call you if she finds it."

She stepped behind the desk in search of a pen and paper while he glanced down the main corridor toward the elevators. The center car chimed its arrival and Chief Wellis stepped out, flanked by Officer Boyd and Sergeant Hyrst, the latter sporting a large adhesive bandage across his forehead. Their hard heels clacked upon the tiles as they marched together down the corridor in unison.

Officer Boyd pointed at Crazy Legs. "That's one of them."

The skinny boy started up the corridor toward them. "Chief

Wellis! I was looking for you," he said. "I forgot to tell you something—"

Sergeant Hyrst brushed him aside. "Save it, Kramer. We got bigger fish to fry."

"Where's Jeff Hollister?" Chief Wellis asked as they sauntered past him.

Crazy Legs trotted after them. "I-I thought he was—"

The nurse smiled at the lawmen as they approached her station. "Good morning, Mr. Wellis," she said cheerfully.

The chief shot back a scornful look. "Nurse, I left specific instructions that my daughter was not to have *any* unapproved visitors."

Her jaw dropped open as she looked about. "Visitors? I didn't—"

Chief Wellis held up his hand to cut her off in midsentence as he rounded the corner with his men at his heels. She bolted from the desk and scurried after them, while Crazy Legs jostled ahead of everyone and turned about to back down the tiled ramp before them.

"Chief, you don't understand!" he gasped. "It's really important!"

The chief refused to look at him. "Officer Boyd, if Mr. Kramer continues to obstruct us, place him under arrest. Sergeant Hyrst, when we locate Jeff Hollister, you are to use whatever means necessary to take him into custody immediately."

"Yes sir!" the two policemen answered.

Officer Boyd reached for Crazy Legs but he darted away, running past the closed door of Cindy's room to a safe distance down the carpeted hallway. Looking back, he saw the chief open the door and enter the room with his subordinates and the nurse filing in behind him.

A cry of despair suddenly filled the hallway. Unnerved, Crazy Legs dashed back to the entrance of the room, nudging his way past the nurse into the center of the room, where he beheld an empty hospital bed and long curtains blowing in a breeze from a window fully open. The two police officers stood dumbfounded at the foot of the bed, while their chief glared out the window at the red taillights of a silver Volvo station wagon vanishing down a side street amid the bustling midday traffic.

Chief Wellis slammed his fist upon the windowsill with a loud curse. He whirled about and barreled past Crazy Legs on a beeline for the door, with the nurse and Officer Boyd both scurrying after him. He tried to follow, but Hyrst blocked his path with eyes bulging and teeth gnashing. The skinny boy bit his lip, trying to maintain a straight face at the sergeant's fuming emotions, but Hyrst simply shoved him back onto the bed before storming out of the room after the others.

Crazy Legs bounced to a rest upon the soft mattress, staring at the ceiling, holding his belly and laughing hysterically.

THE END

ABOUT THE AUTHOR

Set in the fictional town of Salisbury, *Fight or Flight: A South Side Story* is Joe's debut novel. Joe lives with his wife Wendy and rescue cat Cheddar in his lifelong hometown of South Windsor, Connecticut, a suburb of Hartford quite similar to Salisbury. Joe successfully completed the English graduate program at Trinity College in 2015 and the Cinema Arts undergraduate program at the University of Hartford in 2016. He also holds an MS in environmental, health, and safety management from Rensselaer Polytechnic Institute. He is currently employed as a quality inspector and serves as a union safety representative for a large aerospace manufacturing company located in the Hartford area.

josephdurette.com